The Prisoner of Shiverstone

Linette Moore

AMULET BOOKS · NEW YORK

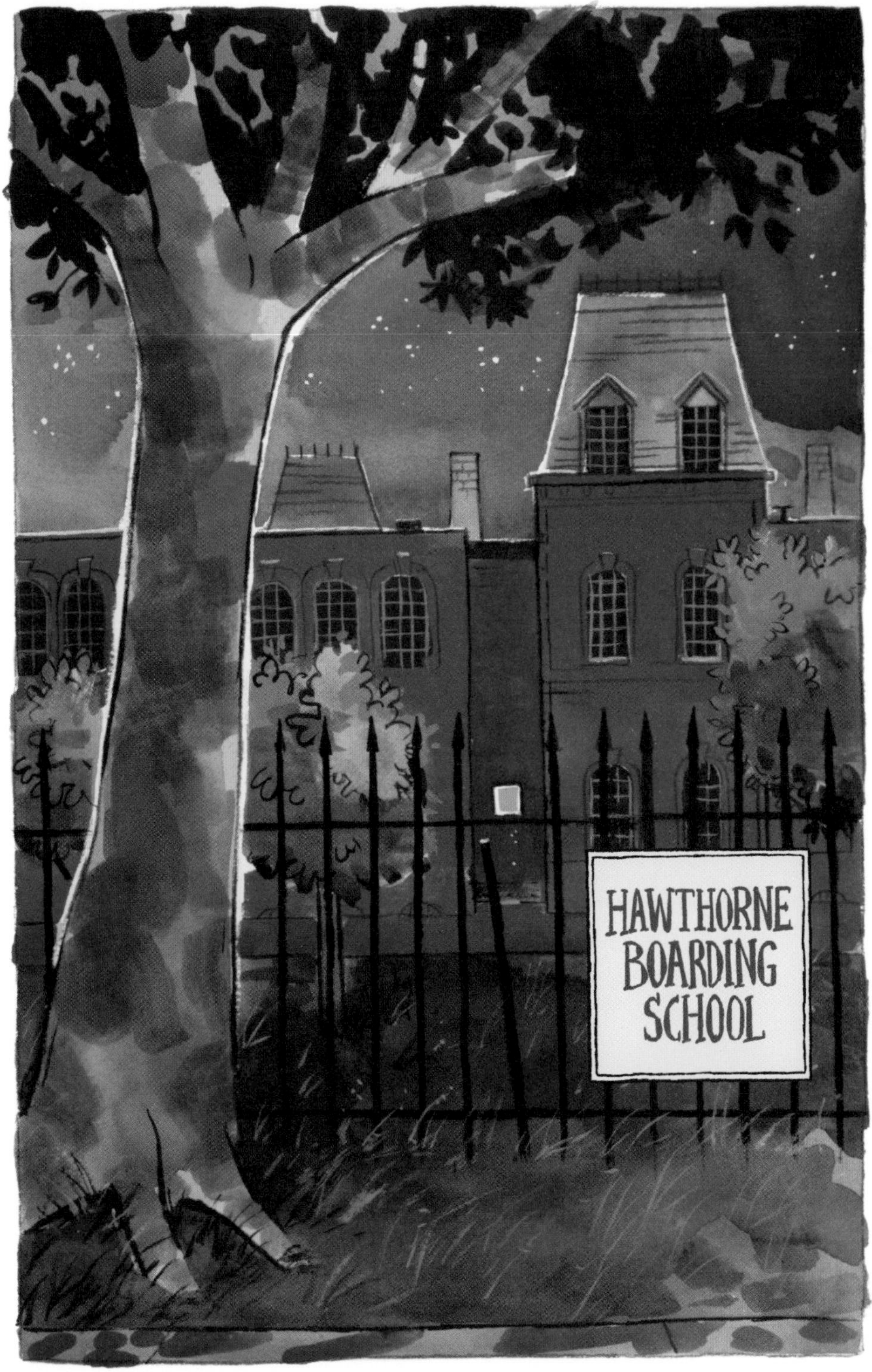
HAWTHORNE
BOARDING
SCHOOL

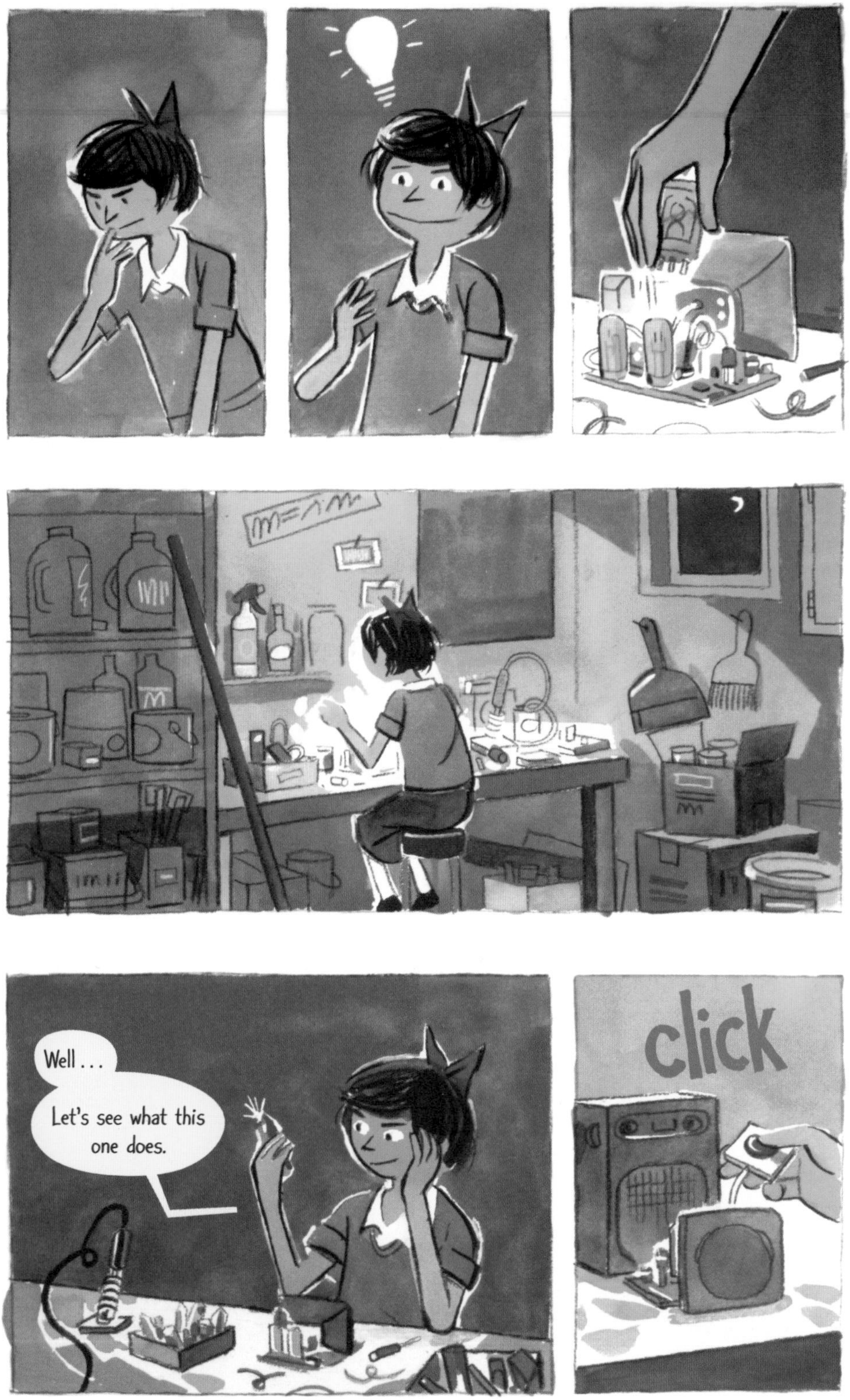
Well . . .
Let's see what this one does.
click

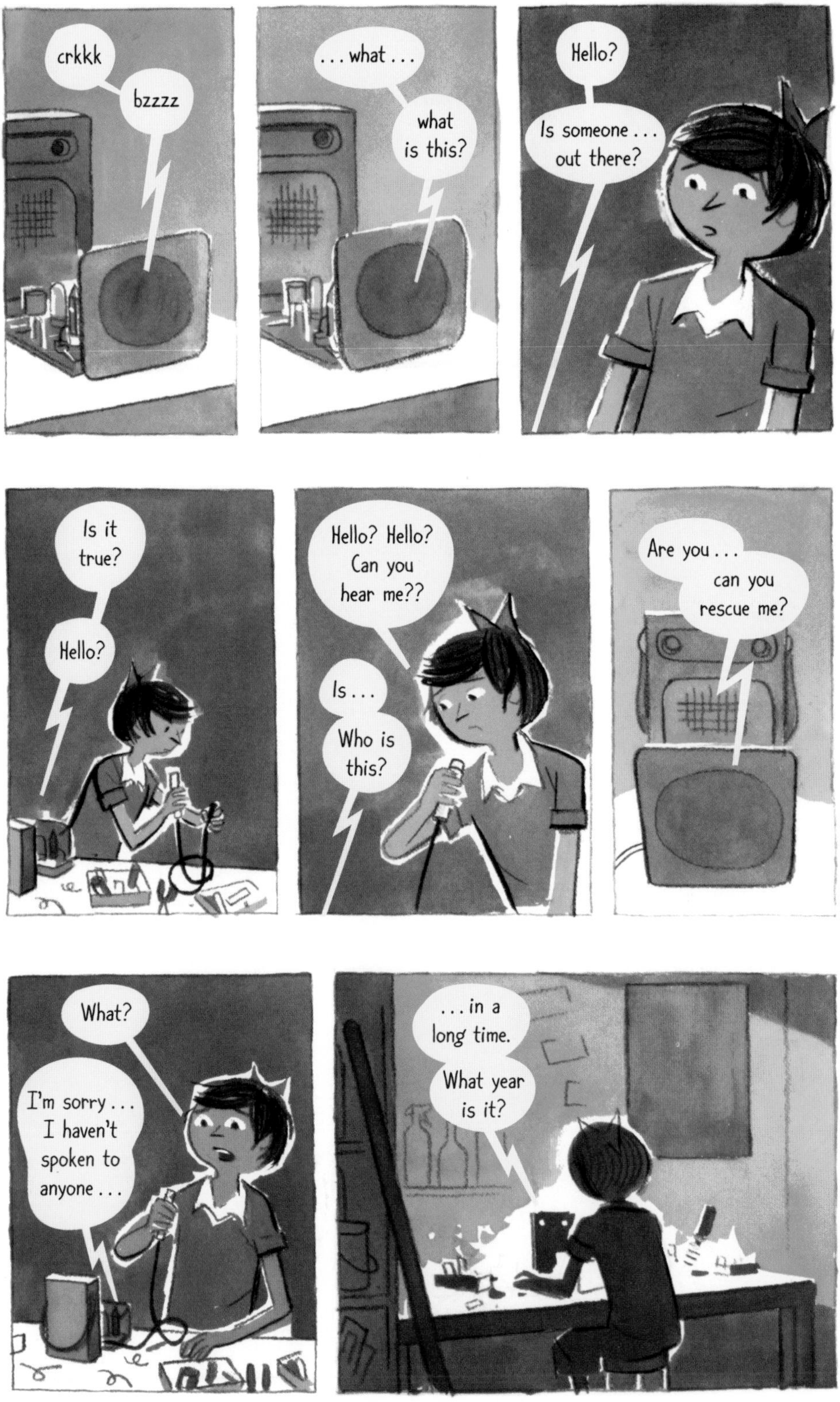
crkkk
bzzzz
. . . what . . .
what is this?
Hello?
Is someone . . . out there?
Is it true?
Hello?
Hello? Hello? Can you hear me??
Is . . .
Who is this?
Are you . . .
can you rescue me?
What?
I'm sorry . . . I haven't spoken to anyone . . .
. . . in a long time.
What year is it?

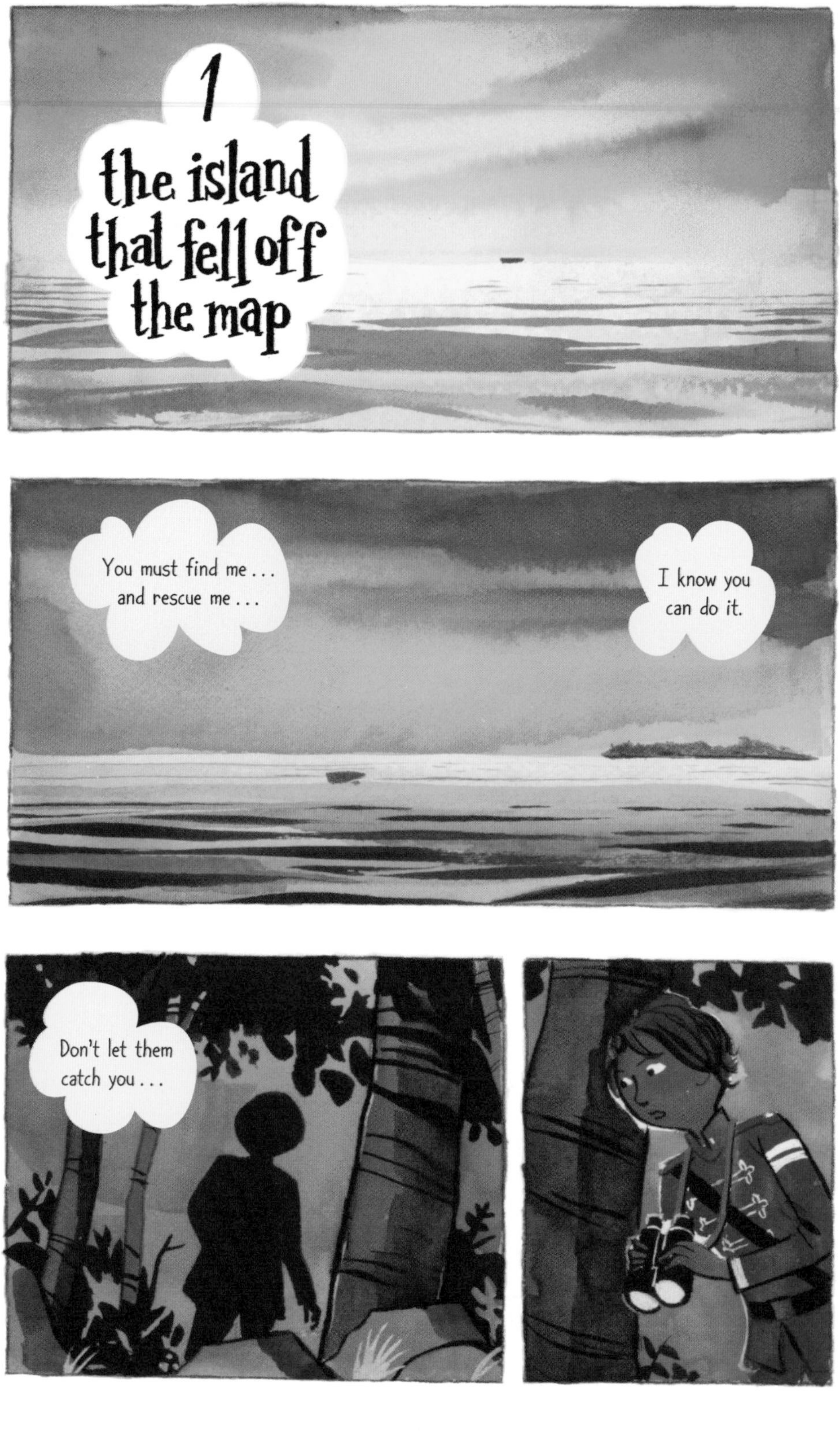
1
the island that fell off the map
You must find me . . . and rescue me . . .
I know you can do it.
Don't let them catch you . . .

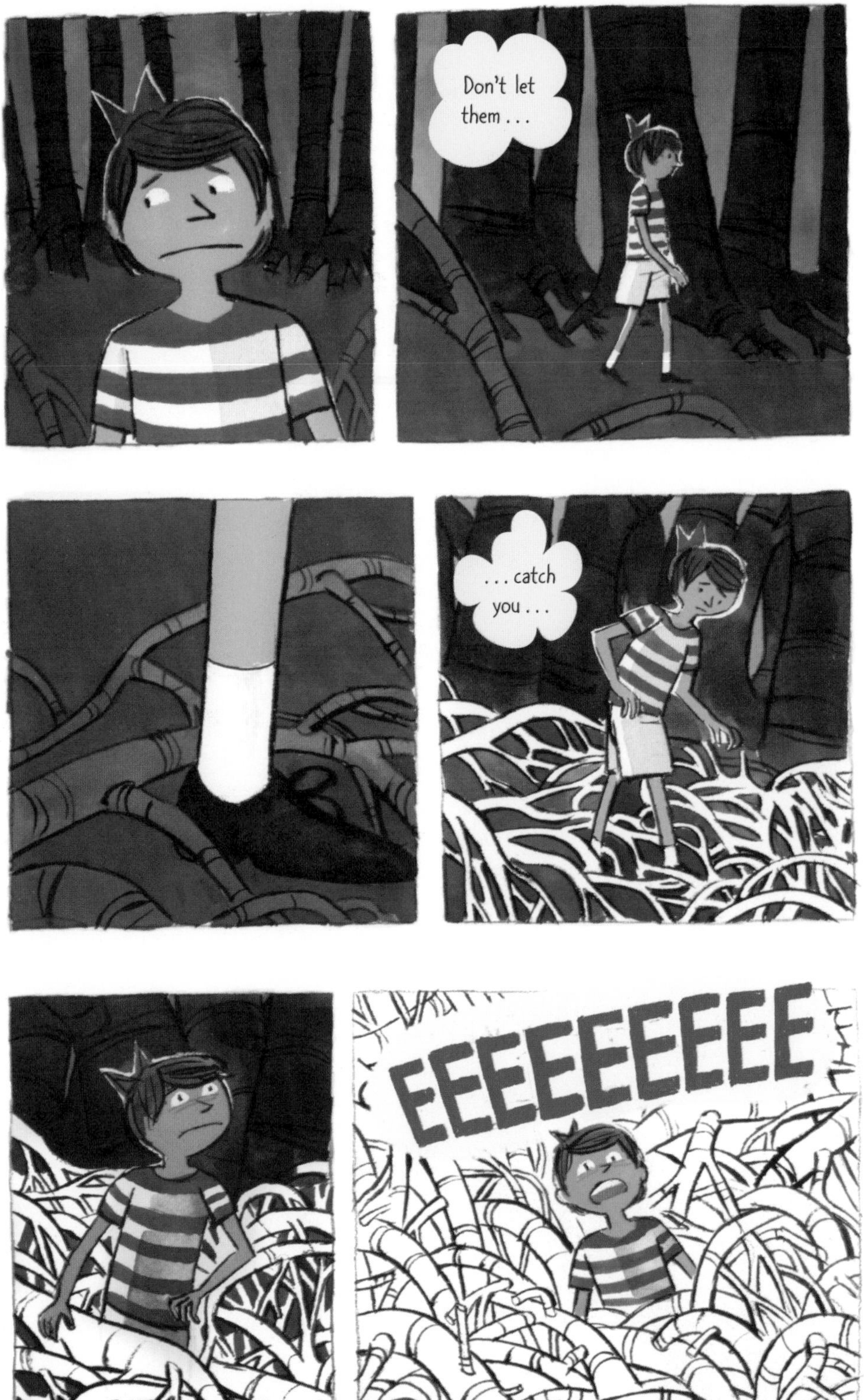
Don't let them . . .
. . . catch you . . .
EEEEEEEEEE

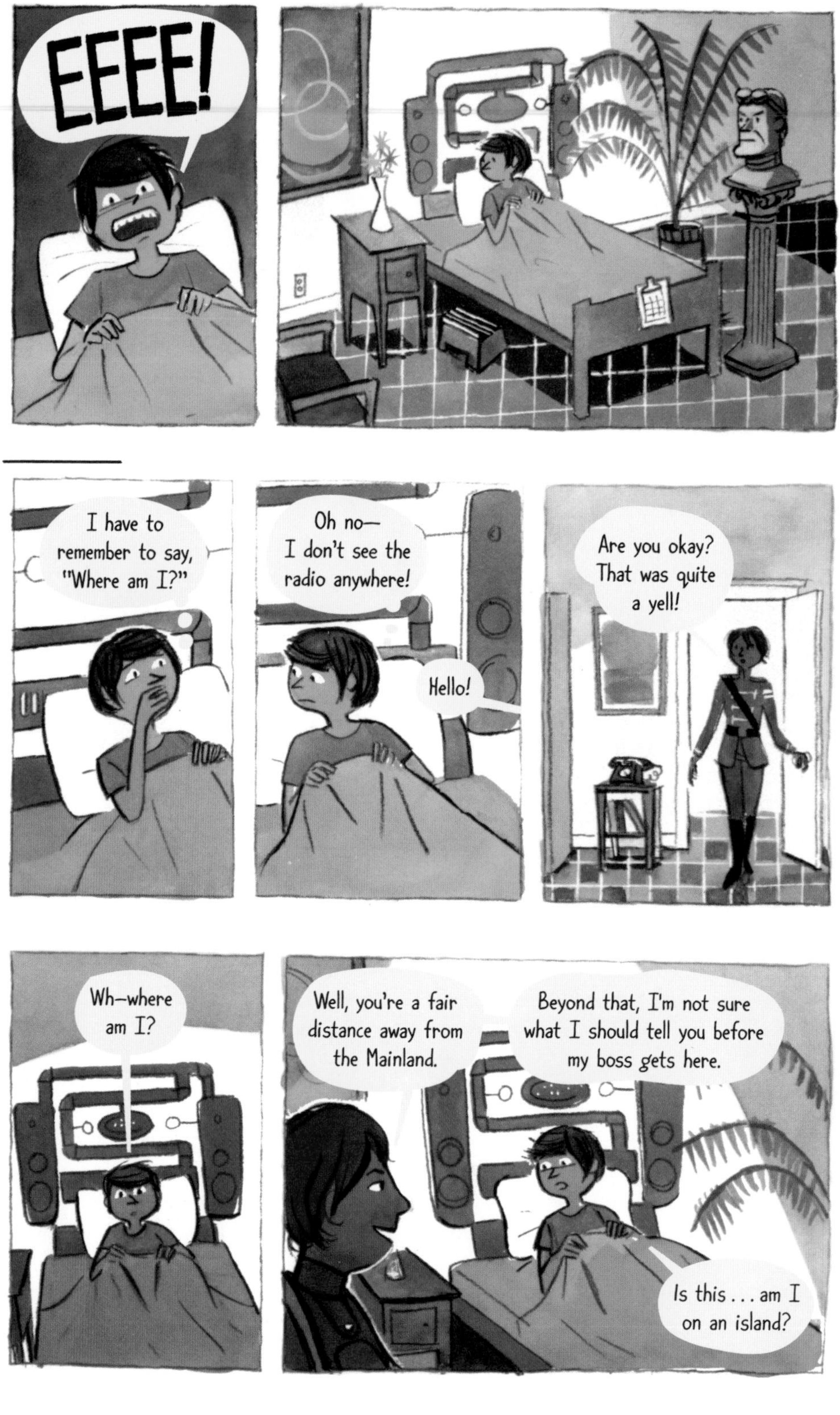
EEEE!
I have to remember to say, "Where am I?"
Oh no— I don't see the radio anywhere!
Hello!
Are you okay? That was quite a yell!
Wh—where am I?
Well, you're a fair distance away from the Mainland.
Beyond that, I'm not sure what I should tell you before my boss gets here.
Is this . . . am I on an island?

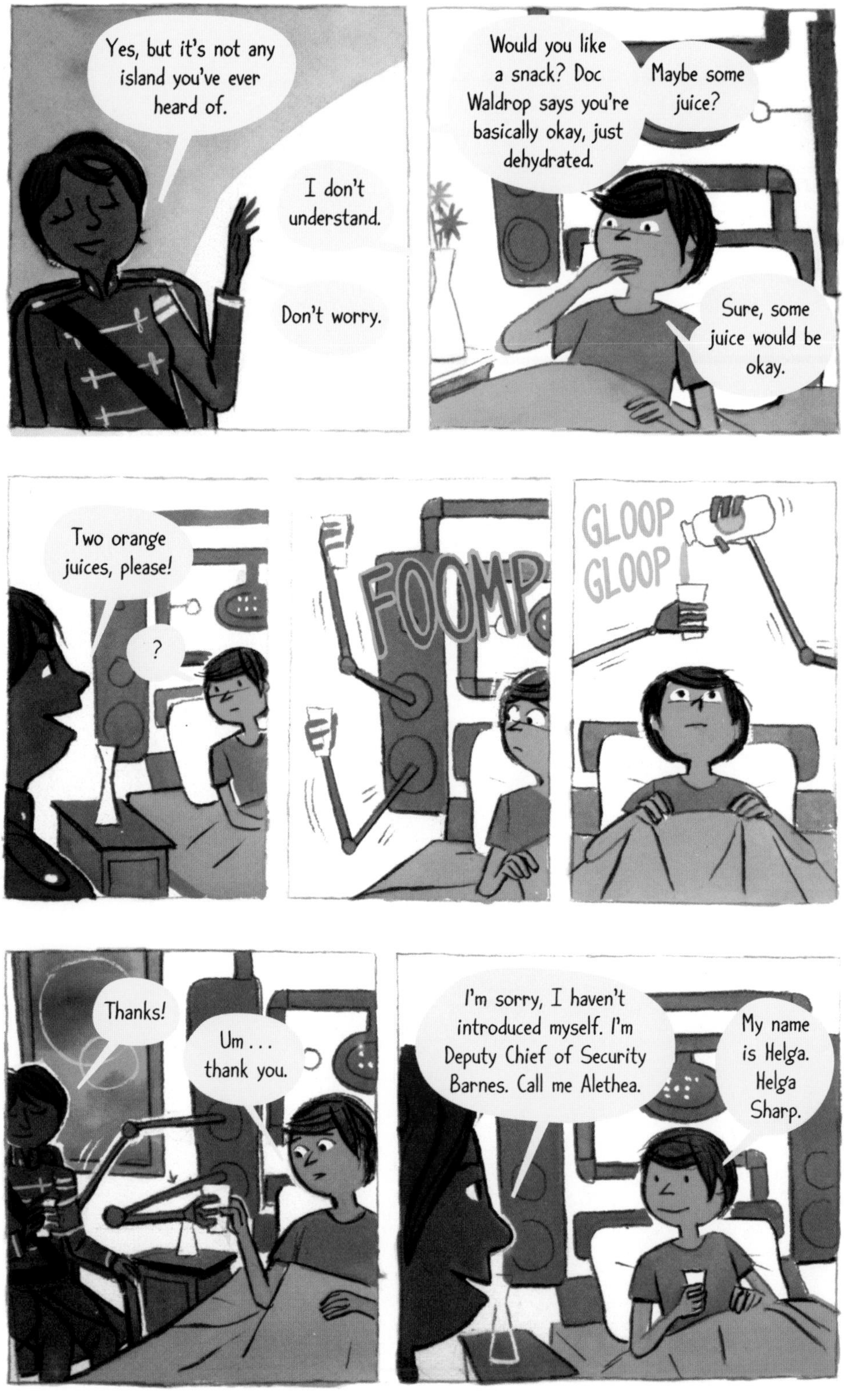
Yes, but it's not any island you've ever heard of.
I don't understand.
Don't worry.
Would you like a snack? Doc Waldrop says you're basically okay, just dehydrated.
Maybe some juice?
Sure, some juice would be okay.
Two orange juices, please!
?
FOOMP
GLOOP
GLOOP
Thanks!
Um . . . thank you.
I'm sorry, I haven't introduced myself. I'm Deputy Chief of Security Barnes. Call me Alethea.
My name is Helga. Helga Sharp.

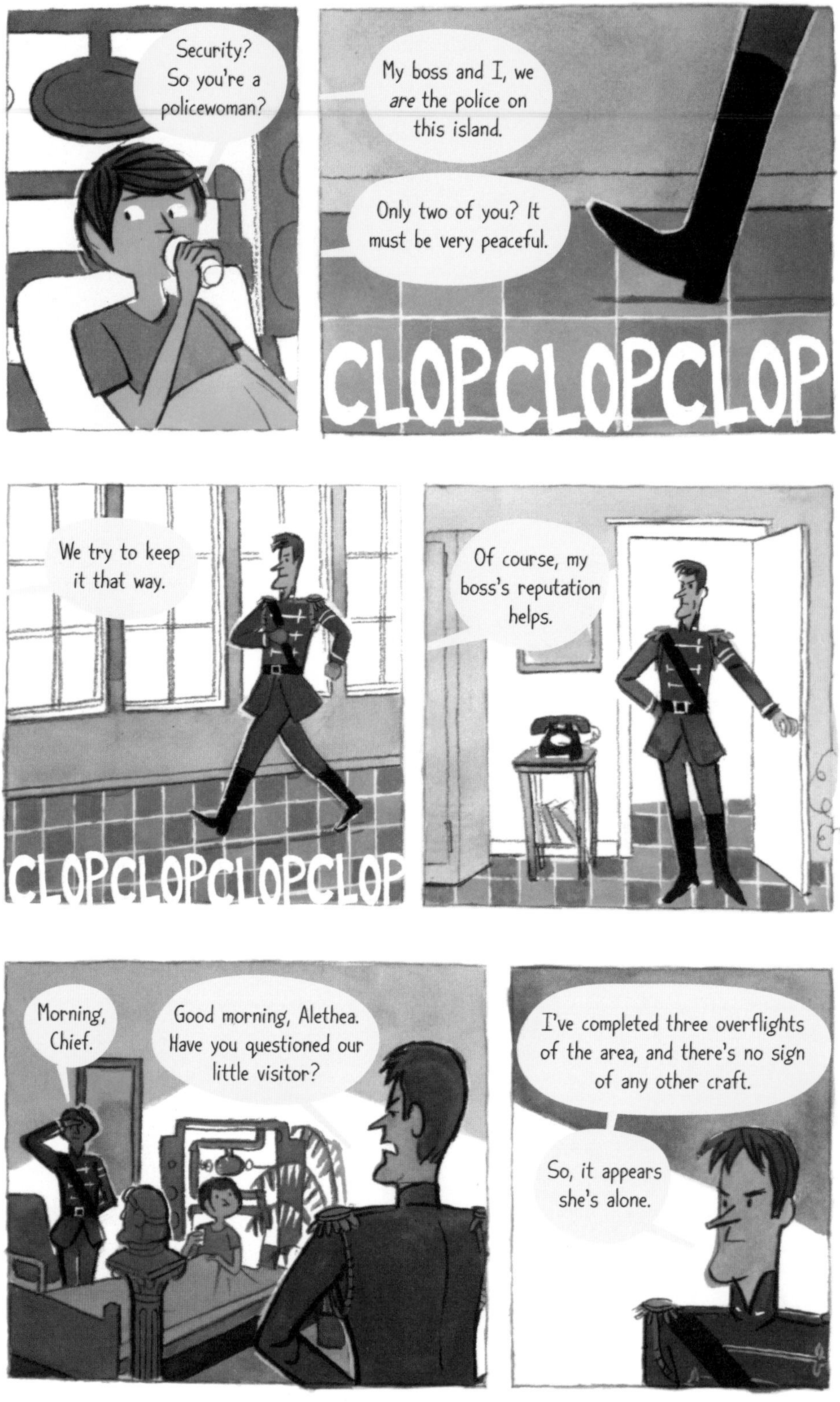
Security? So you're a policewoman?
My boss and I, we *are* the police on this island.
Only two of you? It must be very peaceful.
CLOPCLOPCLOP
We try to keep it that way.
CLOPCLOPCLOPCLOP
Of course, my boss's reputation helps.
Morning, Chief.
Good morning, Alethea. Have you questioned our little visitor?
I've completed three overflights of the area, and there's no sign of any other craft.
So, it appears she's alone.

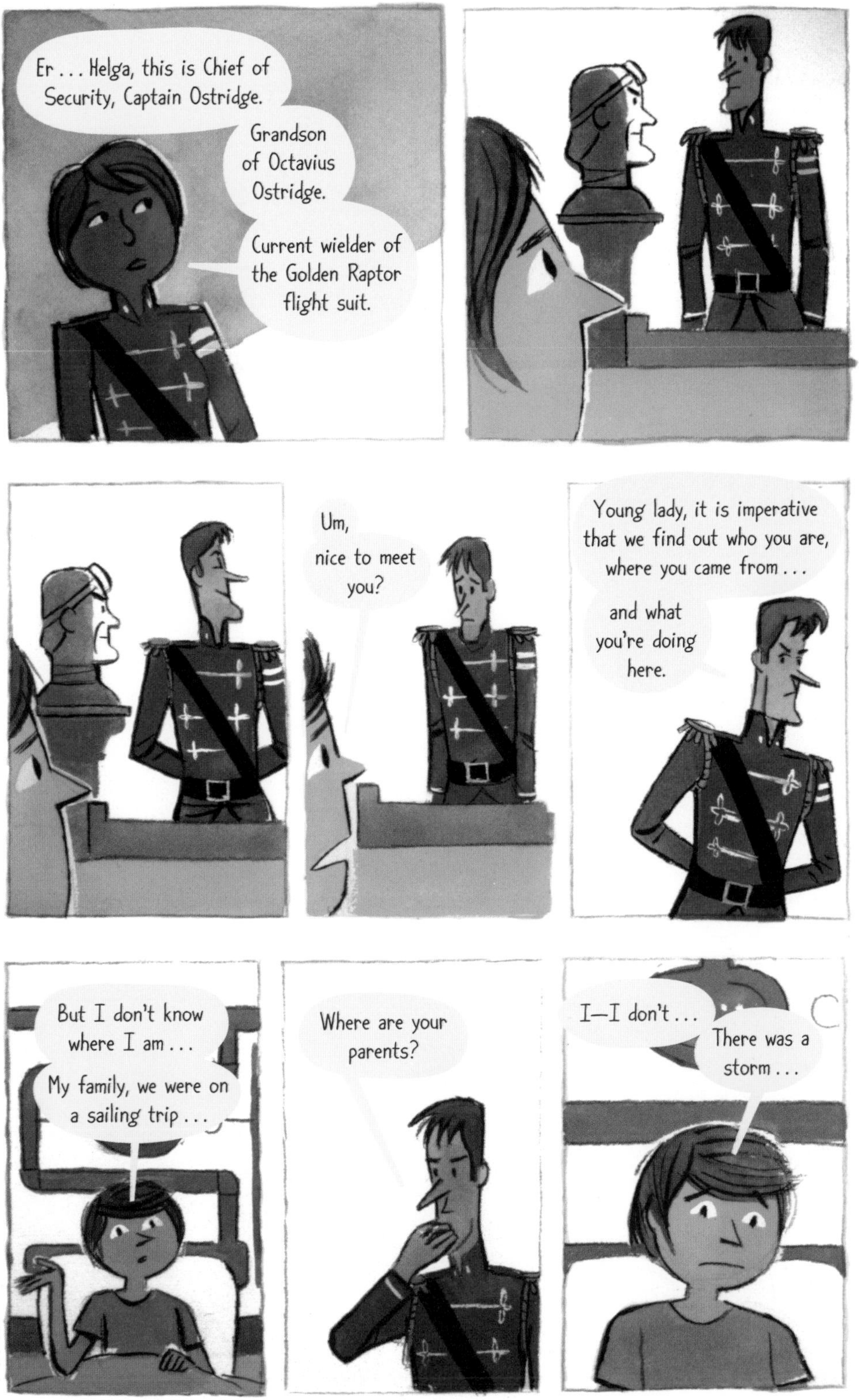

Er . . . Helga, this is Chief of Security, Captain Ostridge.
Grandson of Octavius Ostridge.
Current wielder of the Golden Raptor flight suit.
Um, nice to meet you?
Young lady, it is imperative that we find out who you are, where you came from . . .
and what you're doing here.
But I don't know where I am . . .
My family, we were on a sailing trip . . .
Where are your parents?
I—I don't . . .
There was a storm . . .

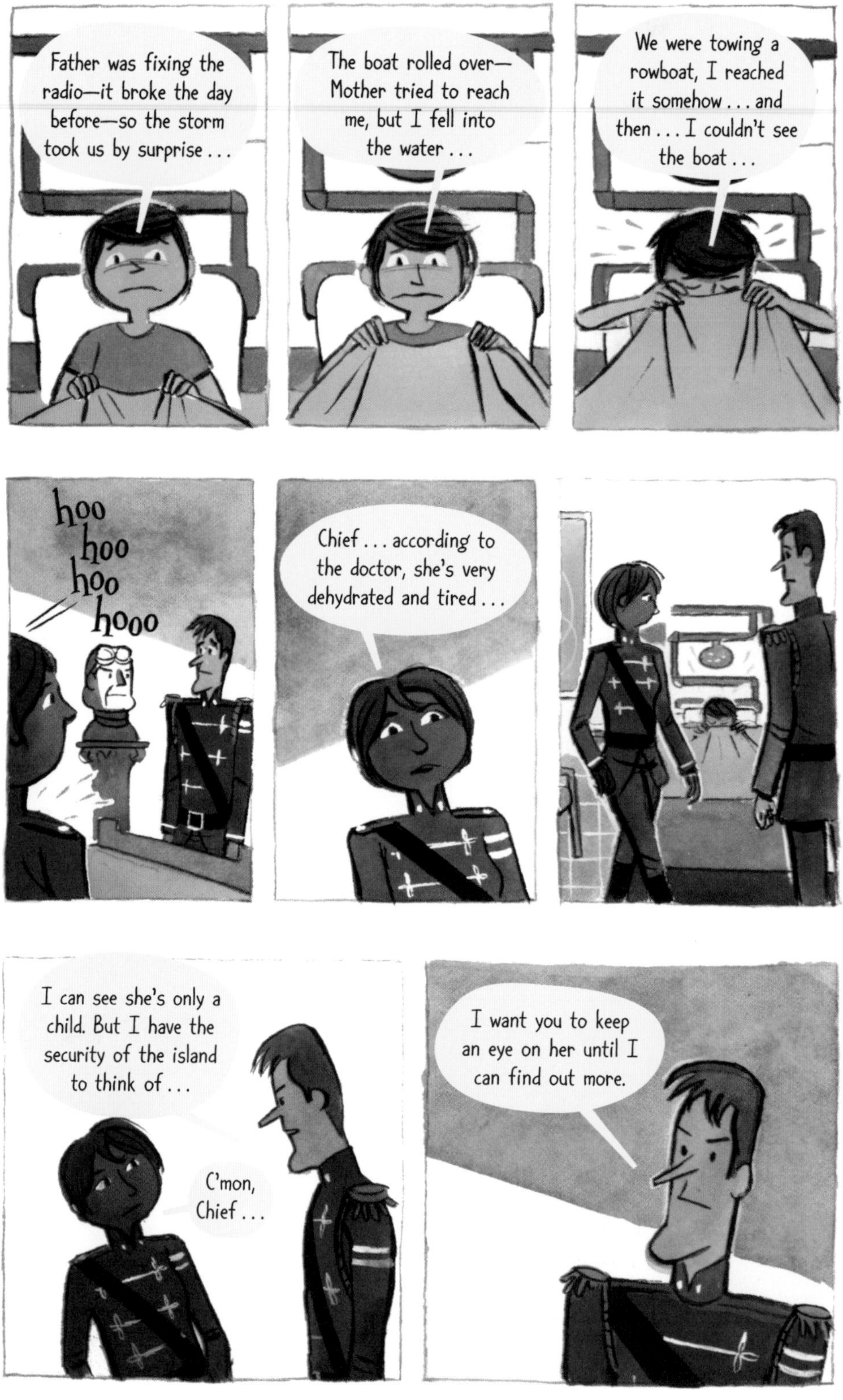
Father was fixing the radio—it broke the day before—so the storm took us by surprise . . .
The boat rolled over—Mother tried to reach me, but I fell into the water . . .
We were towing a rowboat, I reached it somehow . . . and then . . . I couldn't see the boat . . .
hoo hoo hoo hooo
Chief . . . according to the doctor, she's very dehydrated and tired . . .
I can see she's only a child. But I have the security of the island to think of . . .
C'mon, Chief . . .
I want you to keep an eye on her until I can find out more.

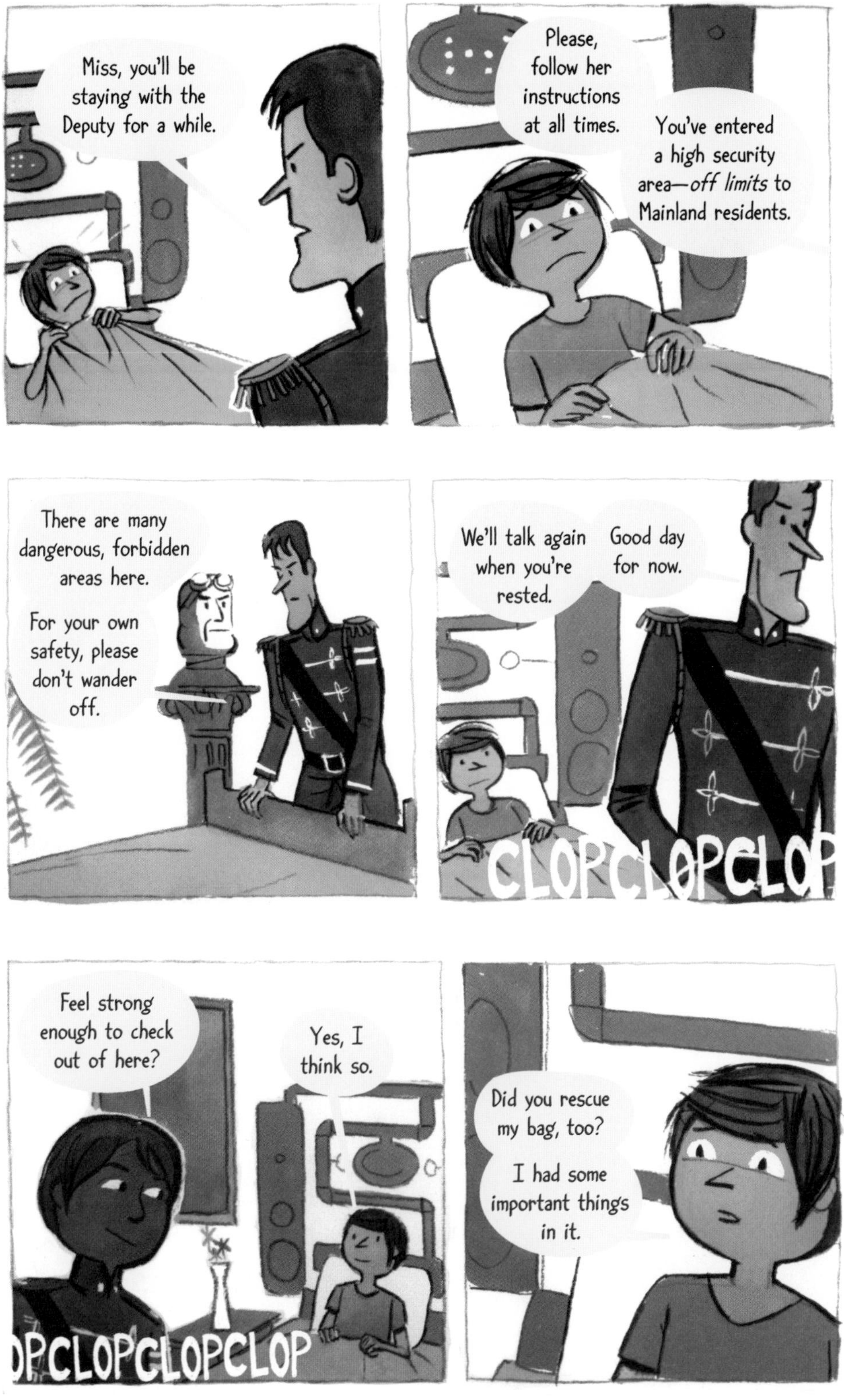

Miss, you'll be staying with the Deputy for a while.
Please, follow her instructions at all times.
You've entered a high security area—*off limits* to Mainland residents.
There are many dangerous, forbidden areas here.
For your own safety, please don't wander off.
We'll talk again when you're rested.
Good day for now.
CLOPCLOPCLOP
Feel strong enough to check out of here?
Yes, I think so.
OPCLOPCLOPCLOP
Did you rescue my bag, too?
I had some important things in it.

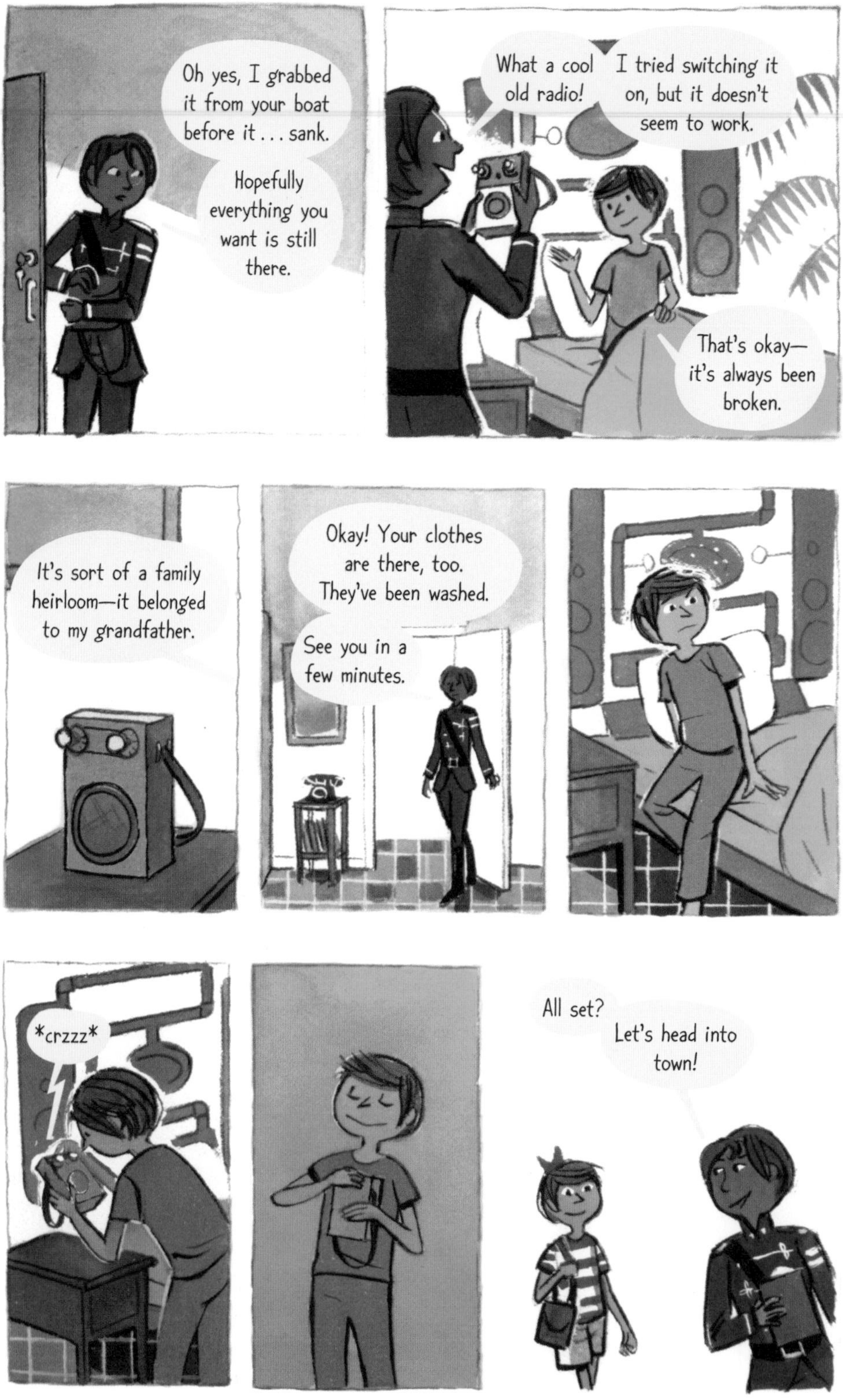
Oh yes, I grabbed it from your boat before it . . . sank.
Hopefully everything you want is still there.
What a cool old radio!
I tried switching it on, but it doesn't seem to work.
That's okay—it's always been broken.
It's sort of a family heirloom—it belonged to my grandfather.
Okay! Your clothes are there, too. They've been washed.
See you in a few minutes.
crzzz
All set?
Let's head into town!

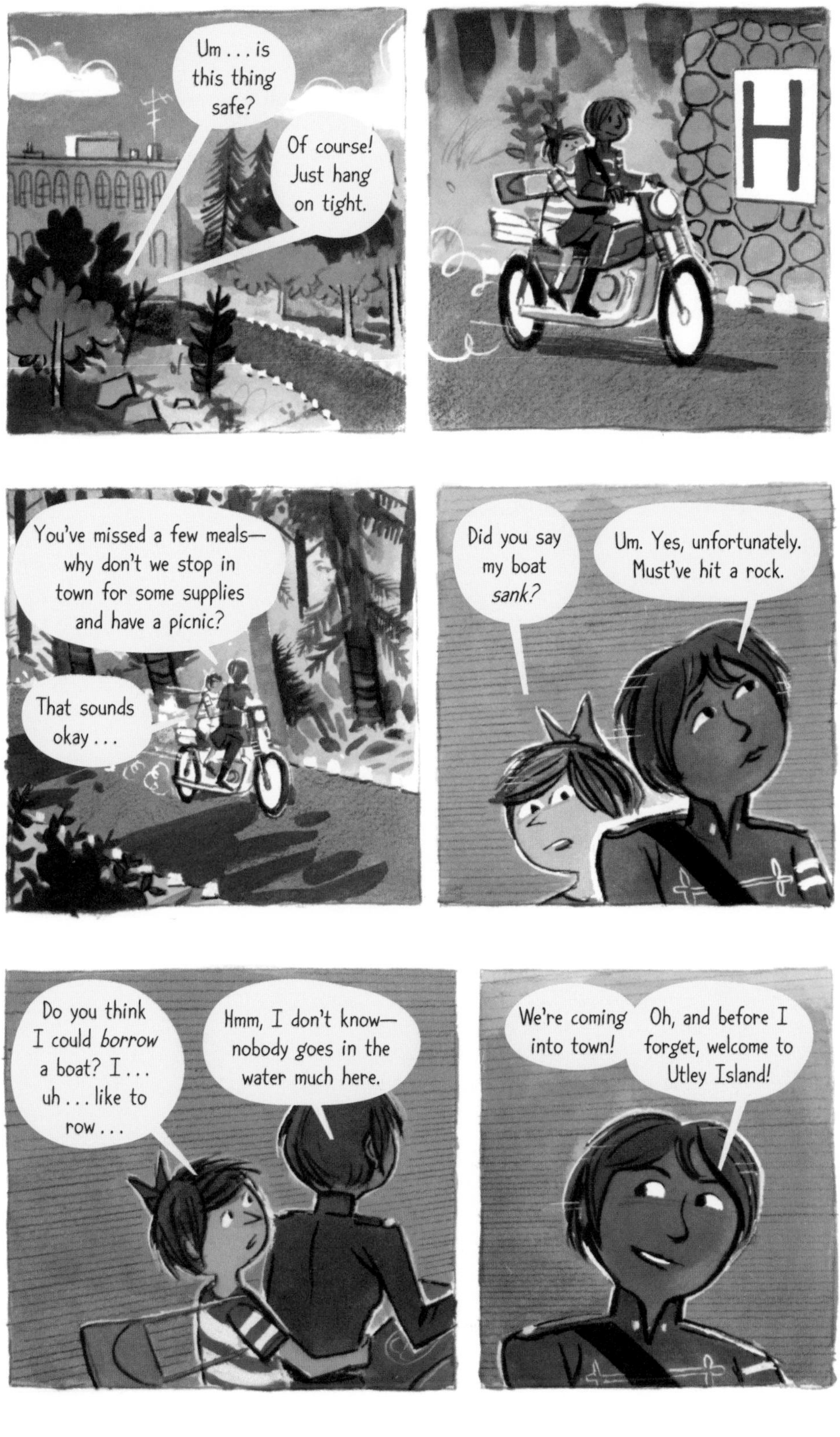
Um . . . is this thing safe?
Of course! Just hang on tight.
H
You've missed a few meals—why don't we stop in town for some supplies and have a picnic?
That sounds okay . . .
Did you say my boat *sank?*
Um. Yes, unfortunately. Must've hit a rock.
Do you think I could *borrow* a boat? I . . . uh . . . like to row . . .
Hmm, I don't know—nobody goes in the water much here.
We're coming into town!
Oh, and before I forget, welcome to Utley Island!

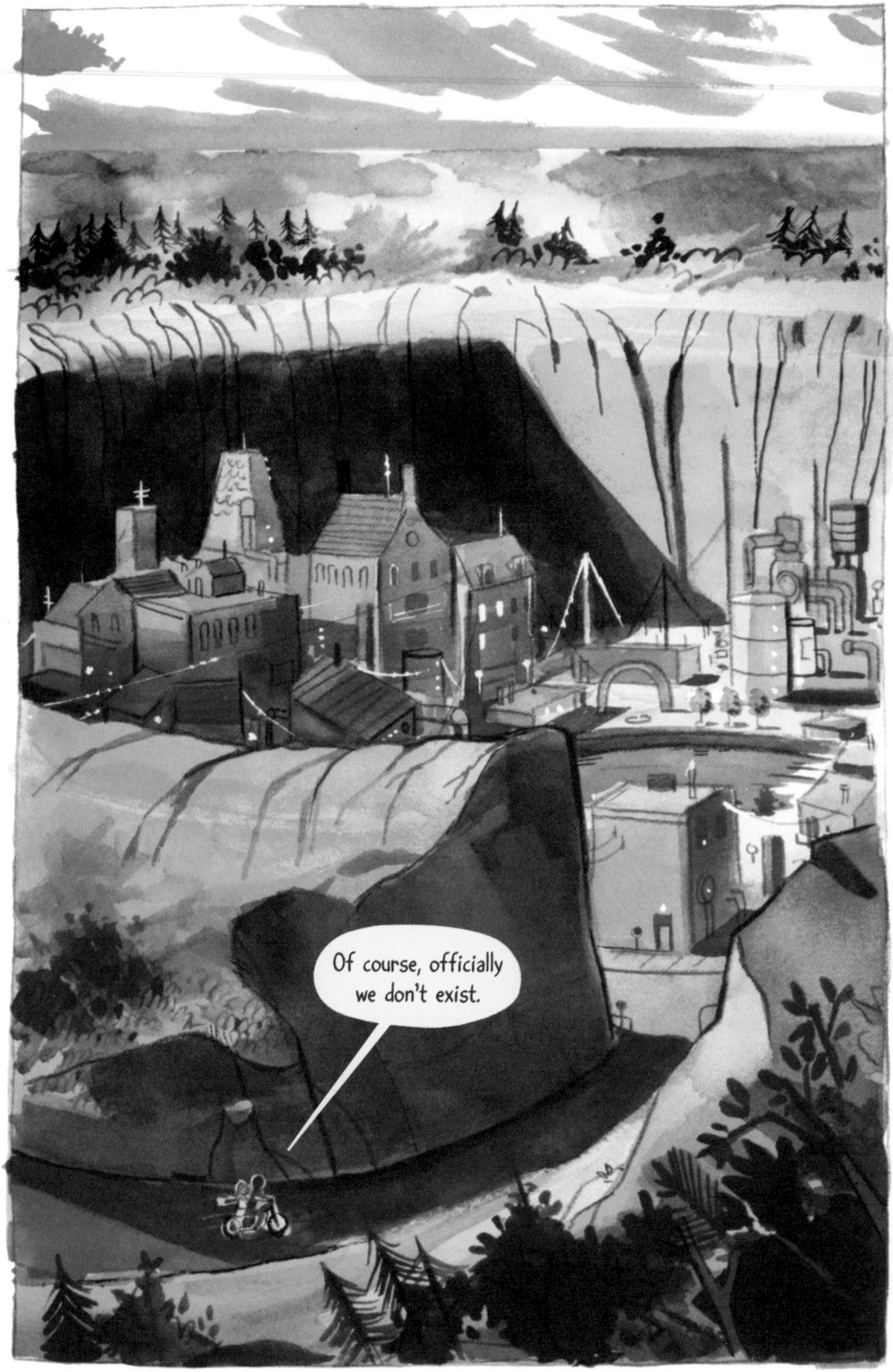
Of course, officially we don't exist.

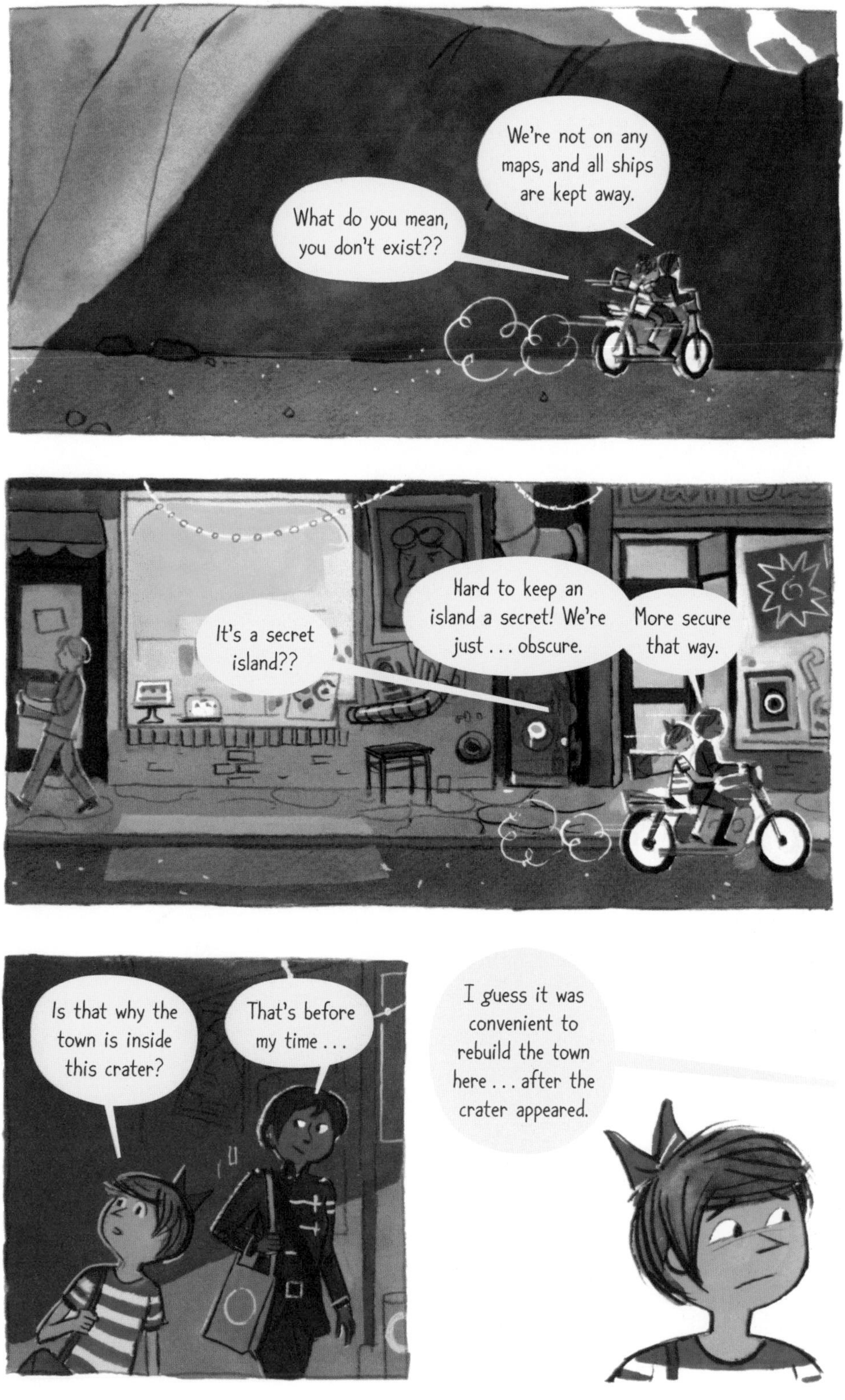
What do you mean, you don't exist??
We're not on any maps, and all ships are kept away.
It's a secret island??
Hard to keep an island a secret! We're just . . . obscure.
More secure that way.
Is that why the town is inside this crater?
That's before my time . . .
I guess it was convenient to rebuild the town here . . . after the crater appeared.

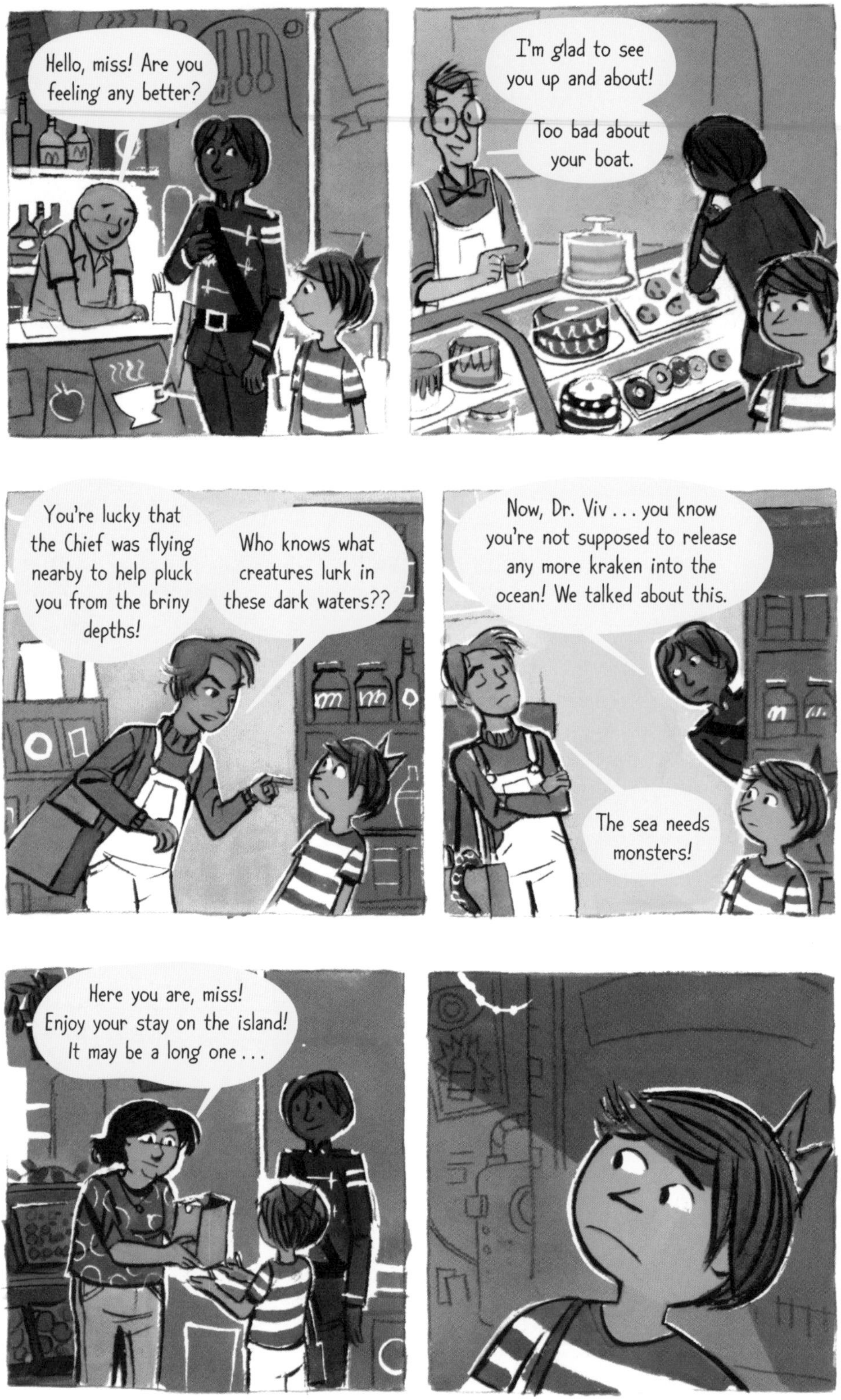
Hello, miss! Are you feeling any better?
I'm glad to see you up and about!
Too bad about your boat.
You're lucky that the Chief was flying nearby to help pluck you from the briny depths!
Who knows what creatures lurk in these dark waters??
Now, Dr. Viv . . . you know you're not supposed to release any more kraken into the ocean! We talked about this.
The sea needs monsters!
Here you are, miss! Enjoy your stay on the island! It may be a long one . . .

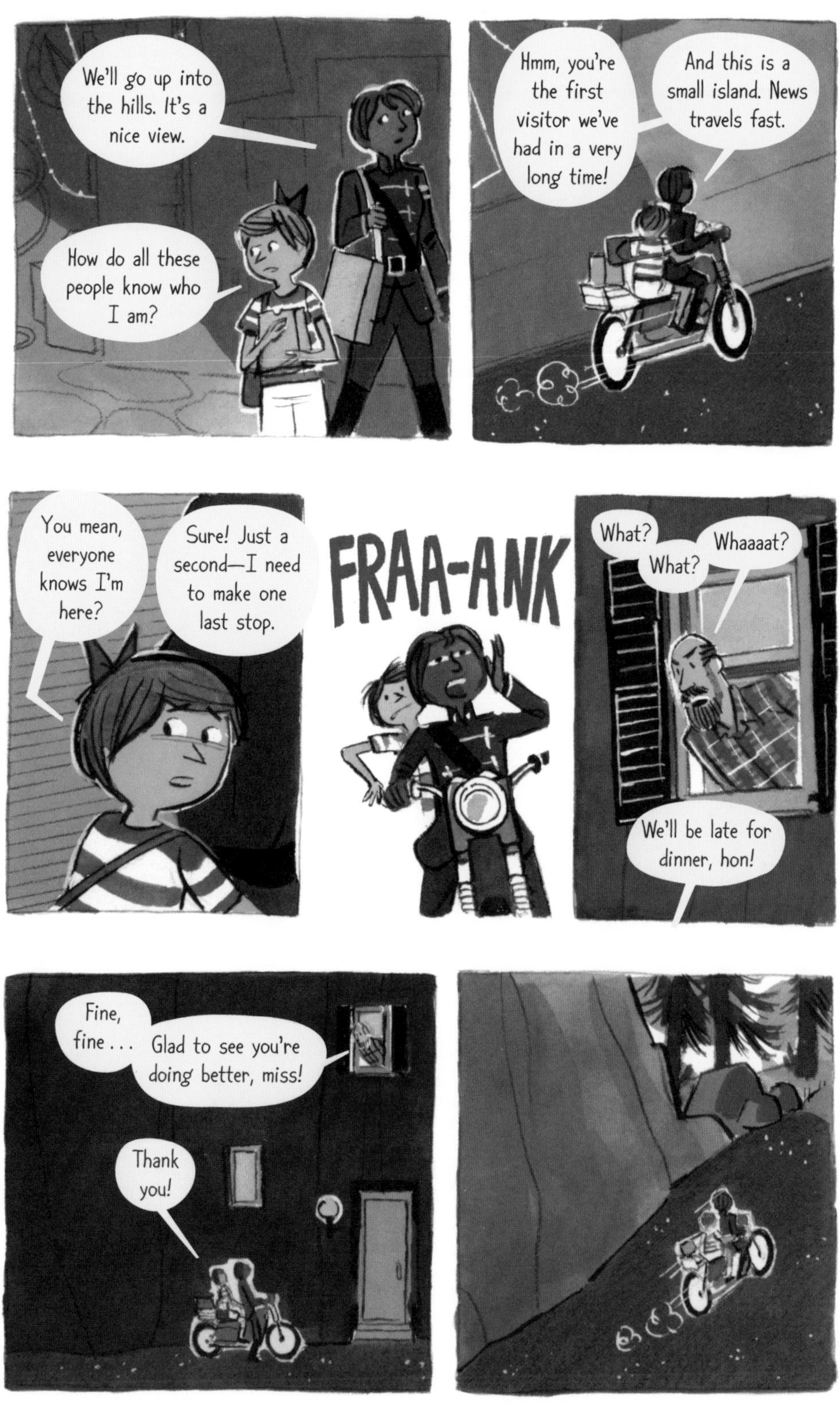
We'll go up into the hills. It's a nice view.
How do all these people know who I am?
Hmm, you're the first visitor we've had in a very long time!
And this is a small island. News travels fast.
You mean, everyone knows I'm here?
Sure! Just a second—I need to make one last stop.
FRAA-ANK
What?
What?
Whaaaat?
We'll be late for dinner, hon!
Fine, fine . . .
Glad to see you're doing better, miss!
Thank you!

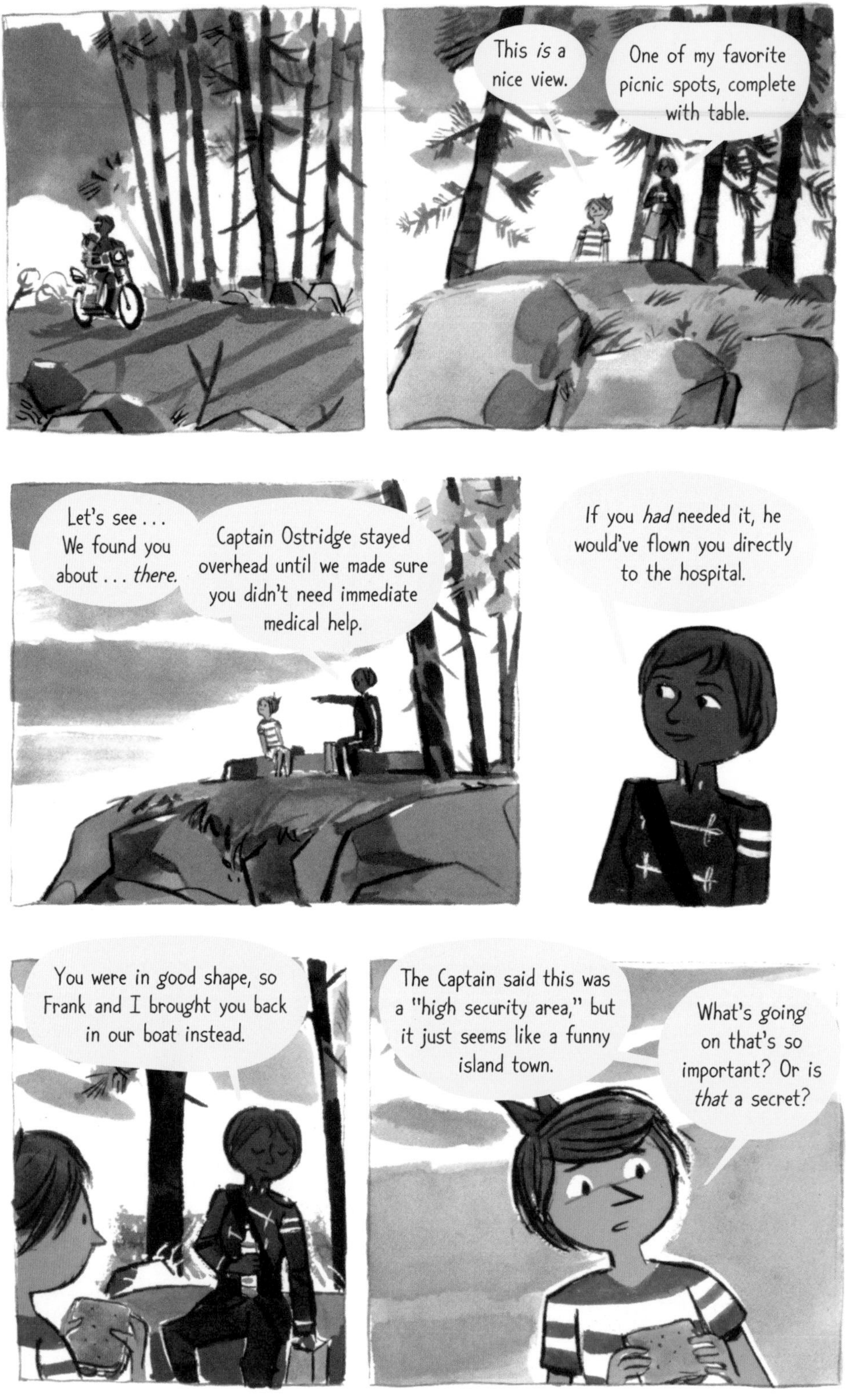
This *is* a nice view.
One of my favorite picnic spots, complete with table.
Let's see . . . We found you about . . . *there.*
Captain Ostridge stayed overhead until we made sure you didn't need immediate medical help.
If you *had* needed it, he would've flown you directly to the hospital.
You were in good shape, so Frank and I brought you back in our boat instead.
The Captain said this was a "high security area," but it just seems like a funny island town.
What's *going* on that's so important? Or is *that* a secret?

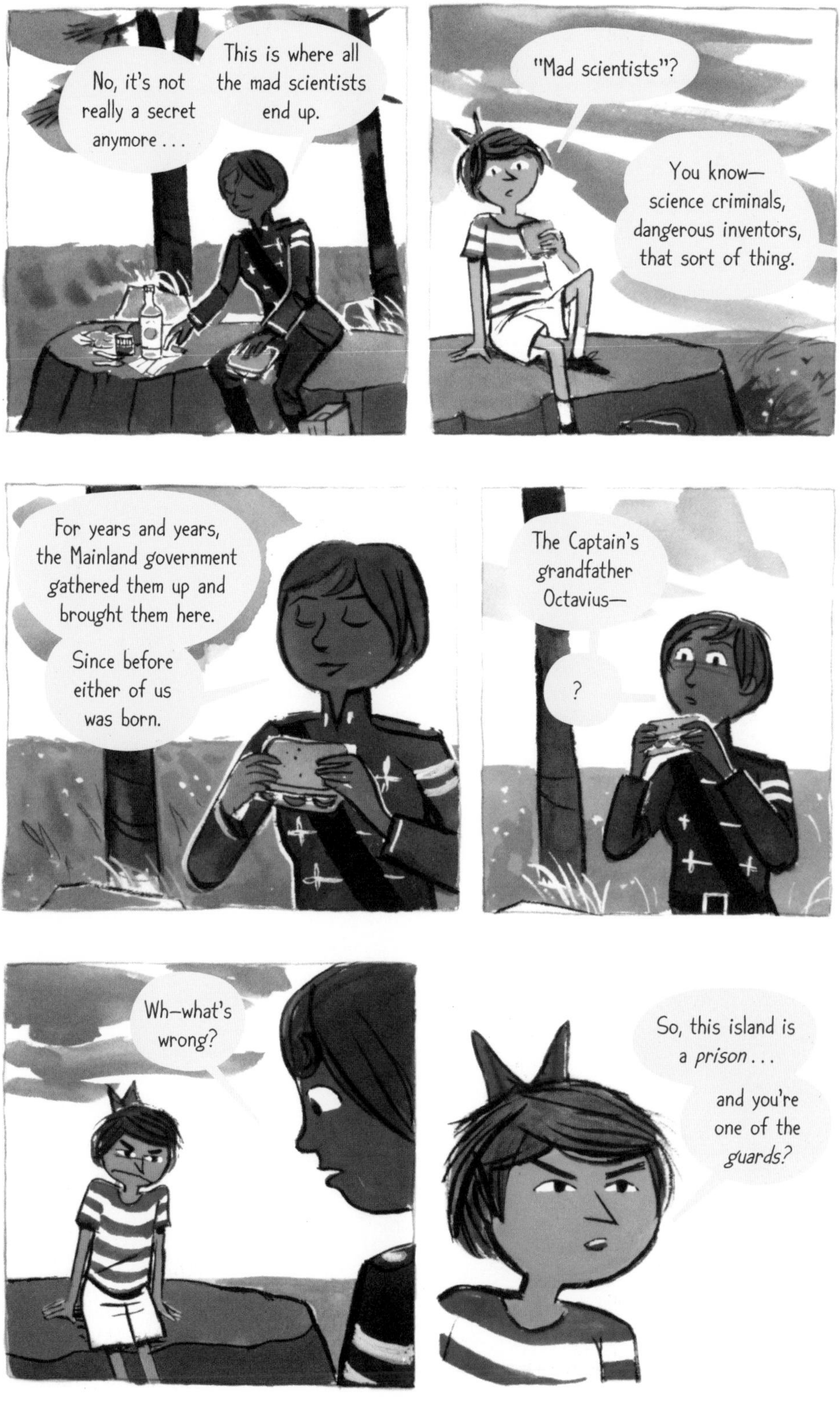
No, it's not really a secret anymore . . .
This is where all the mad scientists end up.
"Mad scientists"?
You know— science criminals, dangerous inventors, that sort of thing.
For years and years, the Mainland government gathered them up and brought them here.
Since before either of us was born.
The Captain's grandfather Octavius—
?
Wh–what's wrong?
So, this island is a *prison* . . .
and you're one of the *guards?*

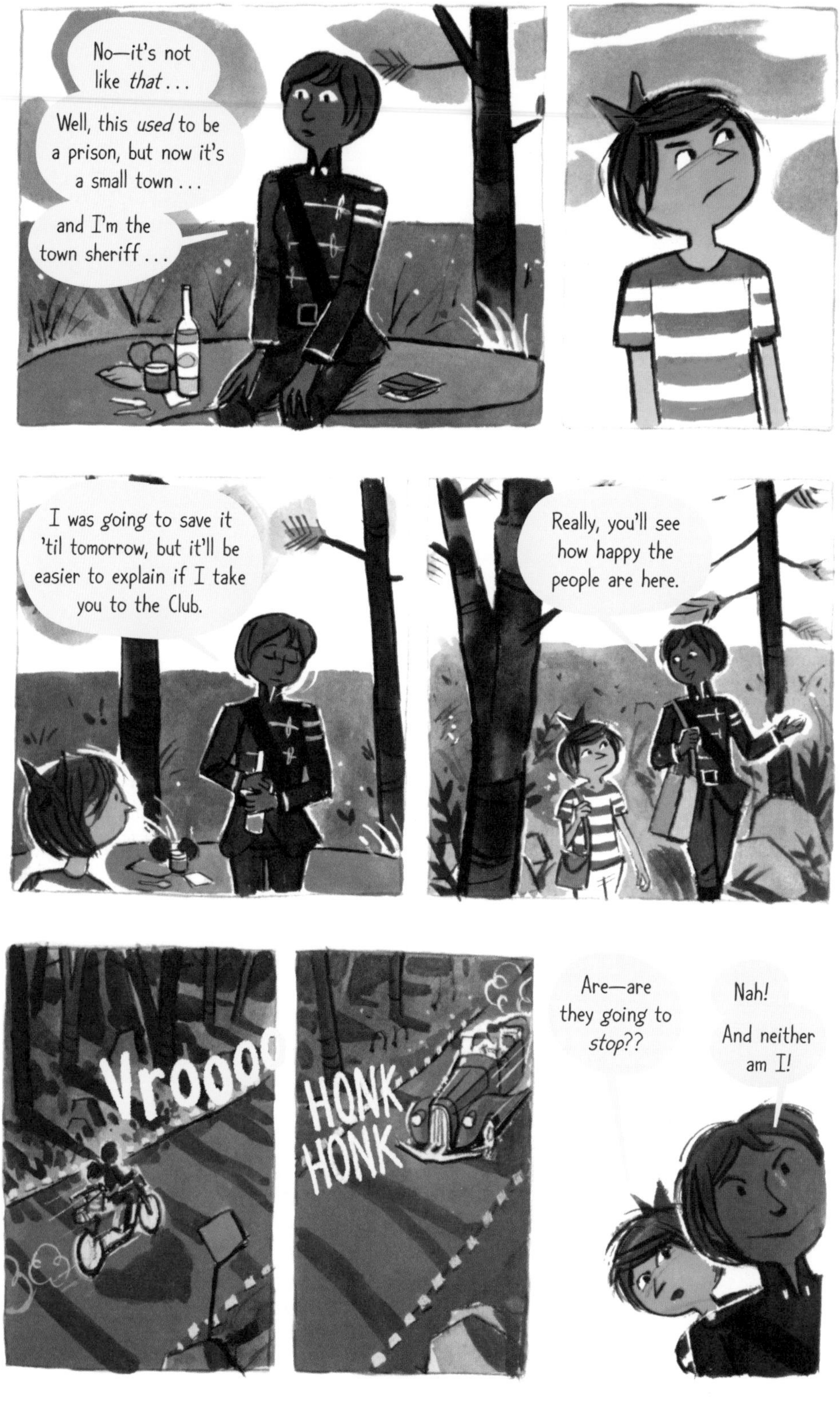
No—it's not like *that*...
Well, this *used* to be a prison, but now it's a small town...
and I'm the town sheriff...
I was going to save it 'til tomorrow, but it'll be easier to explain if I take you to the Club.
Really, you'll see how happy the people are here.
Vroooo
HONK HONK
Are—are they going to *stop*??
Nah!
And neither am I!

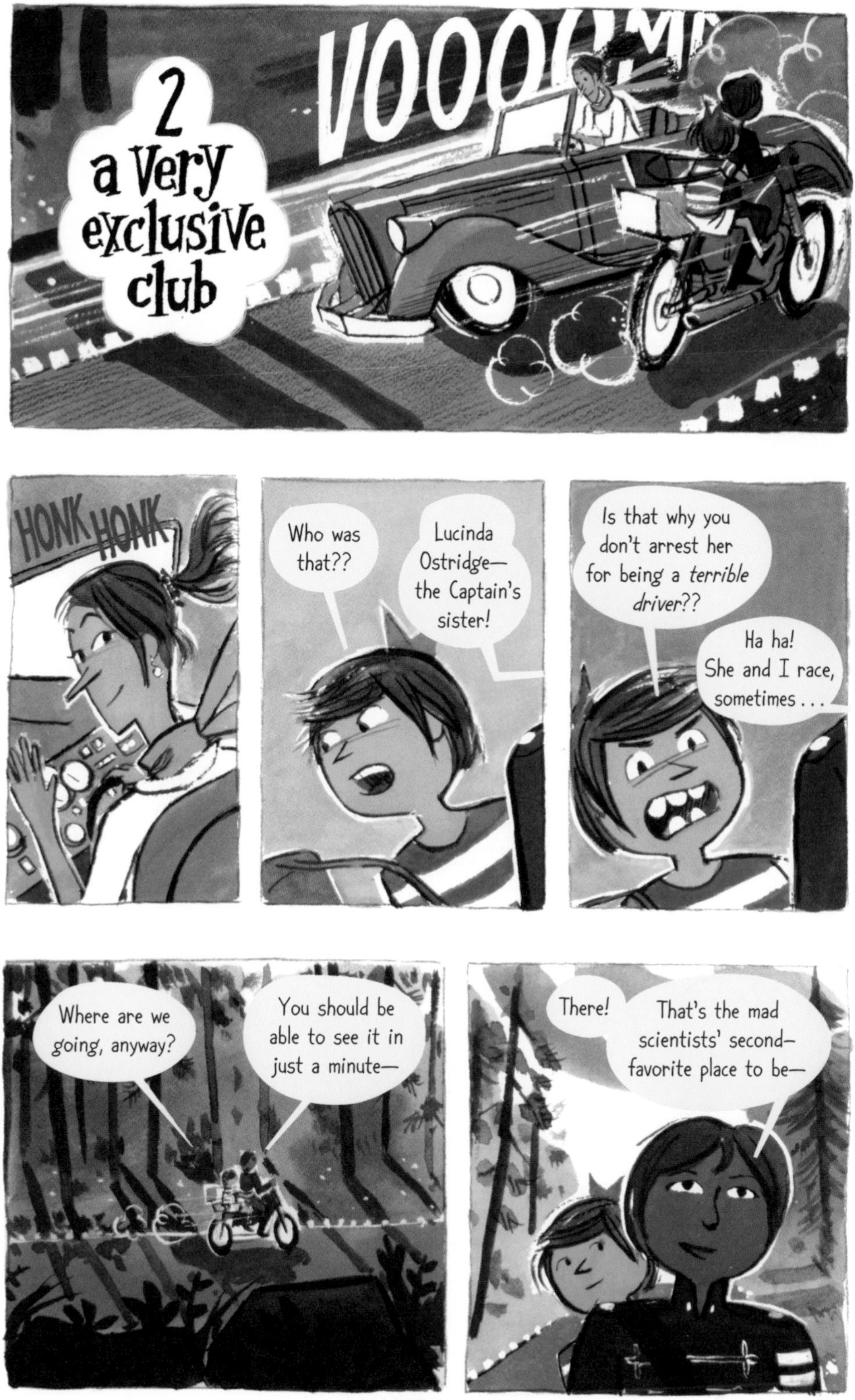
2
a very exclusive club
HONK HONK
Who was that??
Lucinda Ostridge—the Captain's sister!
Is that why you don't arrest her for being a *terrible driver*??
Ha ha! She and I race, sometimes . . .
Where are we going, anyway?
You should be able to see it in just a minute—
There!
That's the mad scientists' second-favorite place to be—

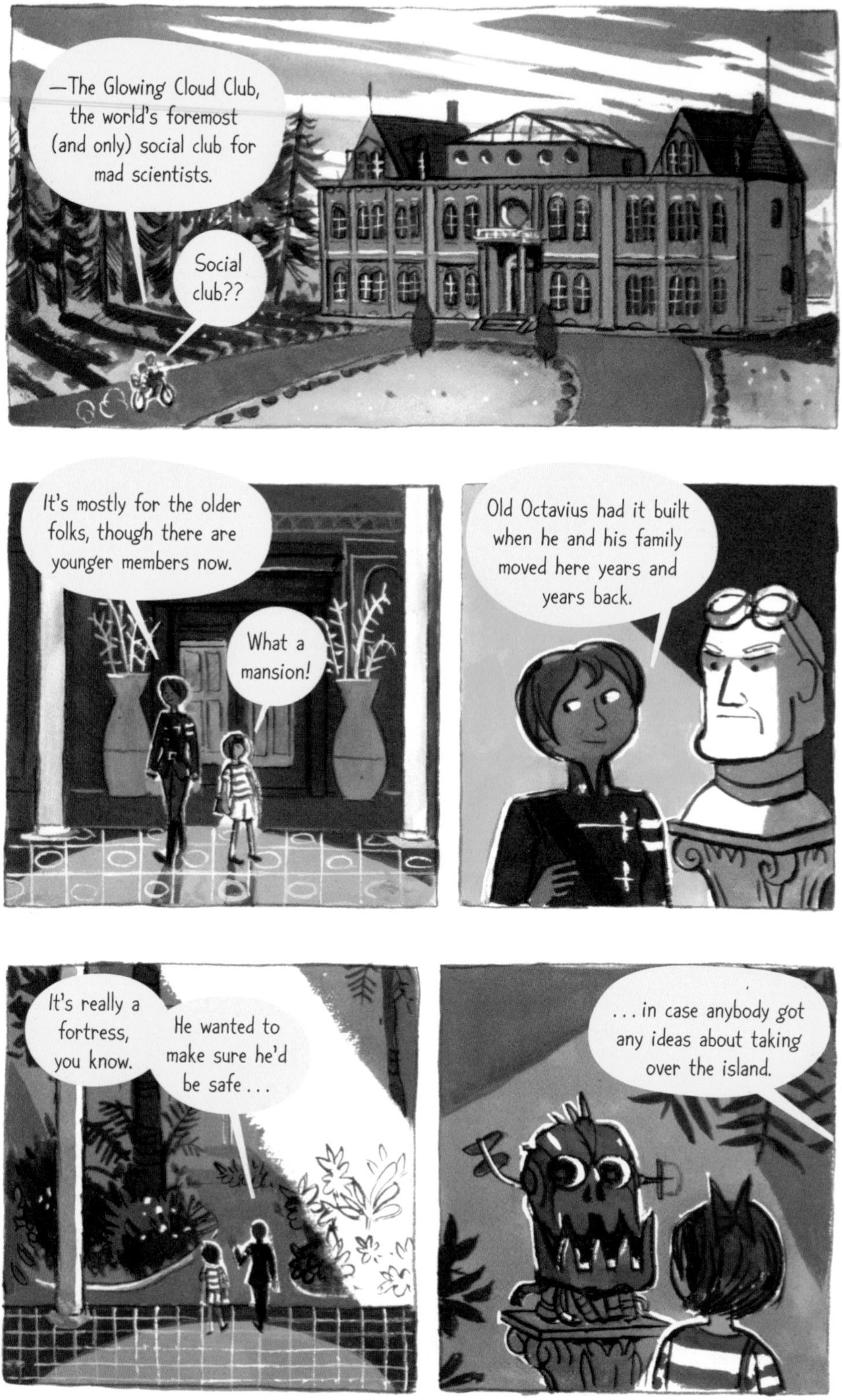
—The Glowing Cloud Club, the world's foremost (and only) social club for mad scientists.
Social club??
It's mostly for the older folks, though there are younger members now.
What a mansion!
Old Octavius had it built when he and his family moved here years and years back.
It's really a fortress, you know.
He wanted to make sure he'd be safe . . .
. . . in case anybody got any ideas about taking over the island.

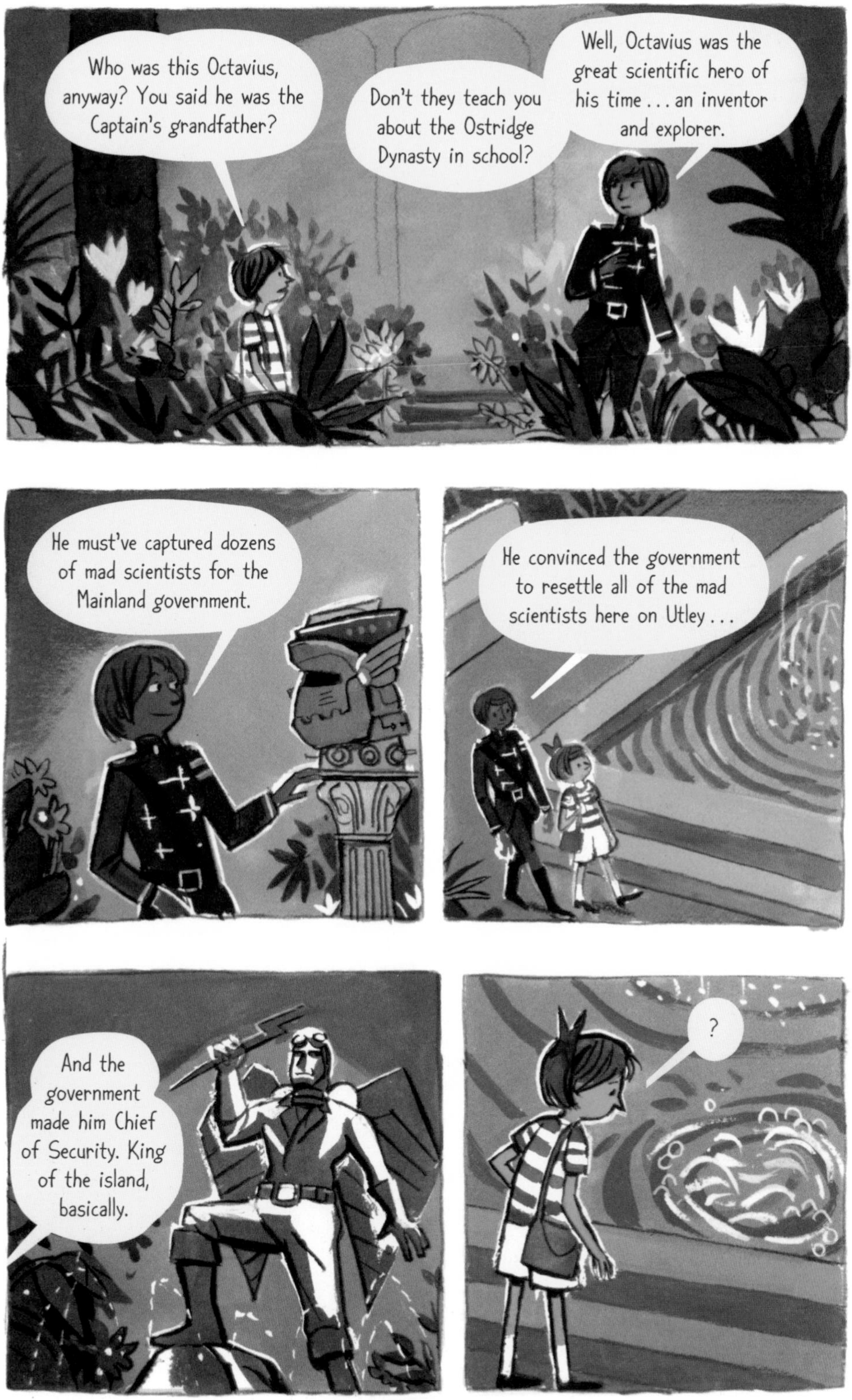
Who was this Octavius, anyway? You said he was the Captain's grandfather?
Don't they teach you about the Ostridge Dynasty in school?
Well, Octavius was the great scientific hero of his time . . . an inventor and explorer.
He must've captured dozens of mad scientists for the Mainland government.
He convinced the government to resettle all of the mad scientists here on Utley . . .
And the government made him Chief of Security. King of the island, basically.
?

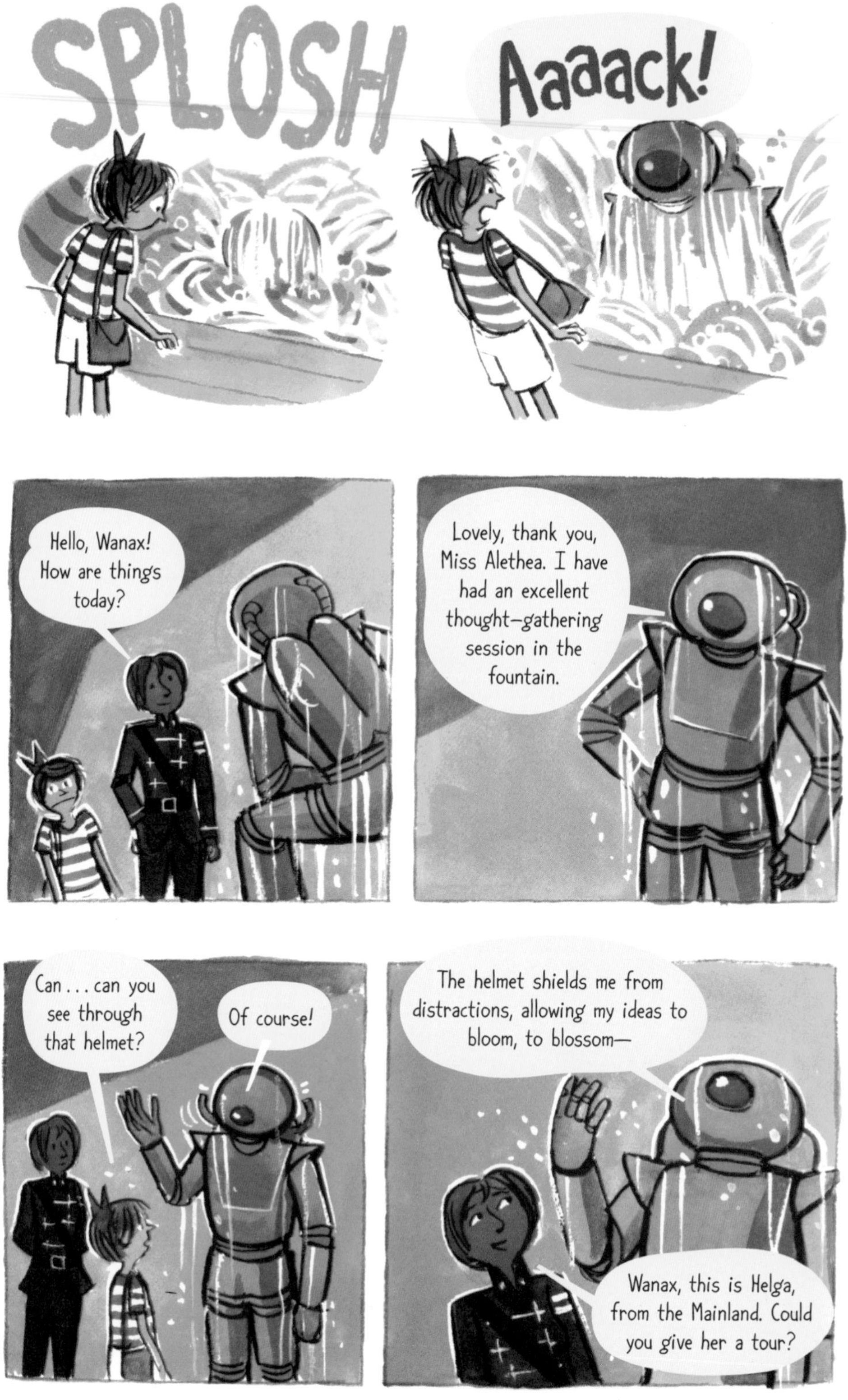
SPLOSH
Aaaack!
Hello, Wanax! How are things today?
Lovely, thank you, Miss Alethea. I have had an excellent thought-gathering session in the fountain.
Can . . . can you see through that helmet?
Of course!
The helmet shields me from distractions, allowing my ideas to bloom, to blossom—
Wanax, this is Helga, from the Mainland. Could you give her a tour?

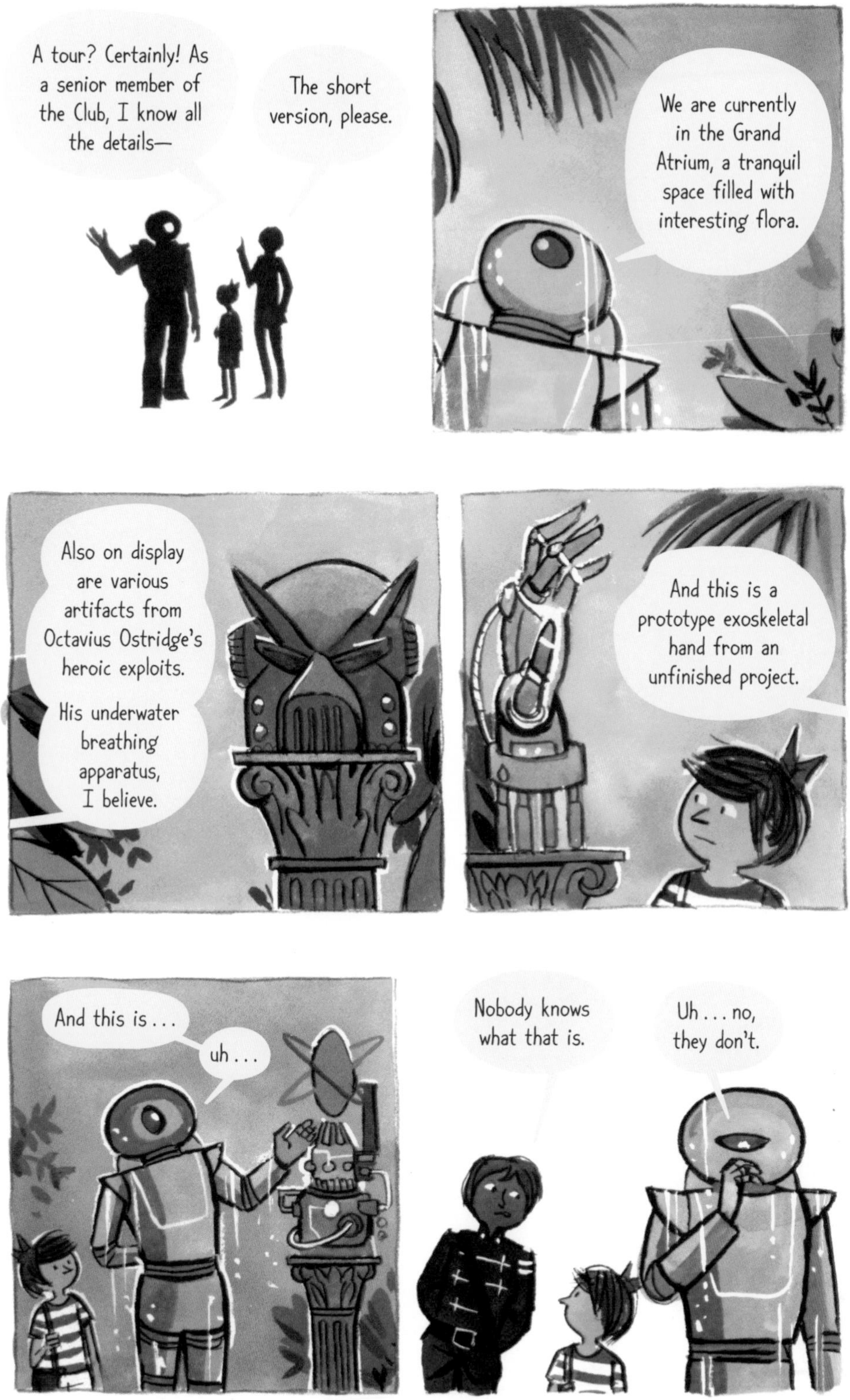
A tour? Certainly! As a senior member of the Club, I know all the details—
The short version, please.
We are currently in the Grand Atrium, a tranquil space filled with interesting flora.
Also on display are various artifacts from Octavius Ostridge's heroic exploits.
His underwater breathing apparatus, I believe.
And this is a prototype exoskeletal hand from an unfinished project.
And this is . . .
uh . . .
Nobody knows what that is.
Uh . . . no, they don't.

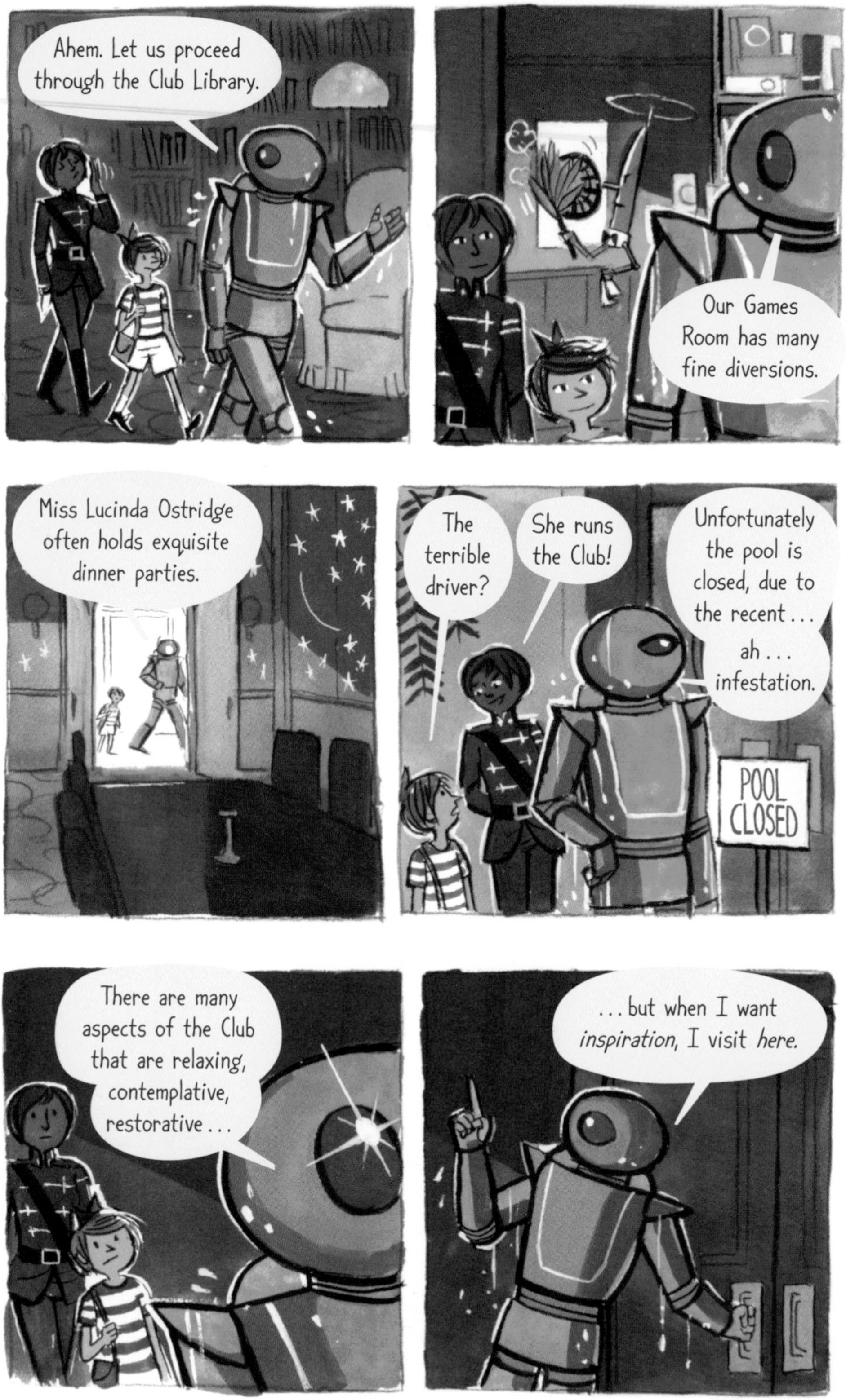
Ahem. Let us proceed through the Club Library.
Our Games Room has many fine diversions.
Miss Lucinda Ostridge often holds exquisite dinner parties.
The terrible driver?
She runs the Club!
Unfortunately the pool is closed, due to the recent . . .
ah . . . infestation.
POOL CLOSED
There are many aspects of the Club that are relaxing, contemplative, restorative . . .
. . . but when I want *inspiration*, I visit *here*.

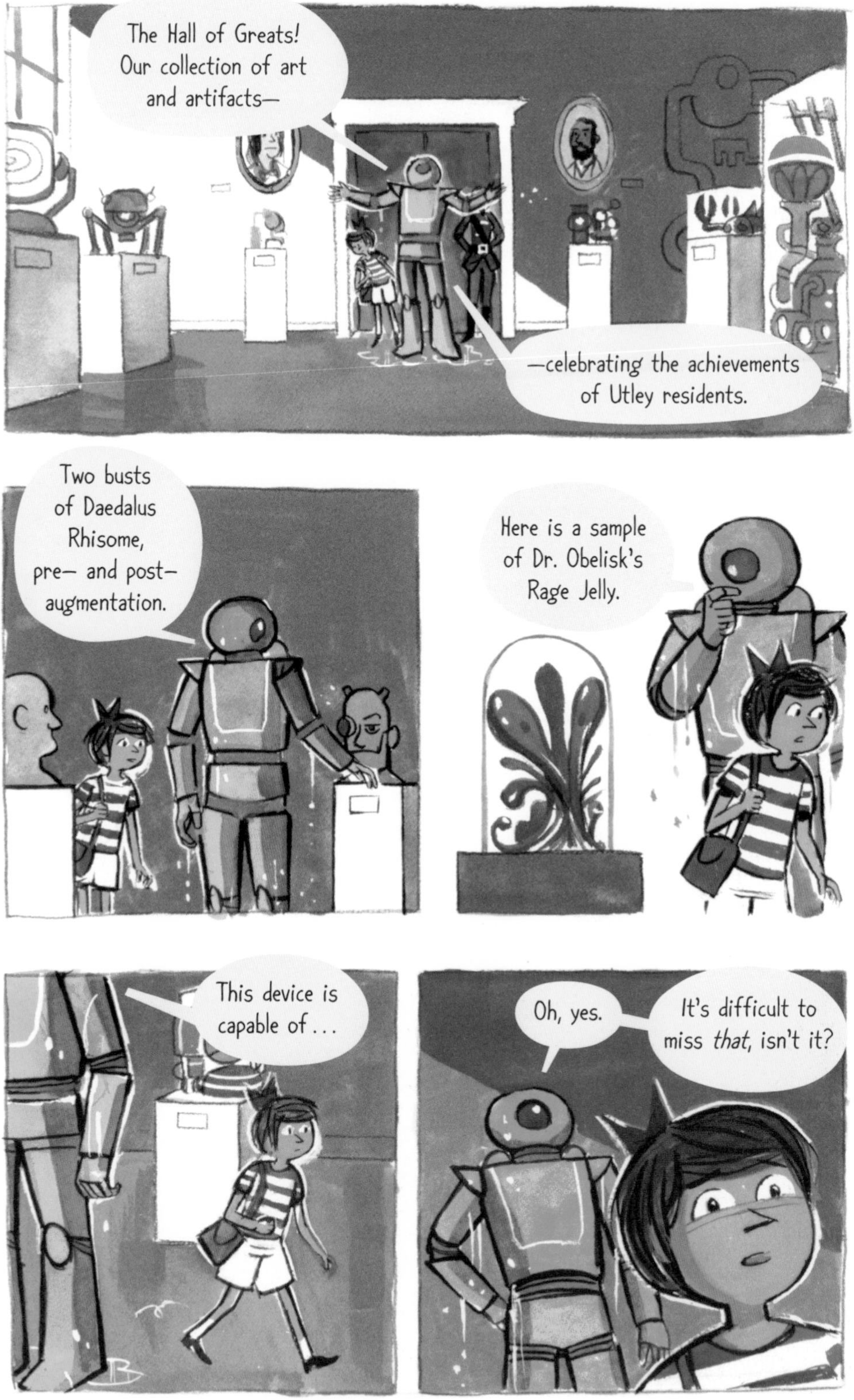
The Hall of Greats! Our collection of art and artifacts—
—celebrating the achievements of Utley residents.
Two busts of Daedalus Rhisome, pre- and post-augmentation.
Here is a sample of Dr. Obelisk's Rage Jelly.
This device is capable of . . .
Oh, yes.
It's difficult to miss *that*, isn't it?

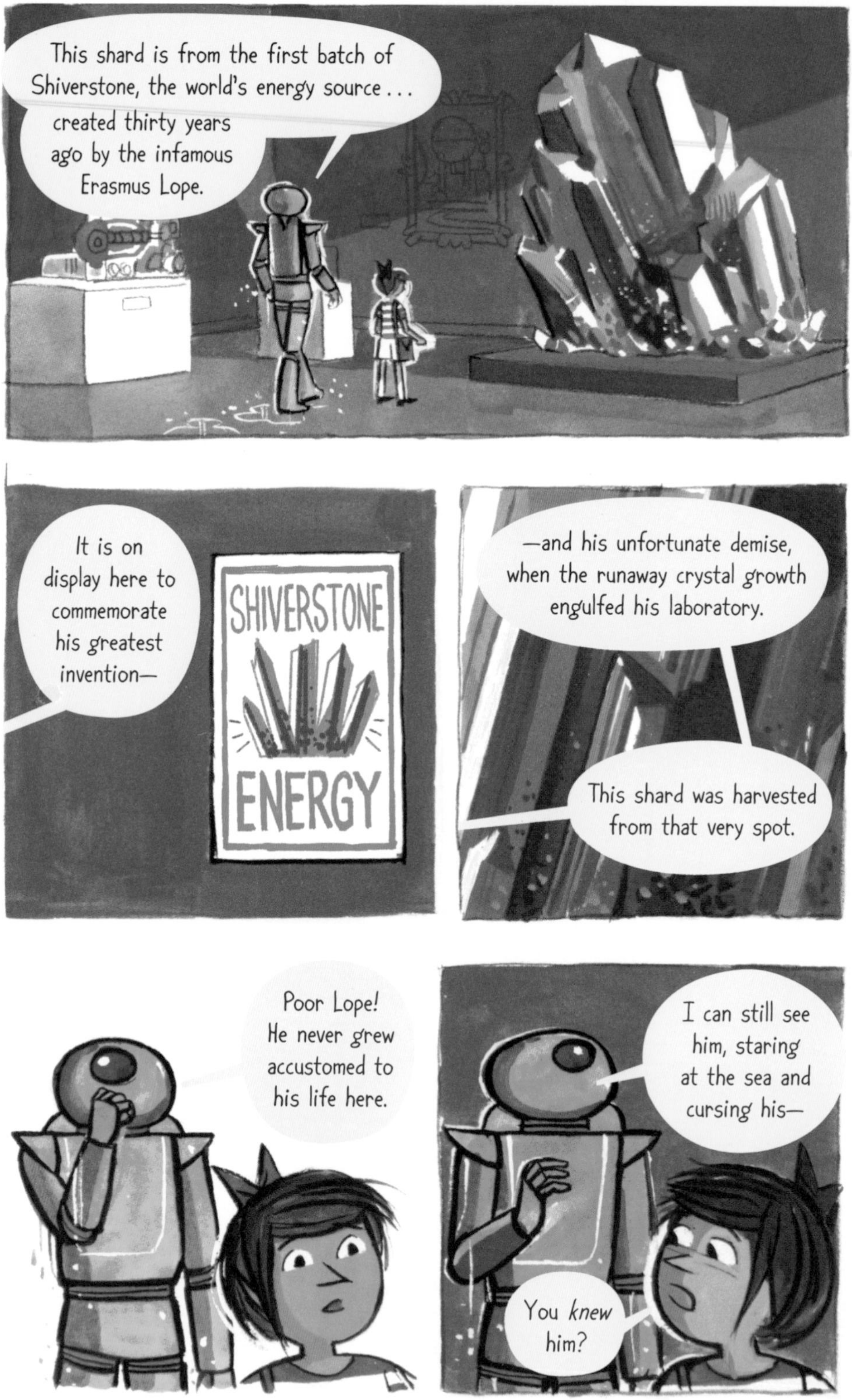
This shard is from the first batch of Shiverstone, the world's energy source . . .
created thirty years ago by the infamous Erasmus Lope.
It is on display here to commemorate his greatest invention—
SHIVERSTONE ENERGY
—and his unfortunate demise, when the runaway crystal growth engulfed his laboratory.
This shard was harvested from that very spot.
Poor Lope! He never grew accustomed to his life here.
I can still see him, staring at the sea and cursing his—
You *knew* him?

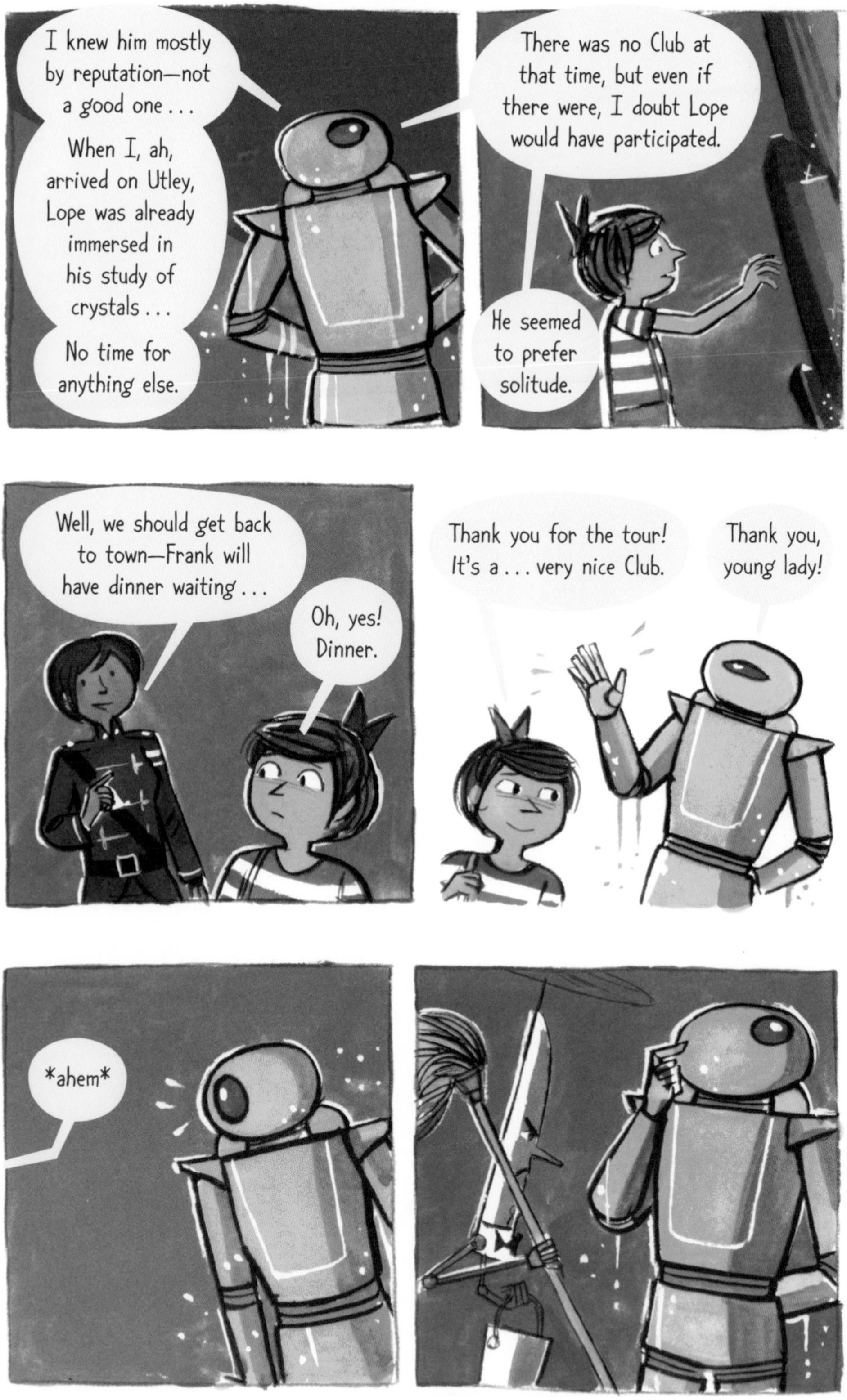
I knew him mostly by reputation—not a good one . . .
When I, ah, arrived on Utley, Lope was already immersed in his study of crystals . . .
No time for anything else.
There was no Club at that time, but even if there were, I doubt Lope would have participated.
He seemed to prefer solitude.
Well, we should get back to town—Frank will have dinner waiting . . .
Oh, yes! Dinner.
Thank you for the tour! It's a . . . very nice Club.
Thank you, young lady!
ahem

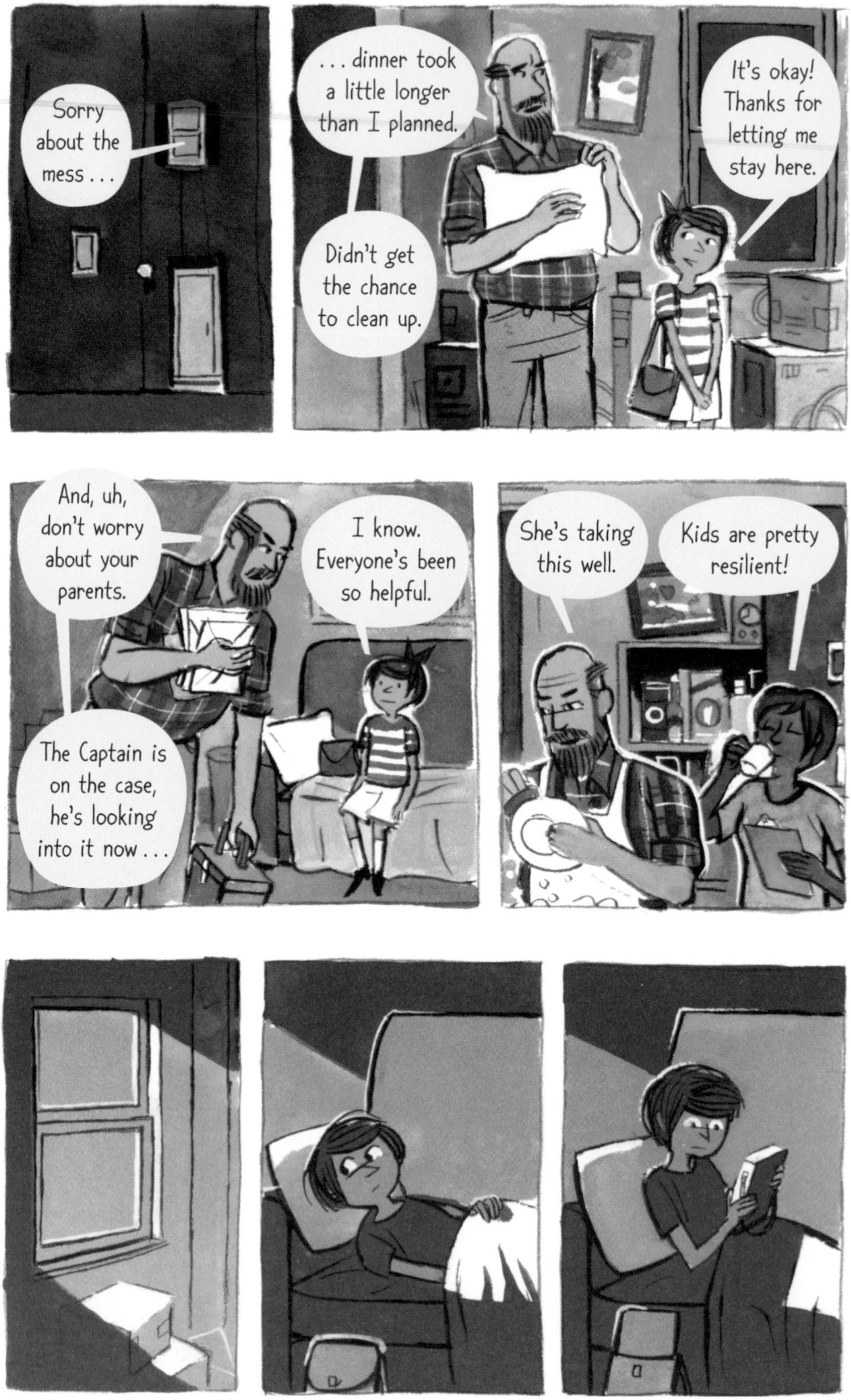
Sorry about the mess . . .
. . . dinner took a little longer than I planned.
Didn't get the chance to clean up.
It's okay! Thanks for letting me stay here.
And, uh, don't worry about your parents.
The Captain is on the case, he's looking into it now . . .
I know. Everyone's been so helpful.
She's taking this well.
Kids are pretty resilient!

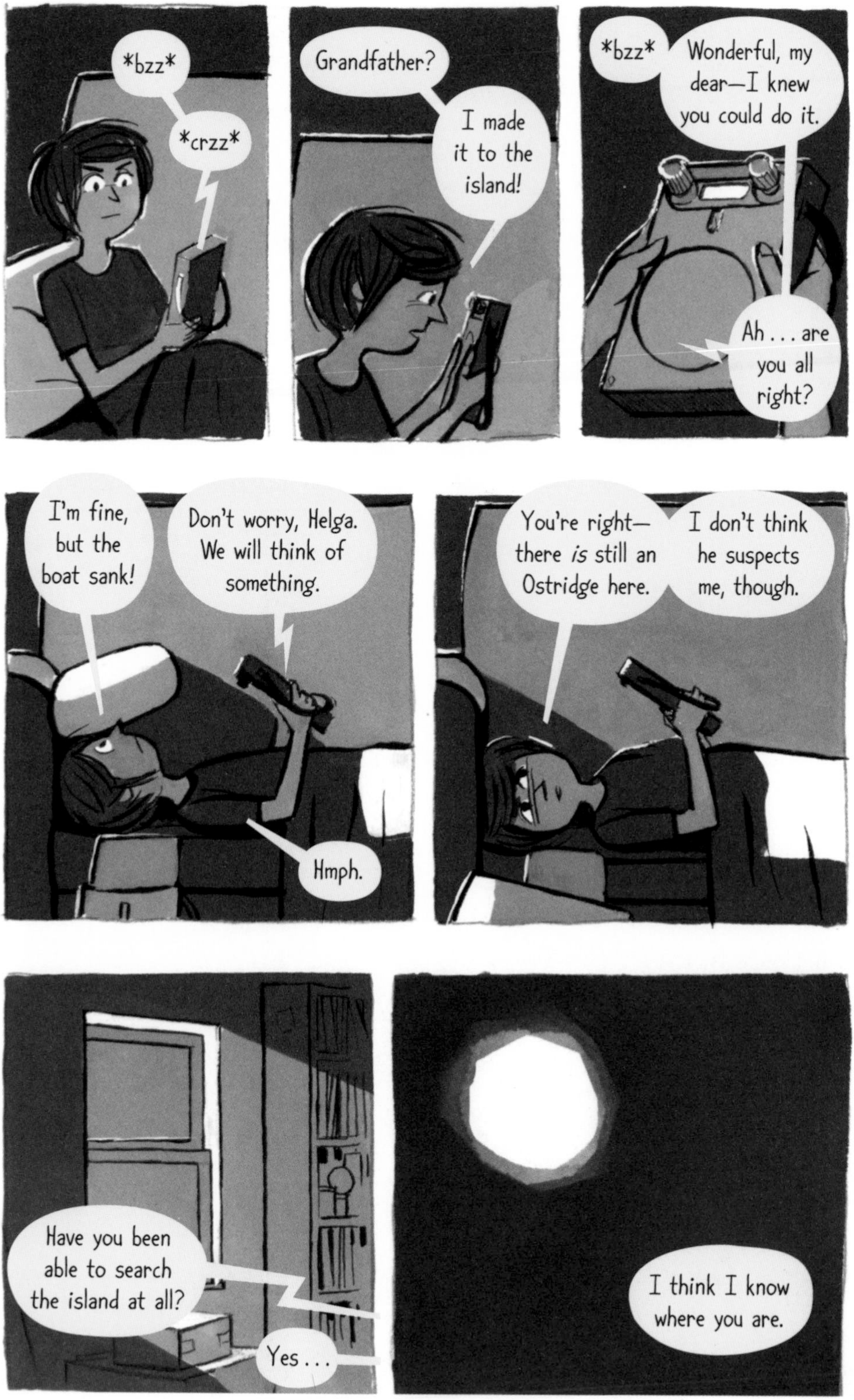
bzz
crzz
Grandfather?
I made it to the island!
bzz
Wonderful, my dear—I knew you could do it.
Ah . . . are you all right?
I'm fine, but the boat sank!
Don't worry, Helga. We will think of something.
Hmph.
You're right—there *is* still an Ostridge here.
I don't think he suspects me, though.
Have you been able to search the island at all?
Yes . . .
I think I know where you are.

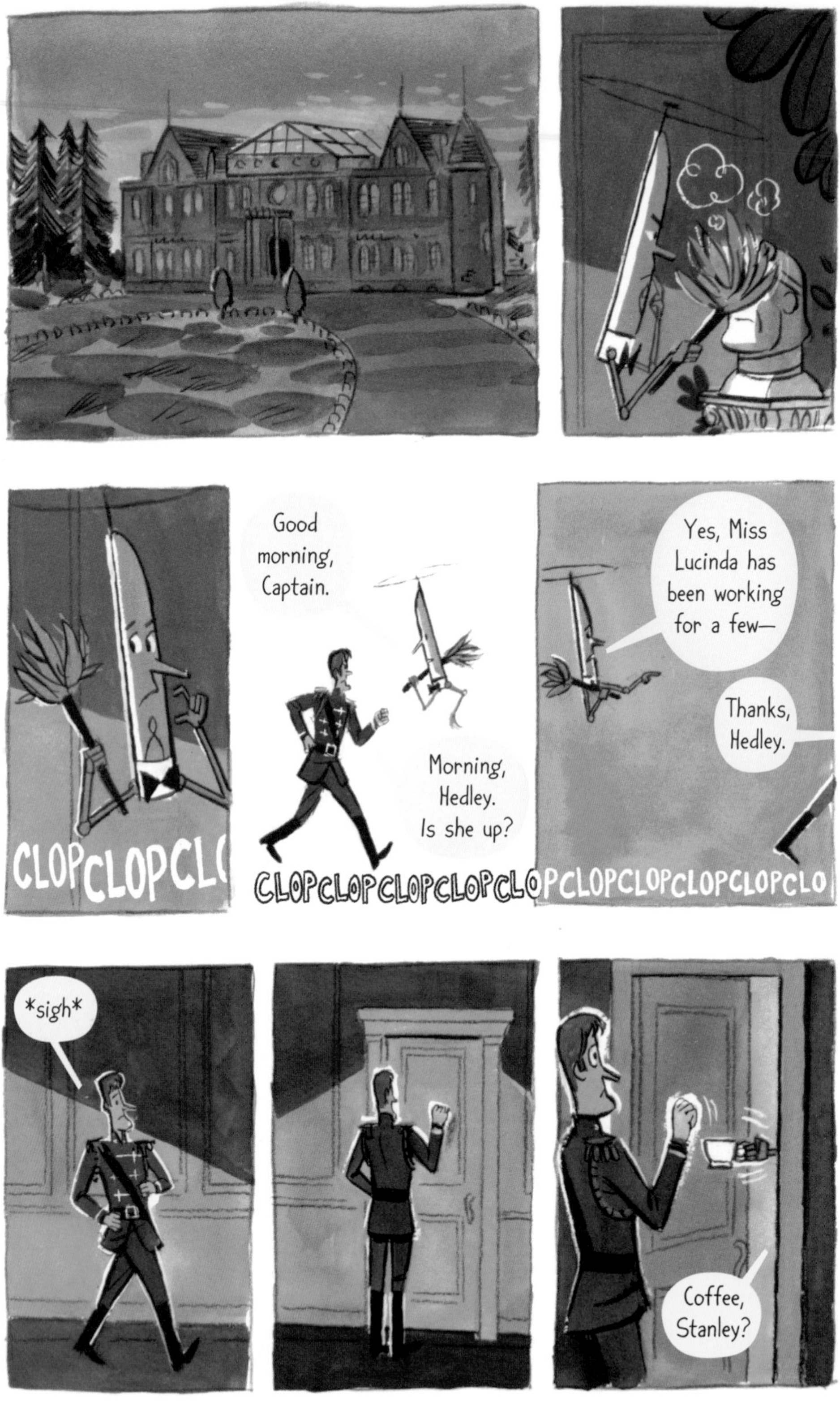
Good morning, Captain.
Morning, Hedley. Is she up?
Yes, Miss Lucinda has been working for a few—
Thanks, Hedley.
CLOPCLOPCLOPCLOPCLOPCLOPCLOPCLOPCLOPCLOPCLOPCLOPCLOPCLO
sigh
Coffee, Stanley?

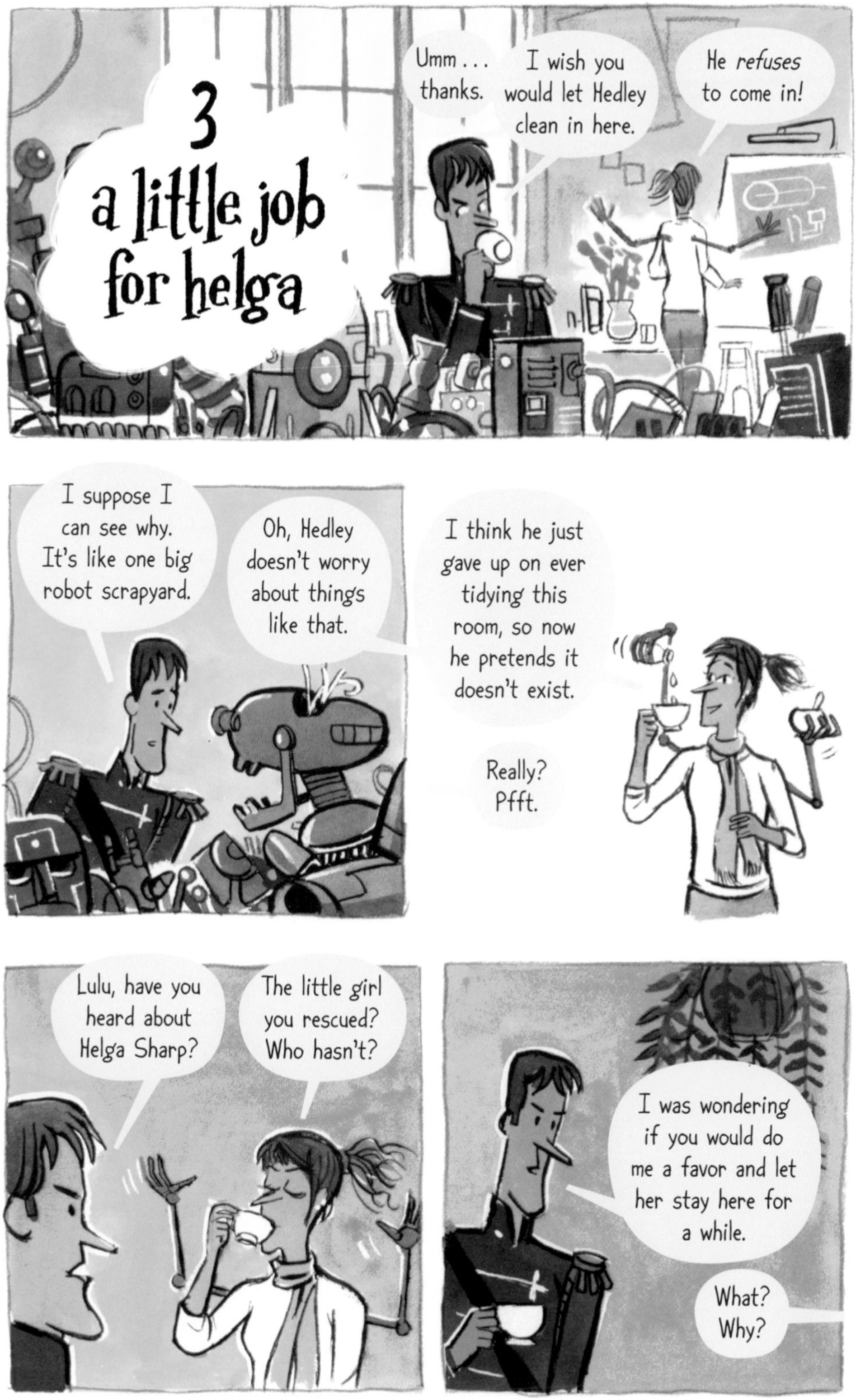
3
a little job for helga
Umm . . . thanks.
I wish you would let Hedley clean in here.
He *refuses* to come in!
I suppose I can see why. It's like one big robot scrapyard.
Oh, Hedley doesn't worry about things like that.
I think he just gave up on ever tidying this room, so now he pretends it doesn't exist.
Really? Pfft.
Lulu, have you heard about Helga Sharp?
The little girl you rescued? Who hasn't?
I was wondering if you would do me a favor and let her stay here for a while.
What? Why?

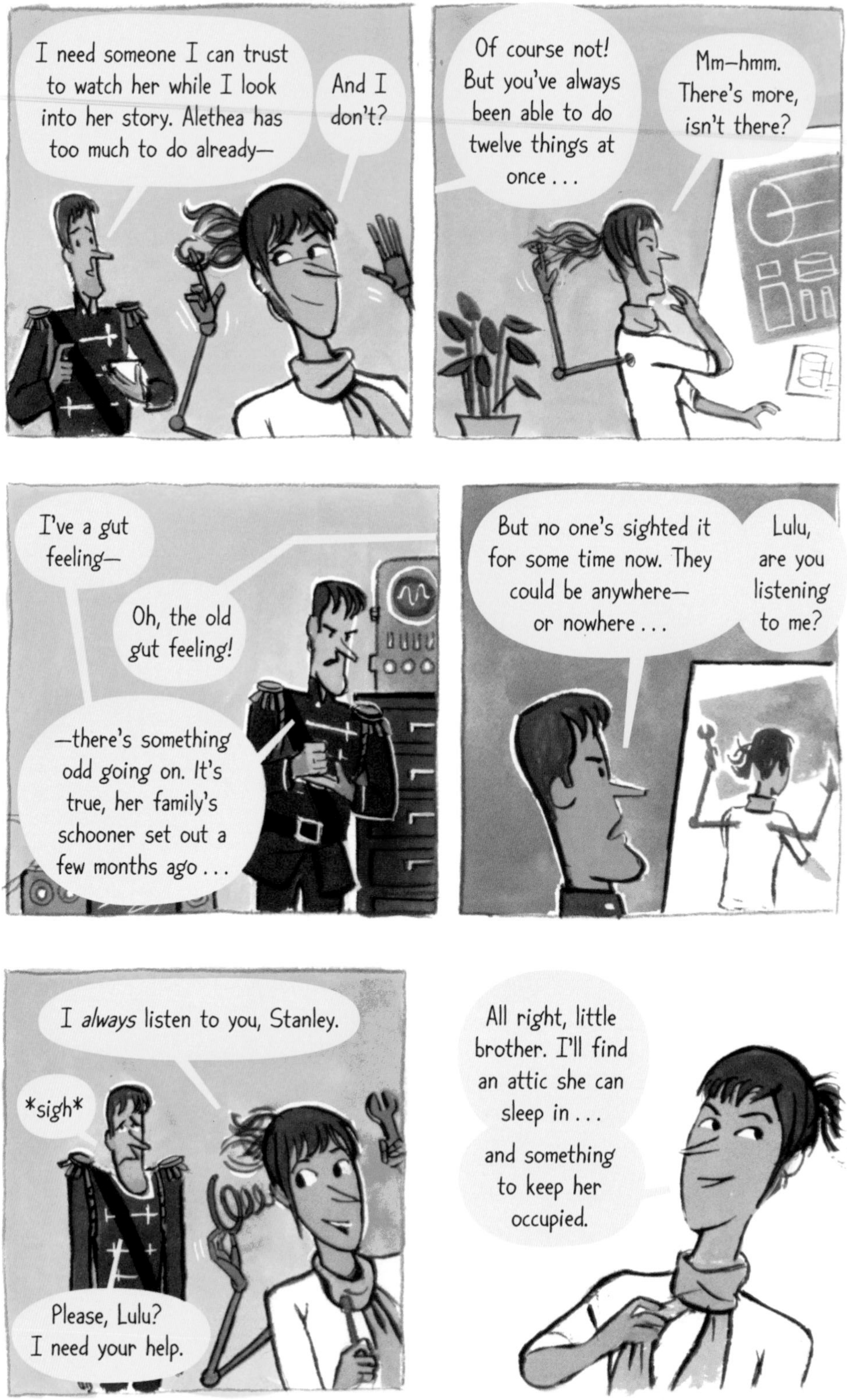
I need someone I can trust to watch her while I look into her story. Alethea has too much to do already—
And I don't?
Of course not! But you've always been able to do twelve things at once . . .
Mm—hmm. There's more, isn't there?
I've a gut feeling—
Oh, the old gut feeling!
—there's something odd going on. It's true, her family's schooner set out a few months ago . . .
But no one's sighted it for some time now. They could be anywhere— or nowhere . . .
Lulu, are you listening to me?
I *always* listen to you, Stanley.
sigh
Please, Lulu? I need your help.
All right, little brother. I'll find an attic she can sleep in . . .
and something to keep her occupied.

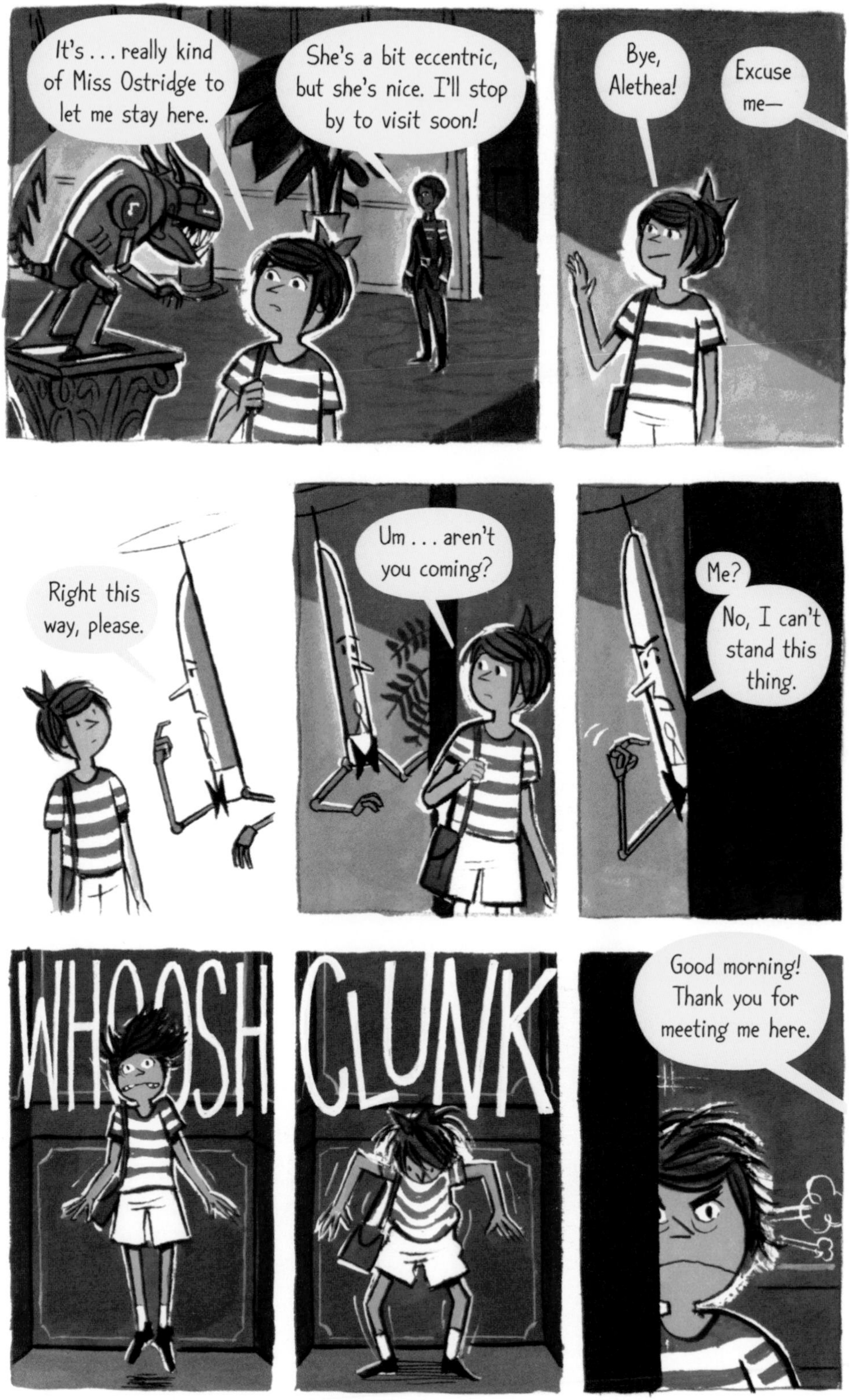
It's . . . really kind of Miss Ostridge to let me stay here.
She's a bit eccentric, but she's nice. I'll stop by to visit soon!
Bye, Alethea!
Excuse me—
Right this way, please.
Um . . . aren't you coming?
Me?
No, I can't stand this thing.
WHOOSH
CLUNK
Good morning! Thank you for meeting me here.

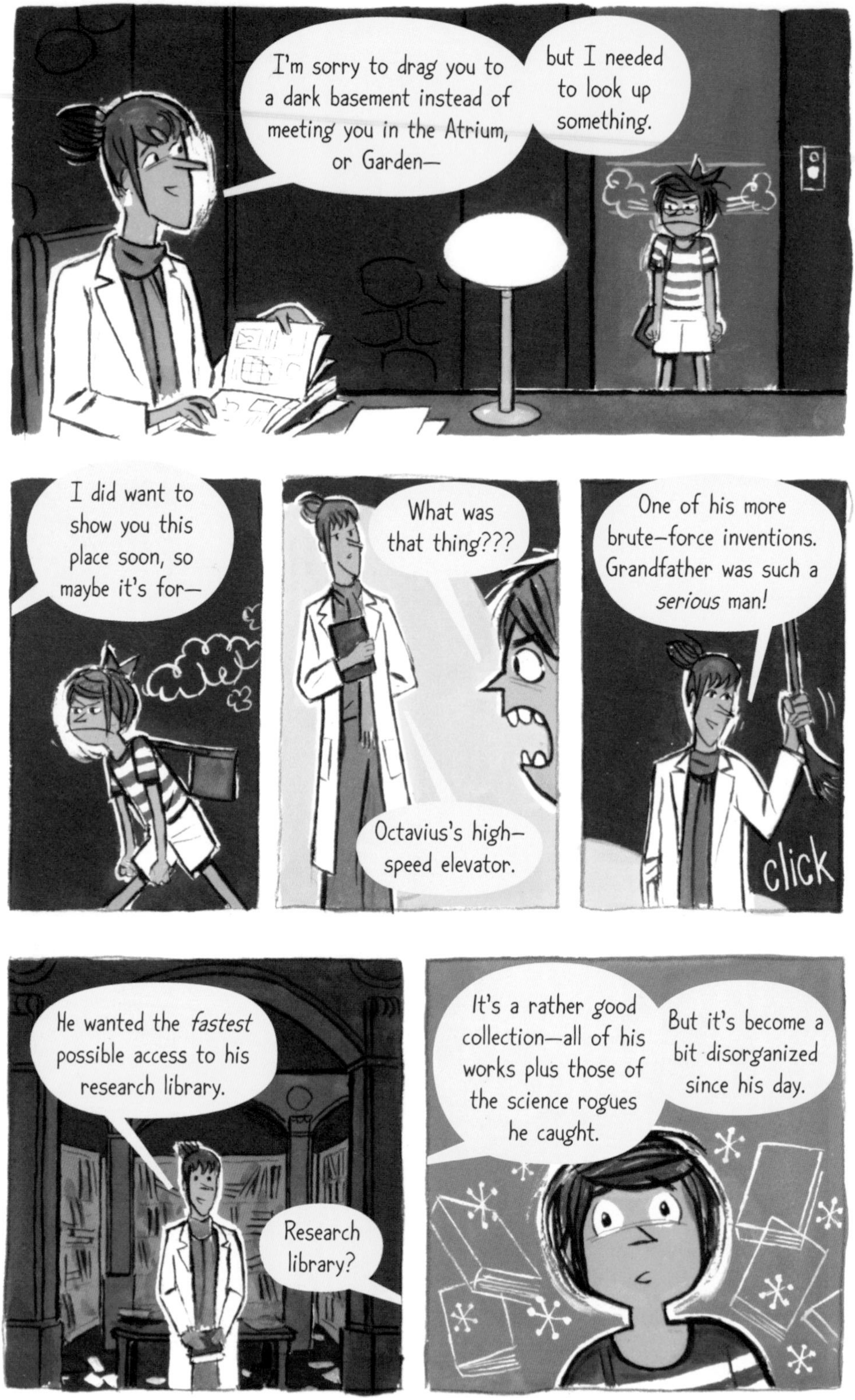
I'm sorry to drag you to a dark basement instead of meeting you in the Atrium, or Garden—
but I needed to look up something.
I did want to show you this place soon, so maybe it's for—
What was that thing???
Octavius's high-speed elevator.
One of his more brute-force inventions. Grandfather was such a *serious* man!
click
He wanted the *fastest* possible access to his research library.
Research library?
It's a rather good collection—all of his works plus those of the science rogues he caught.
But it's become a bit disorganized since his day.

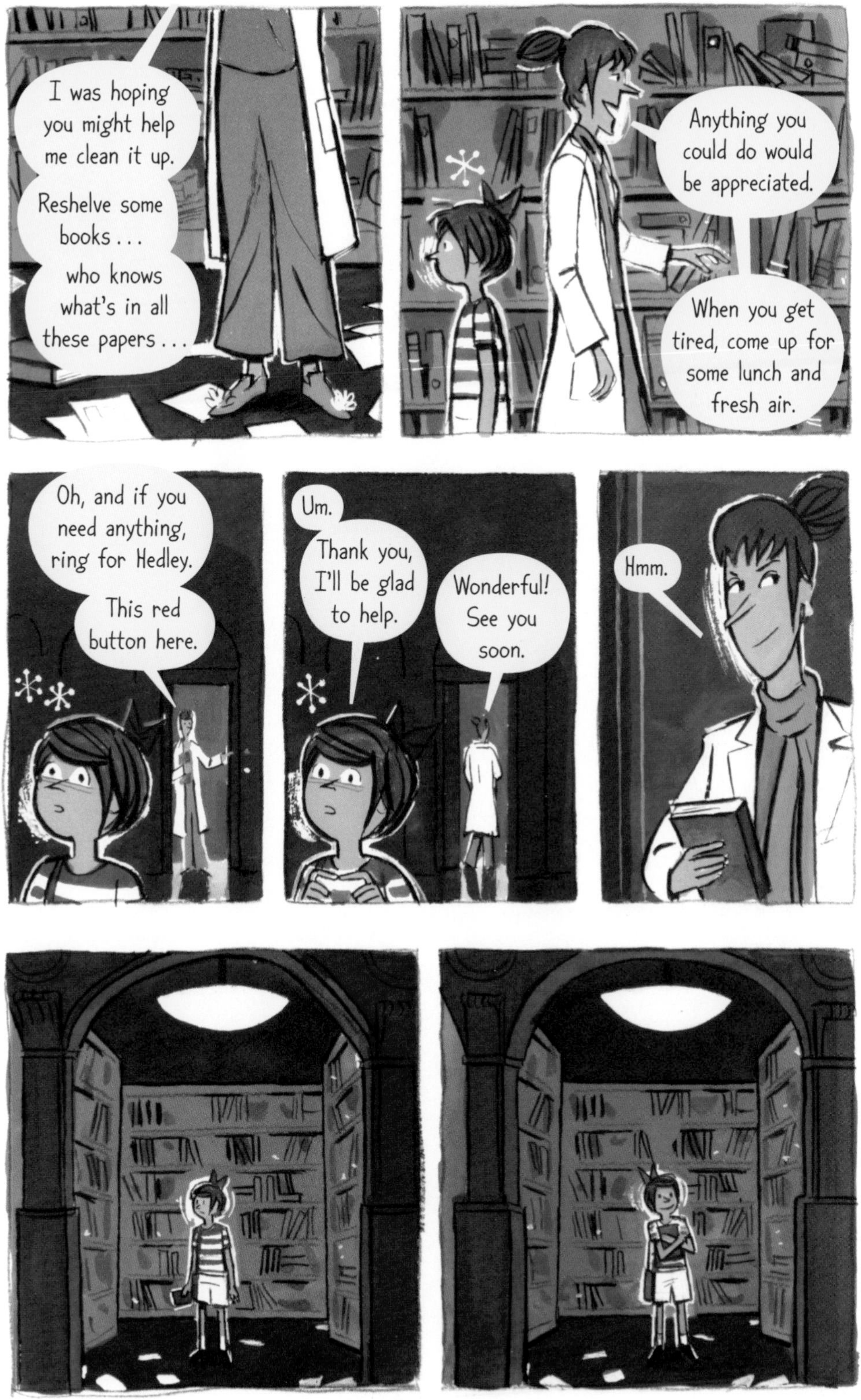
I was hoping you might help me clean it up.
Reshelve some books . . .
who knows what's in all these papers . . .
Anything you could do would be appreciated.
When you get tired, come up for some lunch and fresh air.
Oh, and if you need anything, ring for Hedley.
This red button here.
Um.
Thank you, I'll be glad to help.
Wonderful! See you soon.
Hmm.

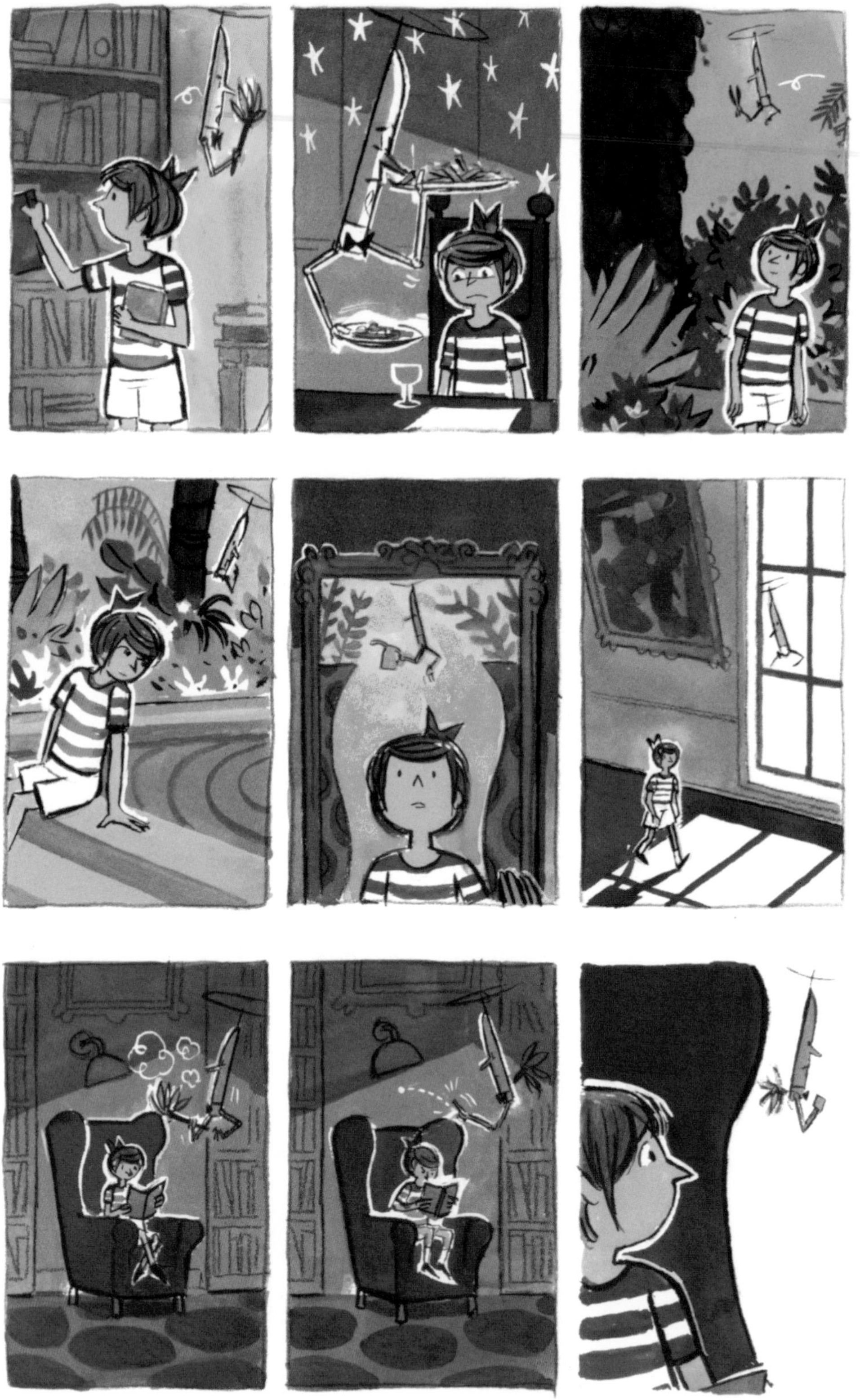

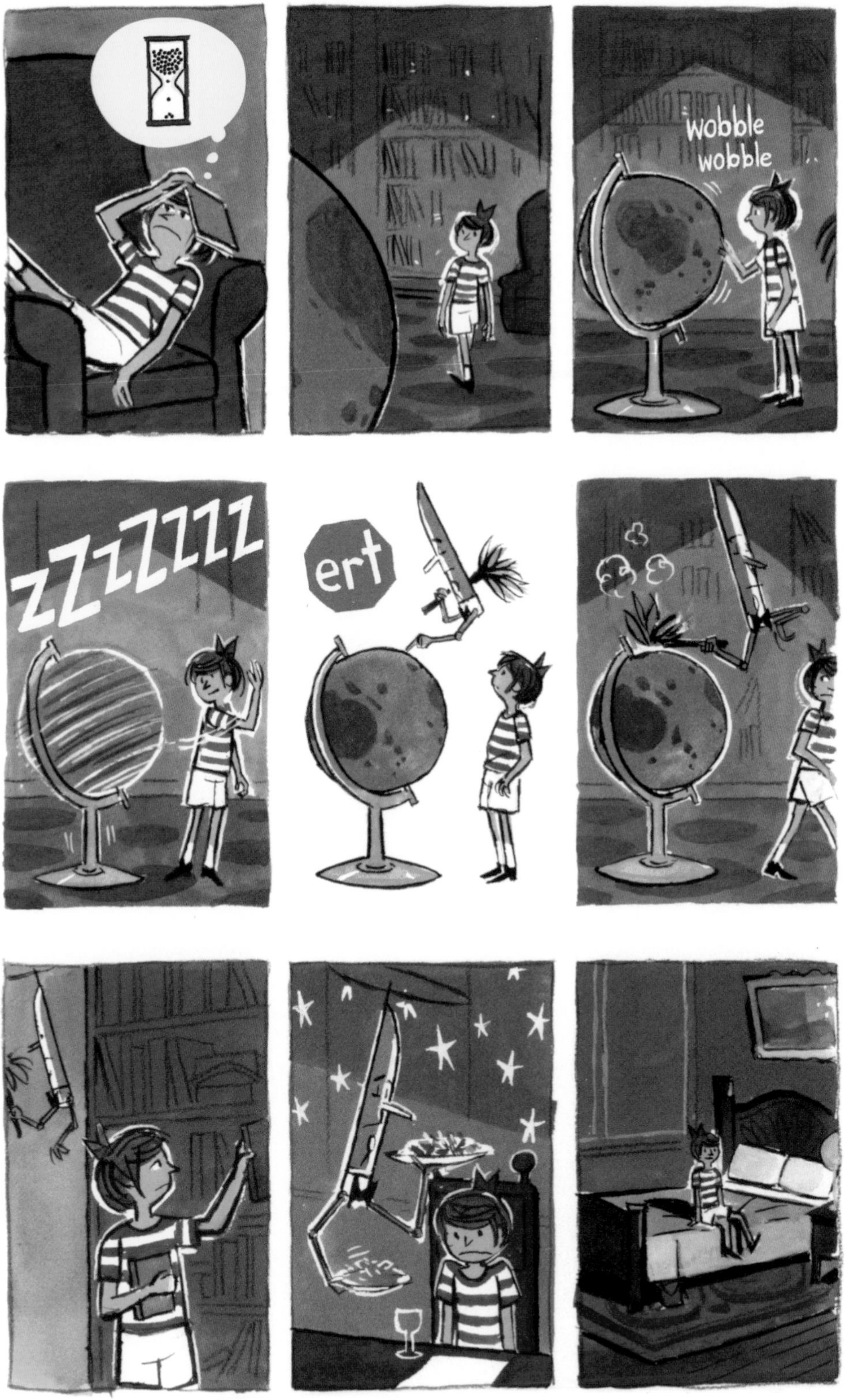
wobble
wobble
zZzzZZZZ
ert

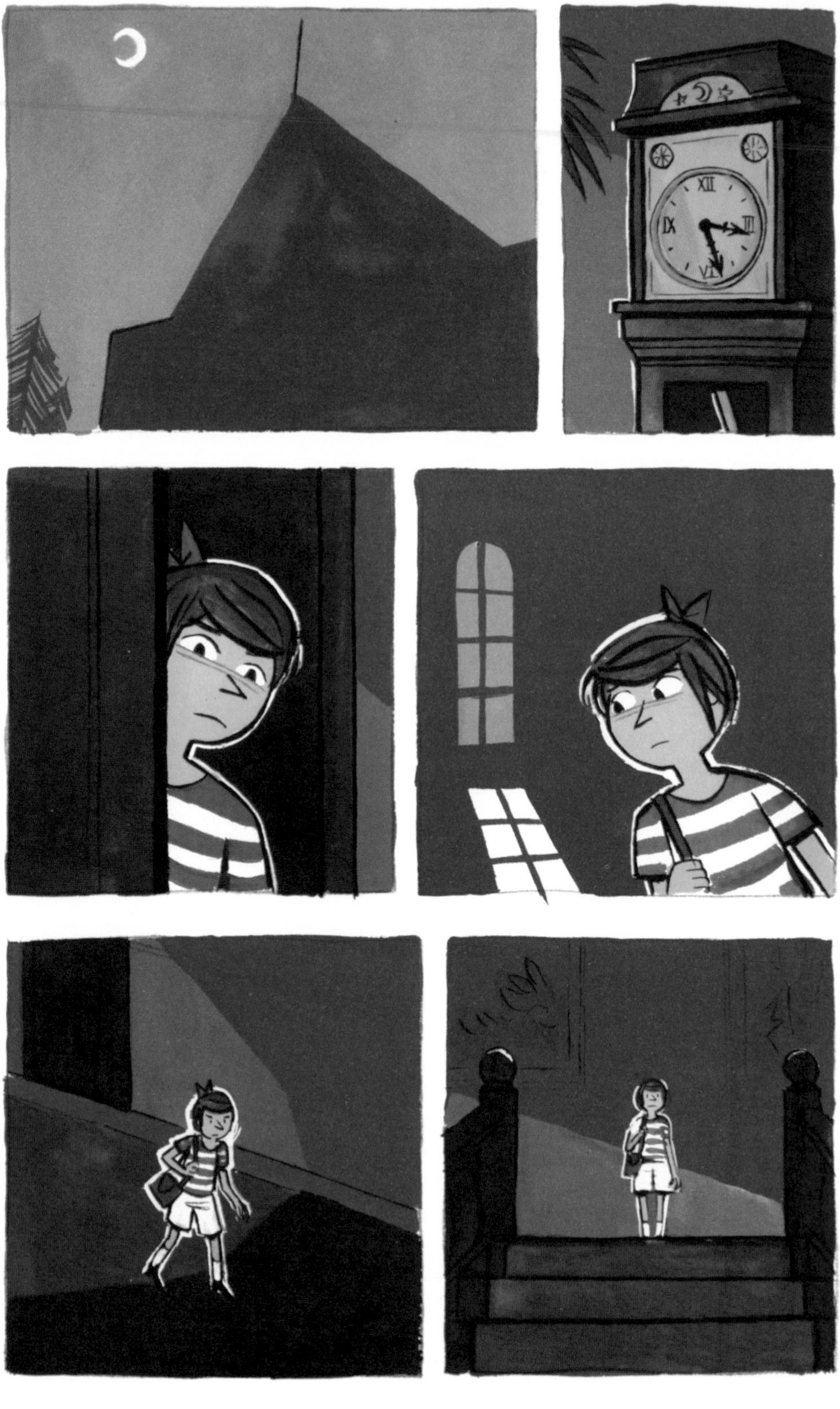

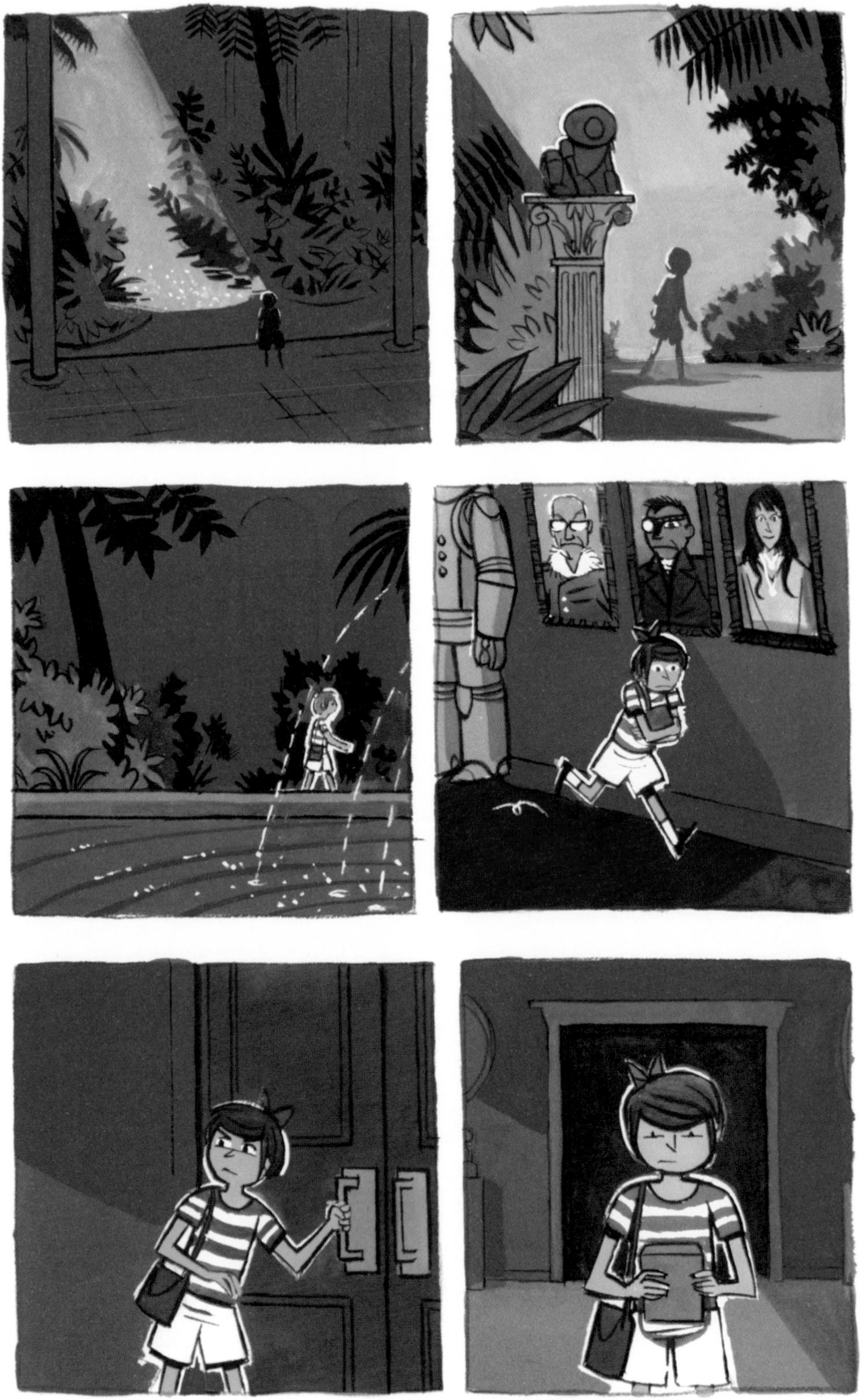

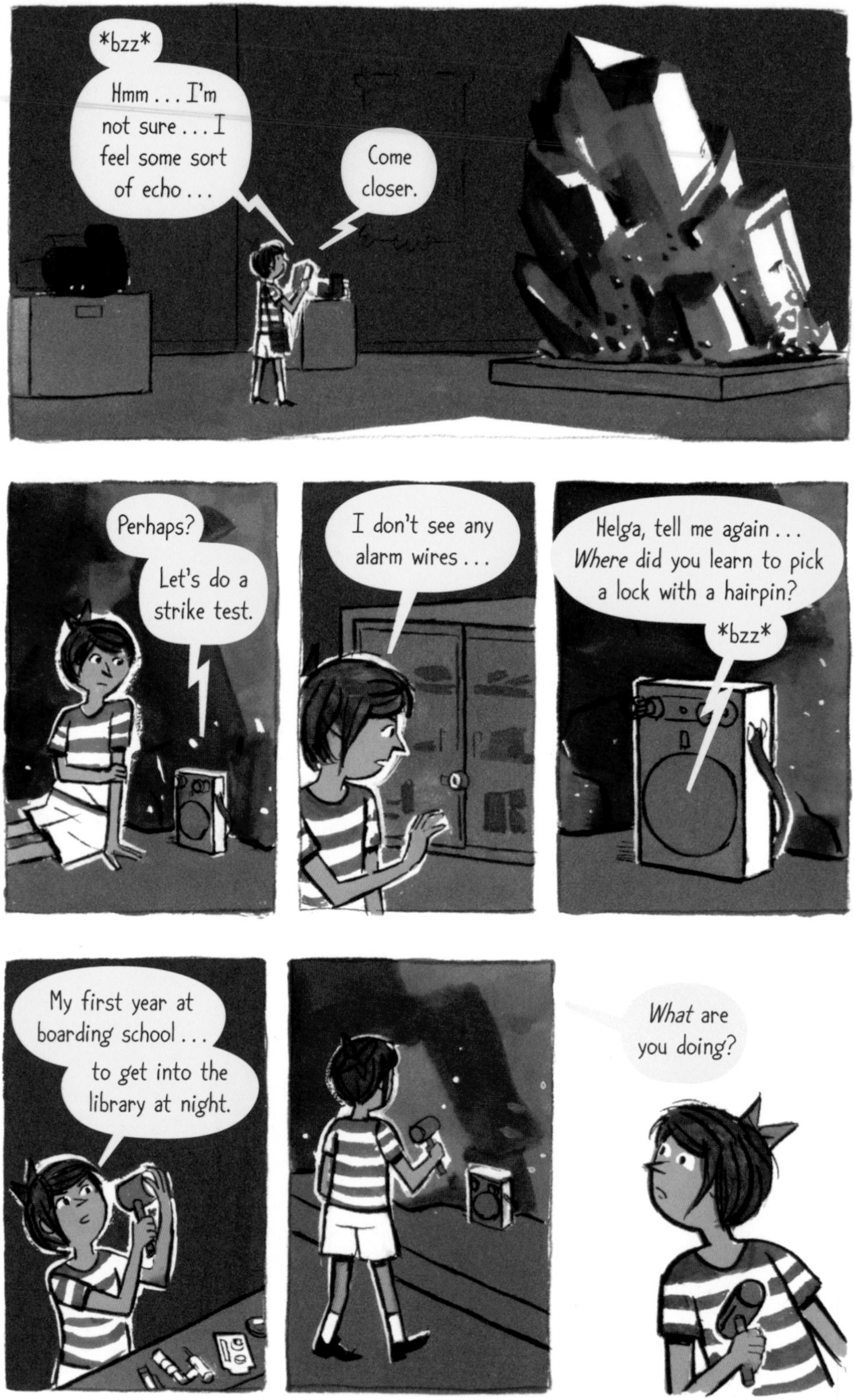
bzz
Hmm . . . I'm not sure . . . I feel some sort of echo . . .
Come closer.
Perhaps?
Let's do a strike test.
I don't see any alarm wires . . .
Helga, tell me again . . . *Where* did you learn to pick a lock with a hairpin?
bzz
My first year at boarding school . . .
to get into the library at night.
What are you doing?

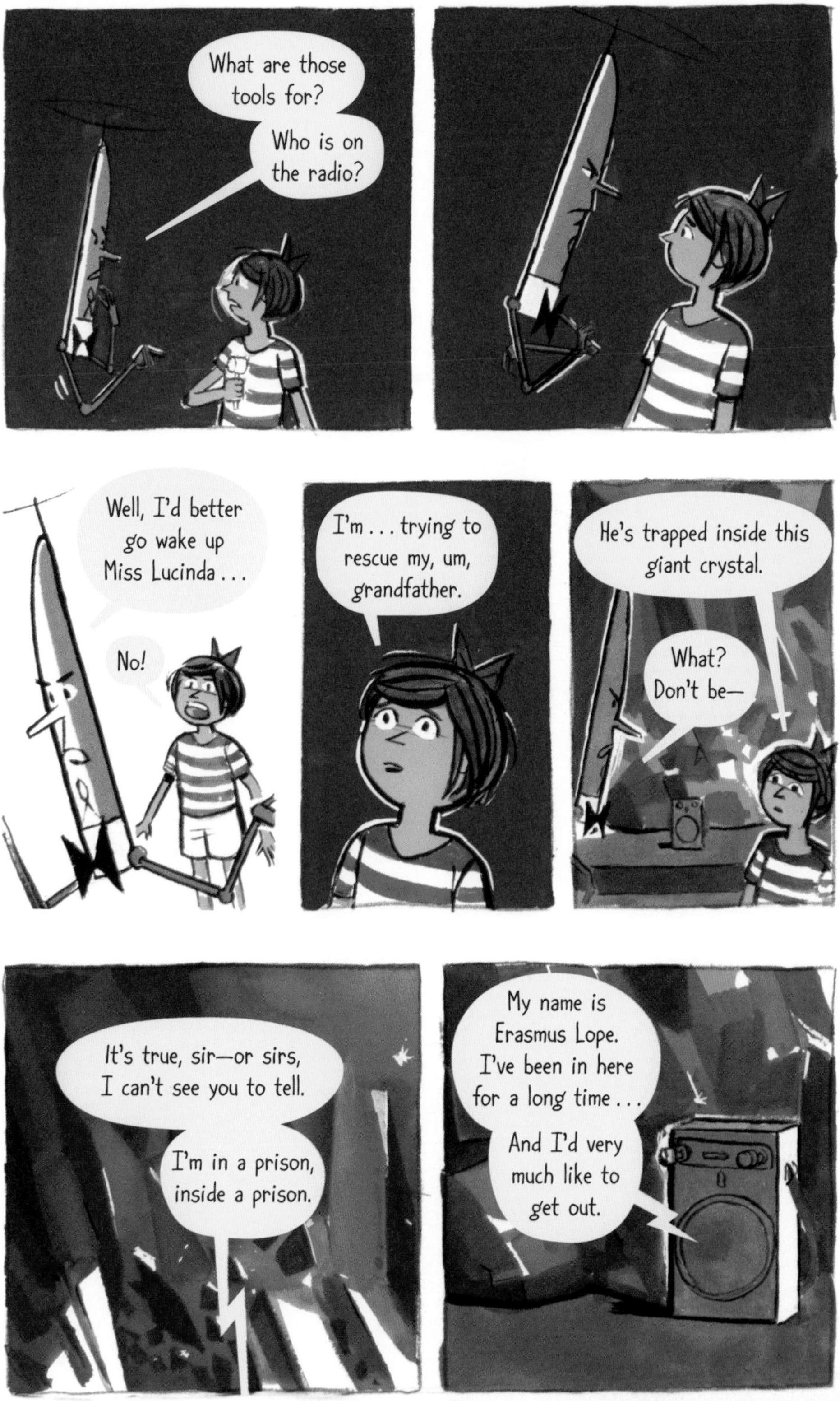
What are those tools for?
Who is on the radio?
Well, I'd better go wake up Miss Lucinda . . .
No!
I'm . . . trying to rescue my, um, grandfather.
He's trapped inside this giant crystal.
What? Don't be—
It's true, sir—or sirs, I can't see you to tell.
I'm in a prison, inside a prison.
My name is Erasmus Lope. I've been in here for a long time . . .
And I'd very much like to get out.

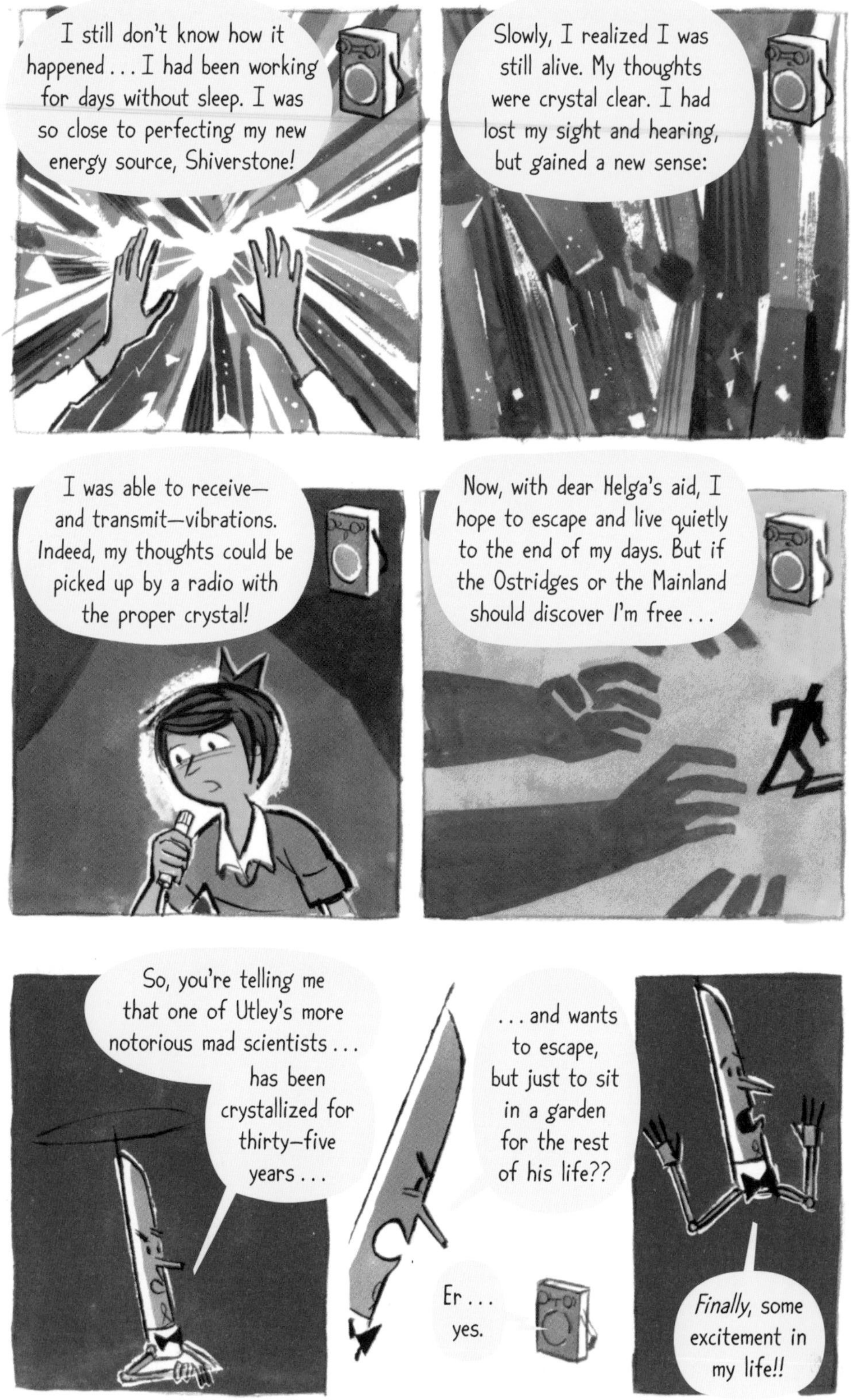
I still don't know how it happened . . . I had been working for days without sleep. I was so close to perfecting my new energy source, Shiverstone!
Slowly, I realized I was still alive. My thoughts were crystal clear. I had lost my sight and hearing, but gained a new sense:
I was able to receive— and transmit—vibrations. Indeed, my thoughts could be picked up by a radio with the proper crystal!
Now, with dear Helga's aid, I hope to escape and live quietly to the end of my days. But if the Ostridges or the Mainland should discover I'm free . . .
So, you're telling me that one of Utley's more notorious mad scientists . . .
has been crystallized for thirty-five years . . .
. . . and wants to escape, but just to sit in a garden for the rest of his life??
Er . . . yes.
Finally, some excitement in my life!!

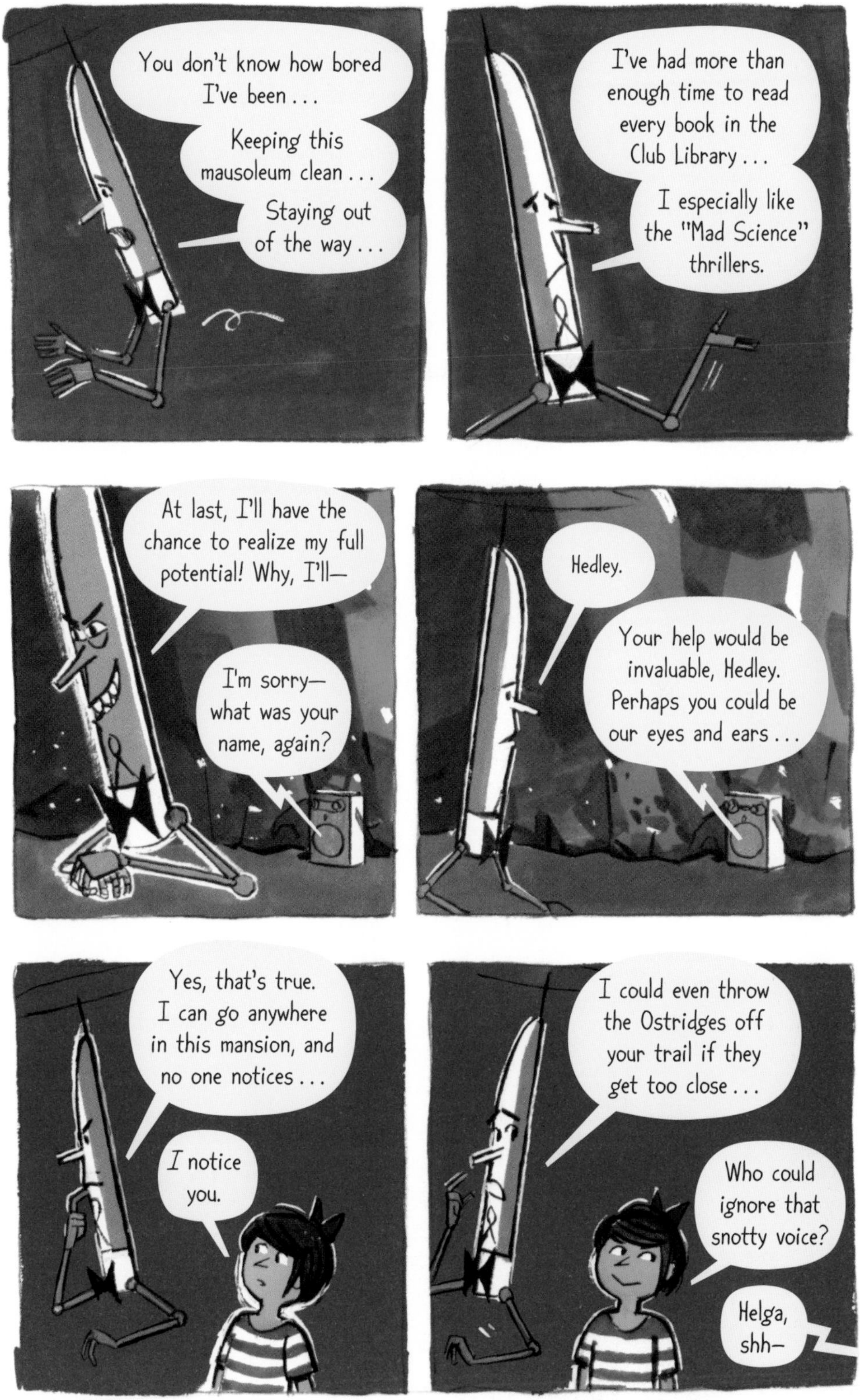
You don't know how bored I've been . . .
Keeping this mausoleum clean . . .
Staying out of the way . . .
I've had more than enough time to read every book in the Club Library . . .
I especially like the "Mad Science" thrillers.
At last, I'll have the chance to realize my full potential! Why, I'll—
I'm sorry— what was your name, again?
Hedley.
Your help would be invaluable, Hedley. Perhaps you could be our eyes and ears . . .
Yes, that's true. I can go anywhere in this mansion, and no one notices . . .
I notice you.
I could even throw the Ostridges off your trail if they get too close . . .
Who could ignore that snotty voice?
Helga, shh—

Hedley, we'll need your help to build the device that will free me—the Sonic Shatterer.

Helga will assemble it, with my guidance.

Some of the parts will be easy to obtain, but some will require . . . ingenuity.

We may have to visit my old lab.

Above all, we must move carefully—find a secure area in which to work, and work only at night.

There's one more thing we should do—make sure that this crystal is the right one.

Go ahead, dear.

Ponk

I felt it.

I felt it!

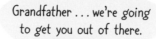

Grandfather . . . we're going to get you out of there.

4
lulu cleans her room

Puff Puff

Do you want to rest a bit?

Yes.

It's amazing . . . you wouldn't even know that there are any people here.

It's so quiet and peaceful.

It *is* nice to get out of town . . . but we need each other here, you know, since we're on our own.

Oh . . . mm–hmm.

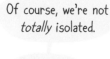

Of course, we're not *totally* isolated.

Supply ship's due to dock in ten days.

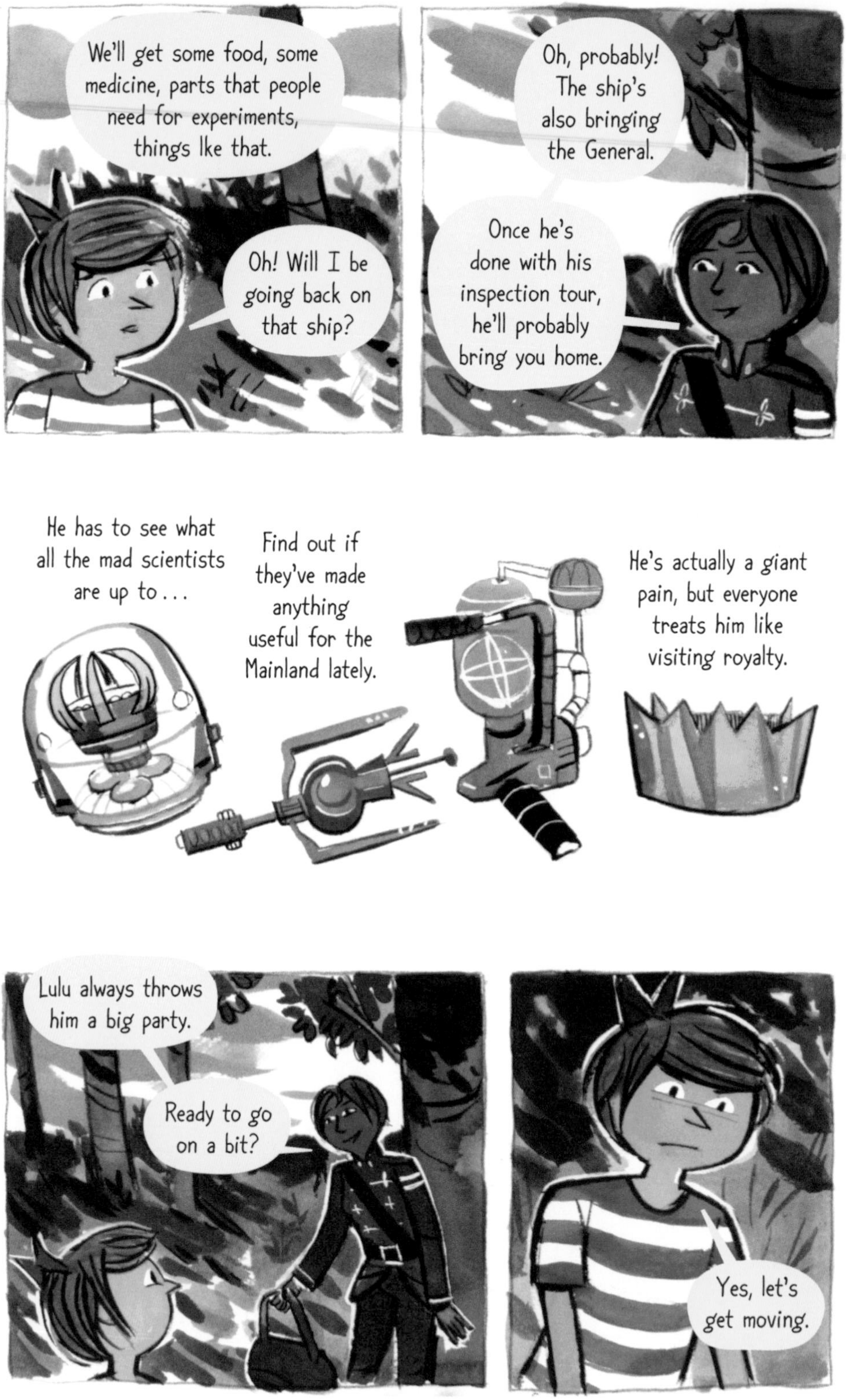
We'll get some food, some medicine, parts that people need for experiments, things lke that.
Oh! Will I be going back on that ship?
Oh, probably! The ship's also bringing the General.
Once he's done with his inspection tour, he'll probably bring you home.
He has to see what all the mad scientists are up to . . .
Find out if they've made anything useful for the Mainland lately.
He's actually a giant pain, but everyone treats him like visiting royalty.
Lulu always throws him a big party.
Ready to go on a bit?
Yes, let's get moving.

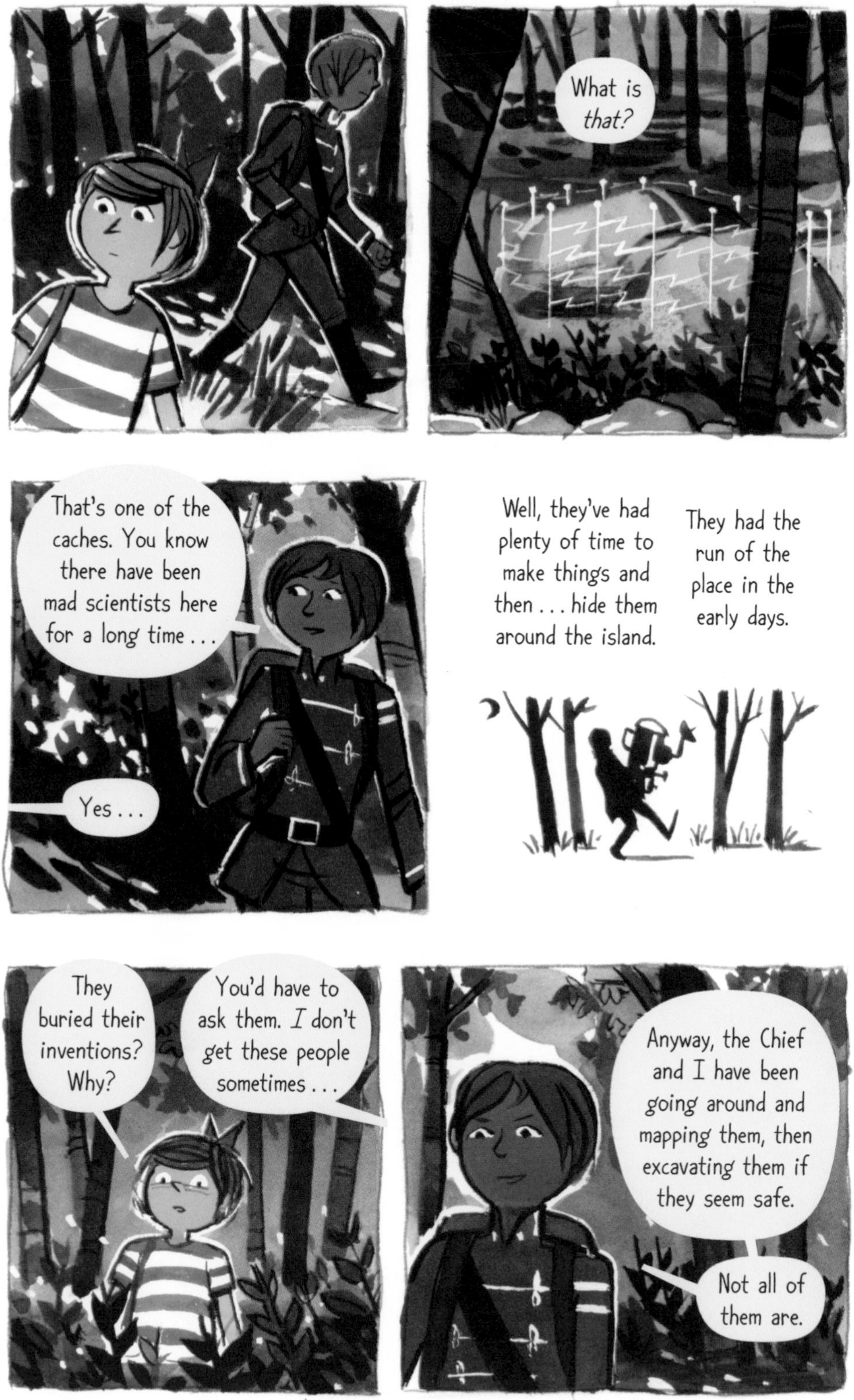

What is *that?*
That's one of the caches. You know there have been mad scientists here for a long time . . .
Yes . . .
Well, they've had plenty of time to make things and then . . . hide them around the island.
They had the run of the place in the early days.
They buried their inventions? Why?
You'd have to ask them. *I* don't get these people sometimes . . .
Anyway, the Chief and I have been going around and mapping them, then excavating them if they seem safe.
Not all of them are.

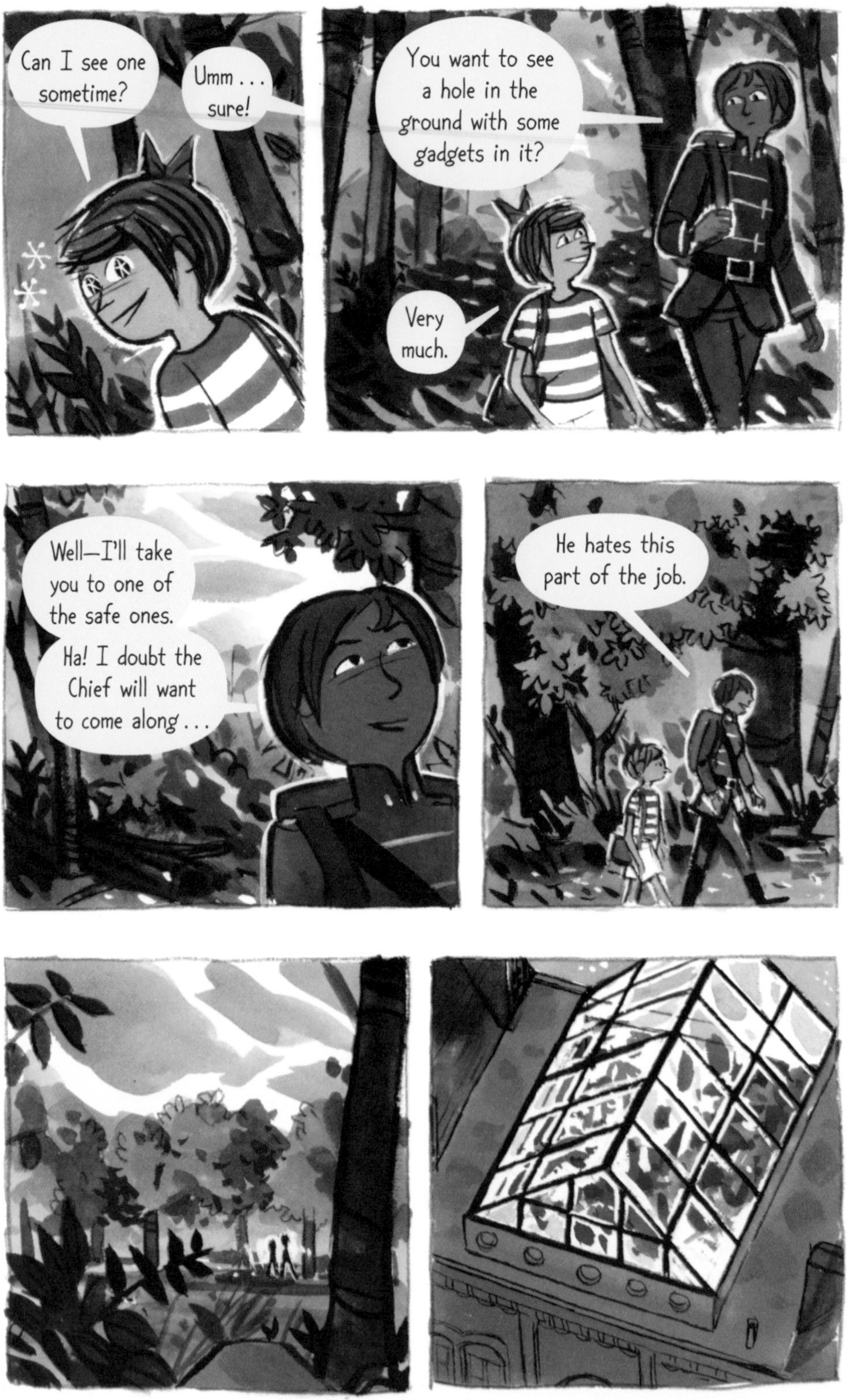
Can I see one sometime?
Umm . . . sure!
You want to see a hole in the ground with some gadgets in it?
Very much.
Well—I'll take you to one of the safe ones.
Ha! I doubt the Chief will want to come along . . .
He hates this part of the job.

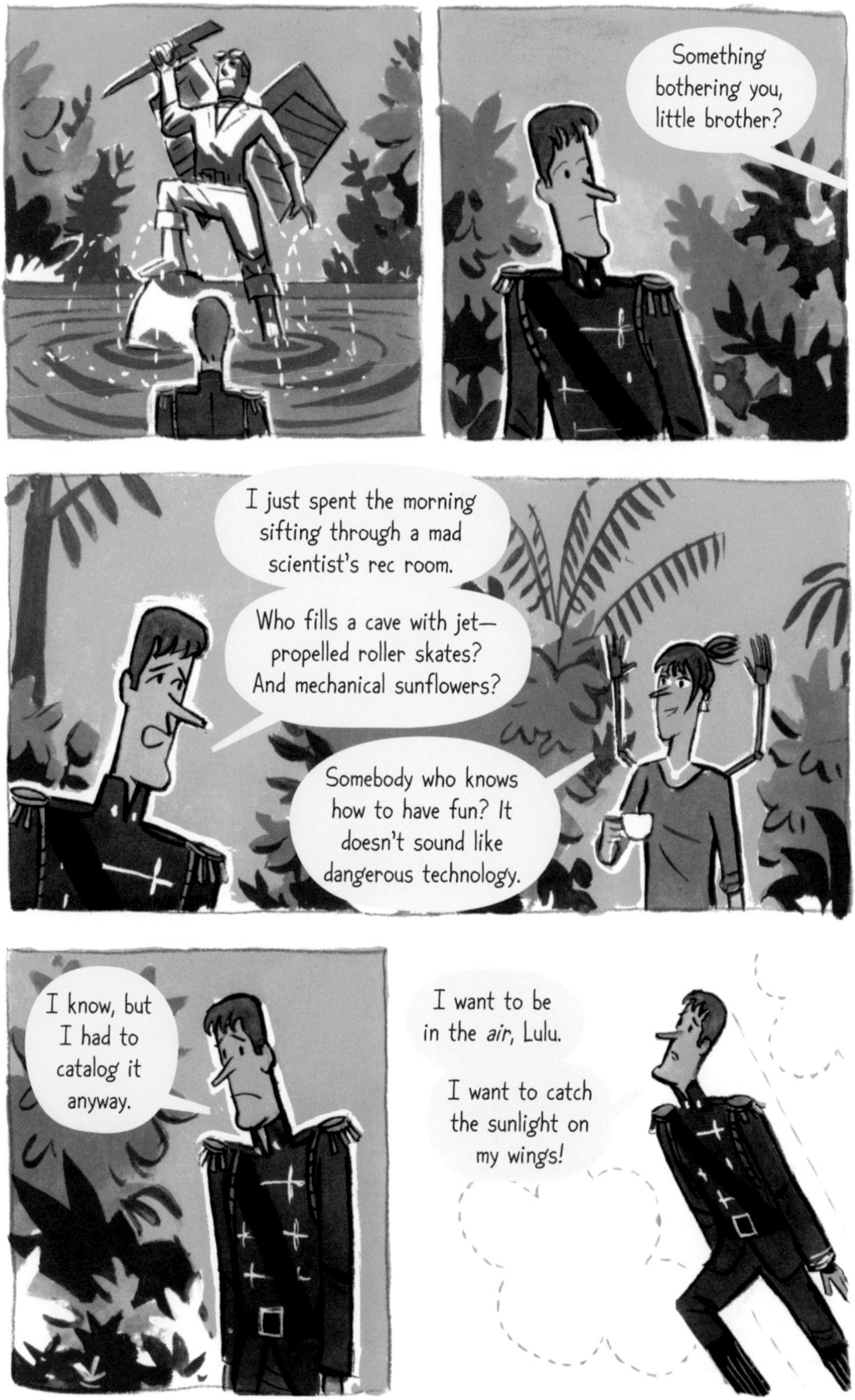
Something bothering you, little brother?
I just spent the morning sifting through a mad scientist's rec room.
Who fills a cave with jet—propelled roller skates? And mechanical sunflowers?
Somebody who knows how to have fun? It doesn't sound like dangerous technology.
I know, but I had to catalog it anyway.
I want to be in the *air*, Lulu.
I want to catch the sunlight on my wings!

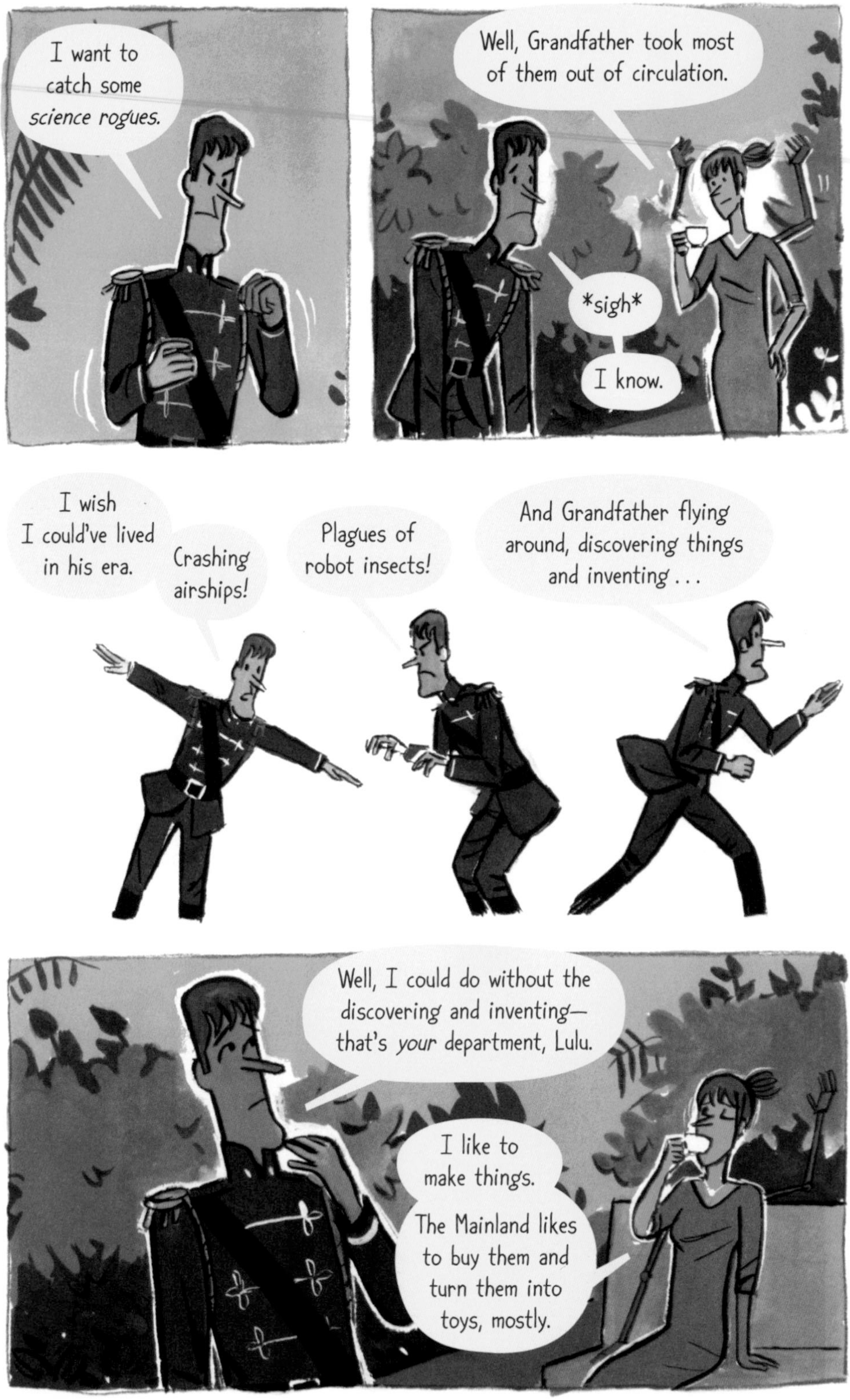

I want to catch some *science rogues.*
Well, Grandfather took most of them out of circulation.
sigh
I know.
I wish I could've lived in his era.
Crashing airships!
Plagues of robot insects!
And Grandfather flying around, discovering things and inventing . . .
Well, I could do without the discovering and inventing—that's *your* department, Lulu.
I like to make things.
The Mainland likes to buy them and turn them into toys, mostly.

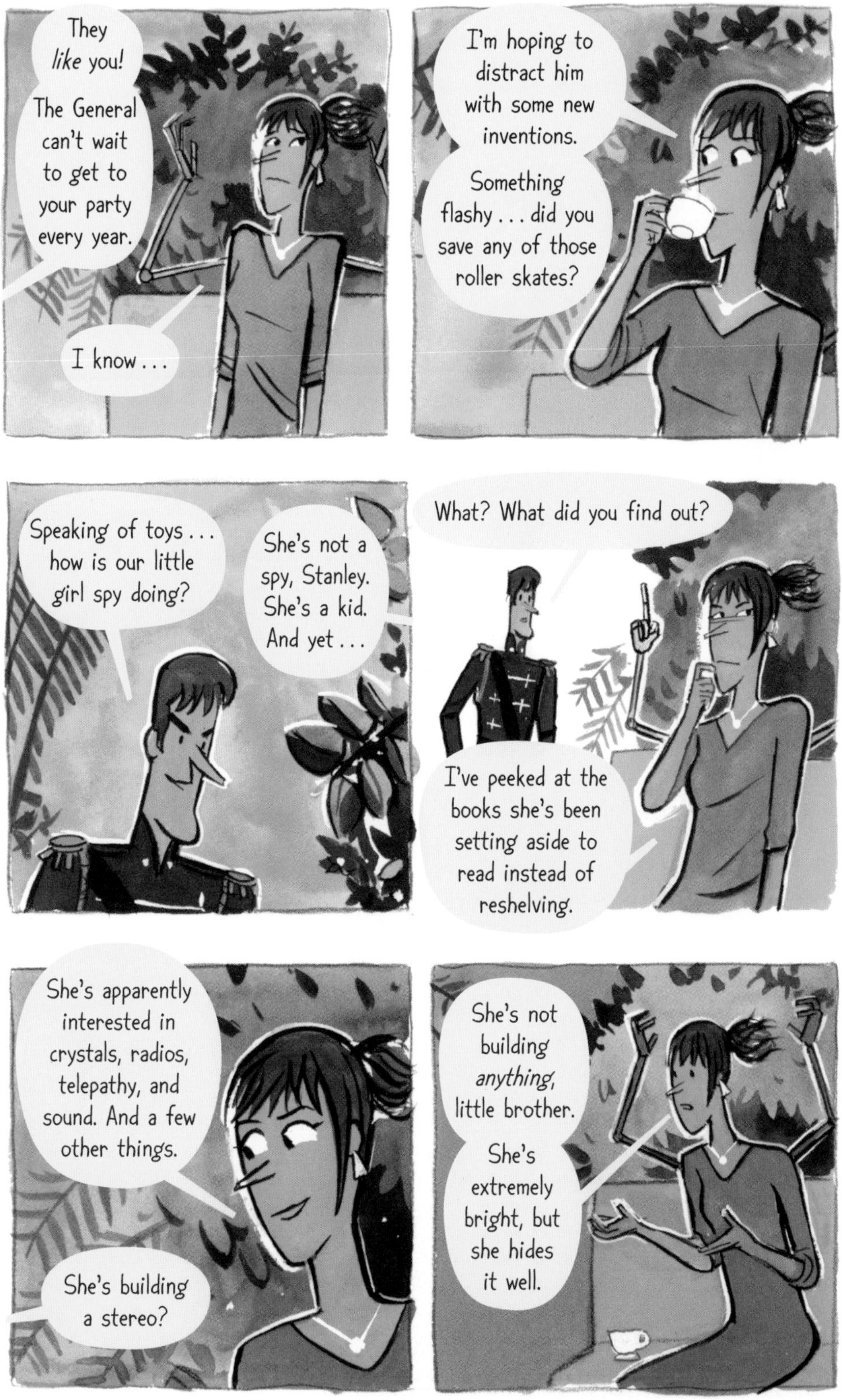
They *like* you!
The General can't wait to get to your party every year.
I know . . .
I'm hoping to distract him with some new inventions.
Something flashy . . . did you save any of those roller skates?
Speaking of toys . . . how is our little girl spy doing?
She's not a spy, Stanley. She's a kid. And yet . . .
What? What did you find out?
I've peeked at the books she's been setting aside to read instead of reshelving.
She's apparently interested in crystals, radios, telepathy, and sound. And a few other things.
She's building a stereo?
She's not building *anything*, little brother.
She's extremely bright, but she hides it well.

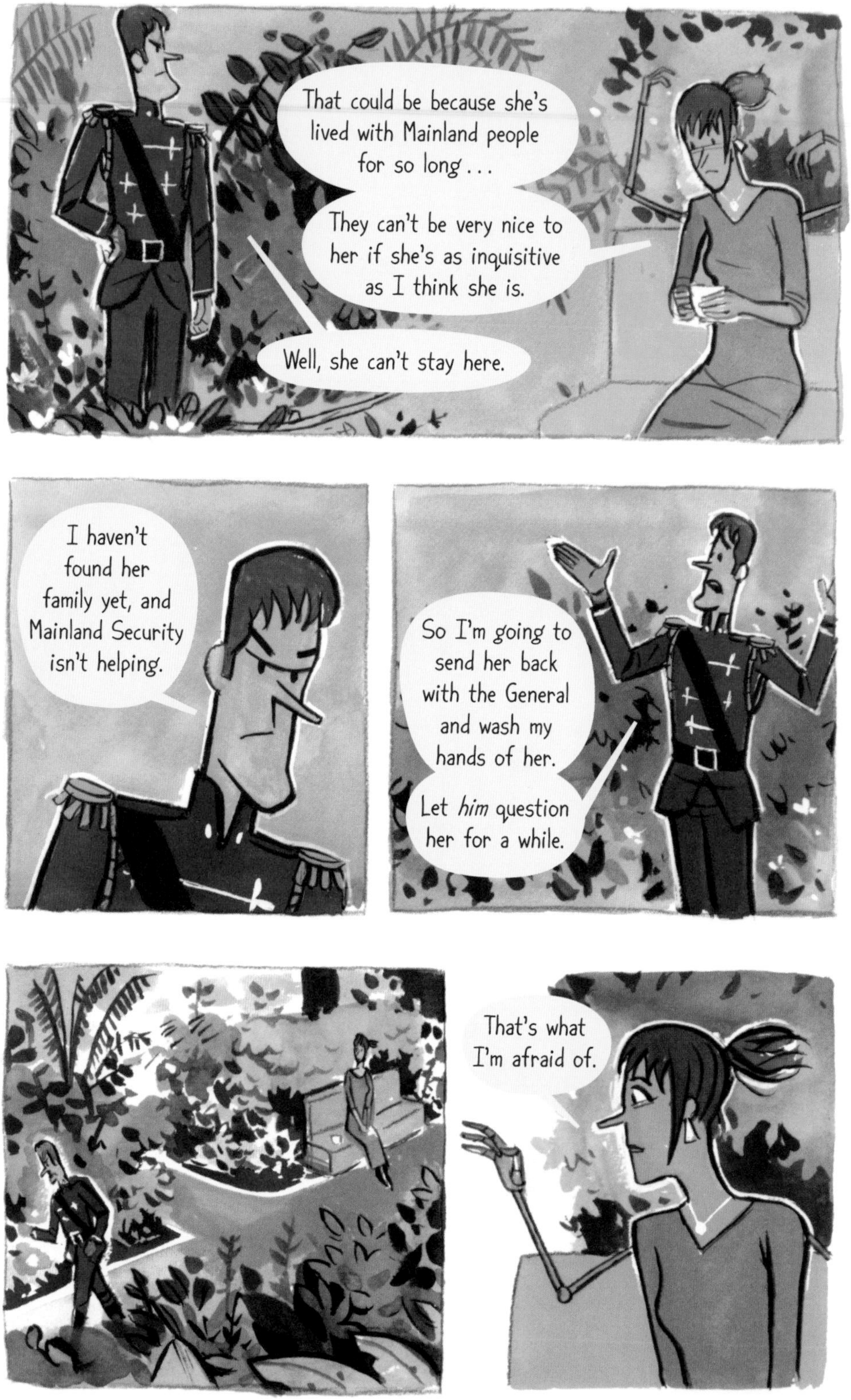
That could be because she's lived with Mainland people for so long...
They can't be very nice to her if she's as inquisitive as I think she is.
Well, she can't stay here.
I haven't found her family yet, and Mainland Security isn't helping.
So I'm going to send her back with the General and wash my hands of her.
Let *him* question her for a while.
That's what I'm afraid of.

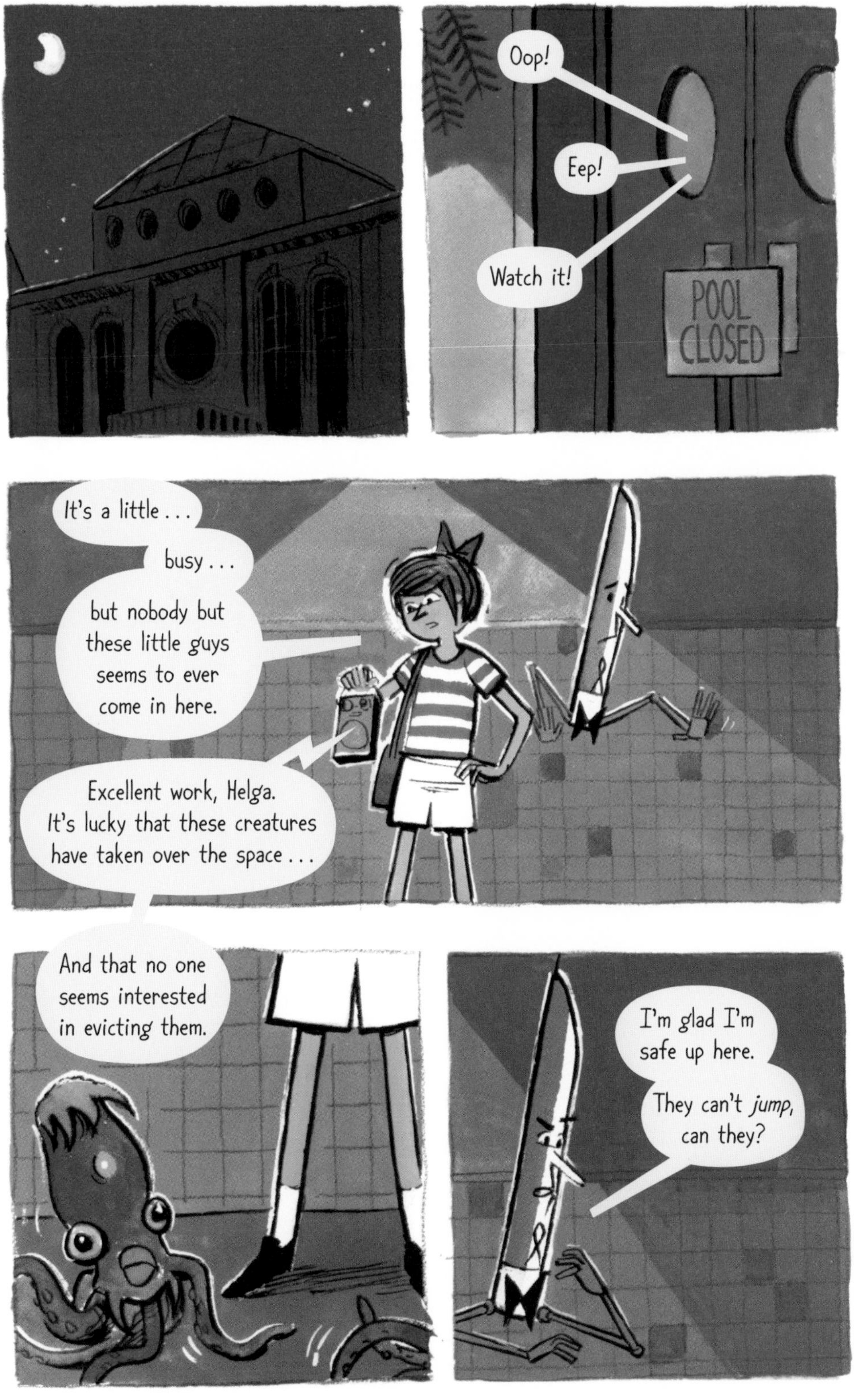
Oop!
Eep!
Watch it!
POOL CLOSED
It's a little . . .
busy . . .
but nobody but these little guys seems to ever come in here.
Excellent work, Helga. It's lucky that these creatures have taken over the space . . .
And that no one seems interested in evicting them.
I'm glad I'm safe up here.
They can't *jump*, can they?

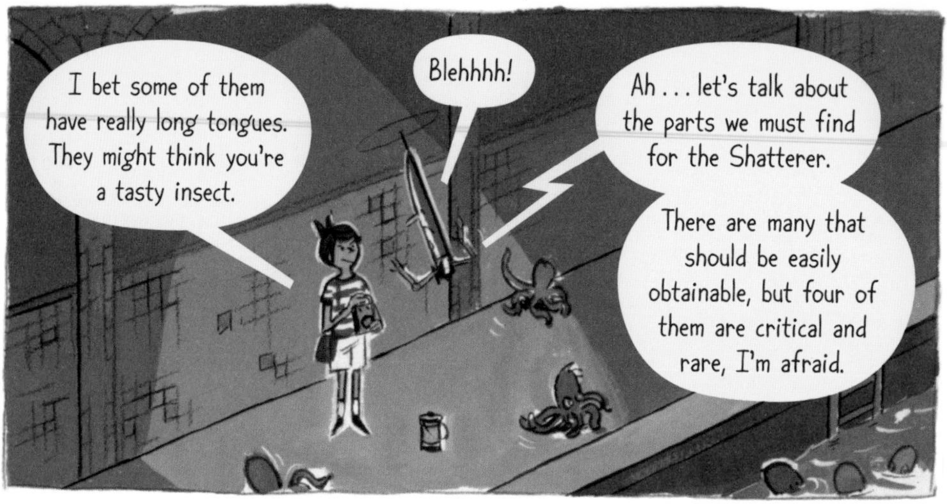
I bet some of them have really long tongues. They might think you're a tasty insect.
Blehhhh!
Ah . . . let's talk about the parts we must find for the Shatterer.
There are many that should be easily obtainable, but four of them are critical and rare, I'm afraid.

We must find:

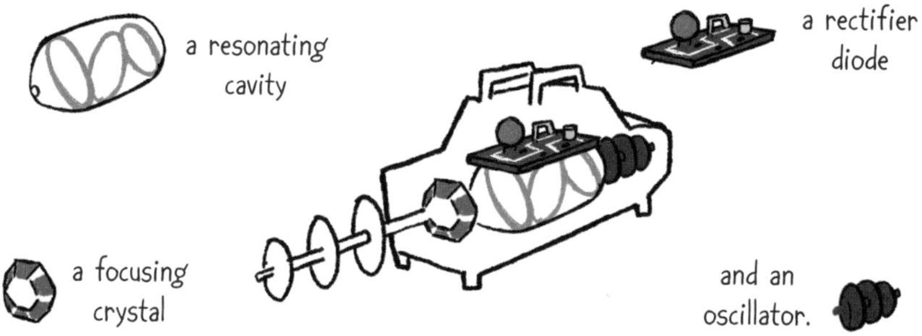
a resonating cavity
a rectifier diode
a focusing crystal
and an oscillator.

Once we have these parts, Helga should be able to complete the device.

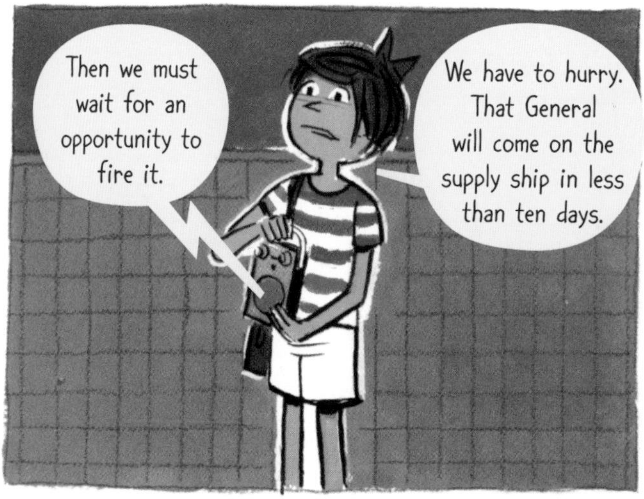
Then we must wait for an opportunity to fire it.
We have to hurry. That General will come on the supply ship in less than ten days.

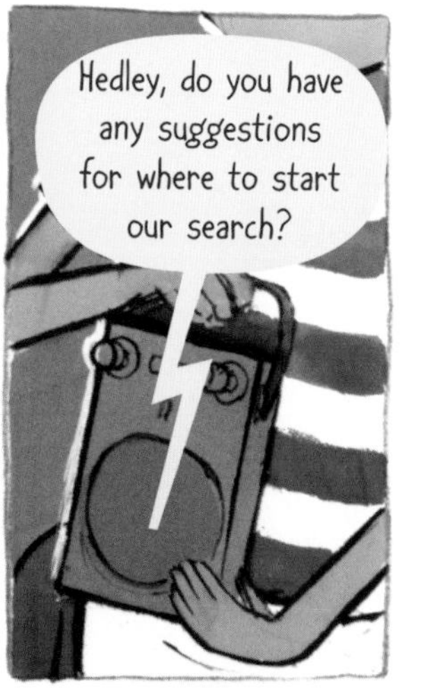
Hedley, do you have any suggestions for where to start our search?

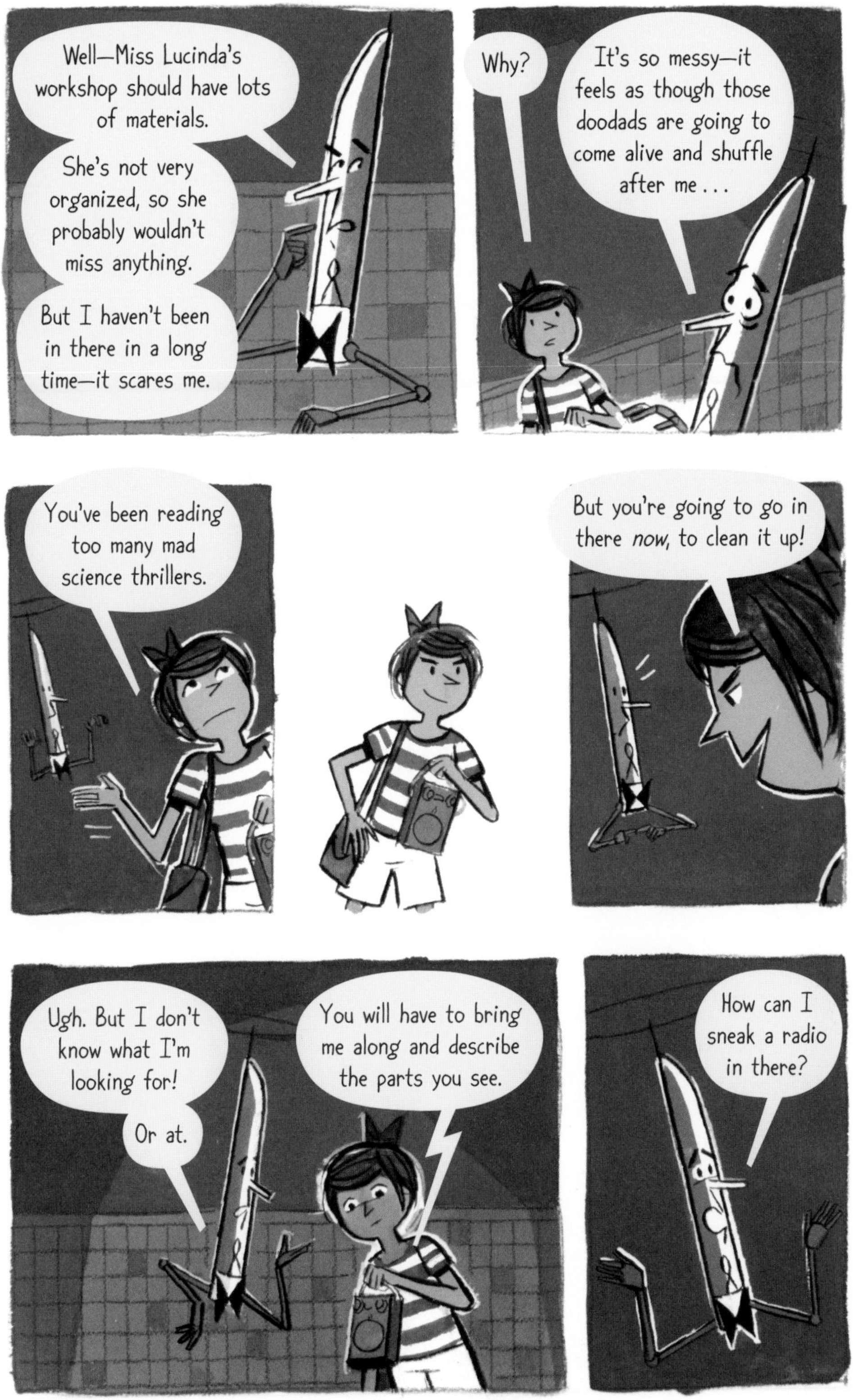
Well—Miss Lucinda's workshop should have lots of materials.
She's not very organized, so she probably wouldn't miss anything.
But I haven't been in there in a long time—it scares me.
Why?
It's so messy—it feels as though those doodads are going to come alive and shuffle after me . . .
You've been reading too many mad science thrillers.
But you're going to go in there *now*, to clean it up!
Ugh. But I don't know what I'm looking for!
Or at.
You will have to bring me along and describe the parts you see.
How can I sneak a radio in there?

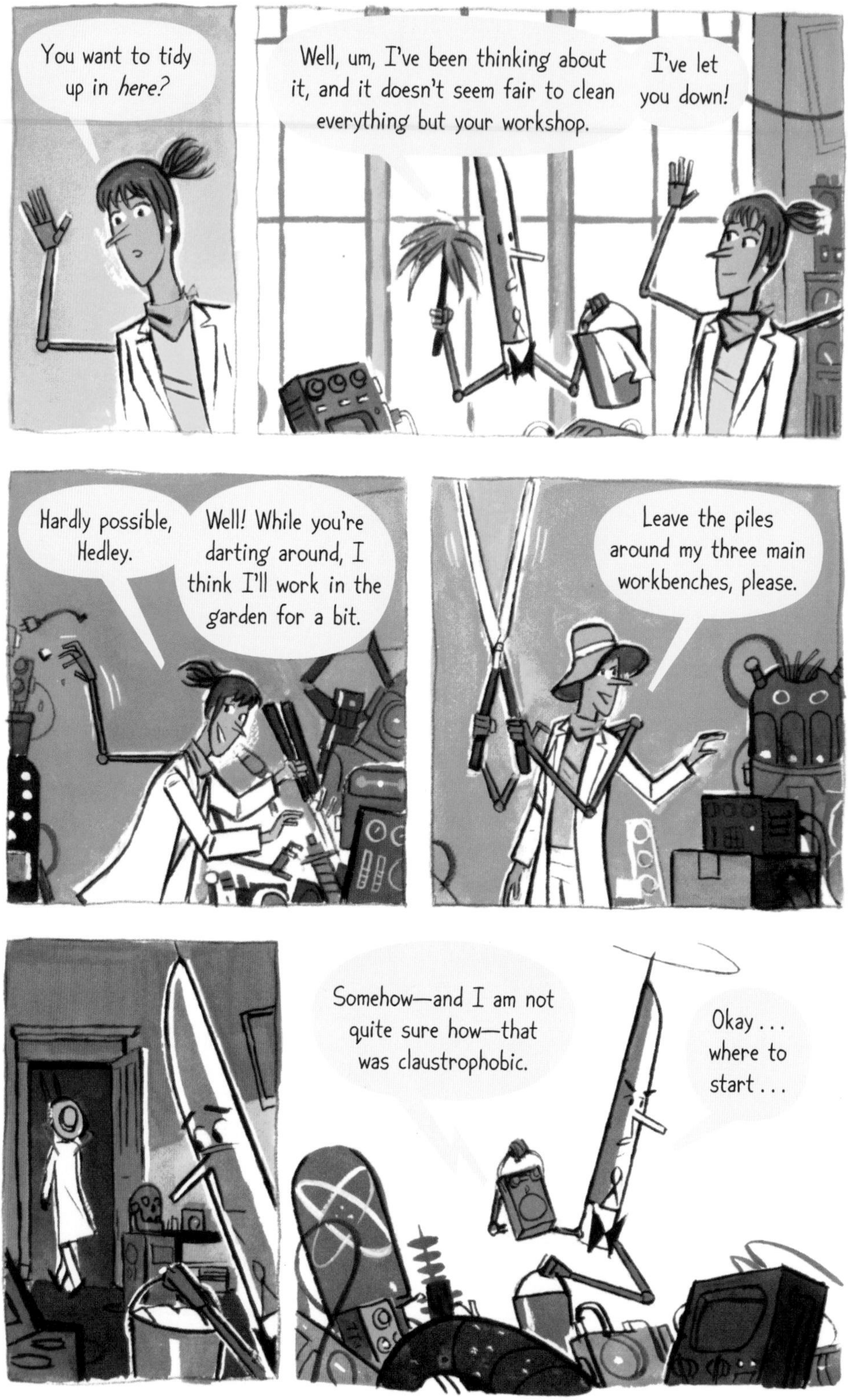
You want to tidy up in *here?*
Well, um, I've been thinking about it, and it doesn't seem fair to clean everything but your workshop.
I've let you down!
Hardly possible, Hedley.
Well! While you're darting around, I think I'll work in the garden for a bit.
Leave the piles around my three main workbenches, please.
Somehow—and I am not quite sure how—that was claustrophobic.
Okay . . . where to start . . .

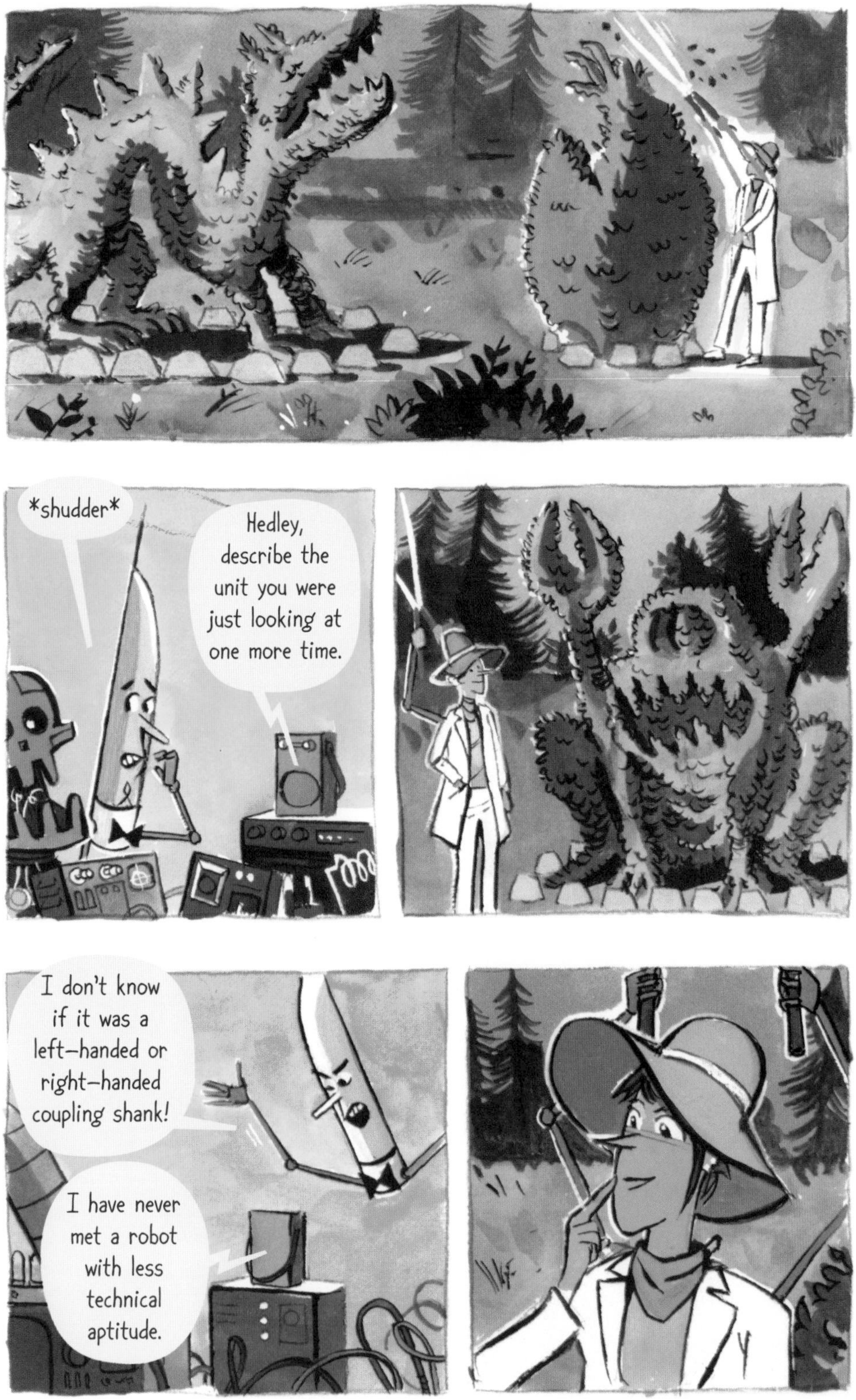

shudder
Hedley, describe the unit you were just looking at one more time.
I don't know if it was a left-handed or right-handed coupling shank!
I have never met a robot with less technical aptitude.

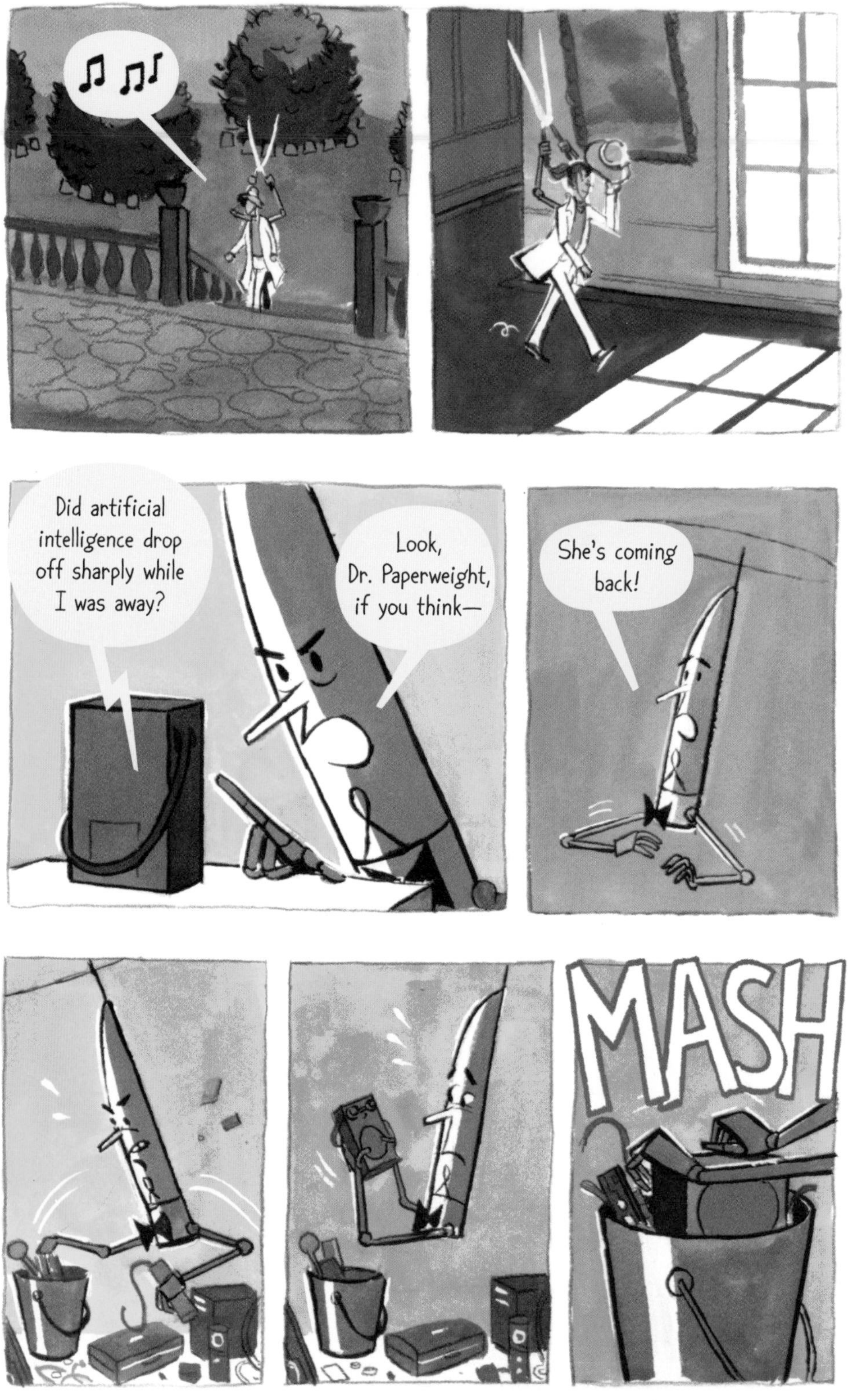
Did artificial intelligence drop off sharply while I was away?
Look, Dr. Paperweight, if you think—
She's coming back!
MASH

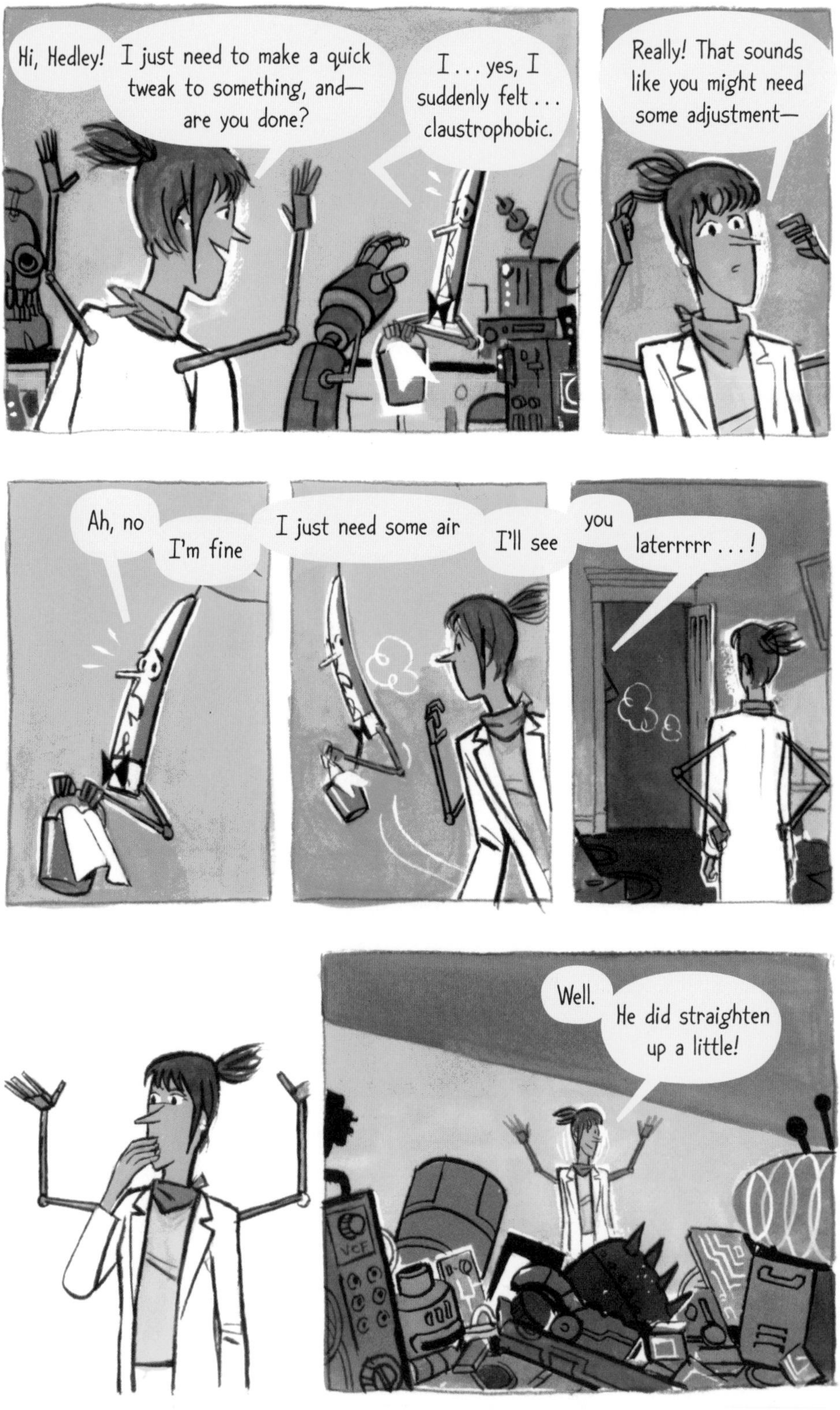
Hi, Hedley!
I just need to make a quick tweak to something, and— are you done?
I . . . yes, I suddenly felt . . . claustrophobic.
Really! That sounds like you might need some adjustment—
Ah, no
I'm fine
I just need some air
I'll see
you
laterrrrr . . . !
Well.
He did straighten up a little!

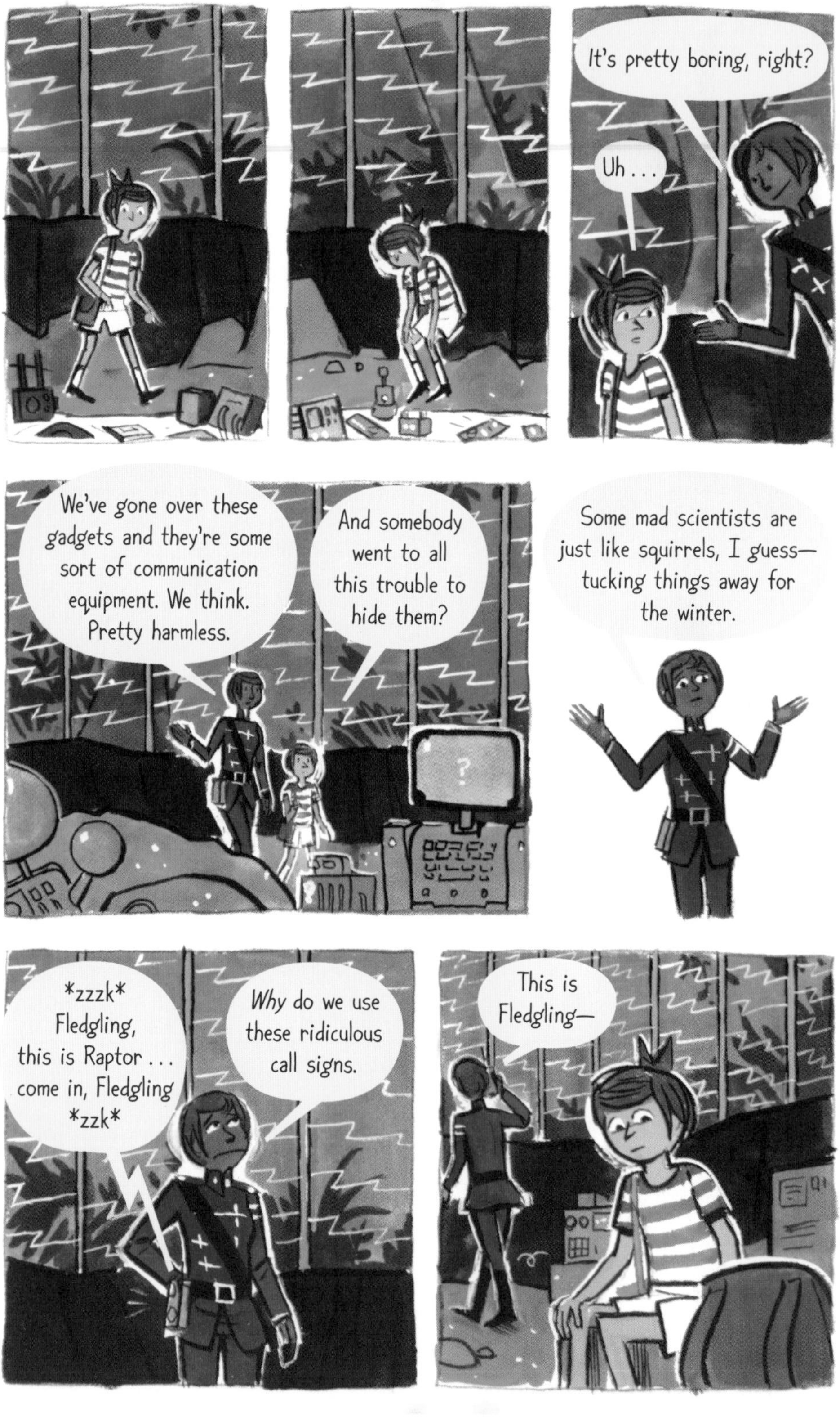
It's pretty boring, right?
Uh . . .
We've gone over these gadgets and they're some sort of communication equipment. We think. Pretty harmless.
And somebody went to all this trouble to hide them?
Some mad scientists are just like squirrels, I guess—tucking things away for the winter.
zzzk Fledgling, this is Raptor . . . come in, Fledgling *zzk*
Why do we use these ridiculous call signs.
This is Fledgling—

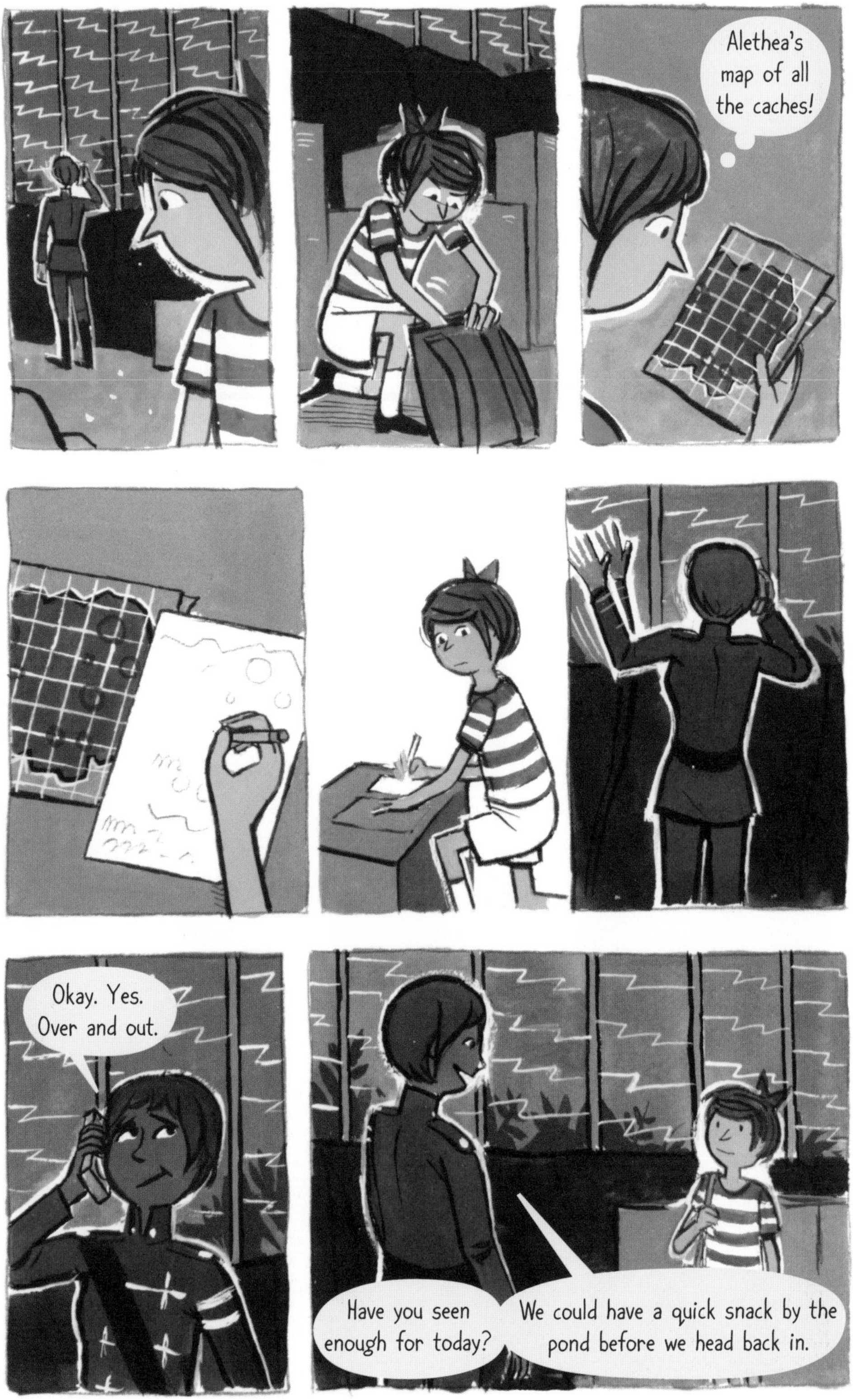
Alethea's map of all the caches!
Okay. Yes. Over and out.
Have you seen enough for today?
We could have a quick snack by the pond before we head back in.

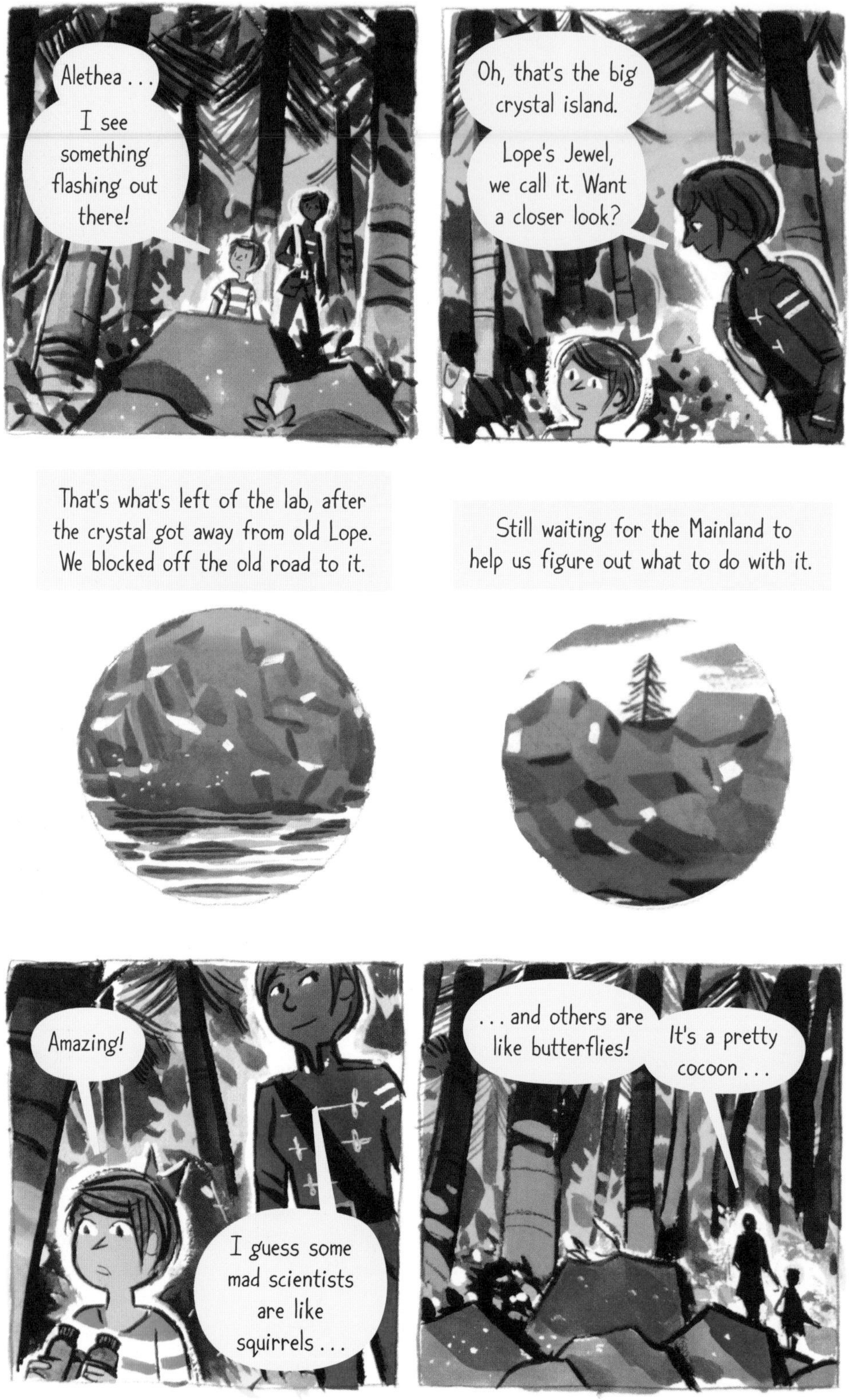
Alethea . . .
I see something flashing out there!
Oh, that's the big crystal island.
Lope's Jewel, we call it. Want a closer look?
That's what's left of the lab, after the crystal got away from old Lope. We blocked off the old road to it.
Still waiting for the Mainland to help us figure out what to do with it.
Amazing!
I guess some mad scientists are like squirrels . . .
. . . and others are like butterflies!
It's a pretty cocoon . . .

5
the life of
the party

zzz

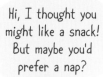

Hi, I thought you might like a snack! But maybe you'd prefer a nap?

Oh... I was just resting my eyes.

I bet you've done a lot of reading down here.

A lot of these books are quite dull, but there are some real treasures hidden here and there.

Oh? What do you like?

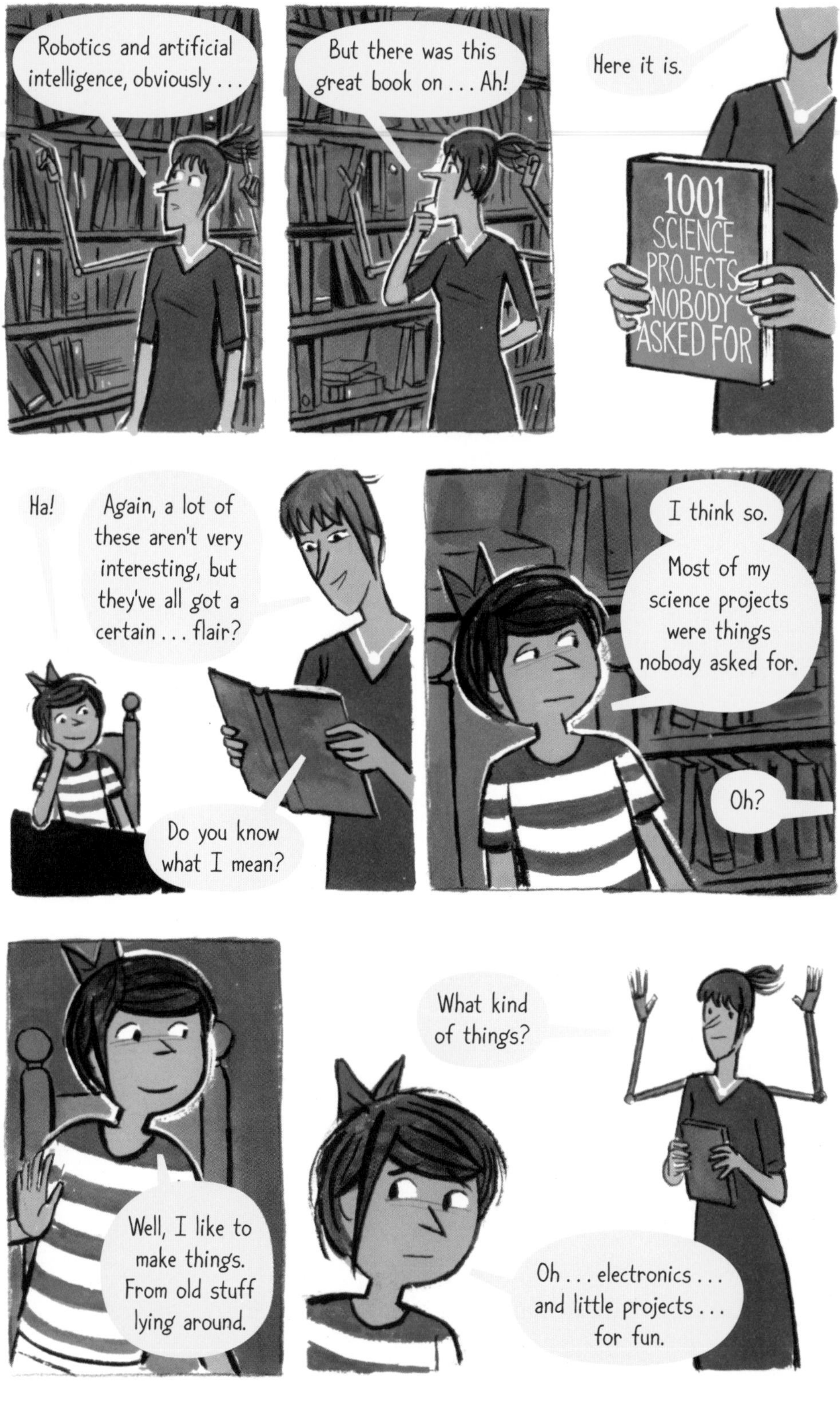
Robotics and artificial intelligence, obviously . . .
But there was this great book on . . . Ah!
Here it is.
1001 SCIENCE PROJECTS NOBODY ASKED FOR
Ha!
Again, a lot of these aren't very interesting, but they've all got a certain . . . flair?
Do you know what I mean?
I think so.
Most of my science projects were things nobody asked for.
Oh?
Well, I like to make things. From old stuff lying around.
What kind of things?
Oh . . . electronics . . . and little projects . . . for fun.

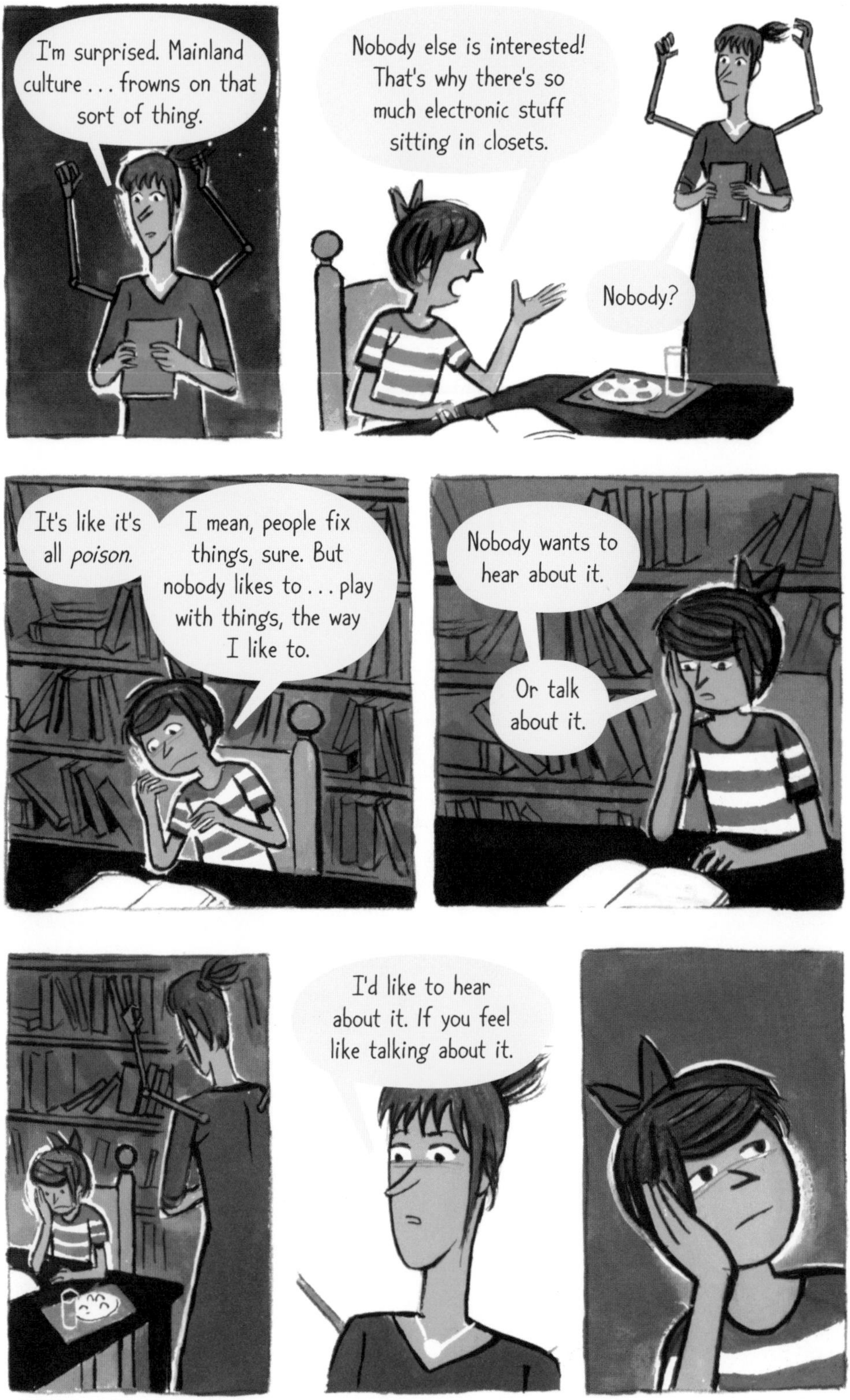
I'm surprised. Mainland culture . . . frowns on that sort of thing.
Nobody else is interested! That's why there's so much electronic stuff sitting in closets.
Nobody?
It's like it's all *poison.*
I mean, people fix things, sure. But nobody likes to . . . play with things, the way I like to.
Nobody wants to hear about it.
Or talk about it.
I'd like to hear about it. If you feel like talking about it.

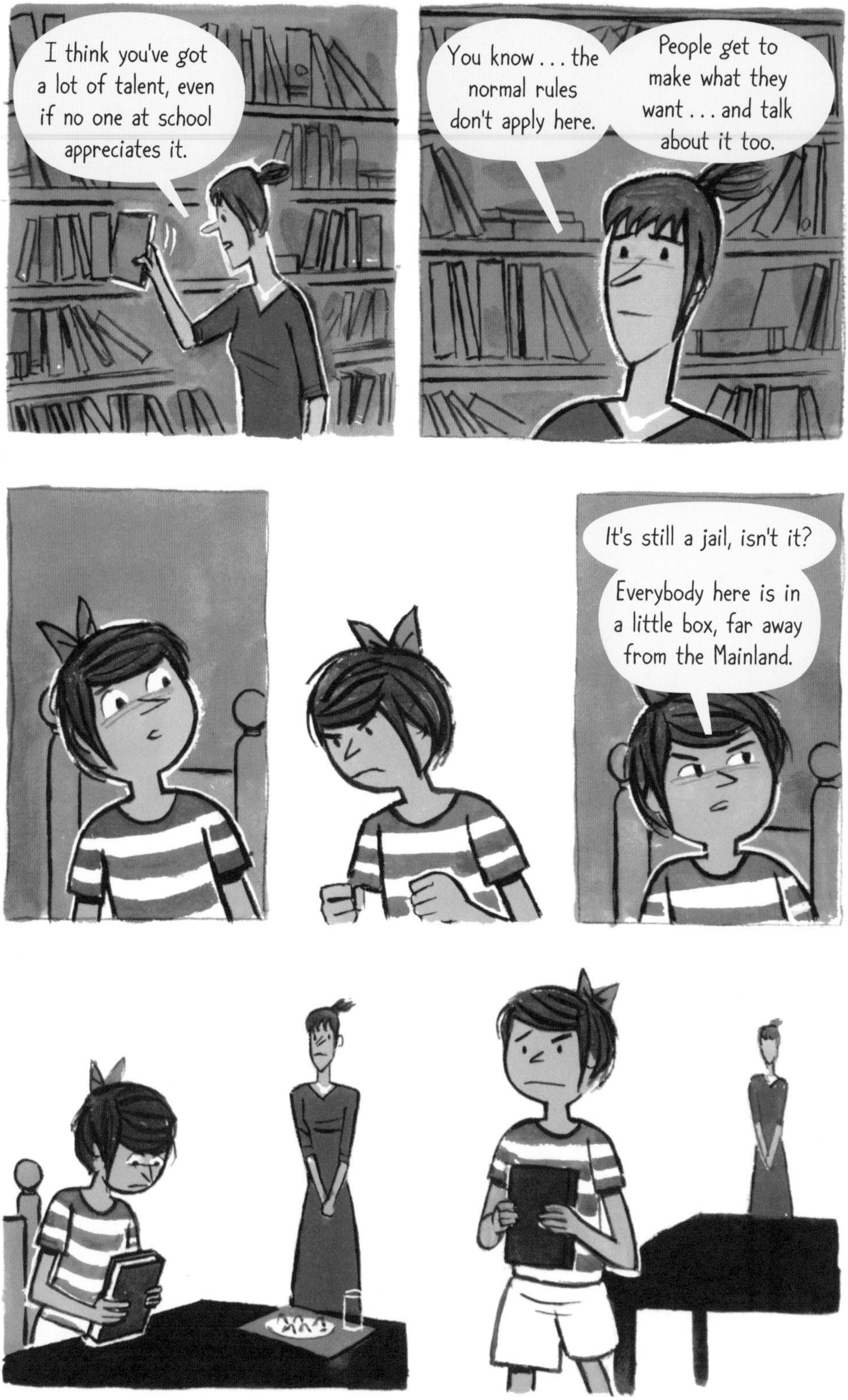
I think you've got a lot of talent, even if no one at school appreciates it.
You know . . . the normal rules don't apply here.
People get to make what they want . . . and talk about it too.
It's still a jail, isn't it?
Everybody here is in a little box, far away from the Mainland.

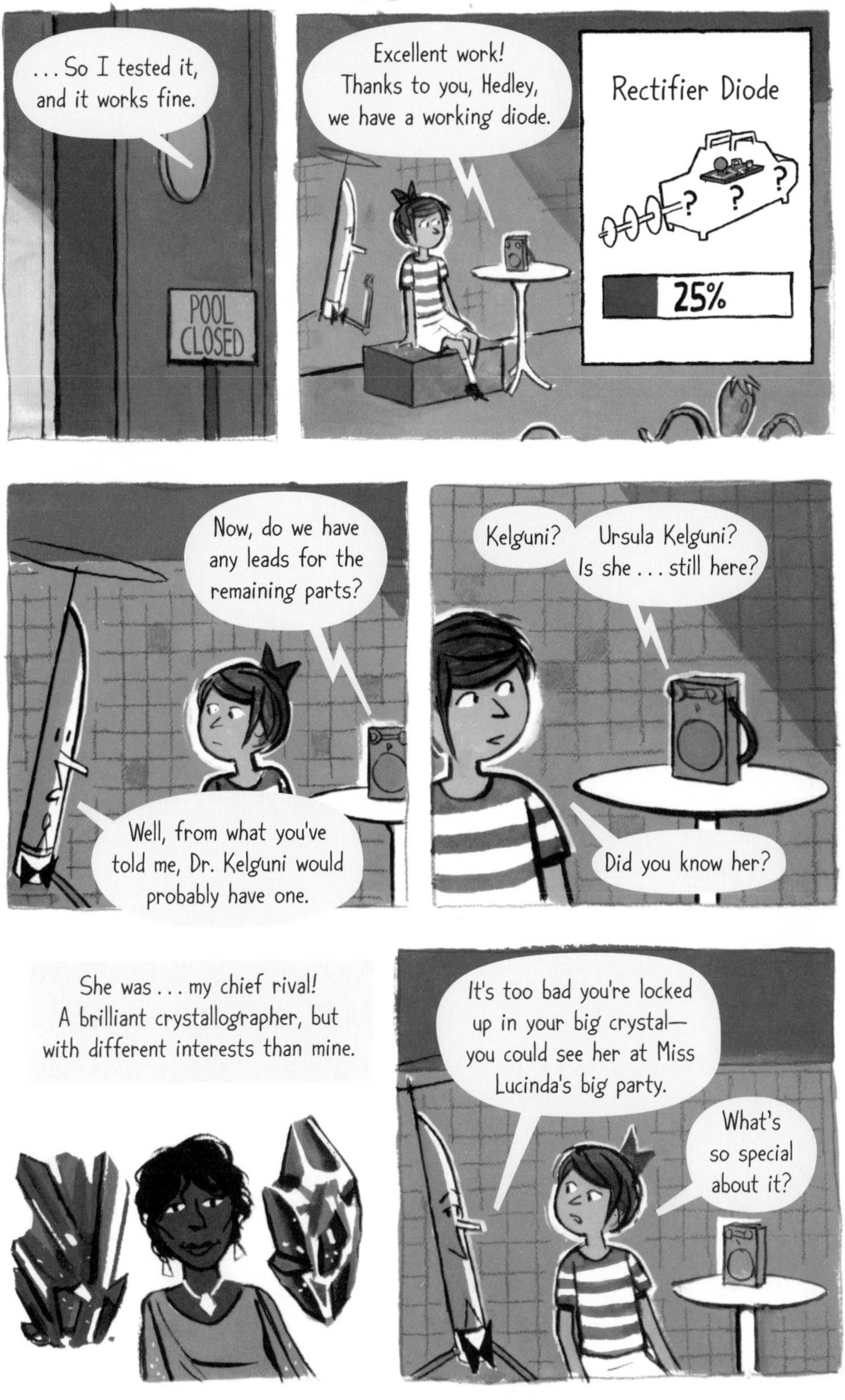

...So I tested it, and it works fine.
POOL CLOSED
Excellent work! Thanks to you, Hedley, we have a working diode.
Rectifier Diode
? ? ?
25%
Now, do we have any leads for the remaining parts?
Well, from what you've told me, Dr. Kelguni would probably have one.
Kelguni?
Ursula Kelguni? Is she... still here?
Did you know her?
She was... my chief rival! A brilliant crystallographer, but with different interests than mine.
It's too bad you're locked up in your big crystal—you could see her at Miss Lucinda's big party.
What's so special about it?

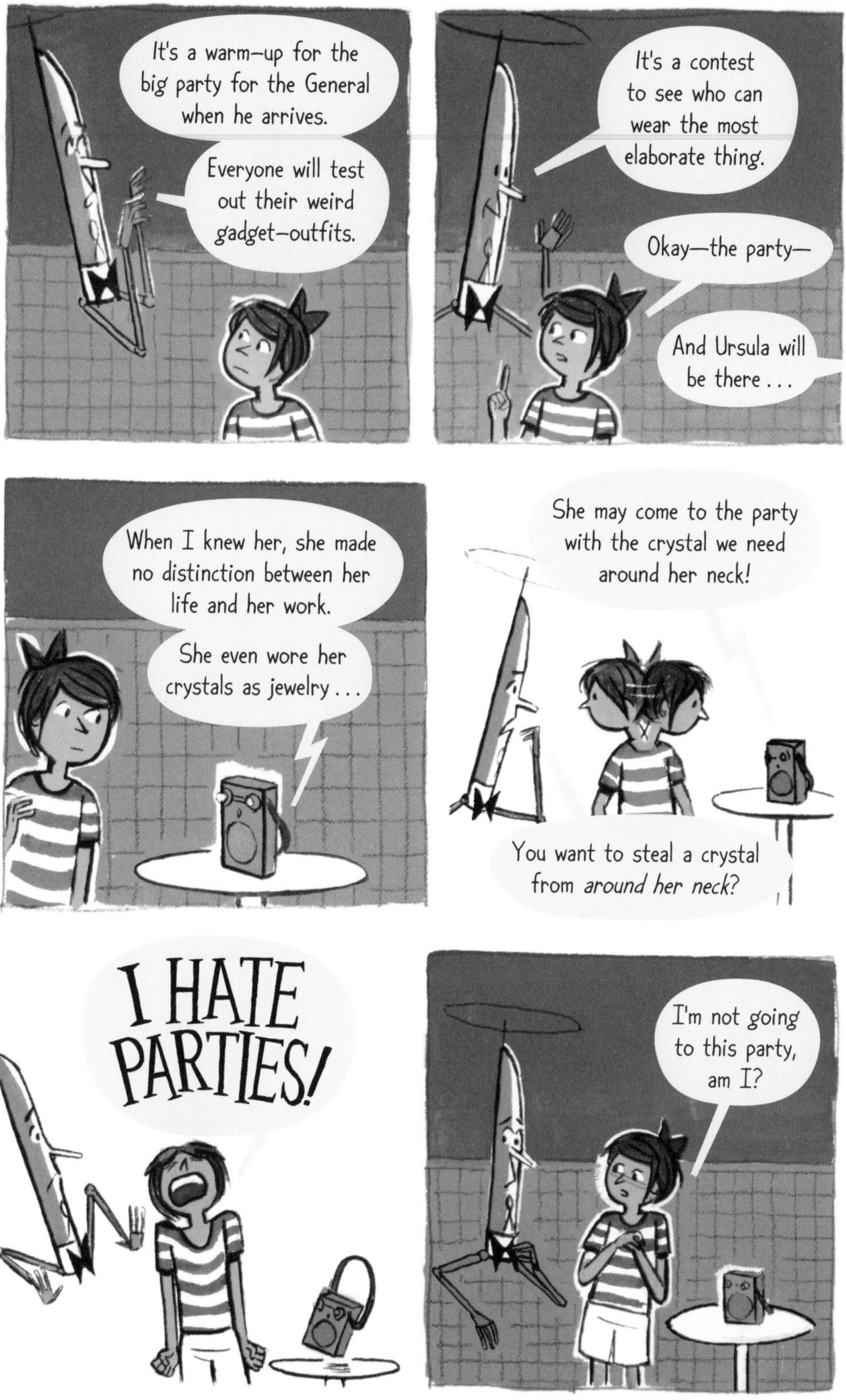
It's a warm-up for the big party for the General when he arrives.
Everyone will test out their weird gadget-outfits.
It's a contest to see who can wear the most elaborate thing.
Okay—the party—
And Ursula will be there . . .
When I knew her, she made no distinction between her life and her work.
She even wore her crystals as jewelry . . .
She may come to the party with the crystal we need around her neck!
You want to steal a crystal from *around her neck?*
I HATE PARTIES!
I'm not going to this party, am I?

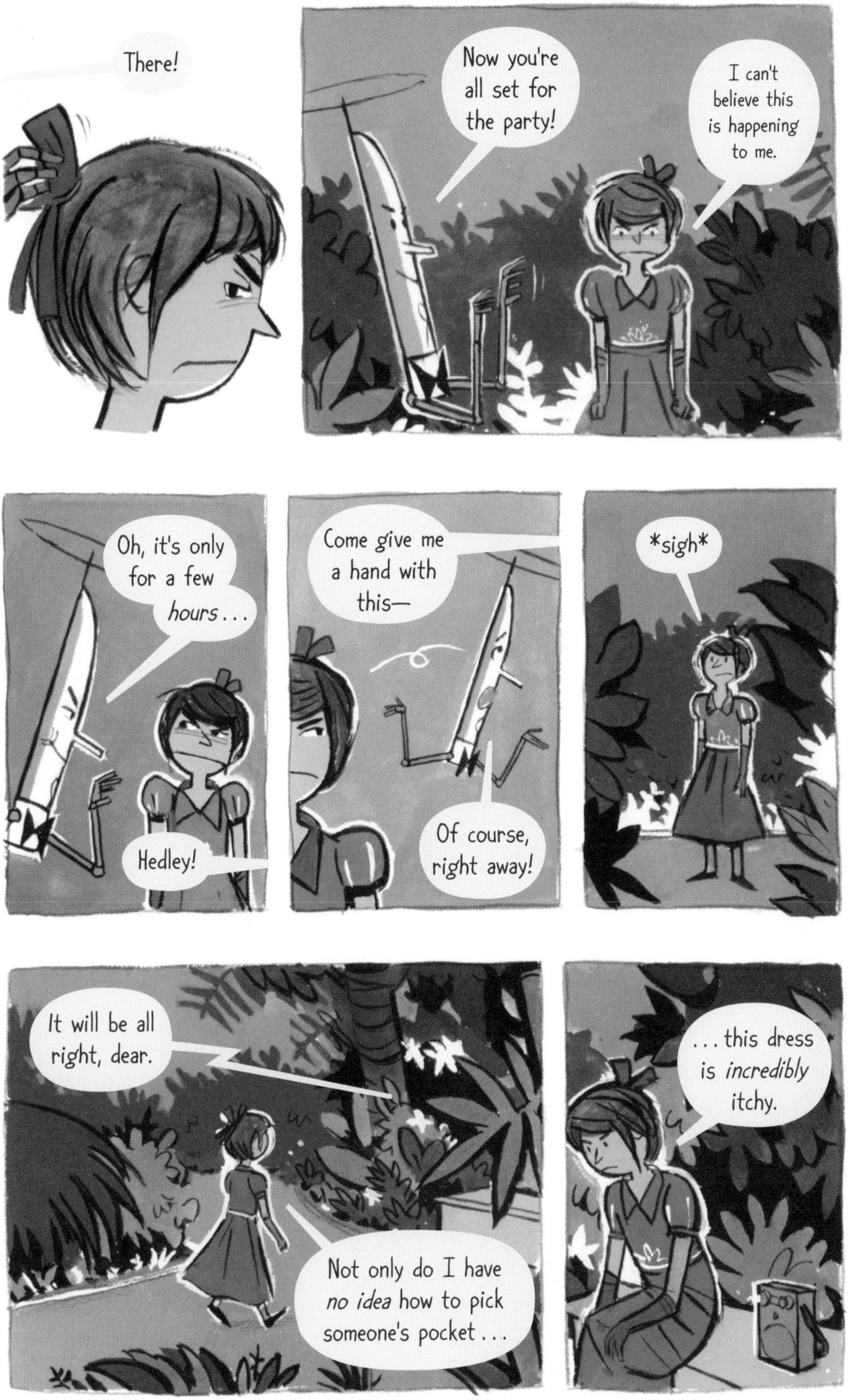
There!
Now you're all set for the party!
I can't believe this is happening to me.
Oh, it's only for a few *hours*...
Hedley!
Come give me a hand with this—
Of course, right away!
sigh
It will be all right, dear.
Not only do I have *no idea* how to pick someone's pocket...
...this dress is *incredibly* itchy.

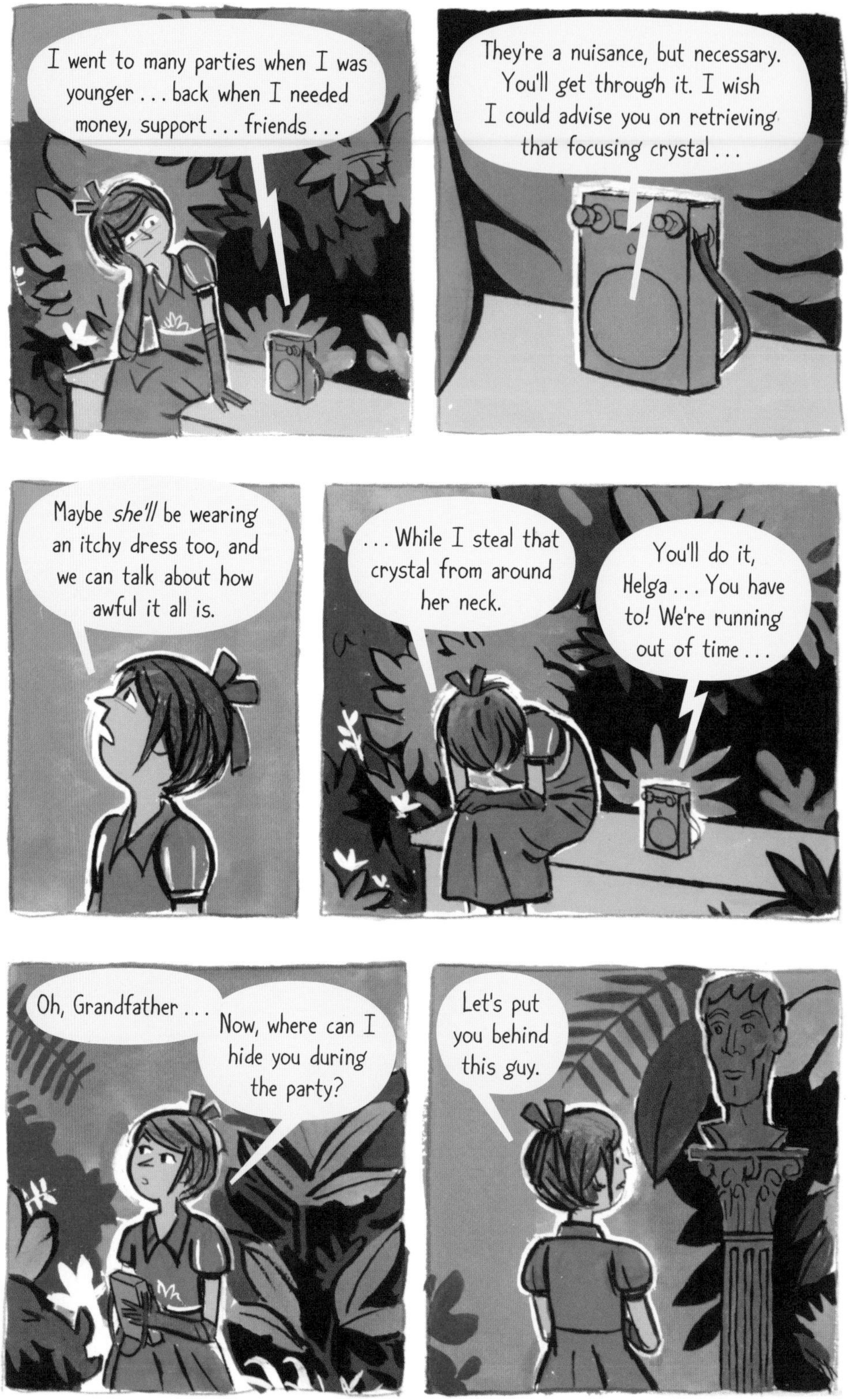
I went to many parties when I was younger . . . back when I needed money, support . . . friends . . .
They're a nuisance, but necessary. You'll get through it. I wish I could advise you on retrieving that focusing crystal . . .
Maybe *she'll* be wearing an itchy dress too, and we can talk about how awful it all is.
. . . While I steal that crystal from around her neck.
You'll do it, Helga . . . You have to! We're running out of time . . .
Oh, Grandfather . . .
Now, where can I hide you during the party?
Let's put you behind this guy.

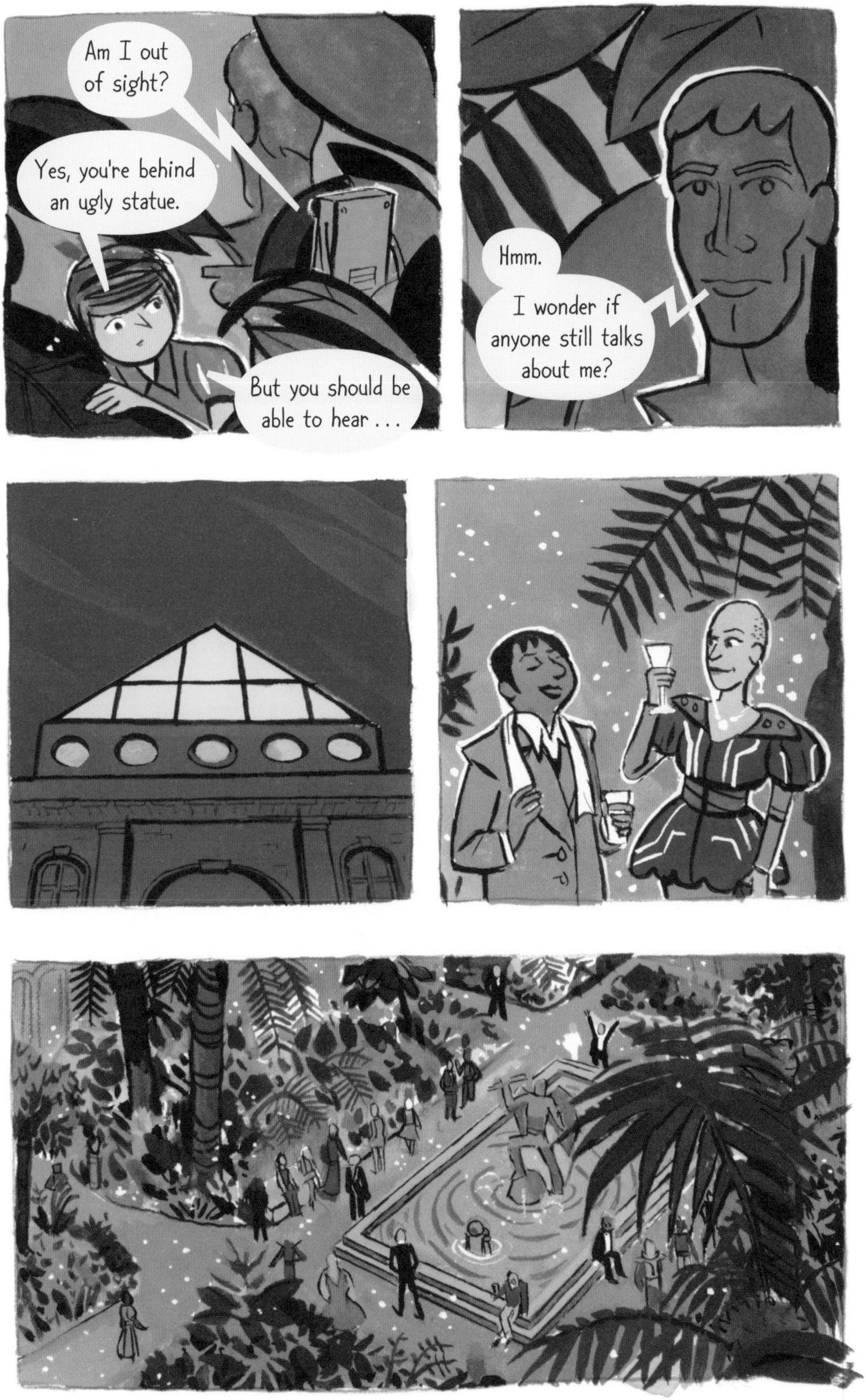
Am I out of sight?
Yes, you're behind an ugly statue.
But you should be able to hear . . .
Hmm.
I wonder if anyone still talks about me?

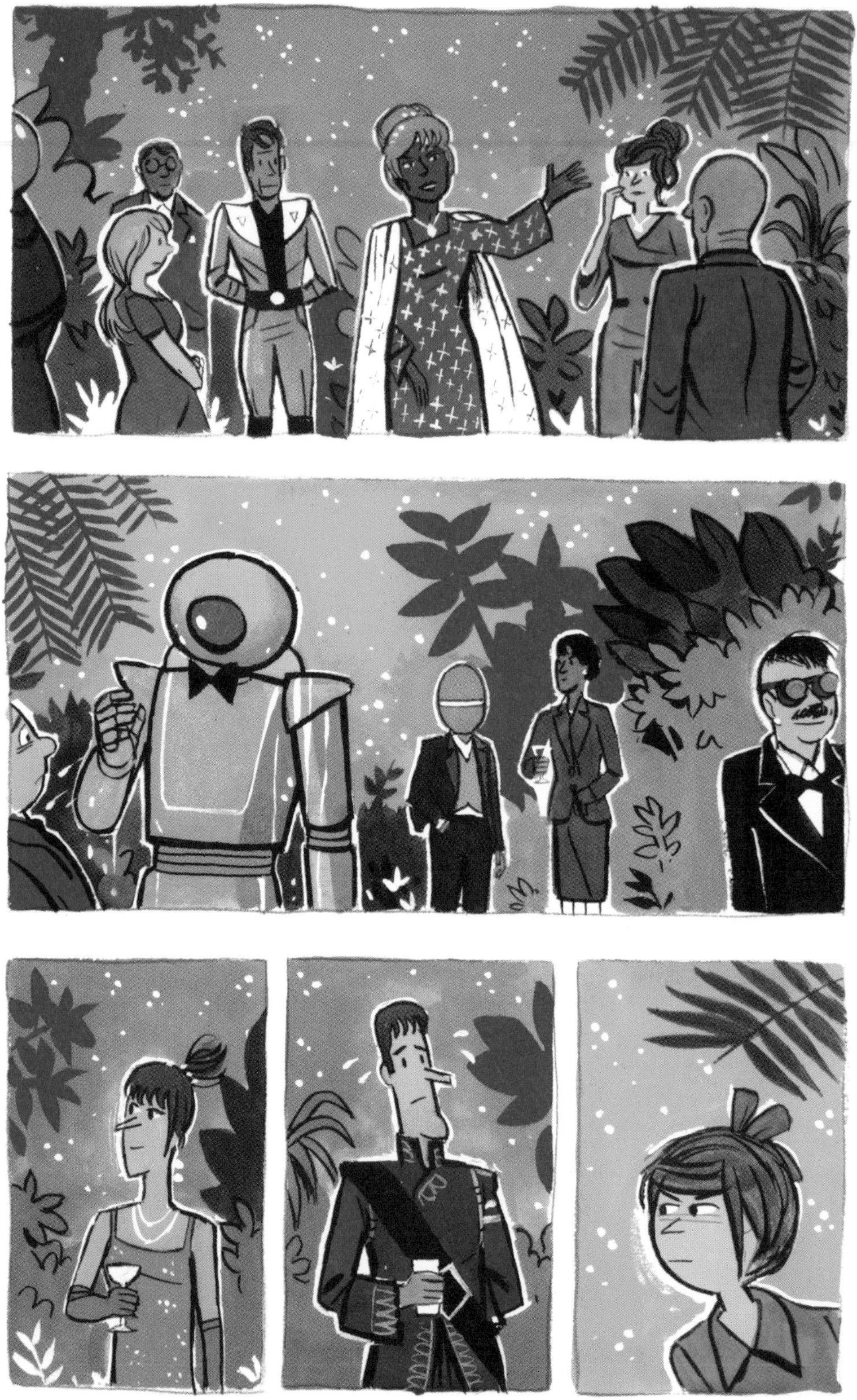

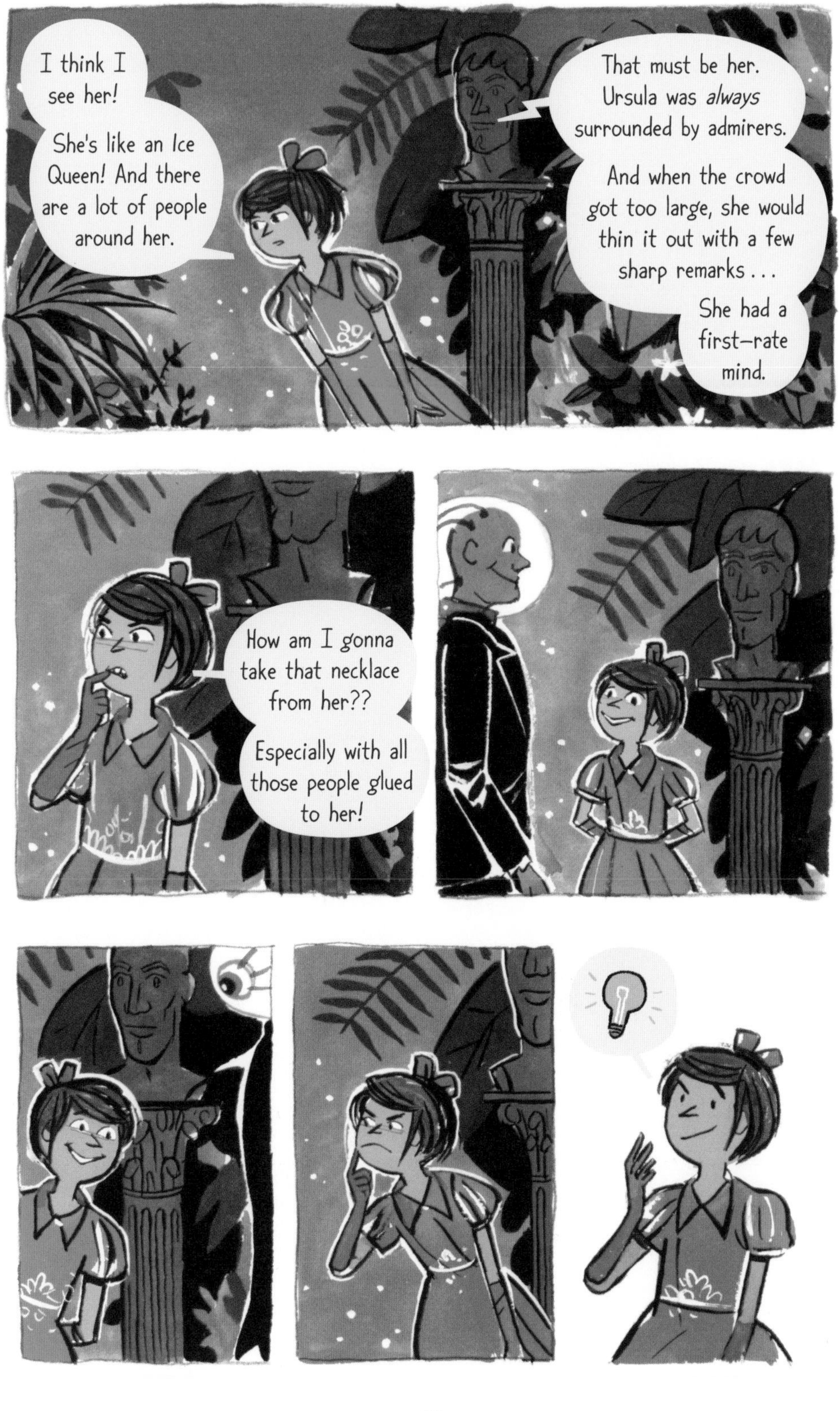
I think I see her!
She's like an Ice Queen! And there are a lot of people around her.
That must be her. Ursula was *always* surrounded by admirers.
And when the crowd got too large, she would thin it out with a few sharp remarks . . .
She had a first-rate mind.
How am I gonna take that necklace from her??
Especially with all those people glued to her!

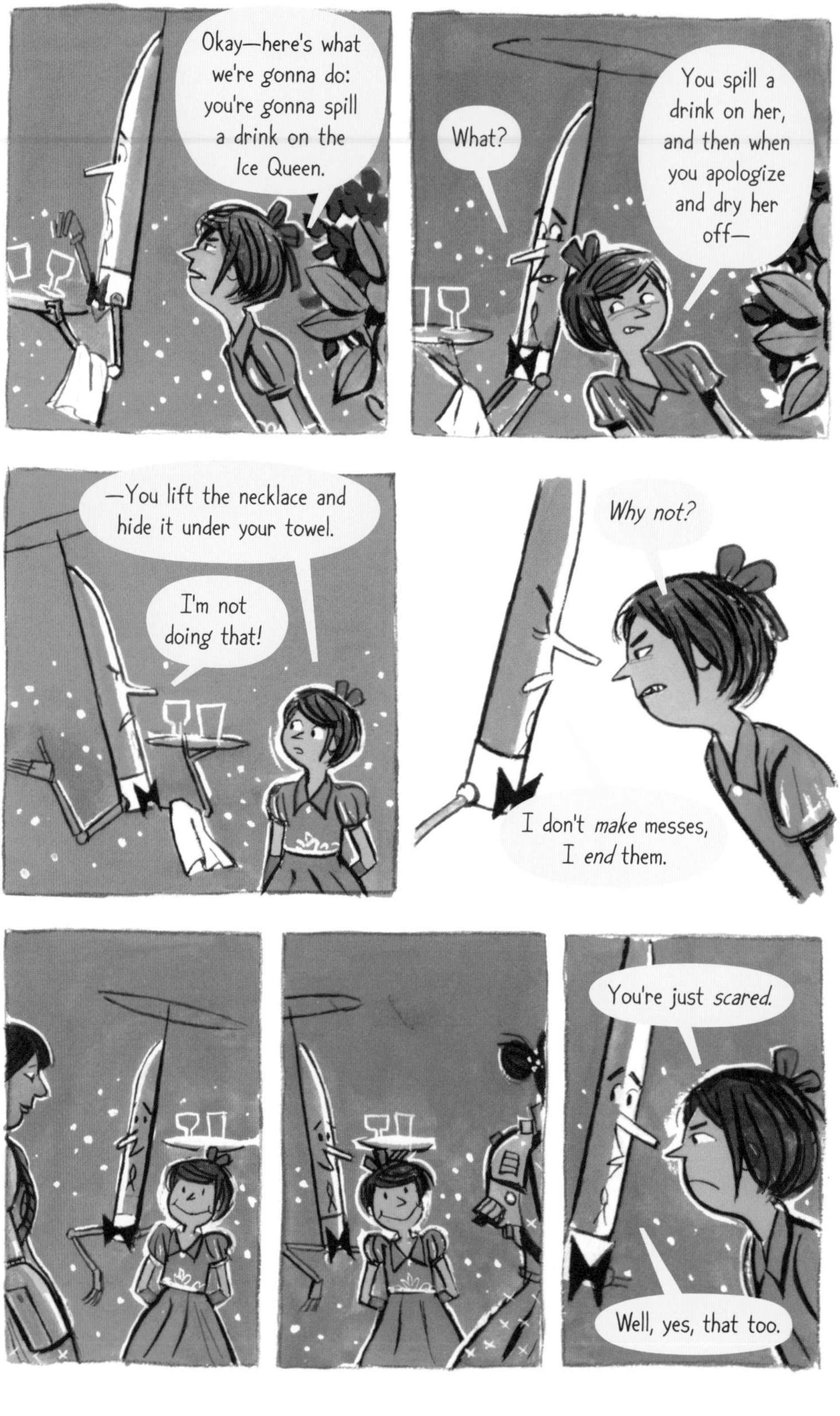
Okay—here's what we're gonna do: you're gonna spill a drink on the Ice Queen.
What?
You spill a drink on her, and then when you apologize and dry her off—
—You lift the necklace and hide it under your towel.
I'm not doing that!
Why not?
I don't *make* messes, I *end* them.
You're just *scared.*
Well, yes, that too.

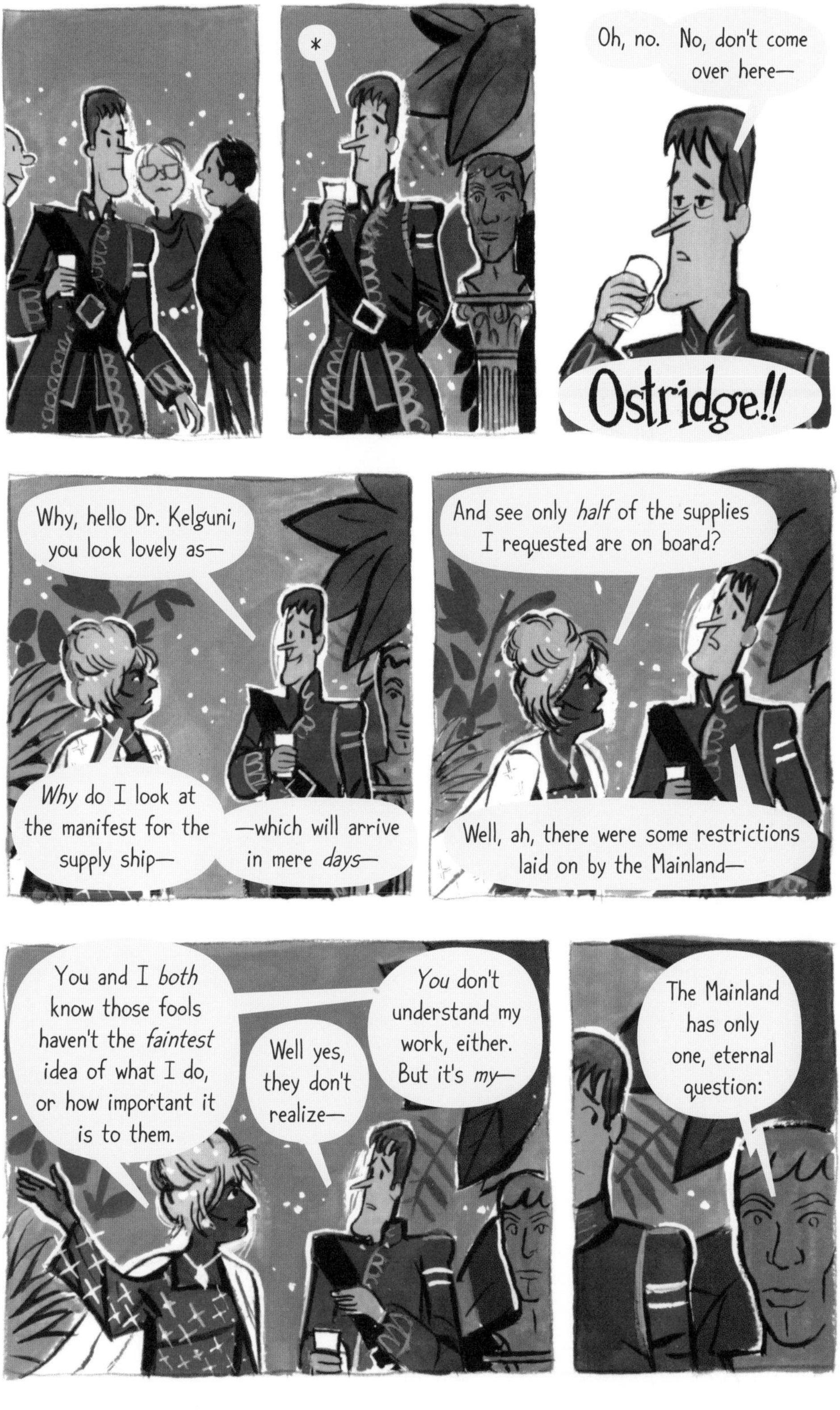
*
Oh, no. No, don't come over here—
Ostridge!!
Why, hello Dr. Kelguni, you look lovely as—
Why do I look at the manifest for the supply ship—
—which will arrive in mere *days*—
And see only *half* of the supplies I requested are on board?
Well, ah, there were some restrictions laid on by the Mainland—
You and I *both* know those fools haven't the *faintest* idea of what I do, or how important it is to them.
Well yes, they don't realize—
You don't understand my work, either. But it's *my*—
The Mainland has only one, eternal question:

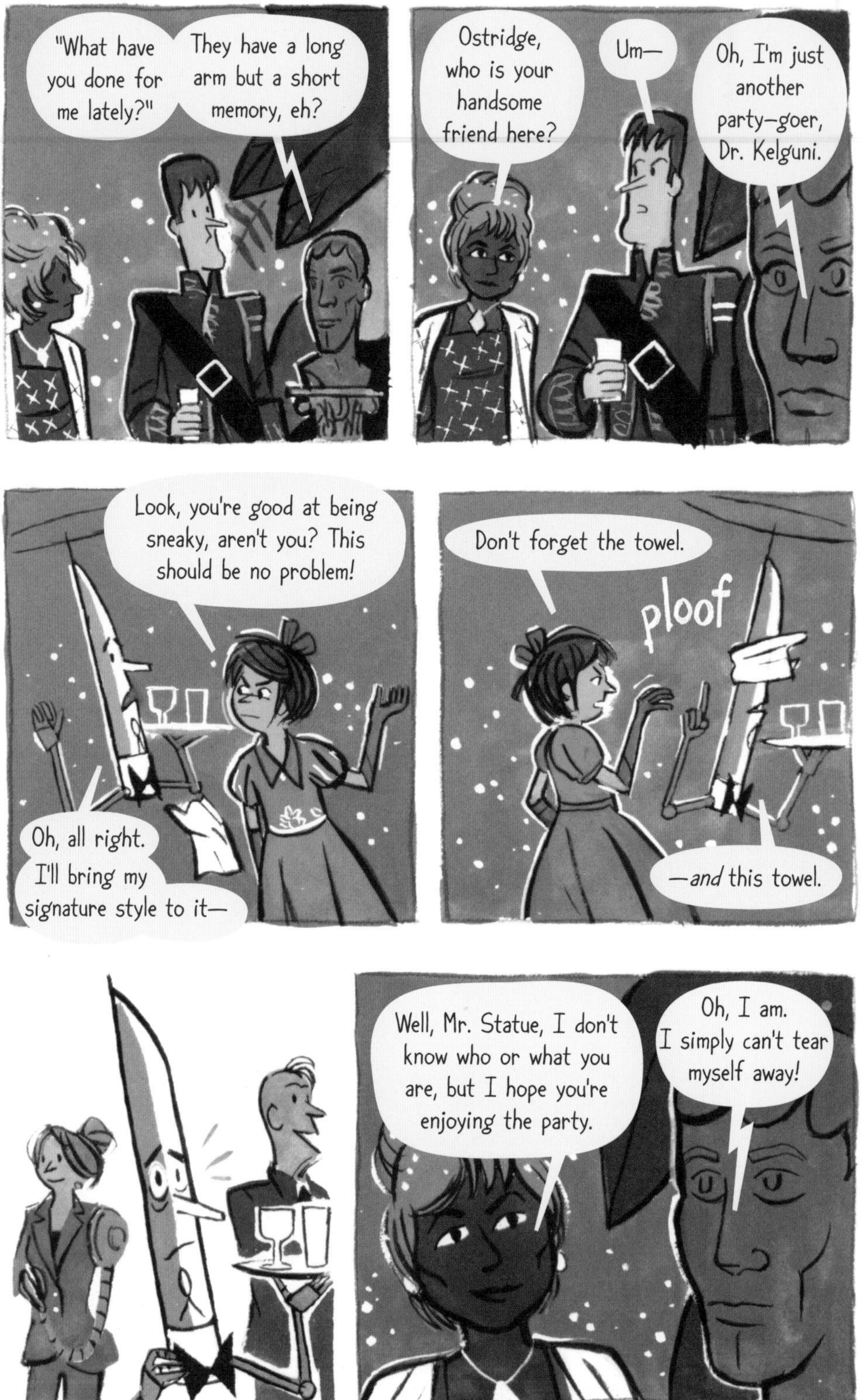
"What have you done for me lately?"
They have a long arm but a short memory, eh?
Ostridge, who is your handsome friend here?
Um—
Oh, I'm just another party-goer, Dr. Kelguni.
Look, you're good at being sneaky, aren't you? This should be no problem!
Oh, all right. I'll bring my signature style to it—
Don't forget the towel.
ploof
—*and* this towel.
Well, Mr. Statue, I don't know who or what you are, but I hope you're enjoying the party.
Oh, I am. I simply can't tear myself away!

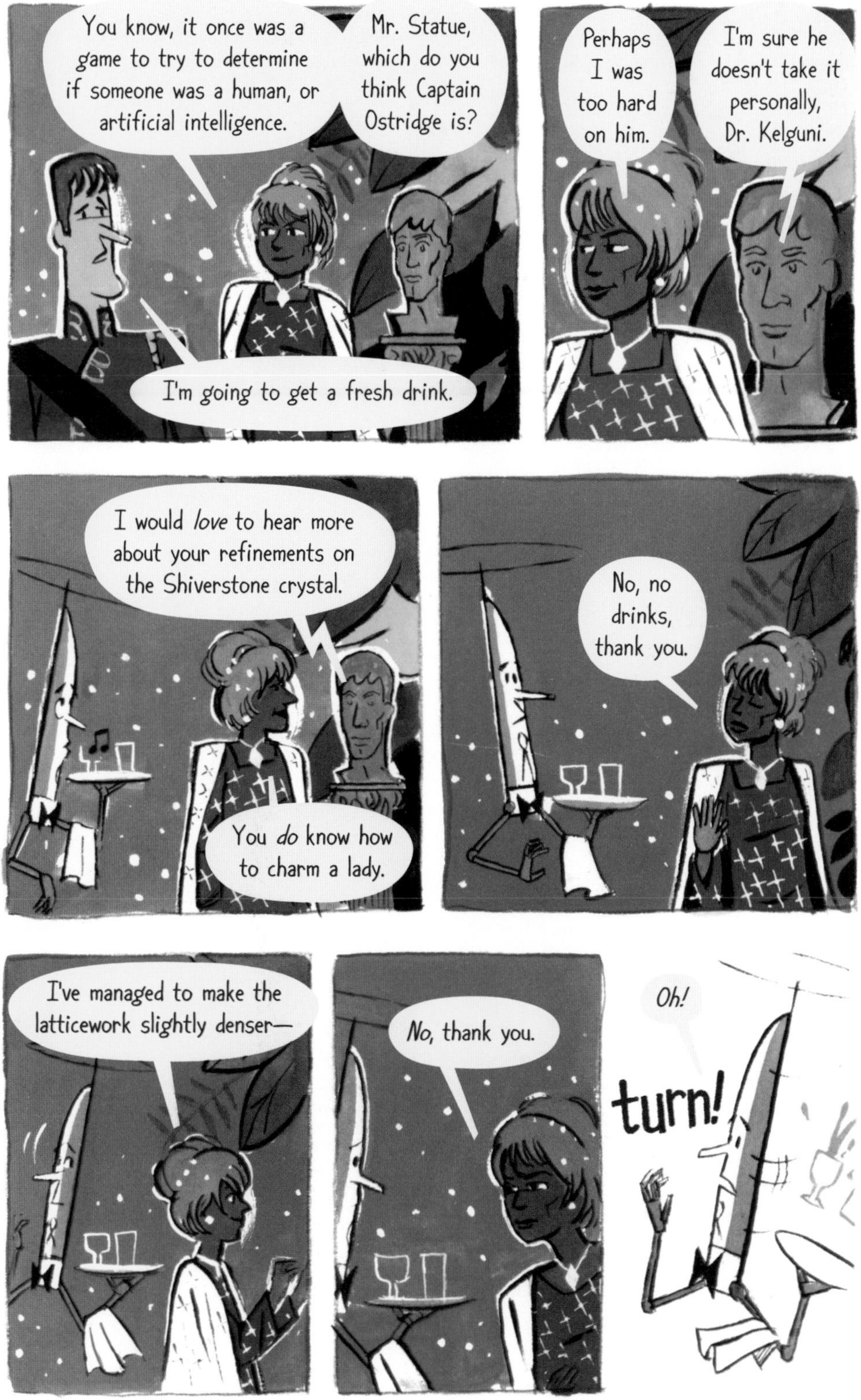
You know, it once was a game to try to determine if someone was a human, or artificial intelligence.
Mr. Statue, which do you think Captain Ostridge is?
I'm going to get a fresh drink.
Perhaps I was too hard on him.
I'm sure he doesn't take it personally, Dr. Kelguni.
I would *love* to hear more about your refinements on the Shiverstone crystal.
You *do* know how to charm a lady.
No, no drinks, thank you.
I've managed to make the latticework slightly denser—
No, thank you.
Oh!
turn!

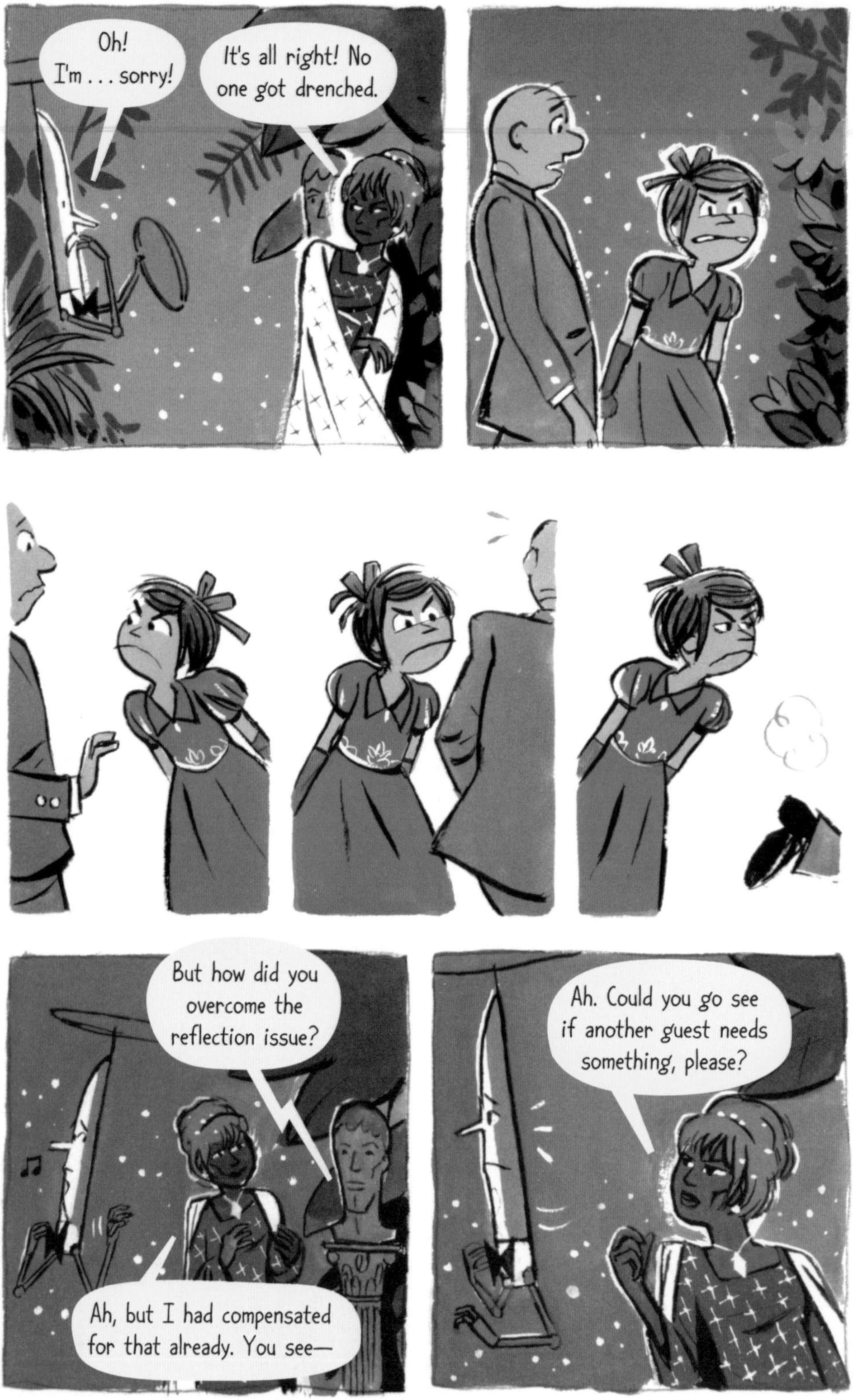
Oh! I'm . . . sorry!
It's all right! No one got drenched.
But how did you overcome the reflection issue?
Ah, but I had compensated for that already. You see—
Ah. Could you go see if another guest needs something, please?

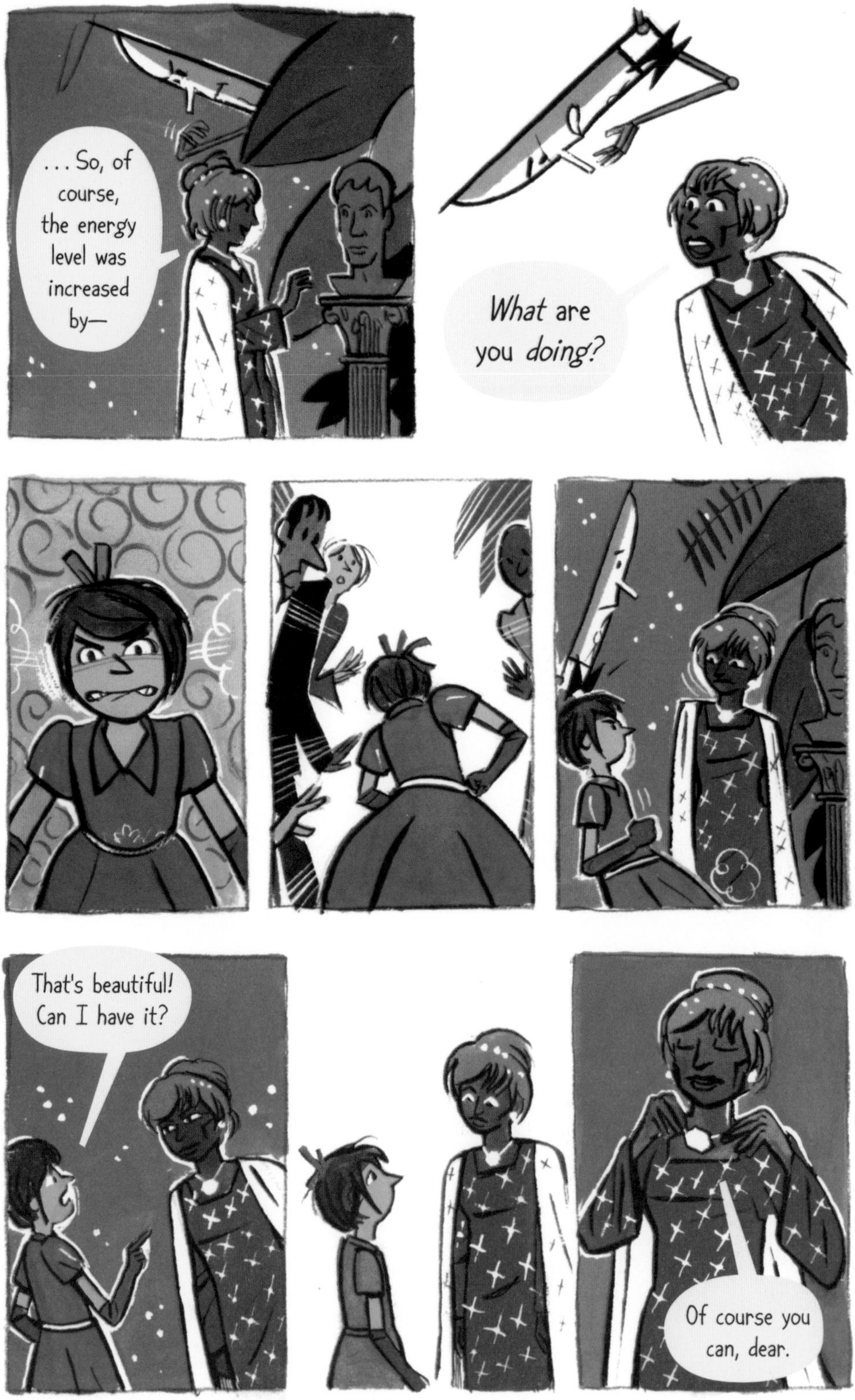

. . . So, of course, the energy level was increased by—
What are you *doing?*
That's beautiful! Can I have it?
Of course you can, dear.

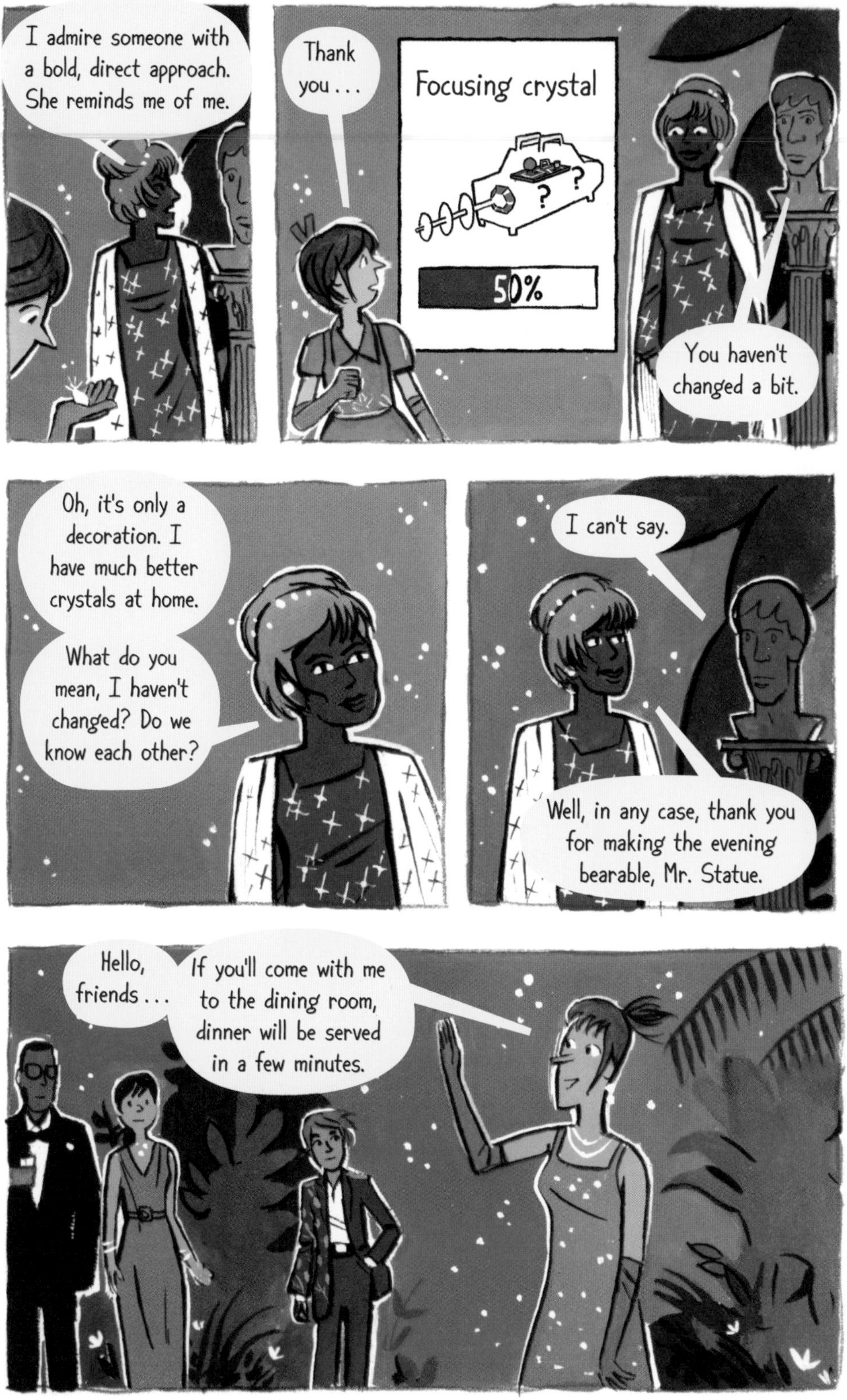
I admire someone with a bold, direct approach. She reminds me of me.
Thank you . . .
Focusing crystal
50%
You haven't changed a bit.
Oh, it's only a decoration. I have much better crystals at home.
What do you mean, I haven't changed? Do we know each other?
I can't say.
Well, in any case, thank you for making the evening bearable, Mr. Statue.
Hello, friends . . .
If you'll come with me to the dining room, dinner will be served in a few minutes.

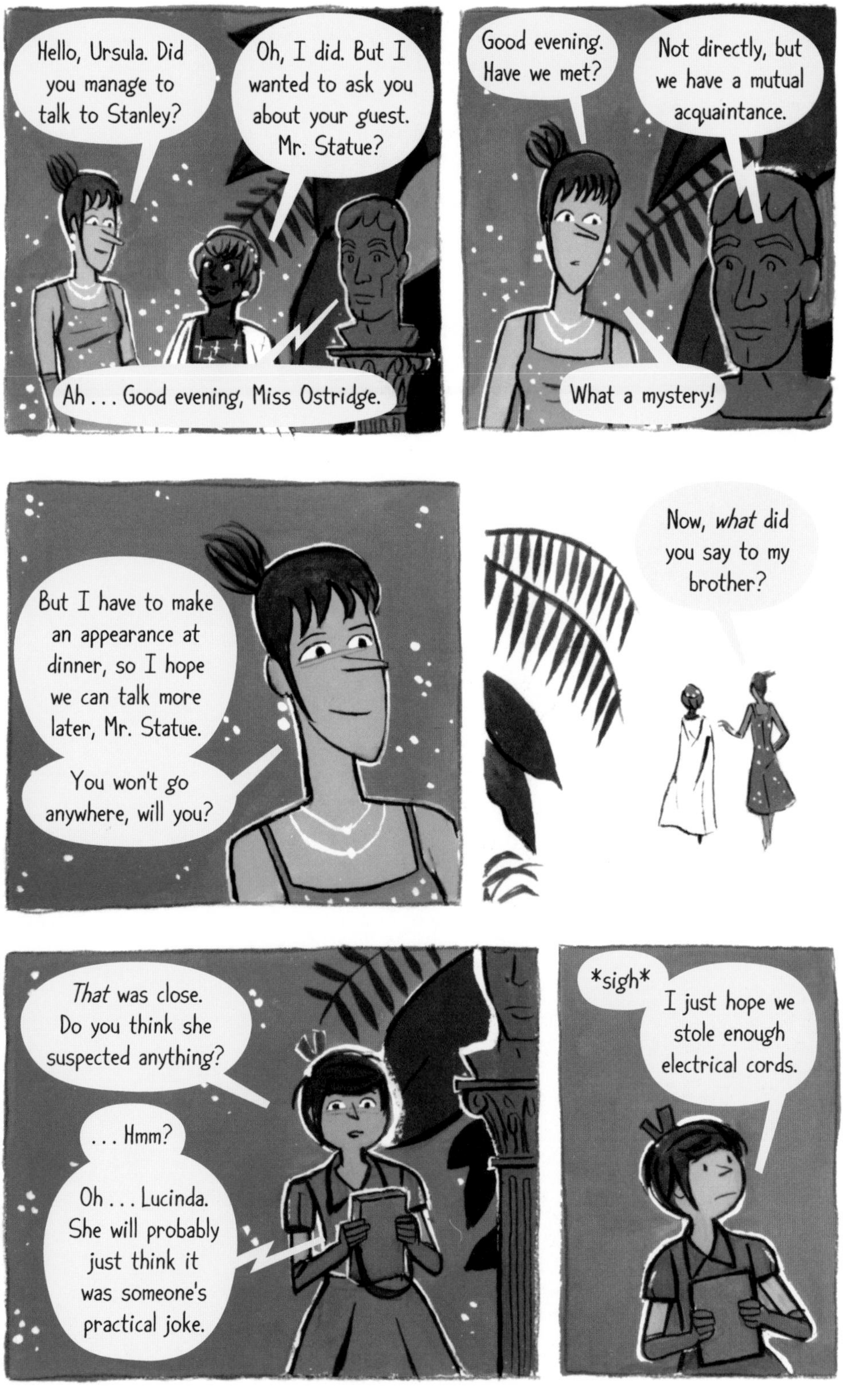
Hello, Ursula. Did you manage to talk to Stanley?
Oh, I did. But I wanted to ask you about your guest. Mr. Statue?
Ah . . . Good evening, Miss Ostridge.
Good evening. Have we met?
Not directly, but we have a mutual acquaintance.
What a mystery!
But I have to make an appearance at dinner, so I hope we can talk more later, Mr. Statue.
You won't go anywhere, will you?
Now, *what* did you say to my brother?
That was close. Do you think she suspected anything?
. . . Hmm?
Oh . . . Lucinda. She will probably just think it was someone's practical joke.
sigh
I just hope we stole enough electrical cords.

6
a stroll in the moonlight

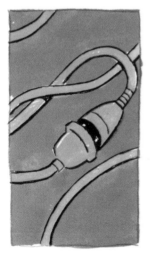

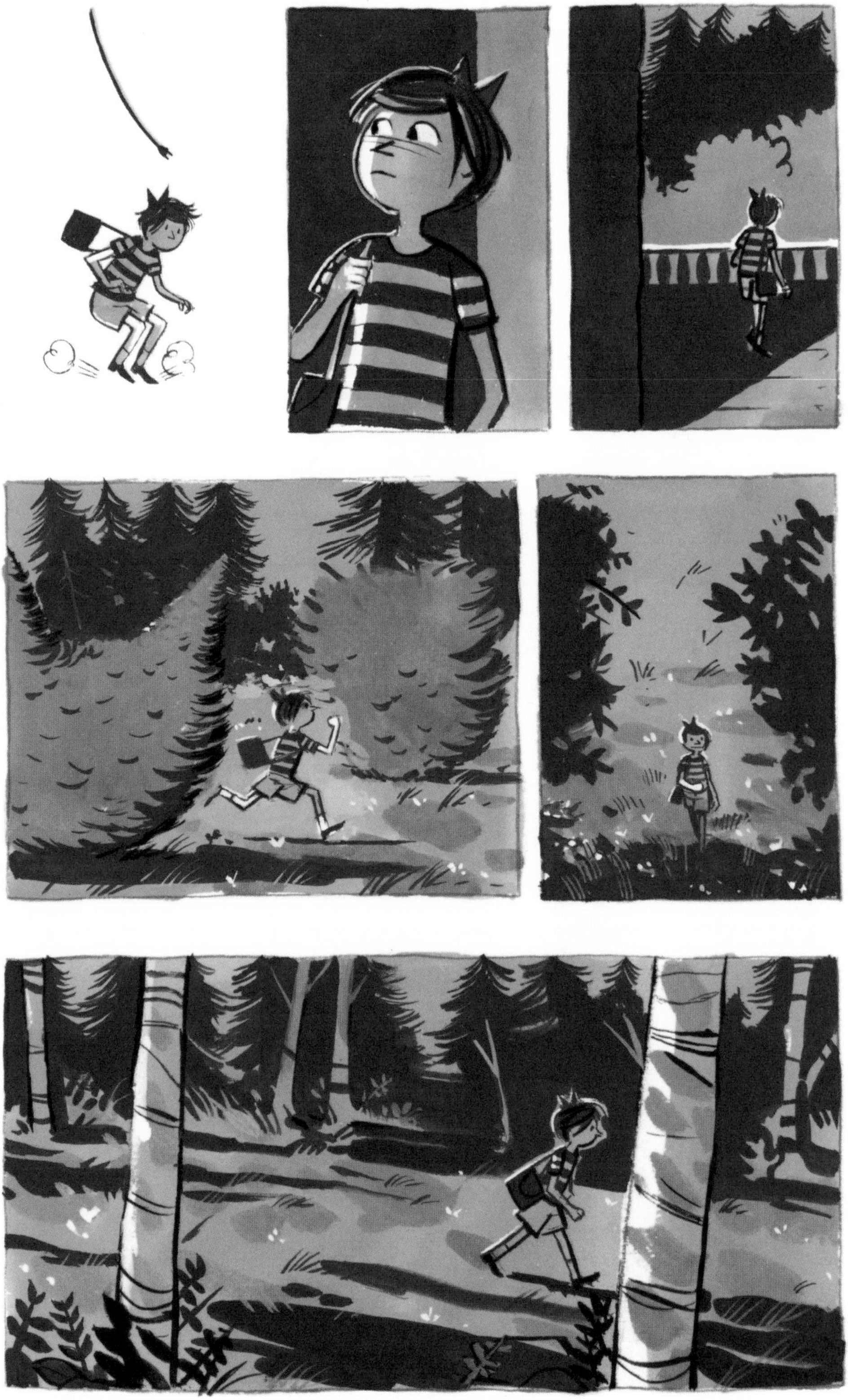

SSSSSS SSSSSS SSSSSS

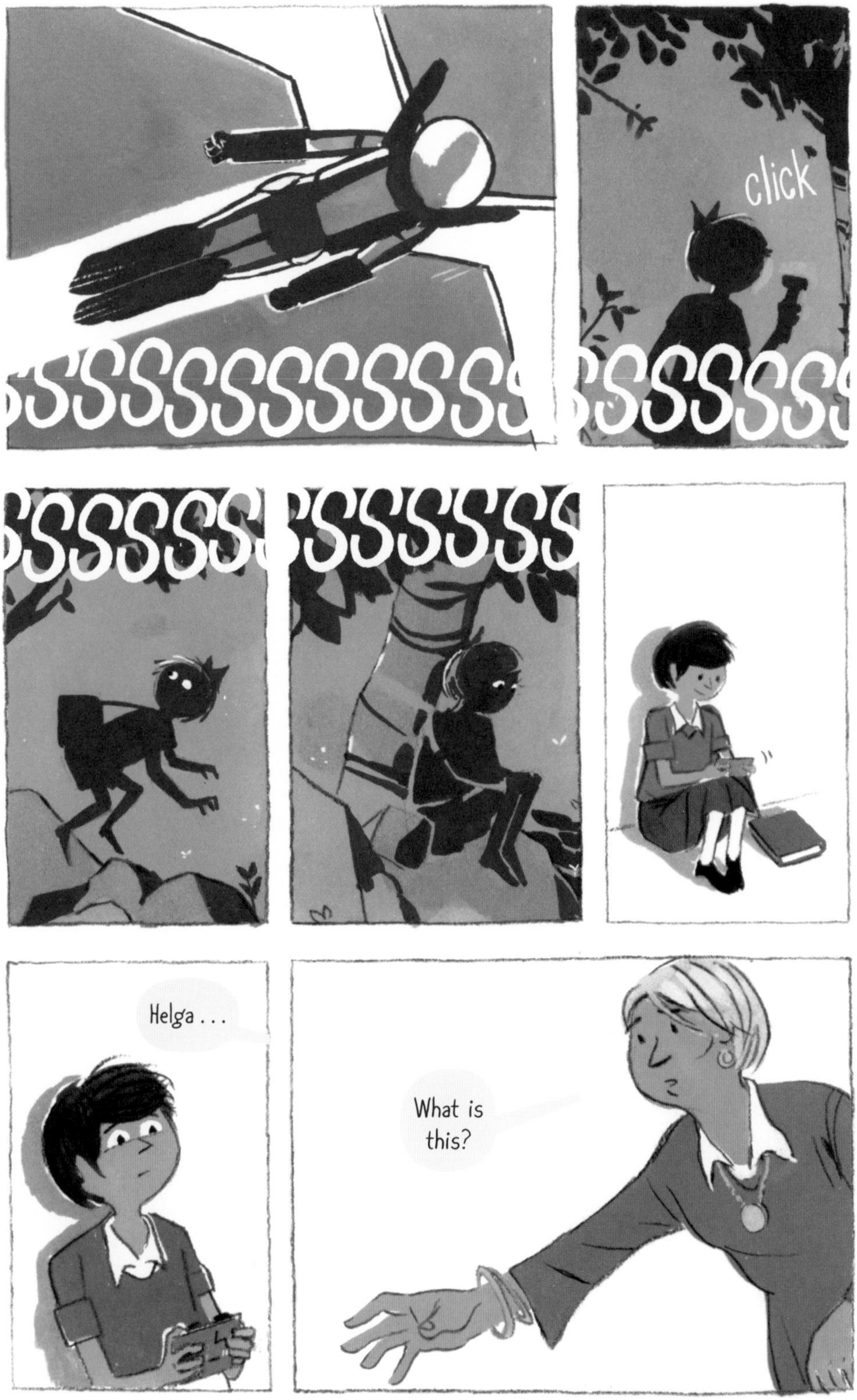
click
SSSSSSSSSSSSSSSSSSSSS
SSSSSSSSSSSSSS
Helga . . .
What is this?

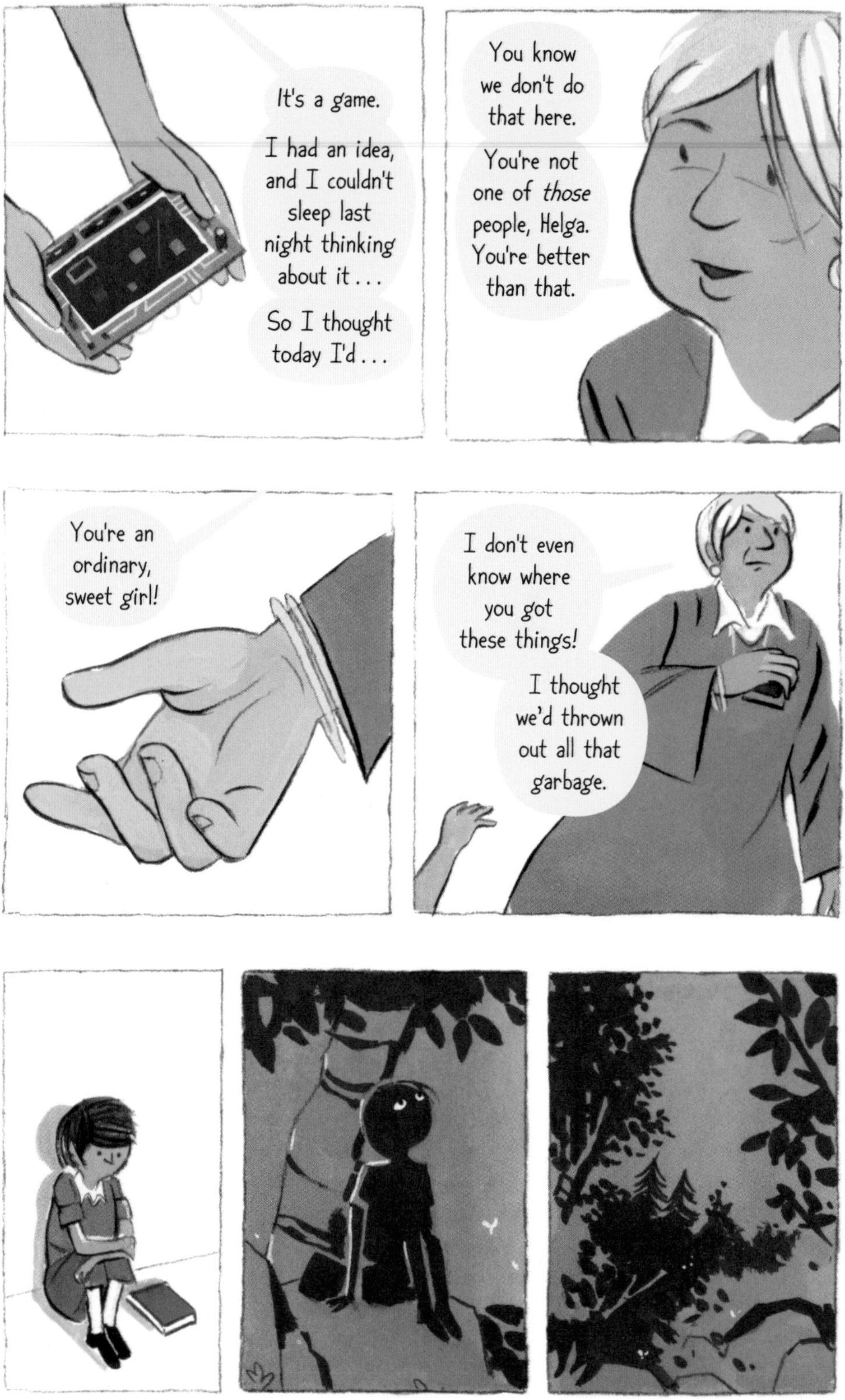
It's a game.
I had an idea, and I couldn't sleep last night thinking about it . . .
So I thought today I'd . . .
You know we don't do that here.
You're not one of *those* people, Helga. You're better than that.
You're an ordinary, sweet girl!
I don't even know where you got these things!
I thought we'd thrown out all that garbage.

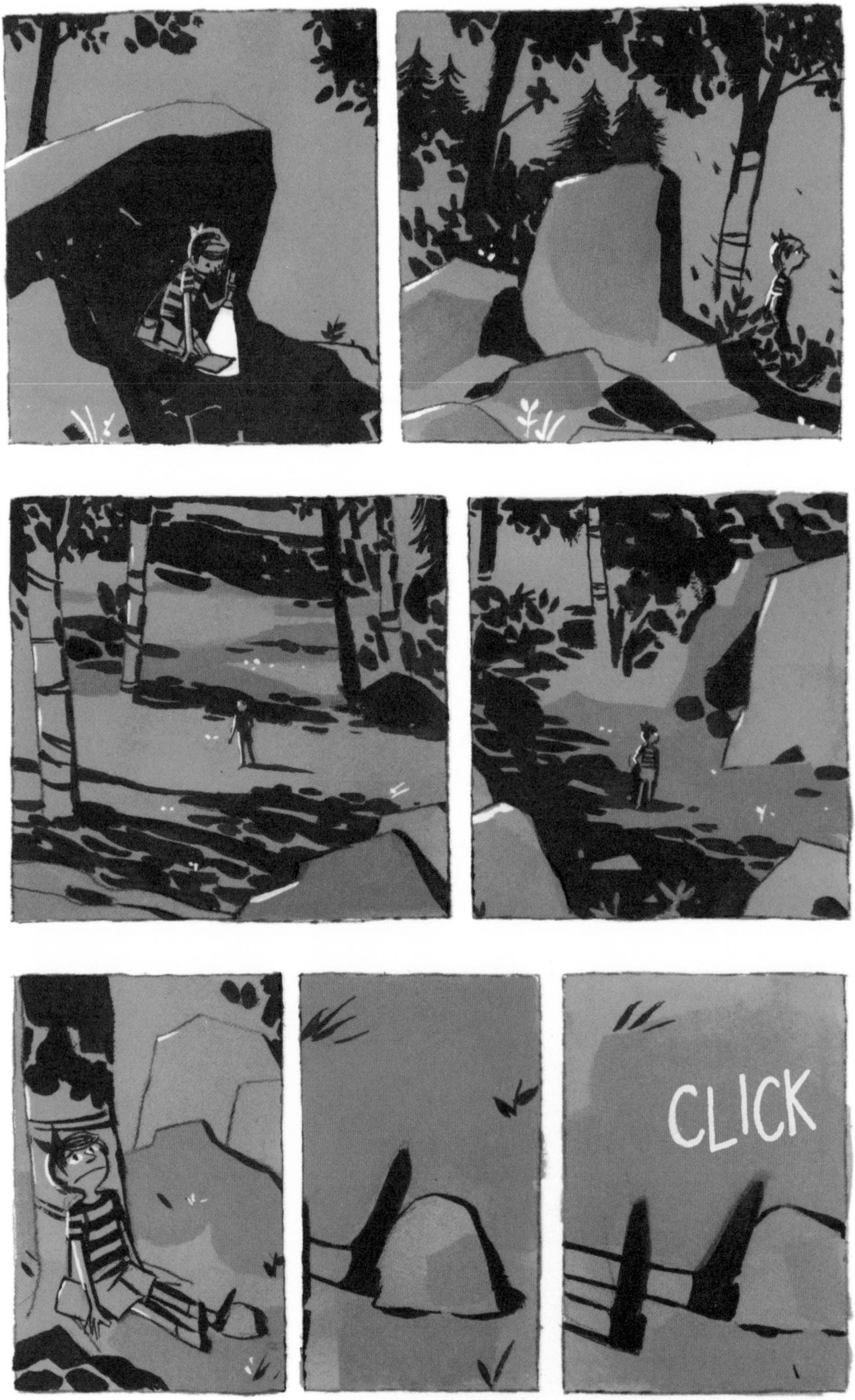
CLICK

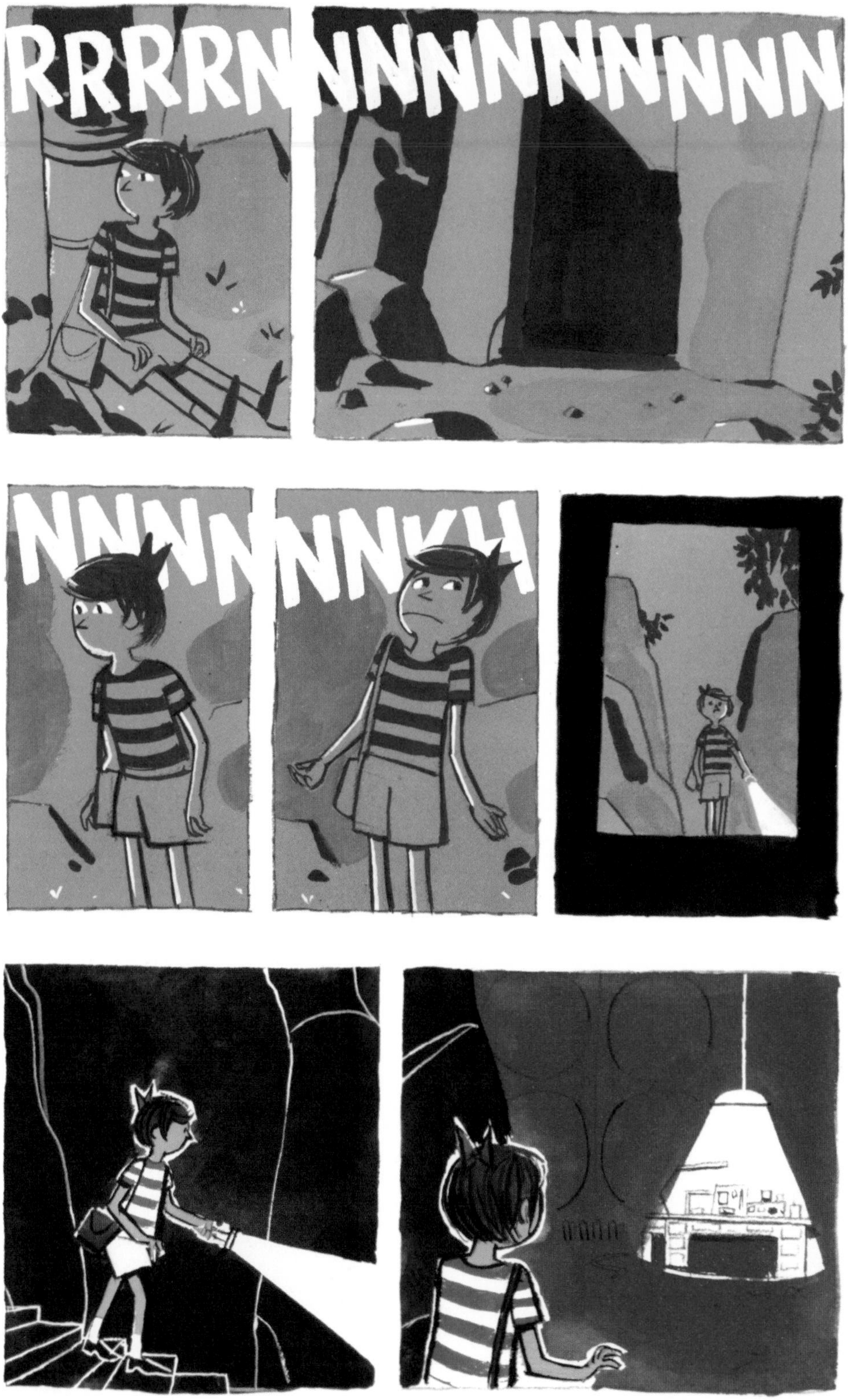
RRRRNNNNNNNNNNNN
NNNNNNKH

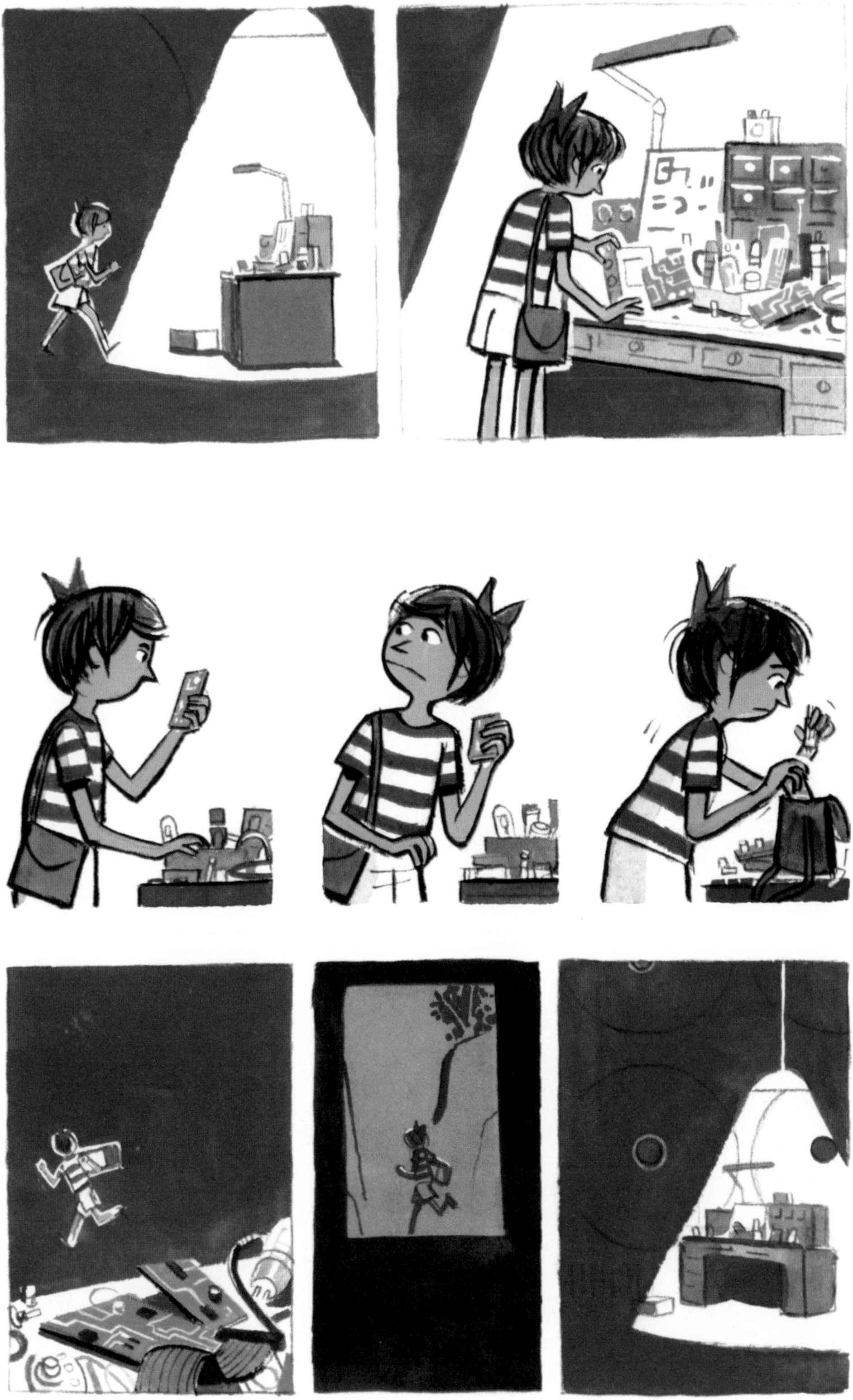

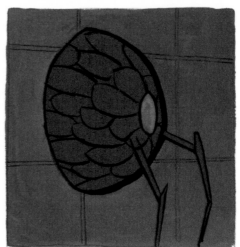

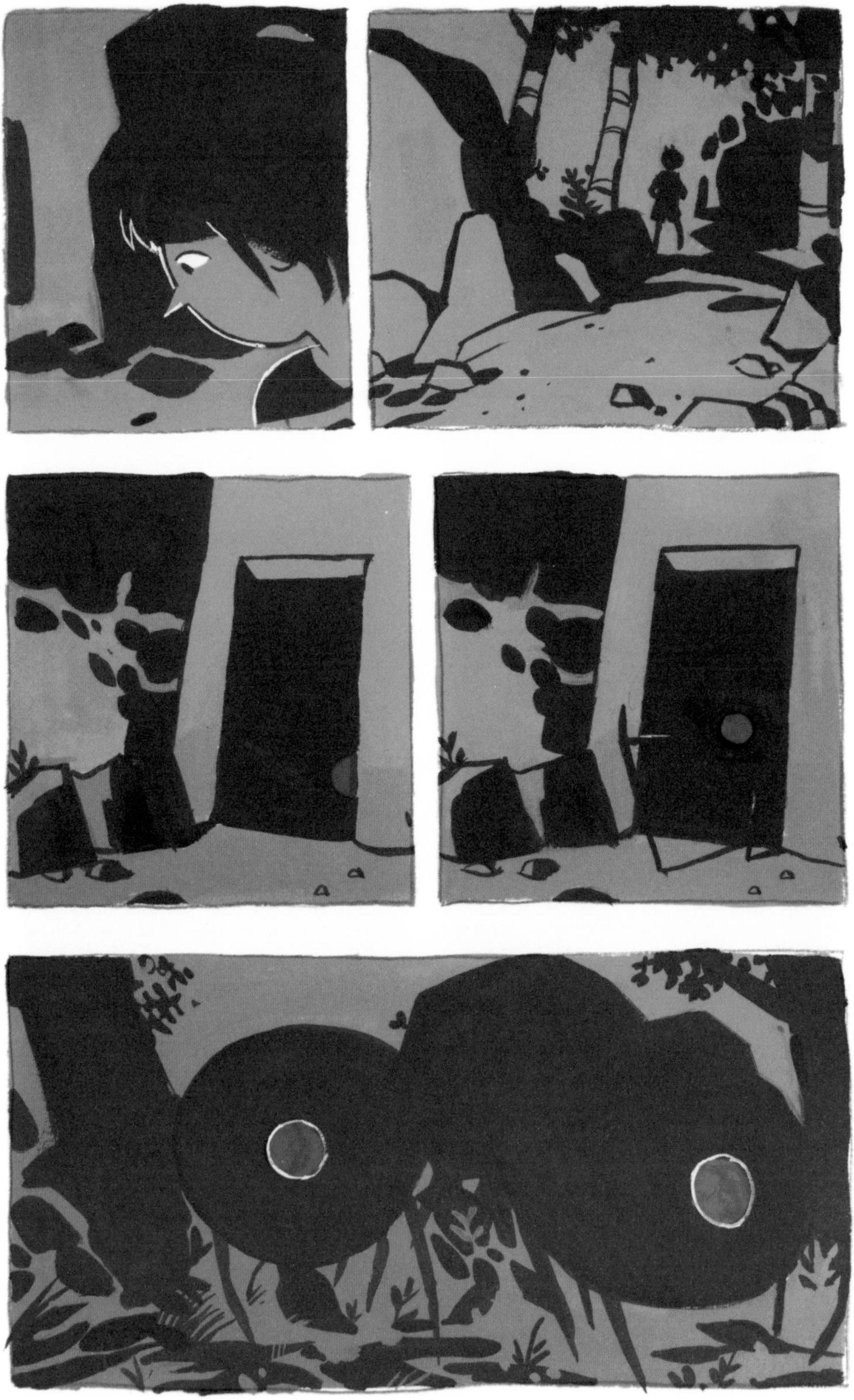

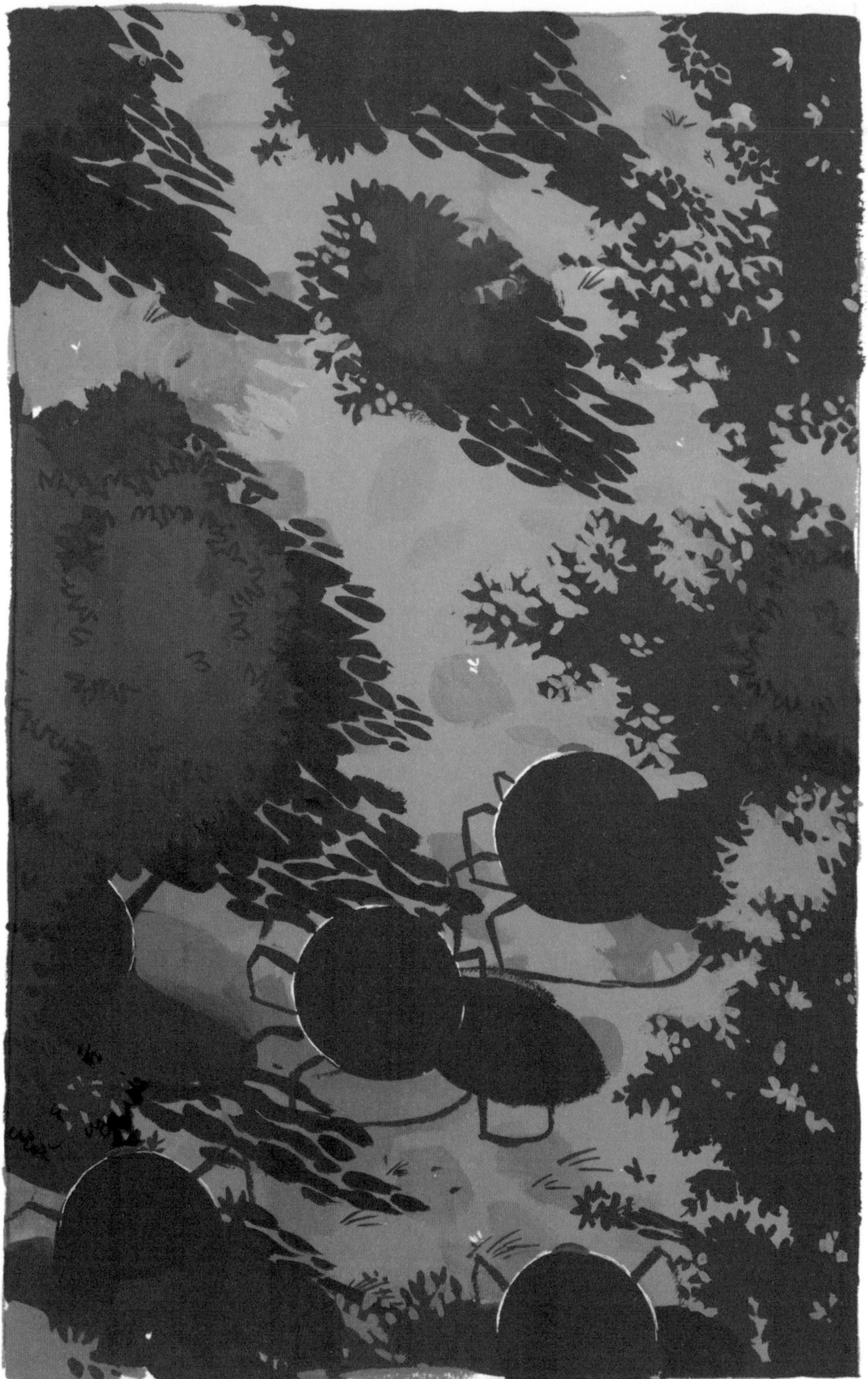

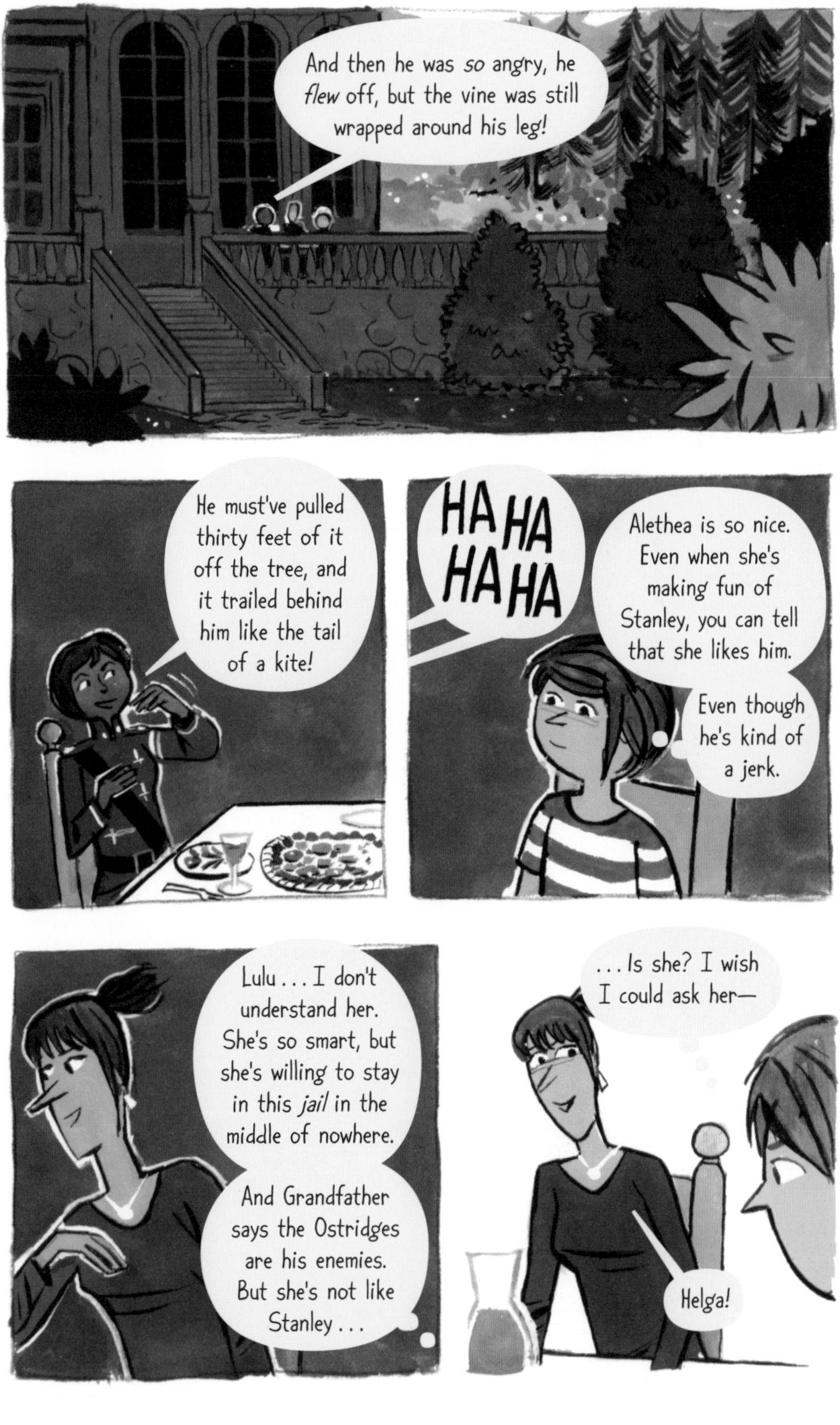
And then he was *so* angry, he *flew* off, but the vine was still wrapped around his leg!
He must've pulled thirty feet of it off the tree, and it trailed behind him like the tail of a kite!
HA HA HA HA
Alethea is so nice. Even when she's making fun of Stanley, you can tell that she likes him.
Even though he's kind of a jerk.
Lulu . . . I don't understand her. She's so smart, but she's willing to stay in this *jail* in the middle of nowhere.
And Grandfather says the Ostridges are his enemies. But she's not like Stanley . . .
. . . Is she? I wish I could ask her—
Helga!

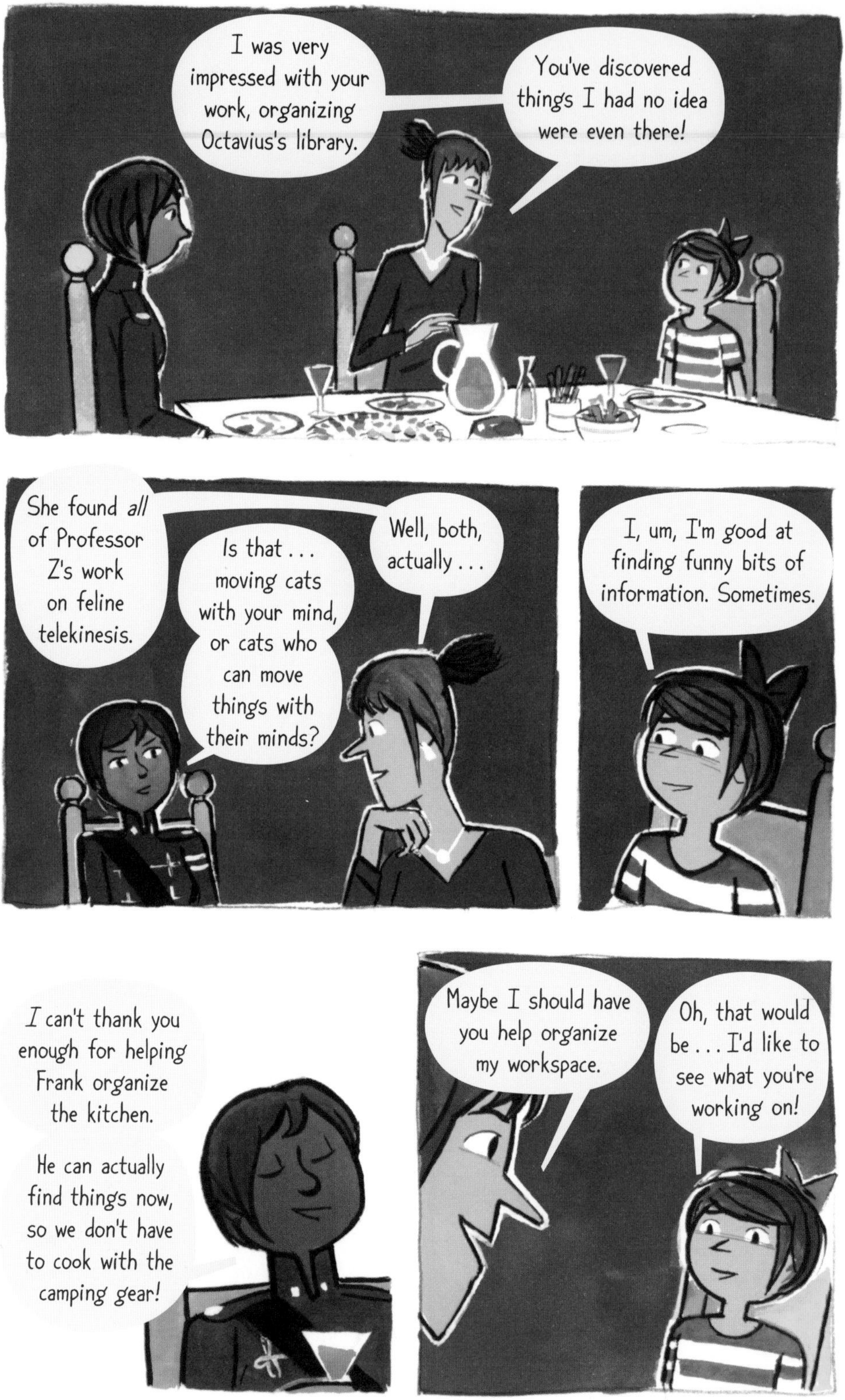
I was very impressed with your work, organizing Octavius's library.
You've discovered things I had no idea were even there!
She found *all* of Professor Z's work on feline telekinesis.
Is that . . . moving cats with your mind, or cats who can move things with their minds?
Well, both, actually . . .
I, um, I'm good at finding funny bits of information. Sometimes.
I can't thank you enough for helping Frank organize the kitchen.
He can actually find things now, so we don't have to cook with the camping gear!
Maybe I should have you help organize my workspace.
Oh, that would be . . . I'd like to see what you're working on!

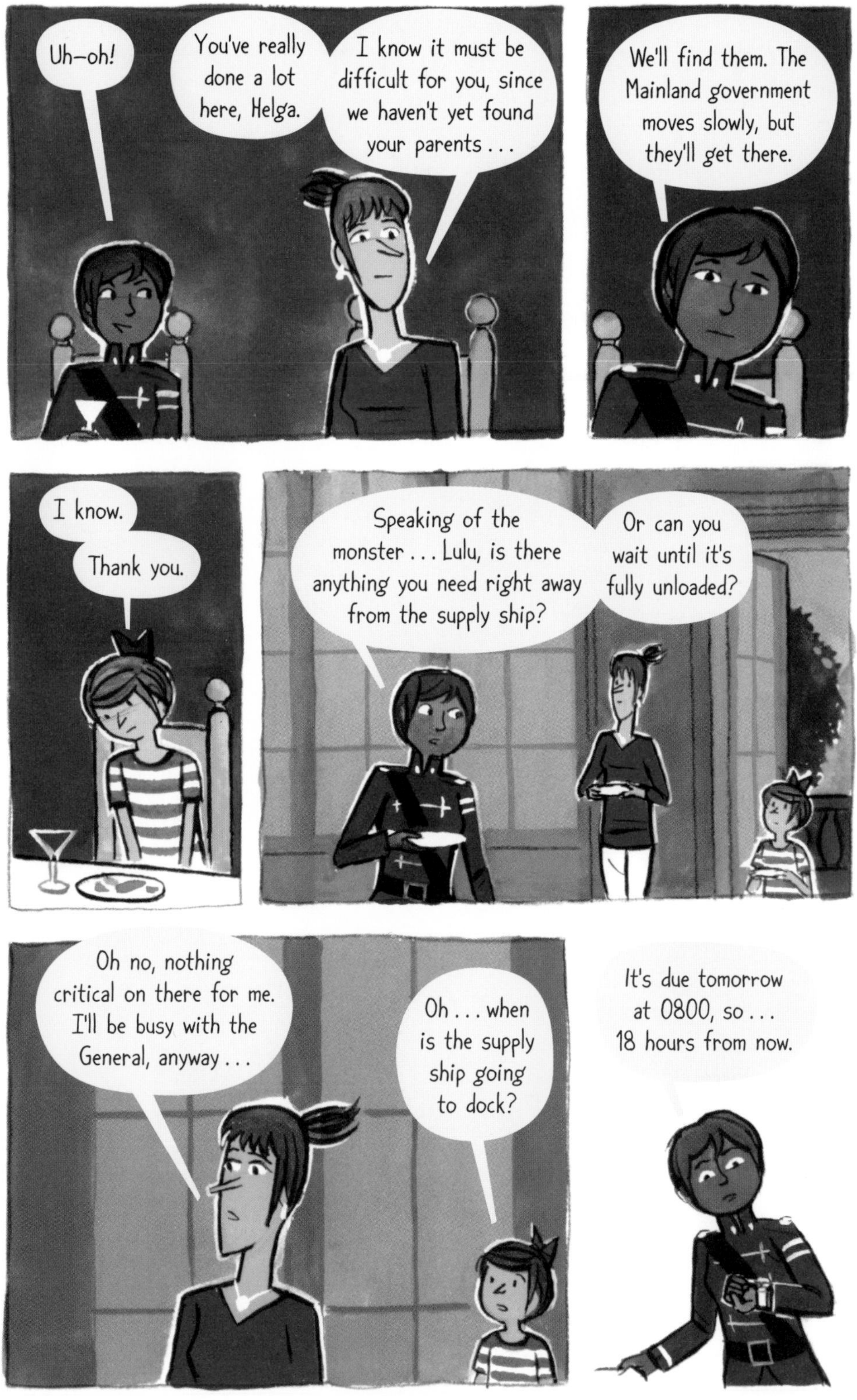
Uh-oh!
You've really done a lot here, Helga.
I know it must be difficult for you, since we haven't yet found your parents . . .
We'll find them. The Mainland government moves slowly, but they'll get there.
I know.
Thank you.
Speaking of the monster . . . Lulu, is there anything you need right away from the supply ship?
Or can you wait until it's fully unloaded?
Oh no, nothing critical on there for me. I'll be busy with the General, anyway . . .
Oh . . . when is the supply ship going to dock?
It's due tomorrow at 0800, so . . . 18 hours from now.

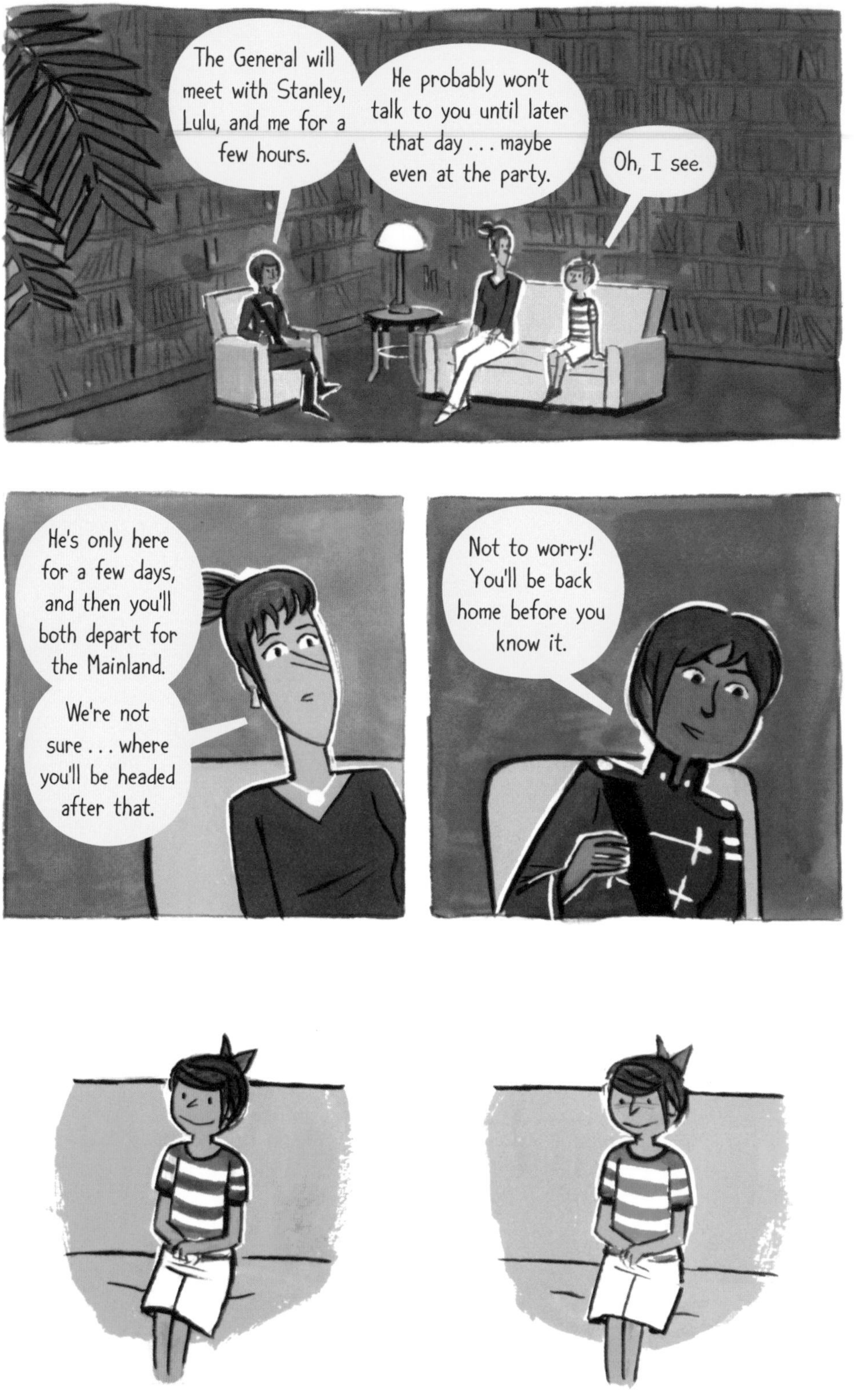
The General will meet with Stanley, Lulu, and me for a few hours.
He probably won't talk to you until later that day . . . maybe even at the party.
Oh, I see.
He's only here for a few days, and then you'll both depart for the Mainland.
We're not sure . . . where you'll be headed after that.
Not to worry! You'll be back home before you know it.

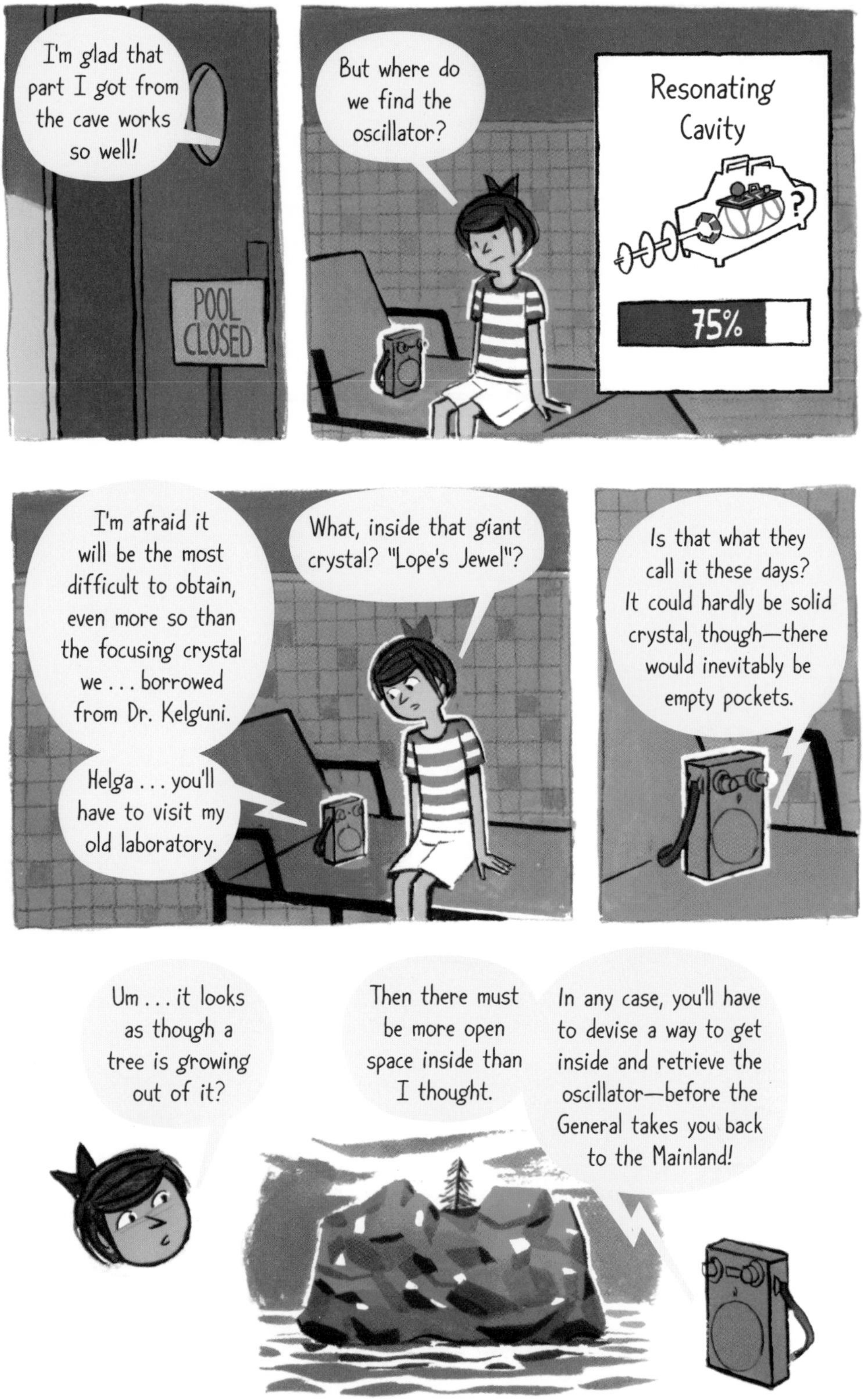
I'm glad that part I got from the cave works so well!
POOL CLOSED
But where do we find the oscillator?
Resonating Cavity
?
75%
I'm afraid it will be the most difficult to obtain, even more so than the focusing crystal we . . . borrowed from Dr. Kelguni.
What, inside that giant crystal? "Lope's Jewel"?
Helga . . . you'll have to visit my old laboratory.
Is that what they call it these days? It could hardly be solid crystal, though—there would inevitably be empty pockets.
Um . . . it looks as though a tree is growing out of it?
Then there must be more open space inside than I thought.
In any case, you'll have to devise a way to get inside and retrieve the oscillator—before the General takes you back to the Mainland!

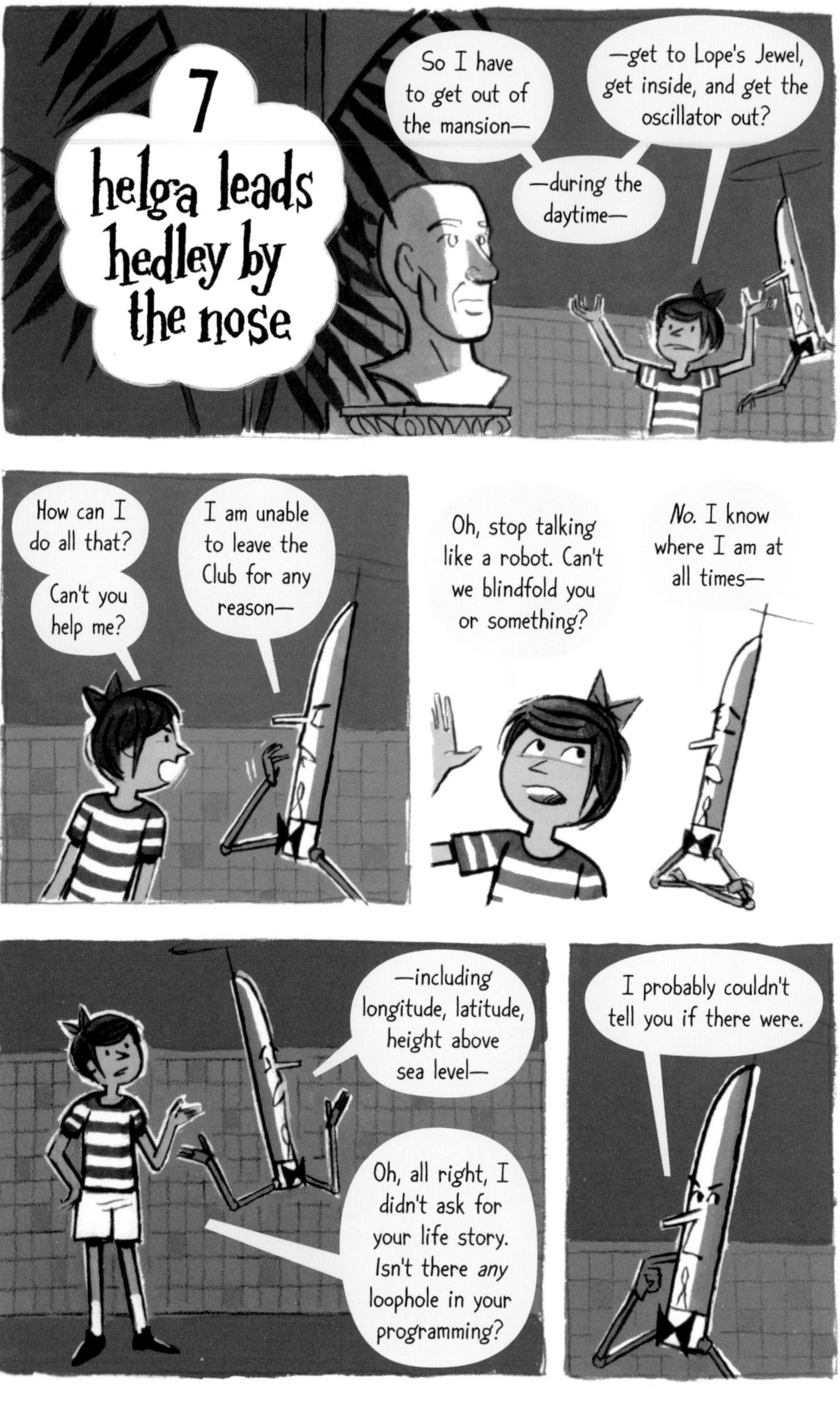
7
helga leads hedley by the nose
So I have to get out of the mansion—
—during the daytime—
—get to Lope's Jewel, get inside, and get the oscillator out?
How can I do all that?
Can't you help me?
I am unable to leave the Club for any reason—
Oh, stop talking like a robot. Can't we blindfold you or something?
No. I know where I am at all times—
—including longitude, latitude, height above sea level—
Oh, all right, I didn't ask for your life story. Isn't there *any* loophole in your programming?
I probably couldn't tell you if there were.

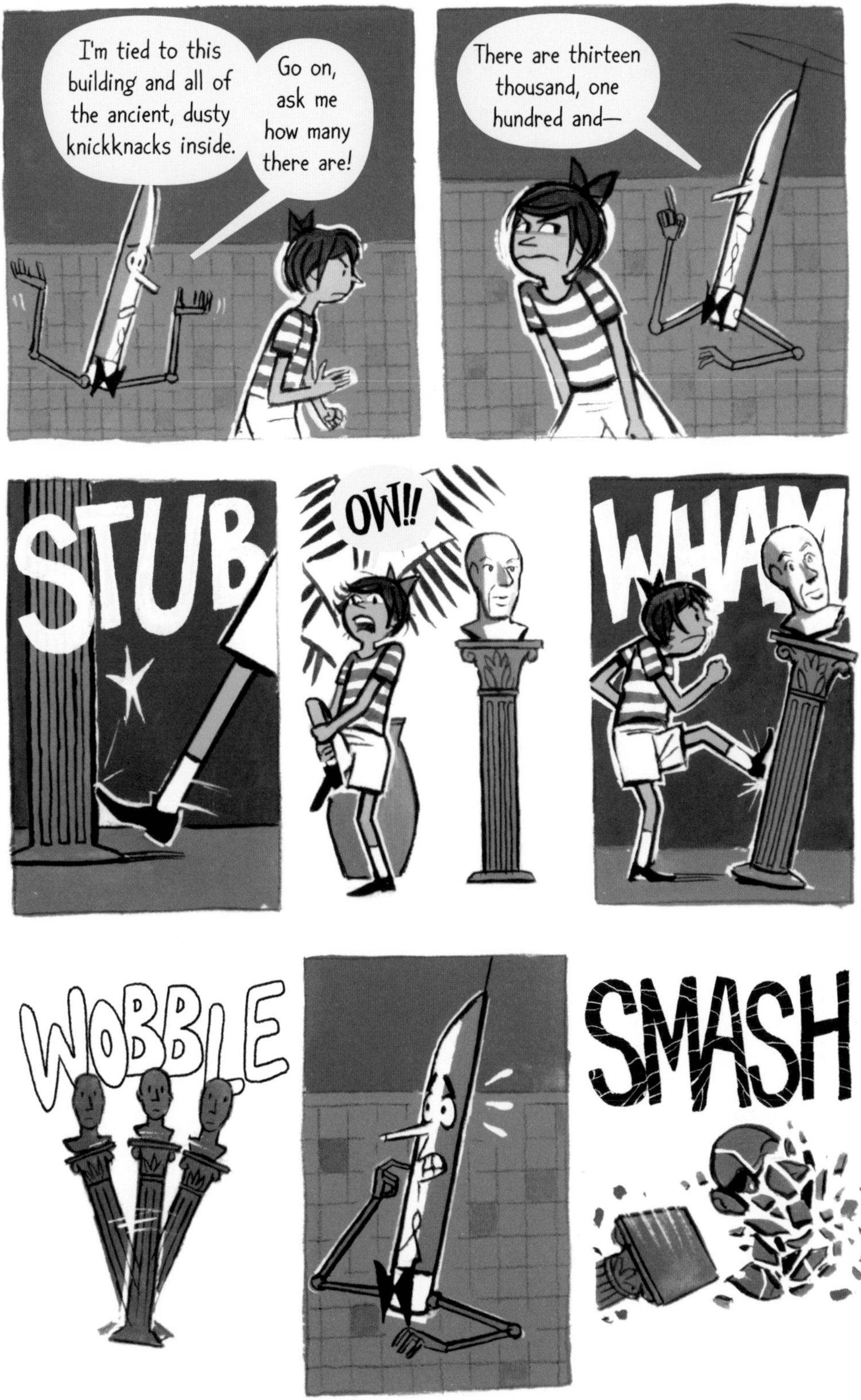
I'm tied to this building and all of the ancient, dusty knickknacks inside.
Go on, ask me how many there are!
There are thirteen thousand, one hundred and—
STUB
OW!!
WHAM
WOBBLE
SMASH

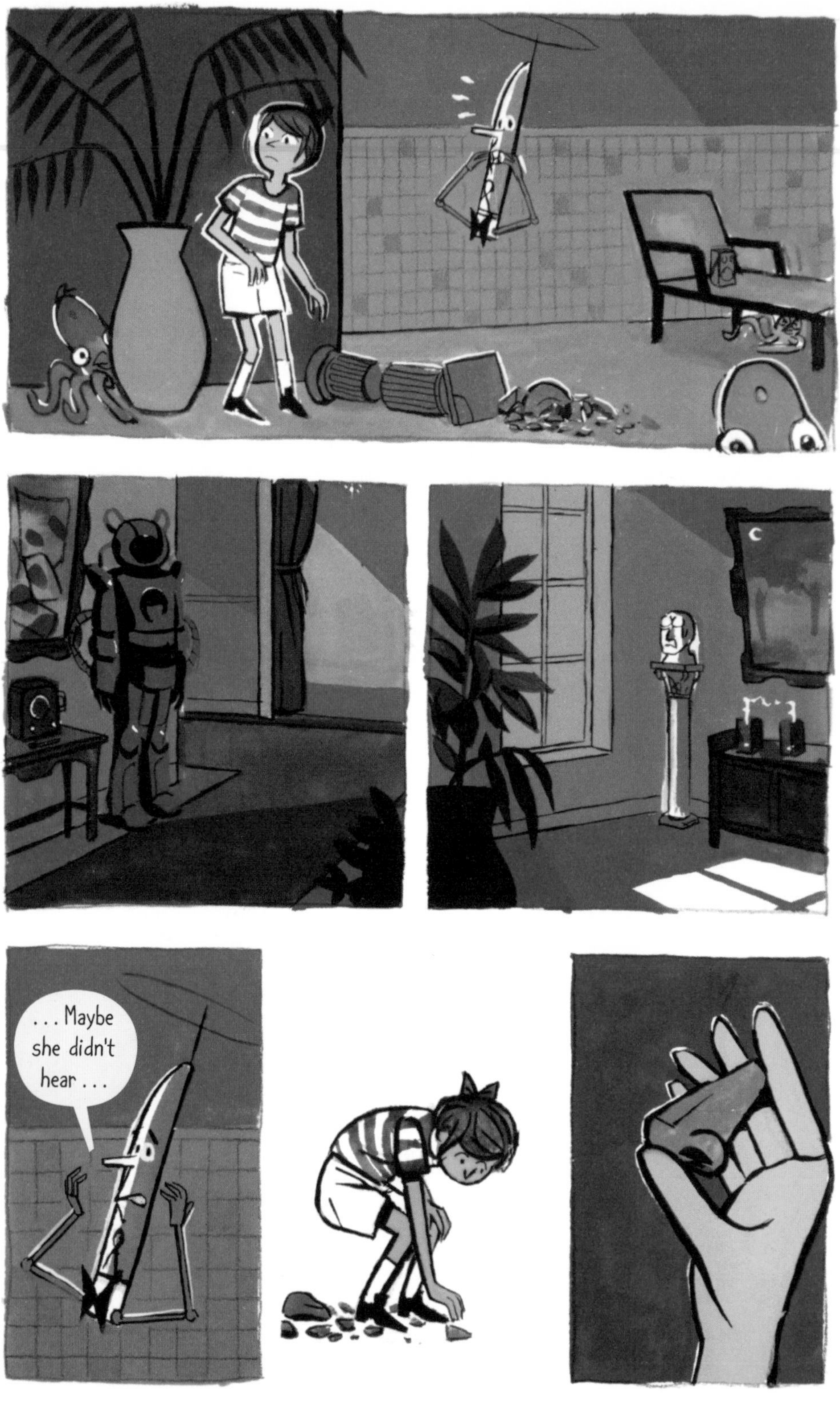
. . . Maybe she didn't hear . . .

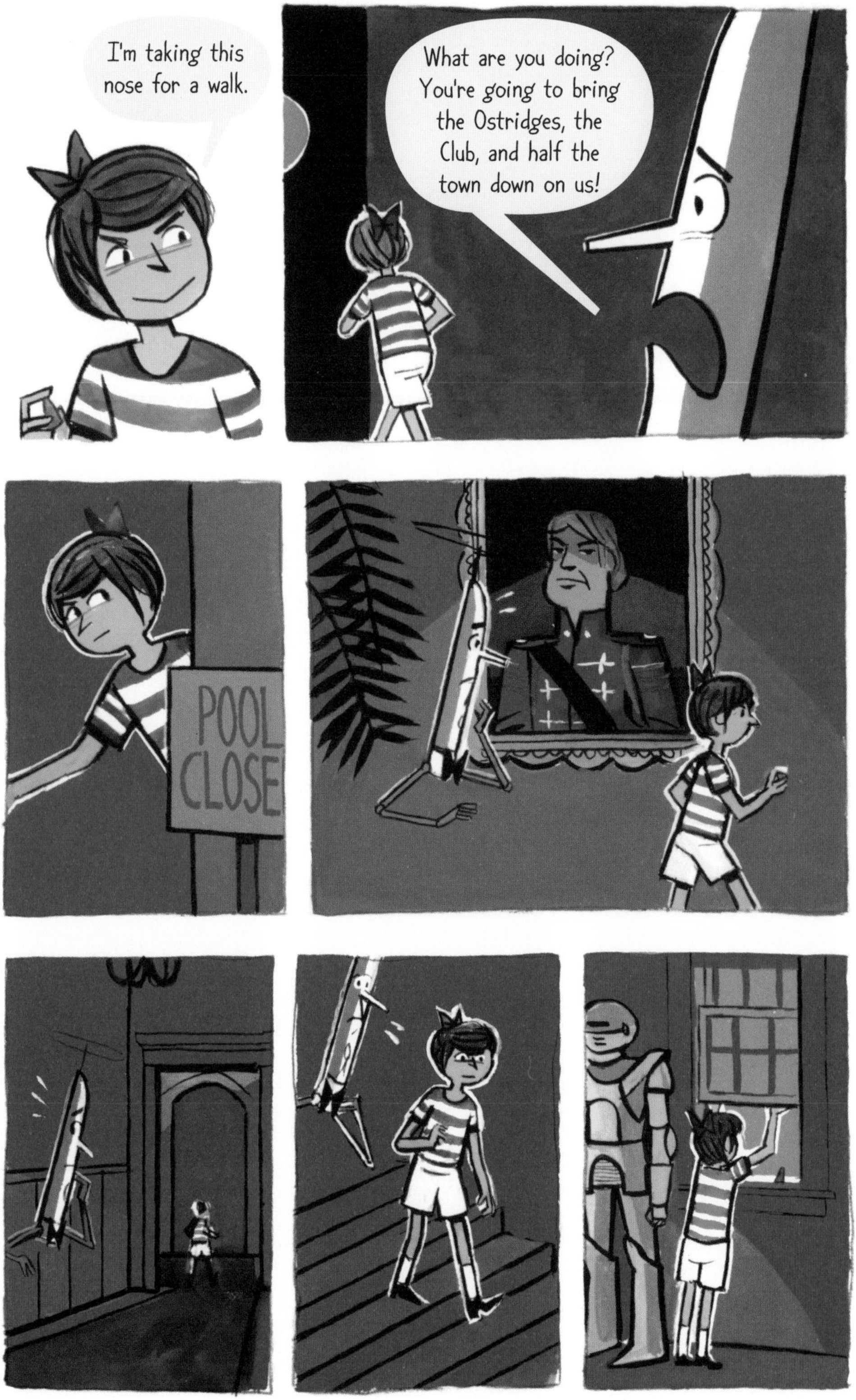
I'm taking this nose for a walk.
What are you doing? You're going to bring the Ostridges, the Club, and half the town down on us!
POOL CLOSE

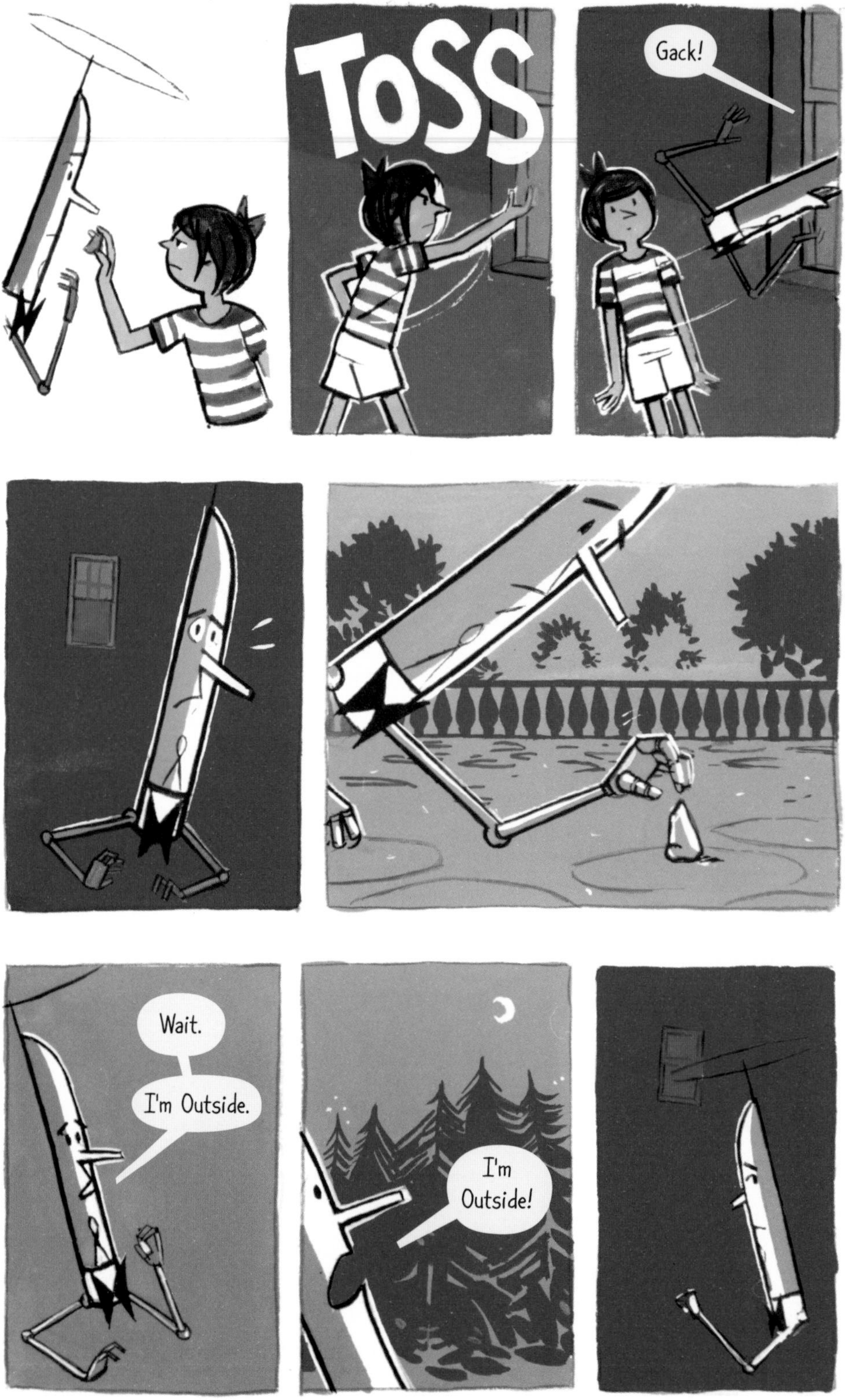
TOSS
Gack!
Wait.
I'm Outside.
I'm Outside!

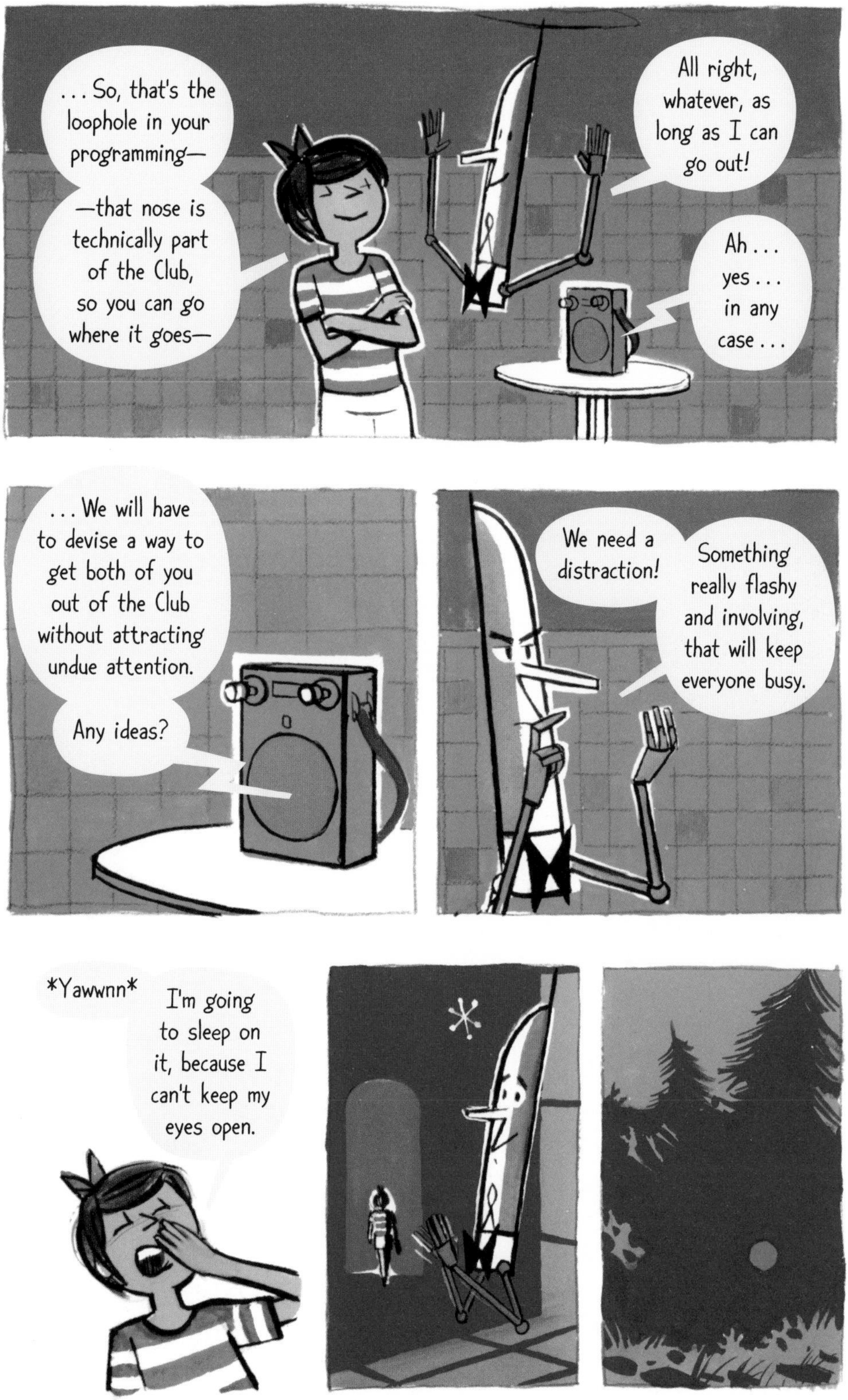
. . . So, that's the loophole in your programming—
—that nose is technically part of the Club, so you can go where it goes—
All right, whatever, as long as I can go out!
Ah . . . yes . . . in any case . . .
. . . We will have to devise a way to get both of you out of the Club without attracting undue attention.
Any ideas?
We need a distraction!
Something really flashy and involving, that will keep everyone busy.
Yawwnn
I'm going to sleep on it, because I can't keep my eyes open.

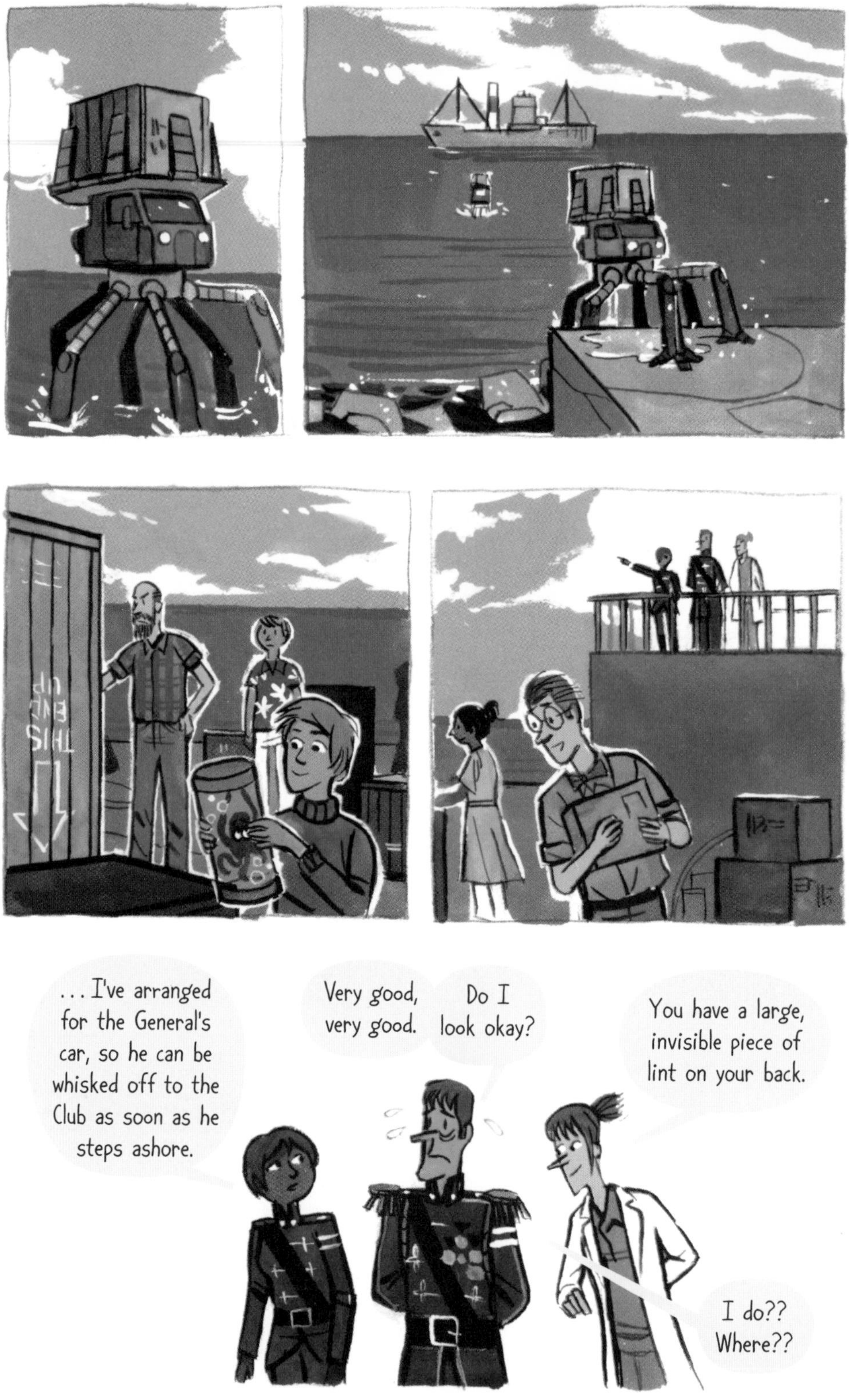
. . . I've arranged for the General's car, so he can be whisked off to the Club as soon as he steps ashore.
Very good, very good.
Do I look okay?
You have a large, invisible piece of lint on your back.
I do?? Where??

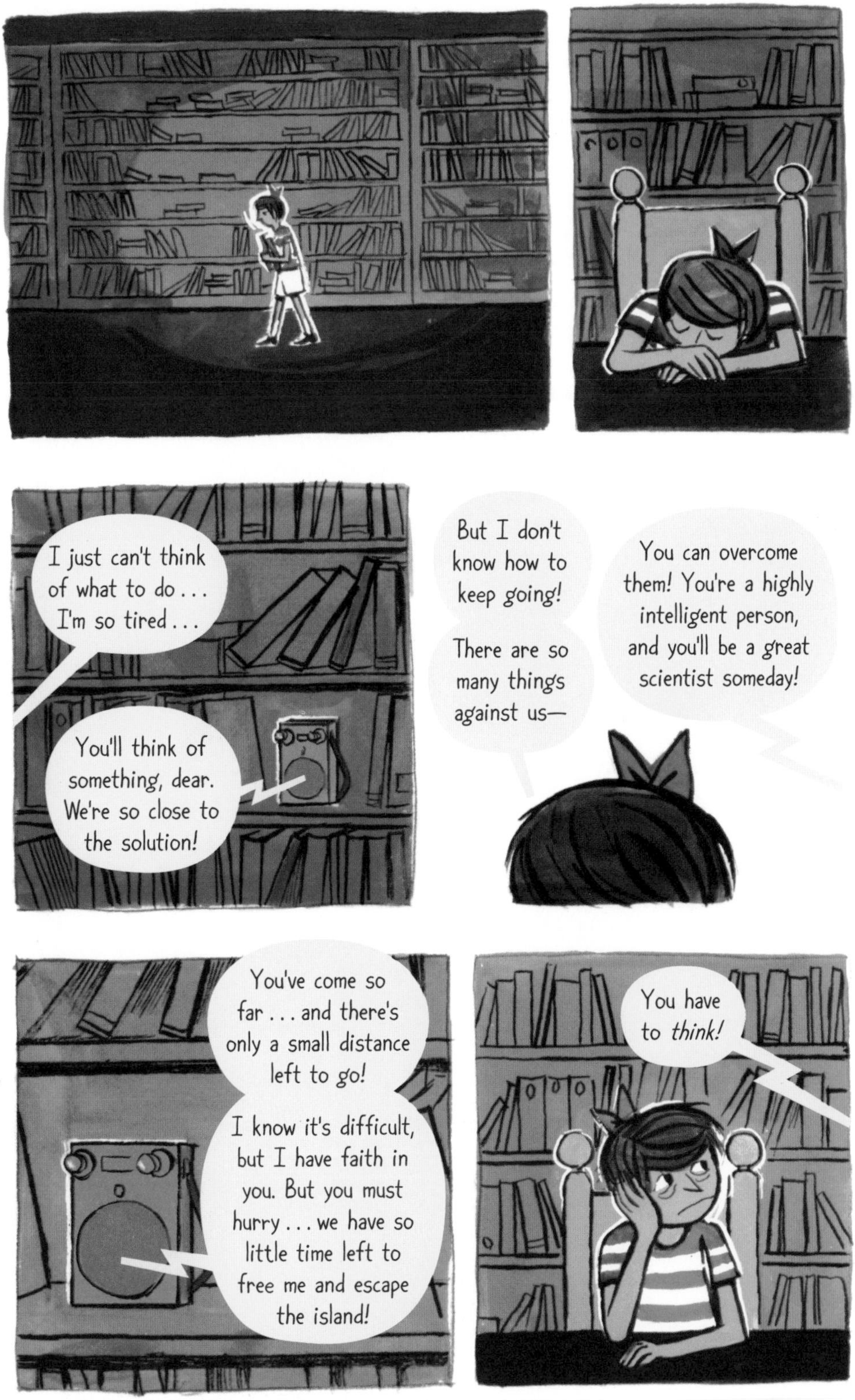
I just can't think of what to do . . . I'm so tired . . .
You'll think of something, dear. We're so close to the solution!
But I don't know how to keep going!
There are so many things against us—
You can overcome them! You're a highly intelligent person, and you'll be a great scientist someday!
You've come so far . . . and there's only a small distance left to go!
I know it's difficult, but I have faith in you. But you must hurry . . . we have so little time left to free me and escape the island!
You have to *think!*

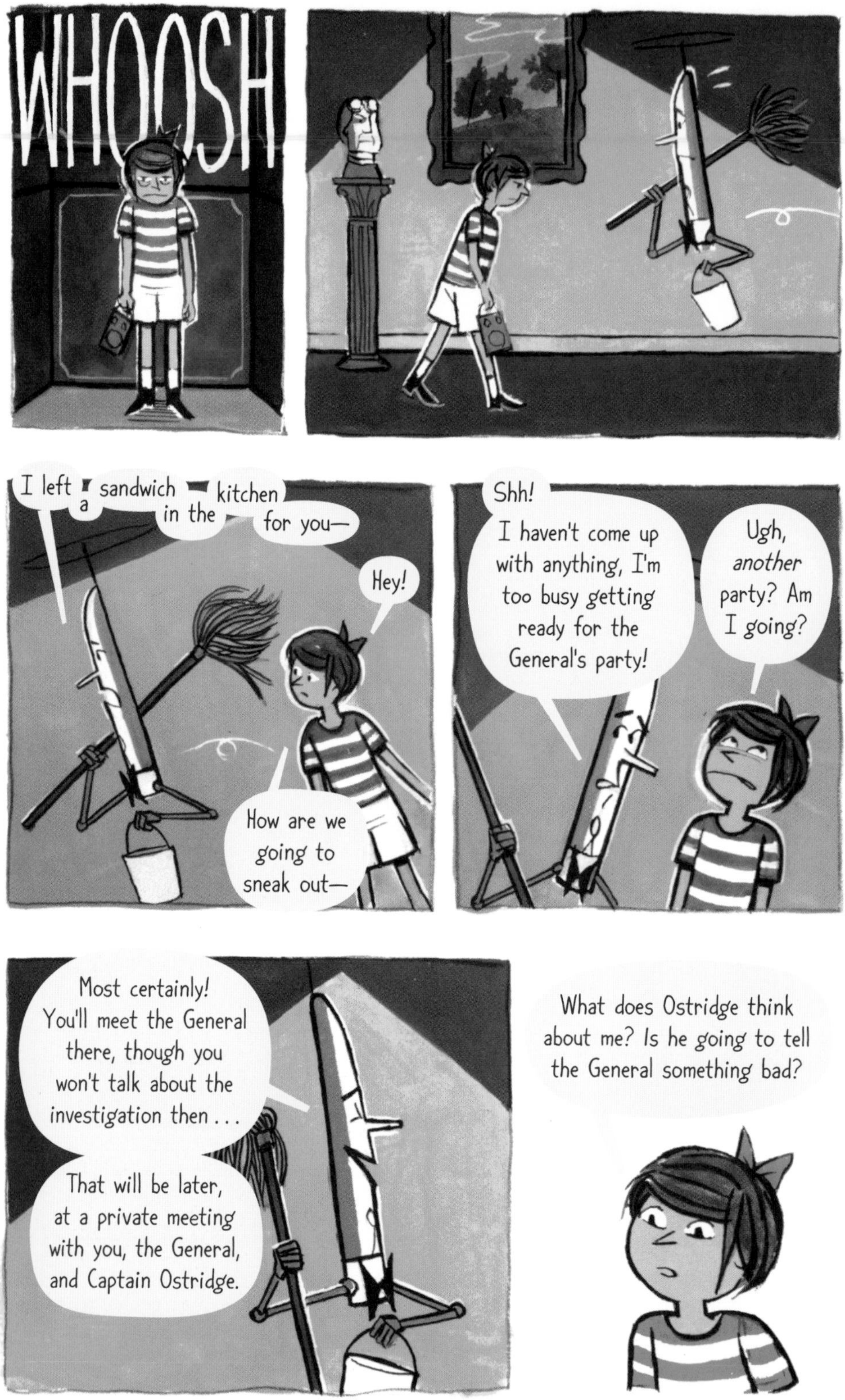
WHOOSH
I left a sandwich in the kitchen for you—
Hey!
How are we going to sneak out—
Shh!
I haven't come up with anything, I'm too busy getting ready for the General's party!
Ugh, *another* party? Am I going?
Most certainly! You'll meet the General there, though you won't talk about the investigation then . . .
That will be later, at a private meeting with you, the General, and Captain Ostridge.
What does Ostridge think about me? Is he going to tell the General something bad?

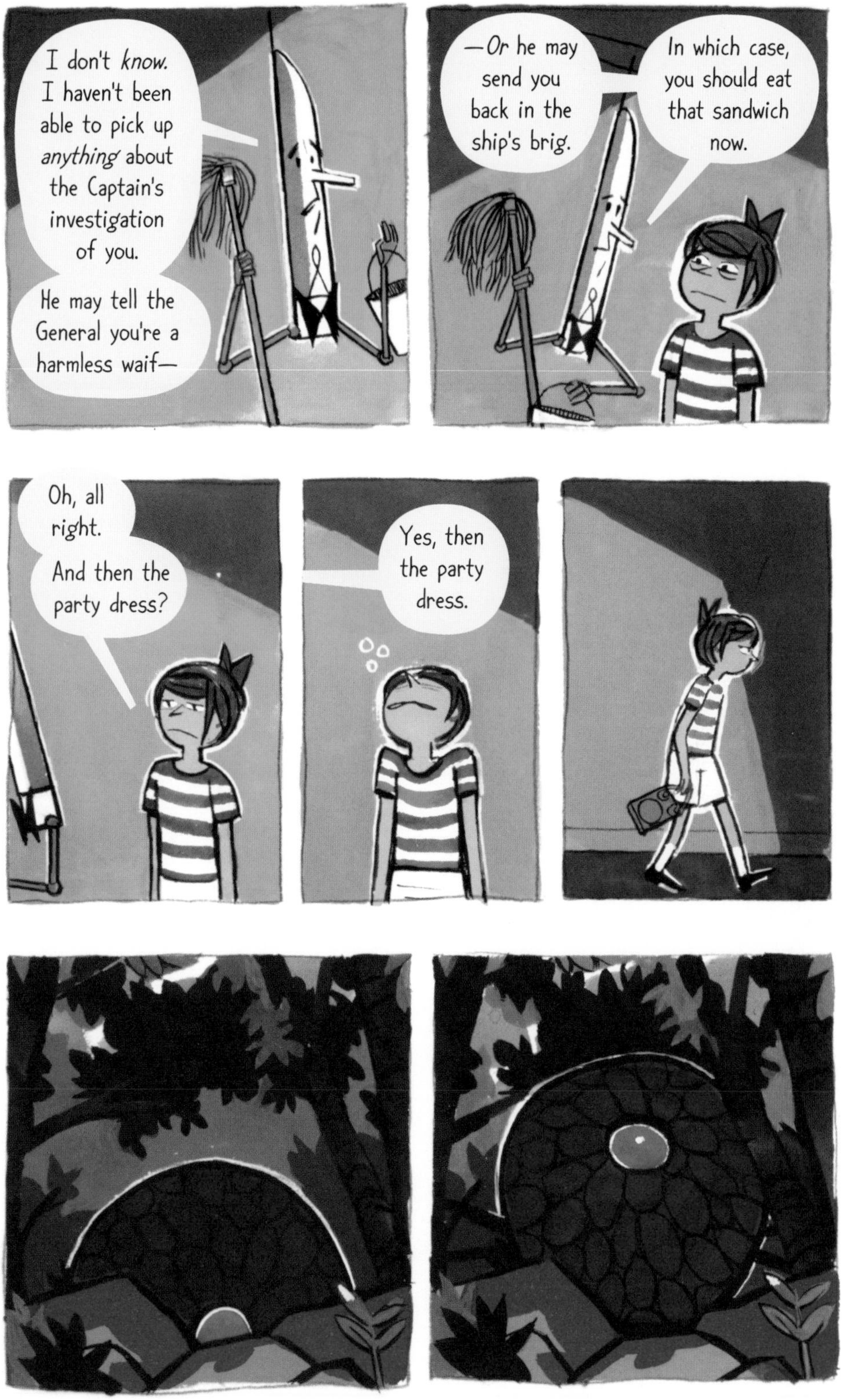

I don't *know.* I haven't been able to pick up *anything* about the Captain's investigation of you.
He may tell the General you're a harmless waif—
—*Or* he may send you back in the ship's brig.
In which case, you should eat that sandwich now.
Oh, all right.
And then the party dress?
Yes, then the party dress.

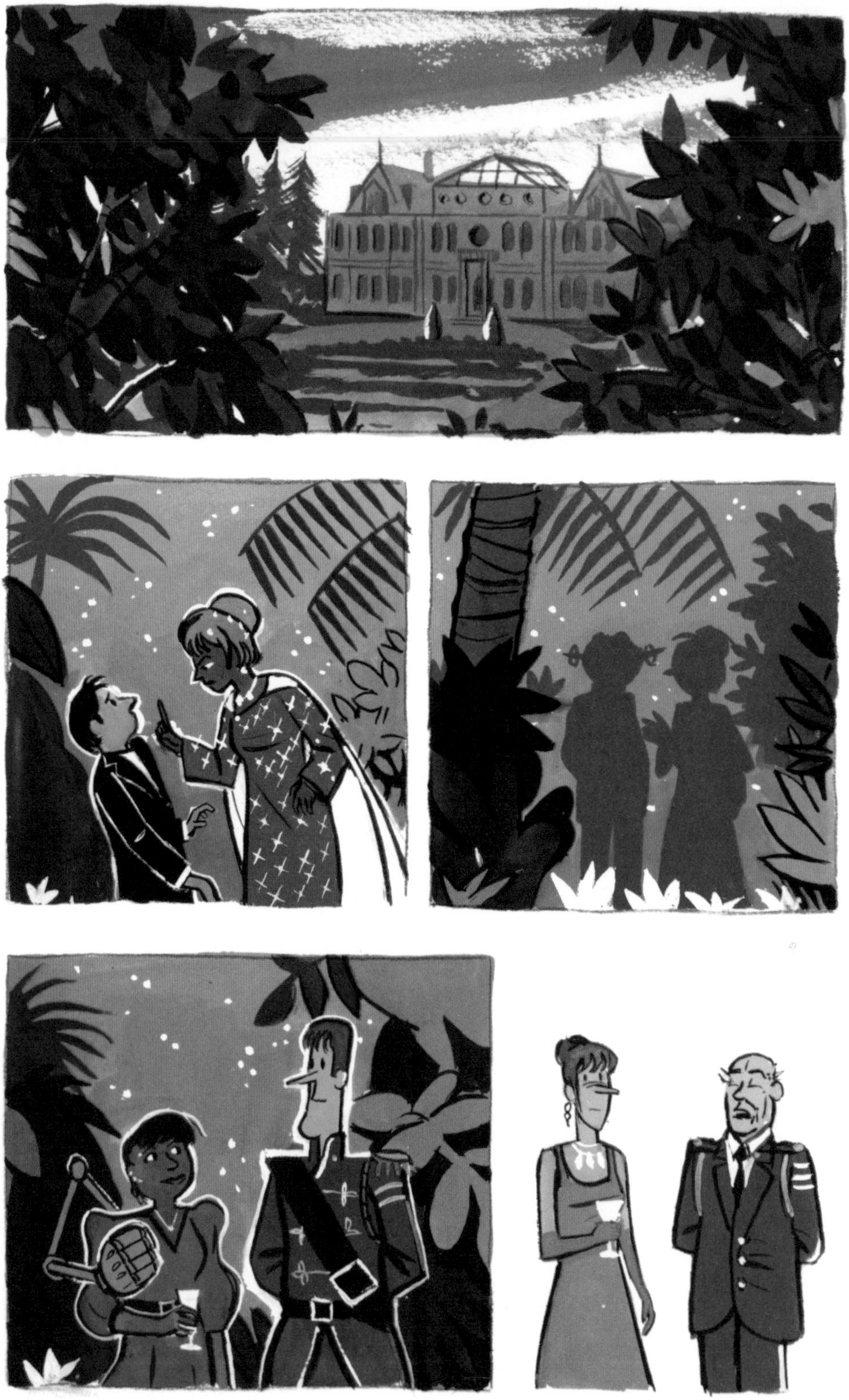

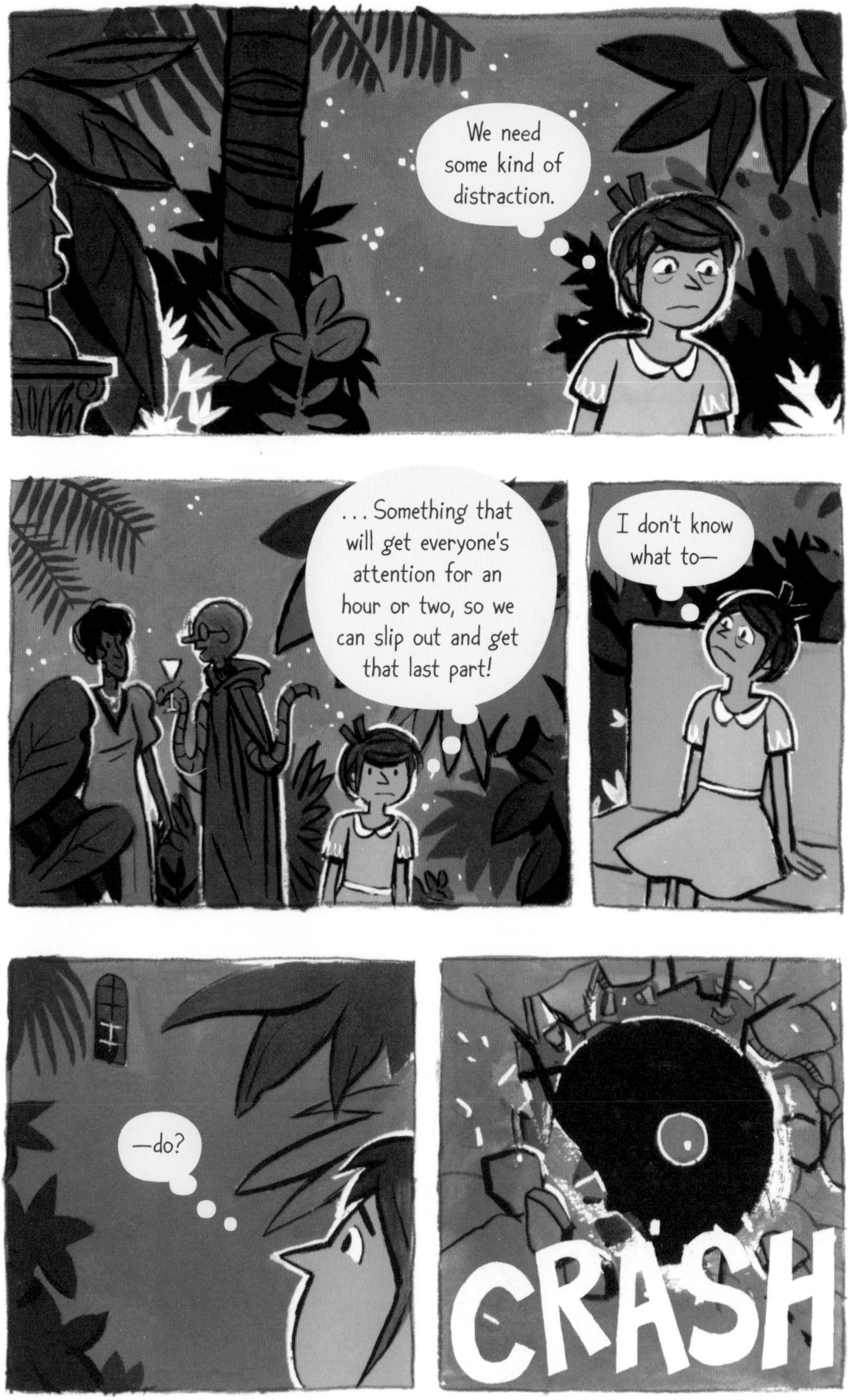
We need some kind of distraction.
. . . Something that will get everyone's attention for an hour or two, so we can slip out and get that last part!
I don't know what to—
—do?
CRASH

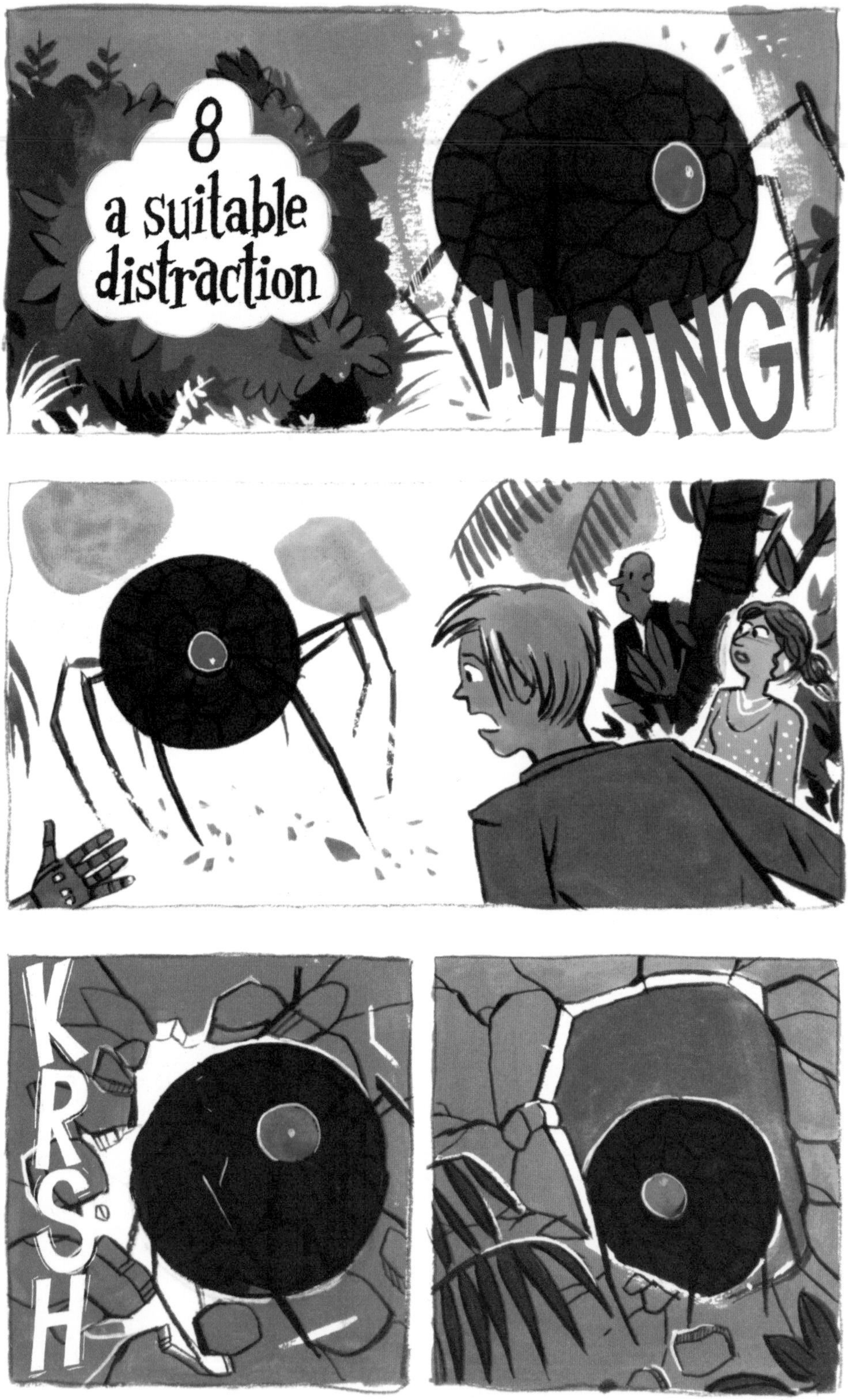
8
a suitable distraction
WHONG
KRSH

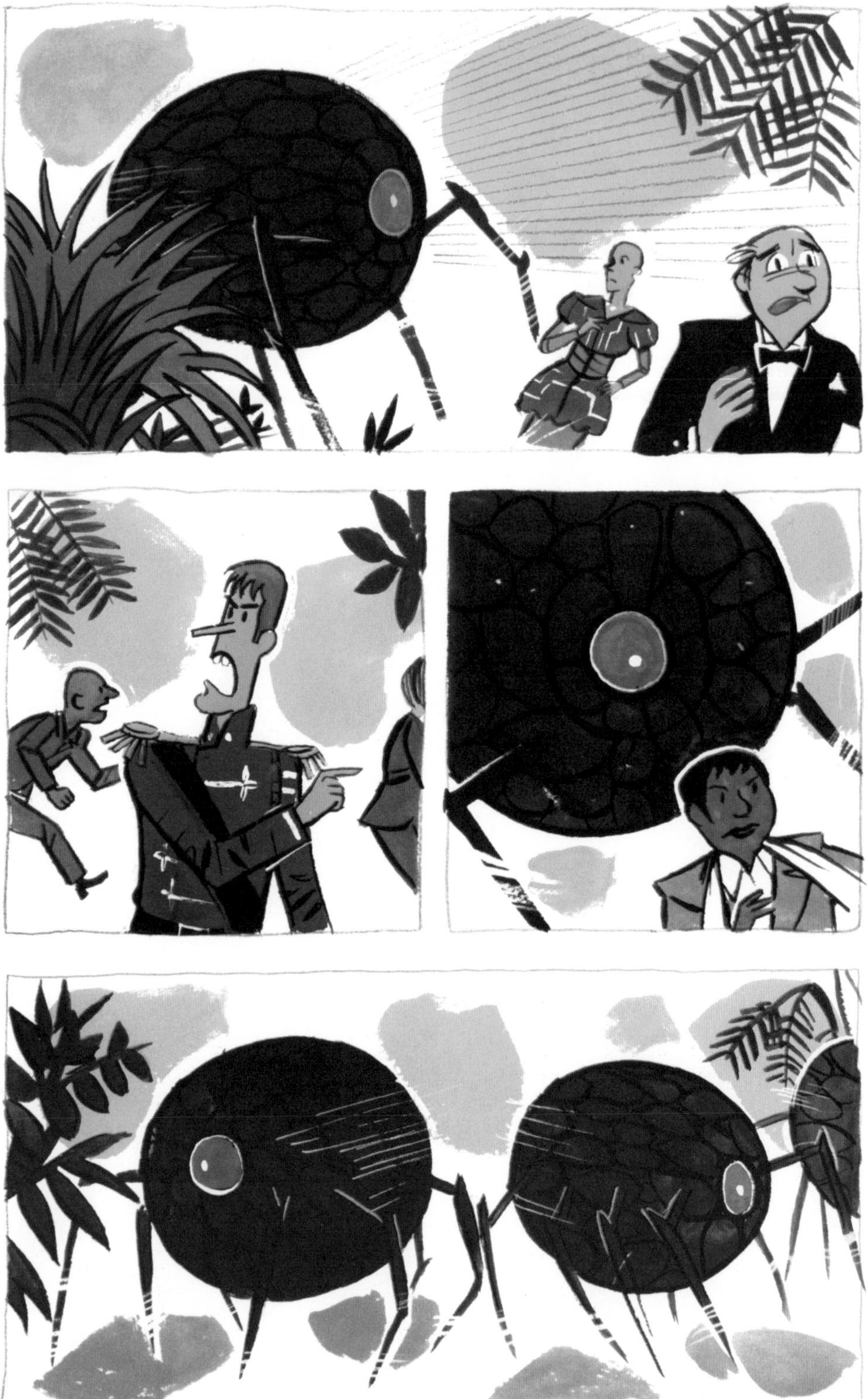

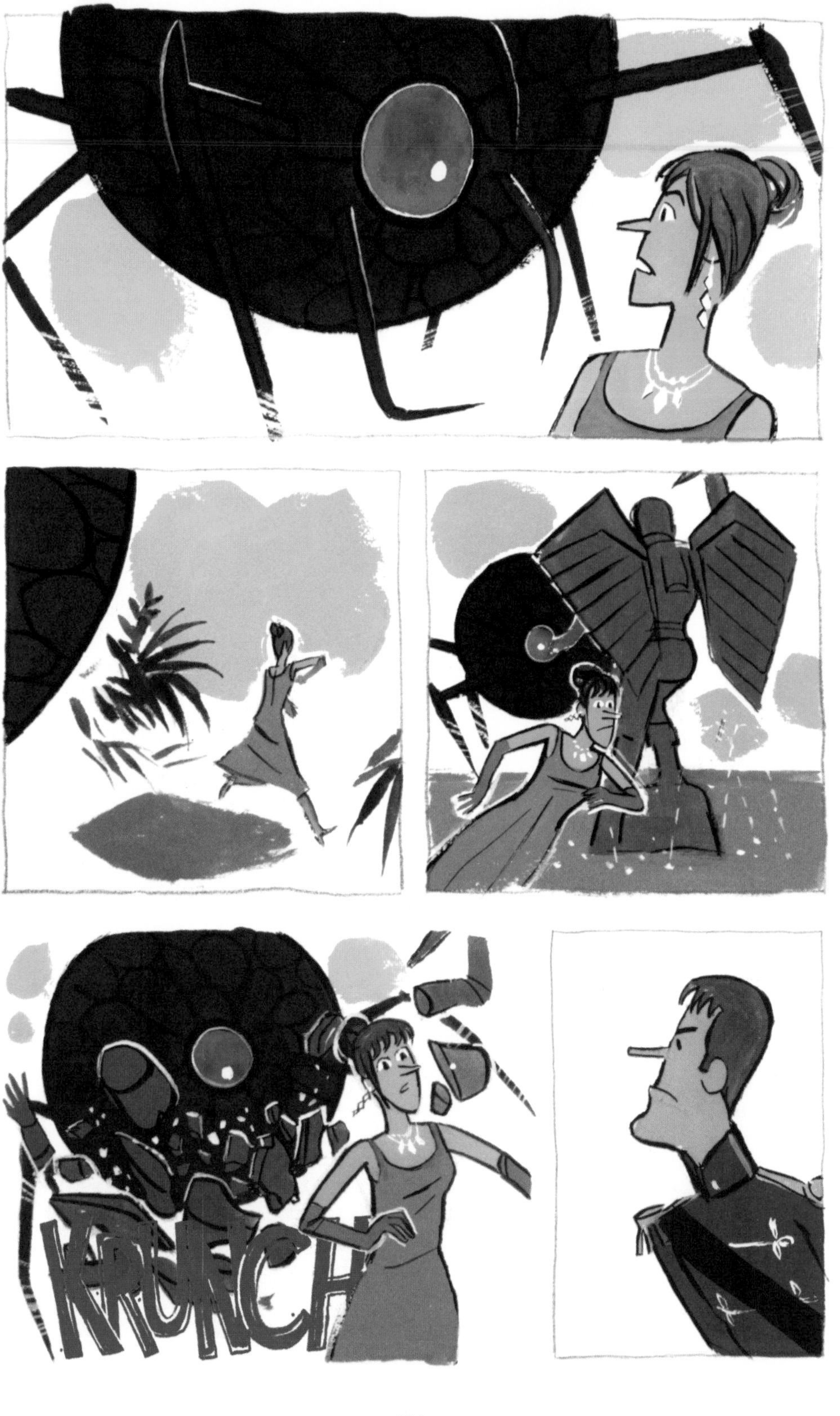
KRUNCH

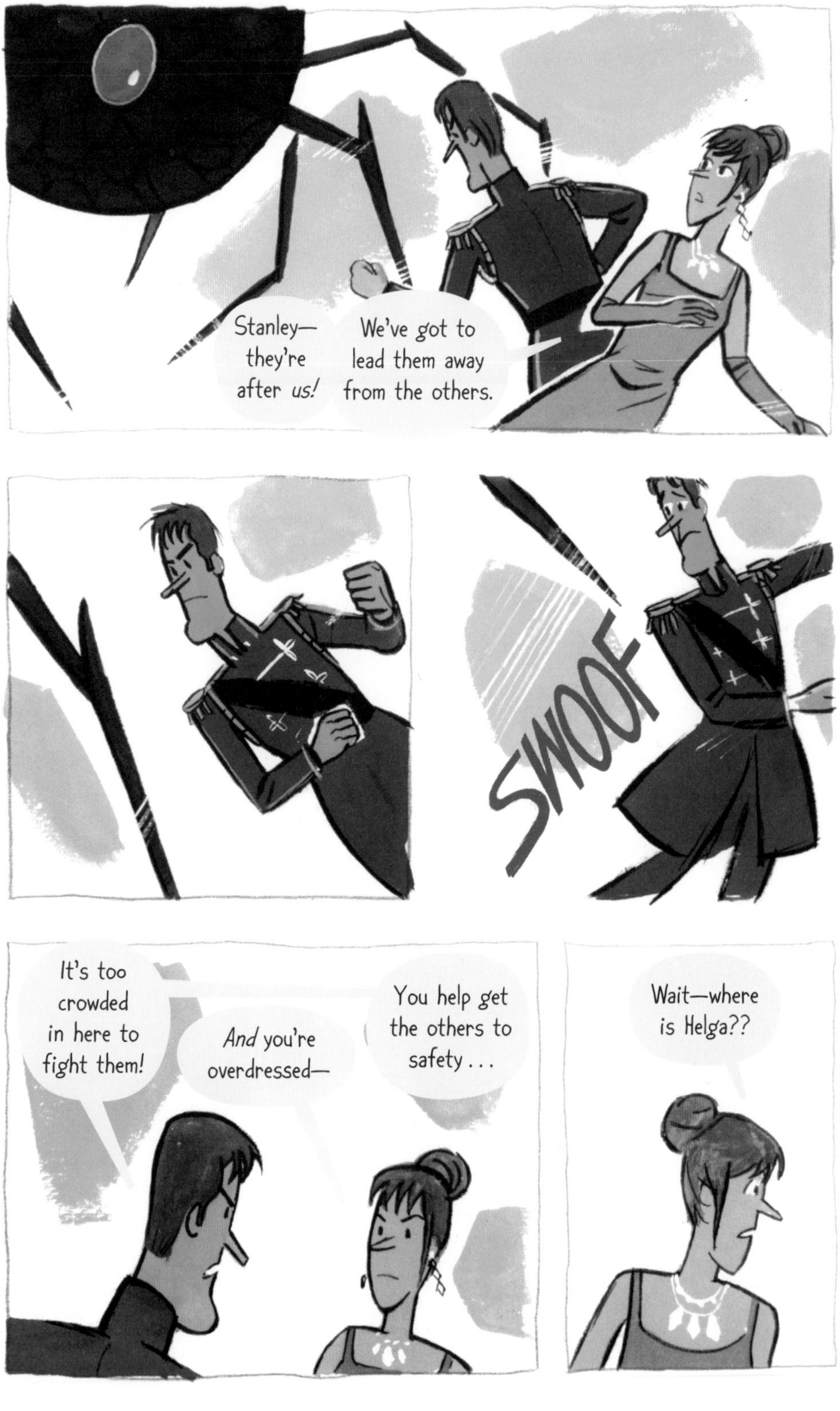
Stanley— they're after *us!*
We've got to lead them away from the others.
SWOOF
It's too crowded in here to fight them!
And you're overdressed—
You help get the others to safety . . .
Wait—where is Helga??

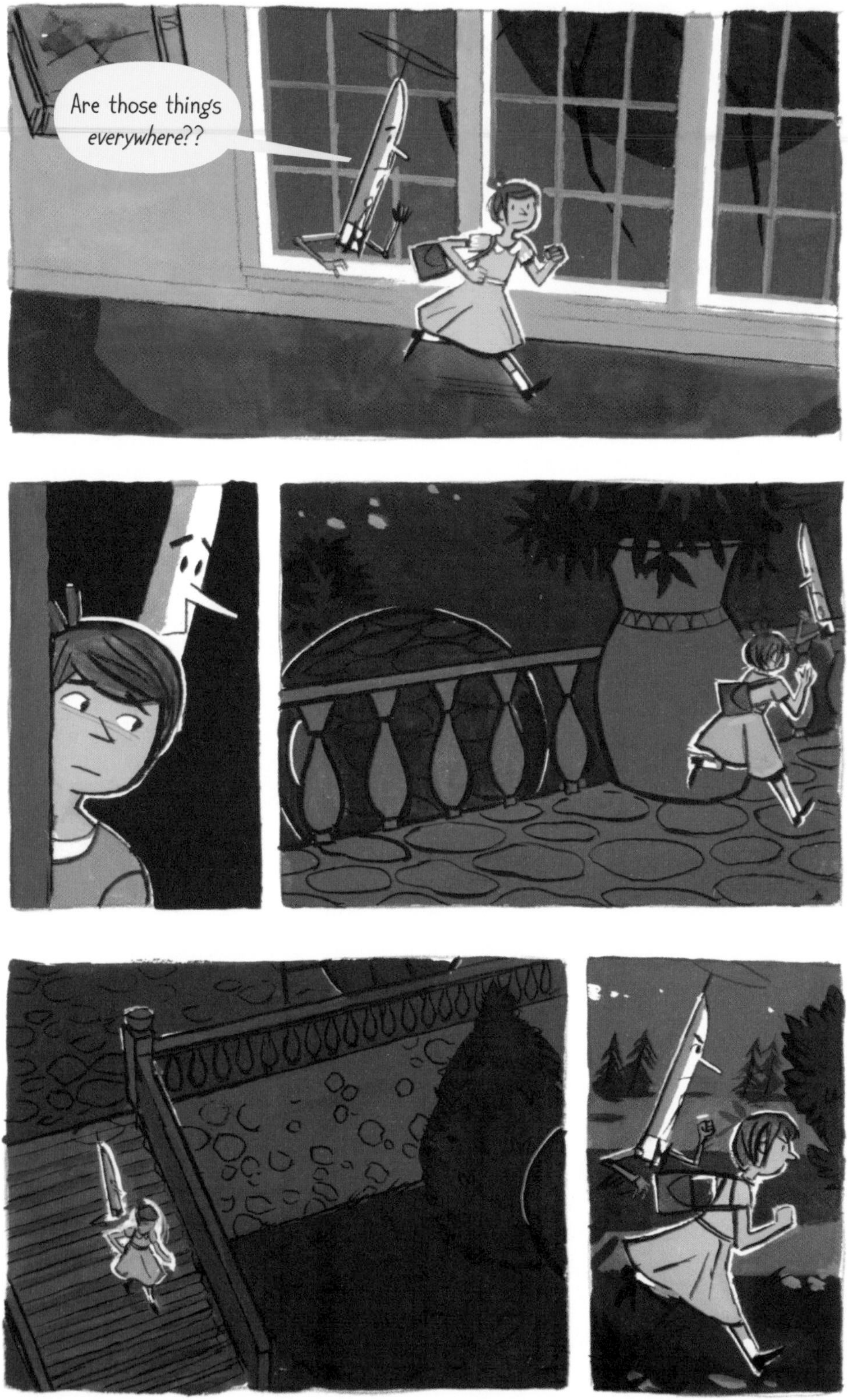
Are those things *everywhere*??

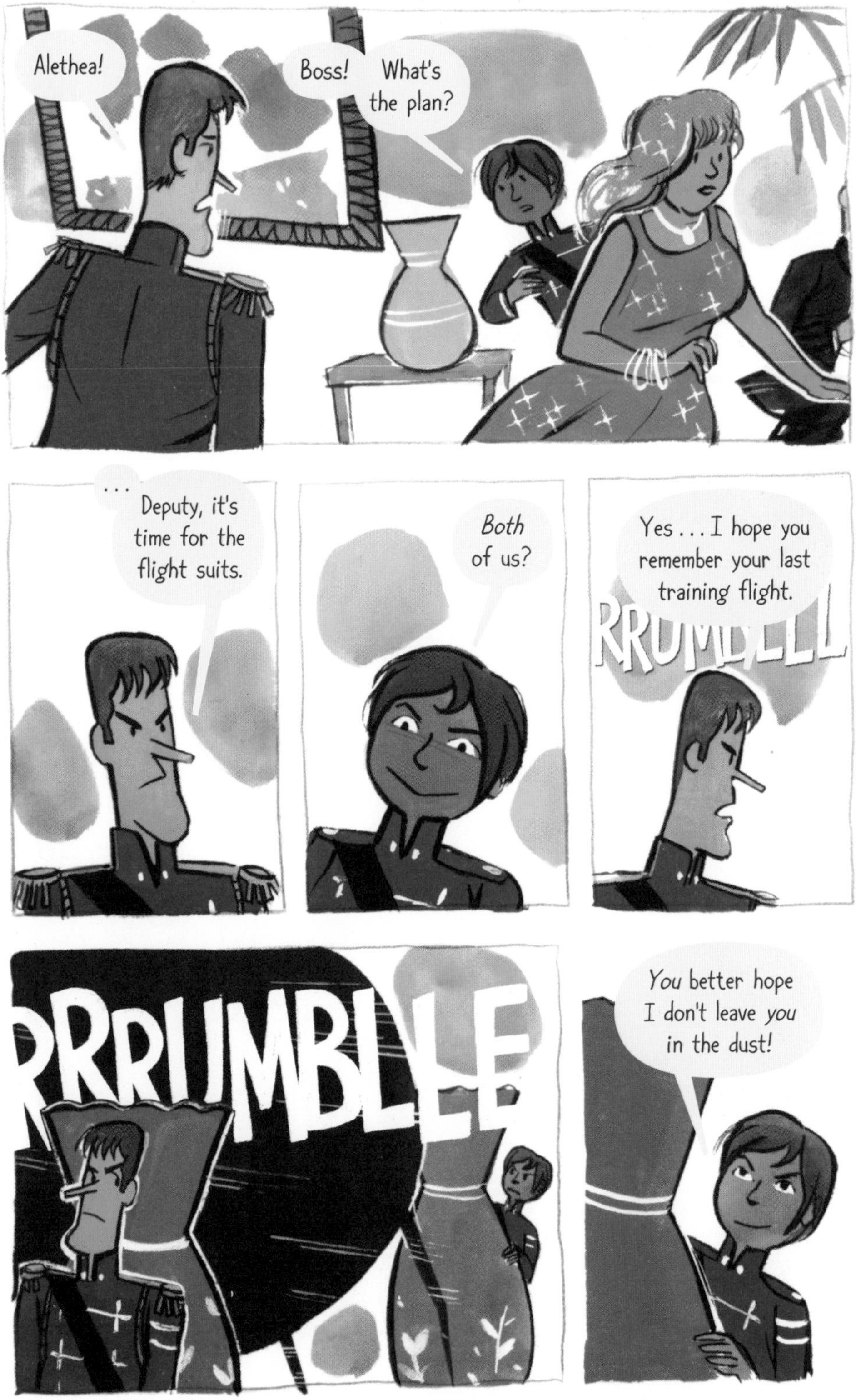

Alethea!
Boss!
What's the plan?
. . .
Deputy, it's time for the flight suits.
Both of us?
Yes . . . I hope you remember your last training flight.
RRUMBLLL
RRRUMBLLE
You better hope I don't leave *you* in the dust!

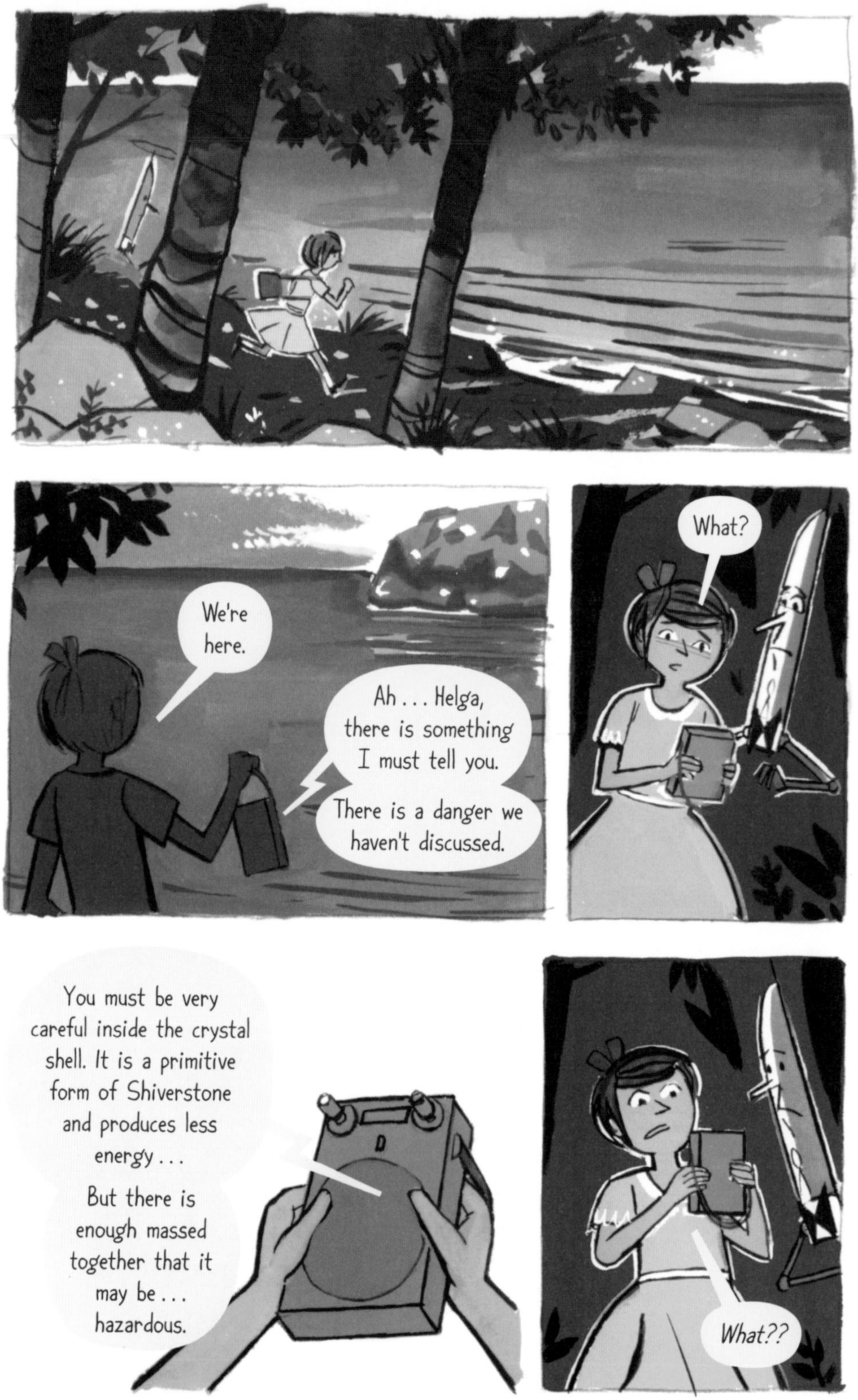
We're here.
Ah . . . Helga, there is something I must tell you.
There is a danger we haven't discussed.
What?
You must be very careful inside the crystal shell. It is a primitive form of Shiverstone and produces less energy . . .
But there is enough massed together that it may be . . . hazardous.
D
What??

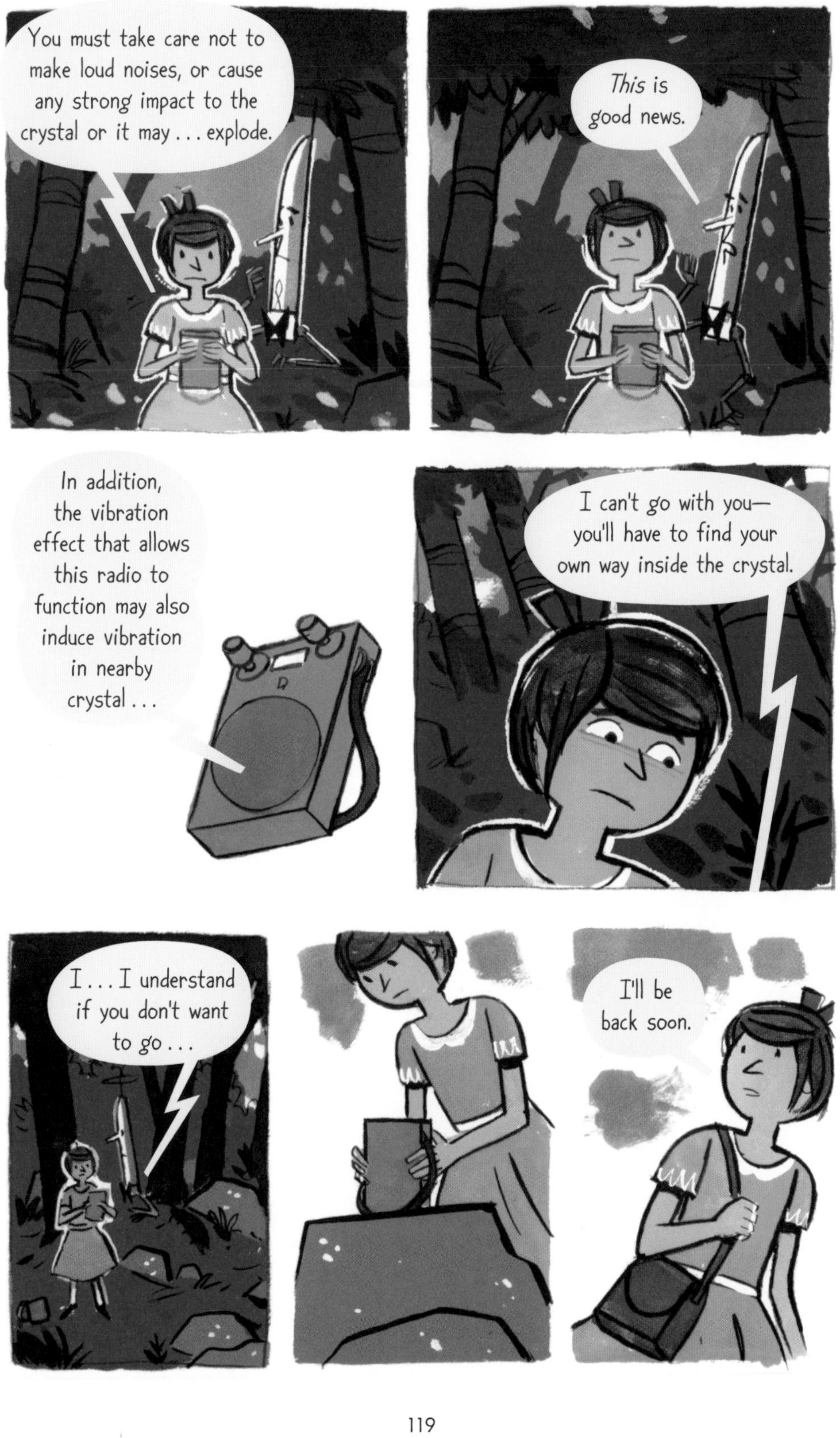
You must take care not to make loud noises, or cause any strong impact to the crystal or it may . . . explode.
This is good news.
In addition, the vibration effect that allows this radio to function may also induce vibration in nearby crystal . . .
I can't go with you— you'll have to find your own way inside the crystal.
I . . . I understand if you don't want to go . . .
I'll be back soon.

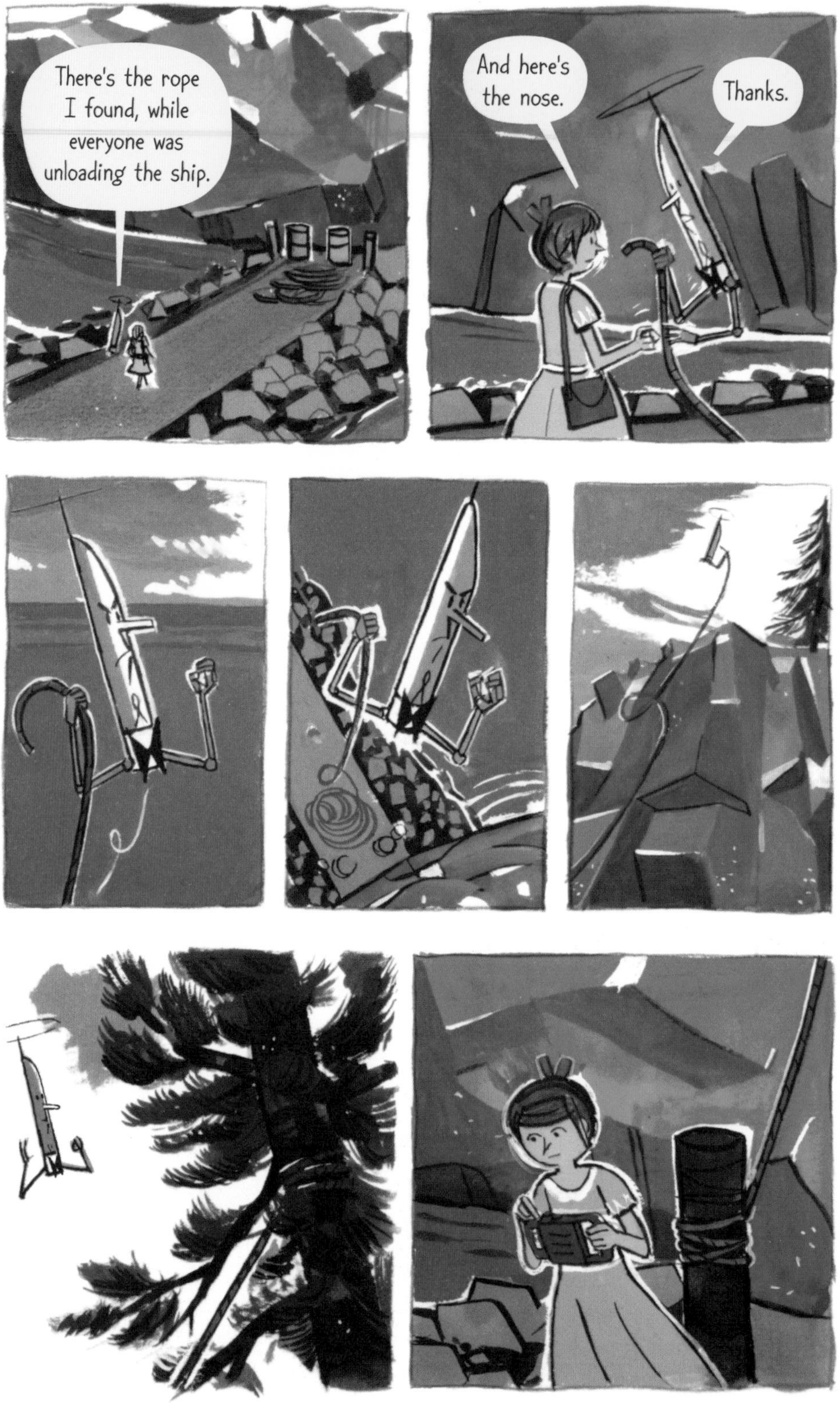
There's the rope I found, while everyone was unloading the ship.
And here's the nose.
Thanks.

RRRRRRR

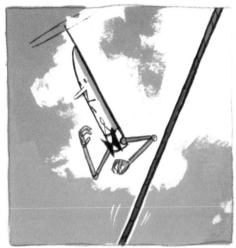

RRRRR RRRRR

RRRR RRRR

She's climbed up . . .
now she's reached
the treetop . . .
She's climbed over
the edge of the shell.
She's inside.

Be careful,
Helga.

Be safe.

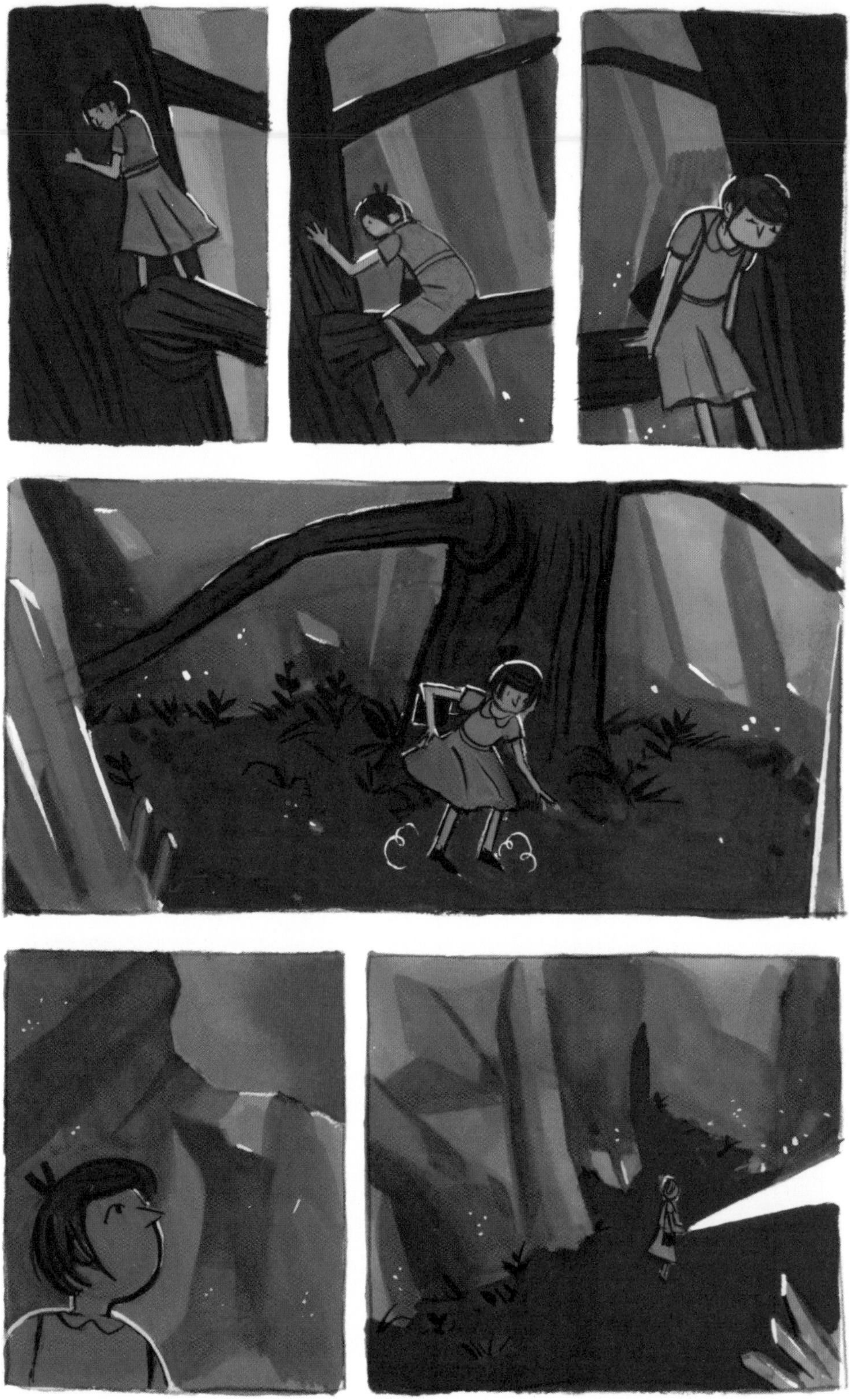

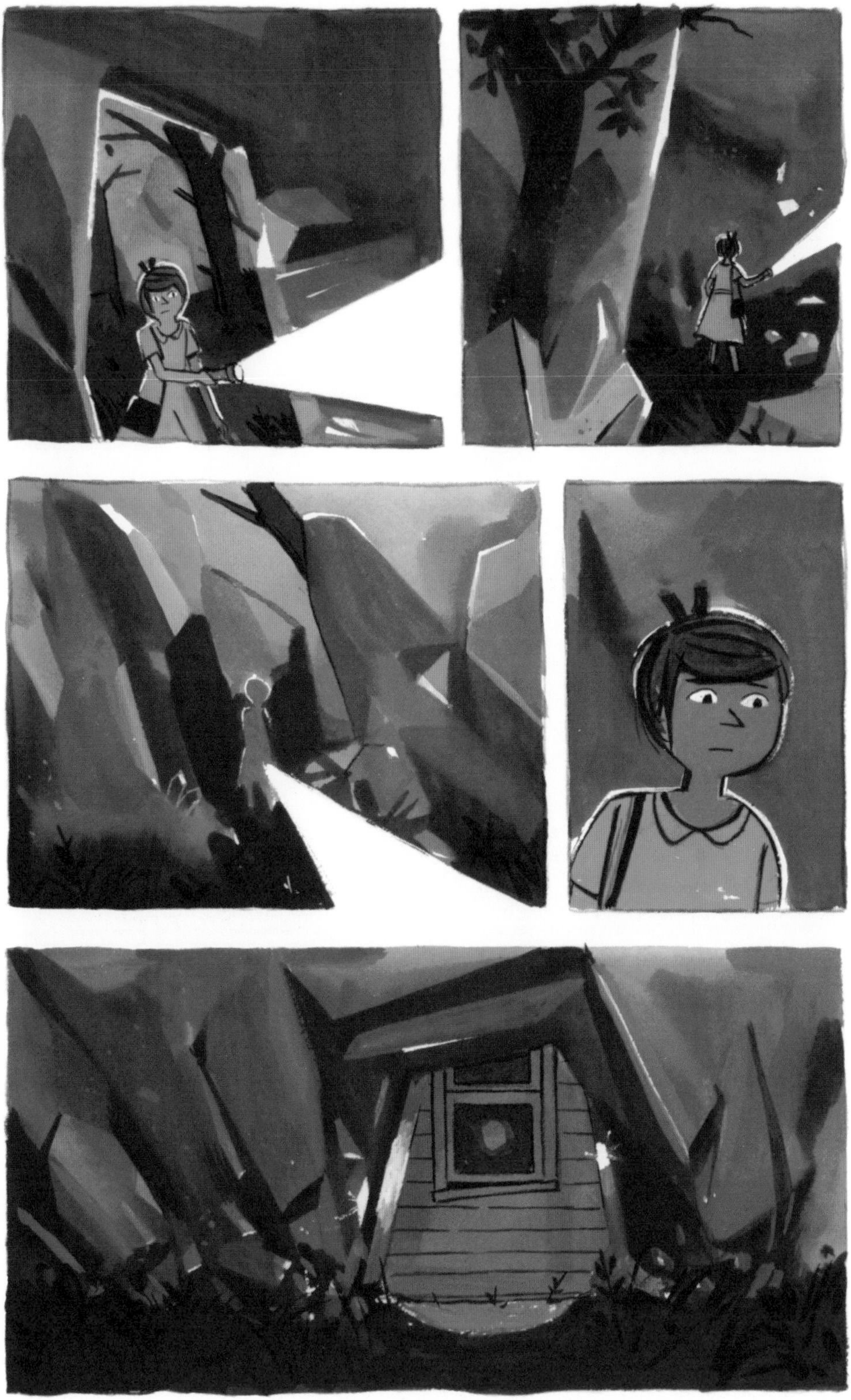

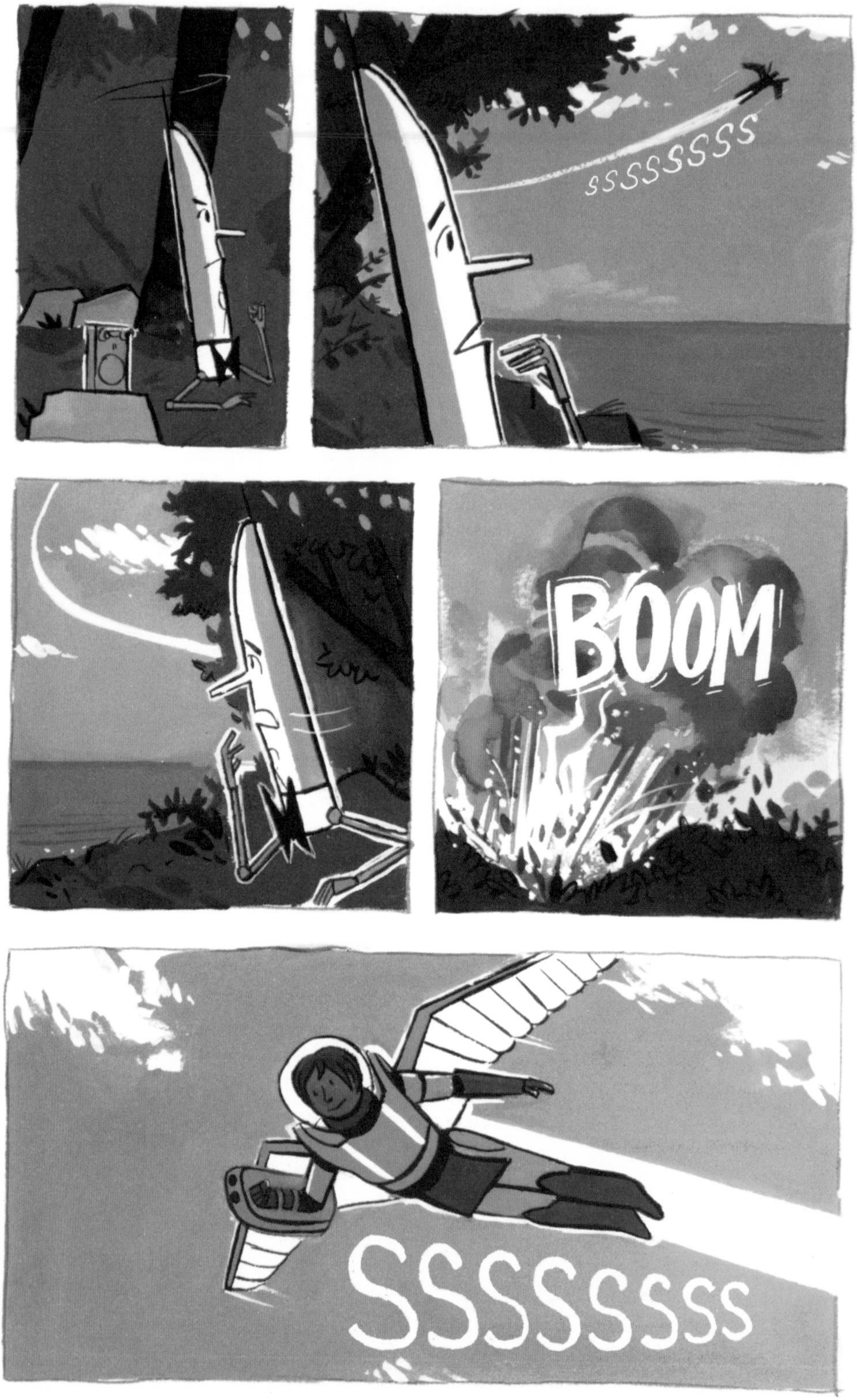
SSSSSSSSS
BOOM
SSSSSSSS

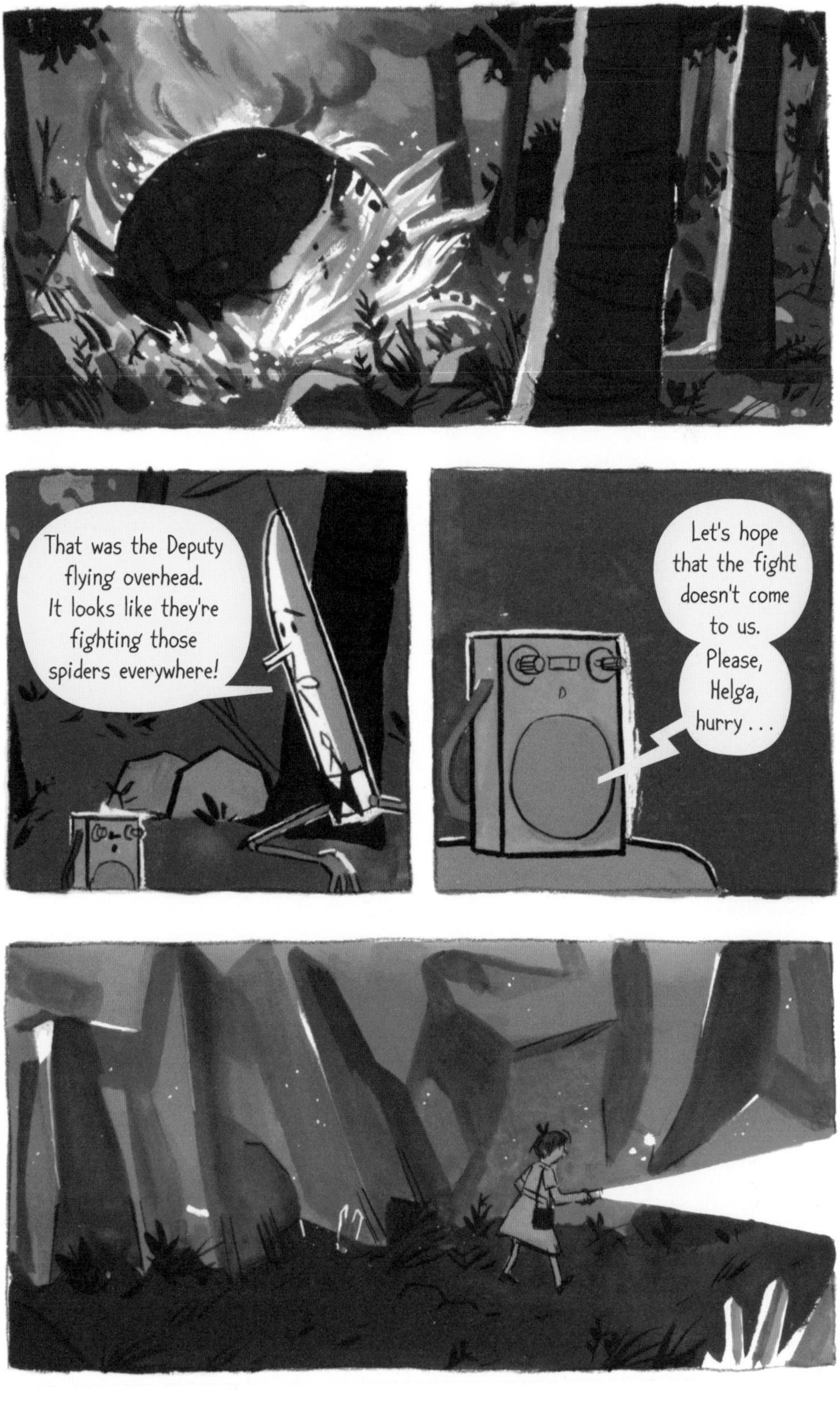
That was the Deputy flying overhead. It looks like they're fighting those spiders everywhere!
Let's hope that the fight doesn't come to us.
Please, Helga, hurry . . .

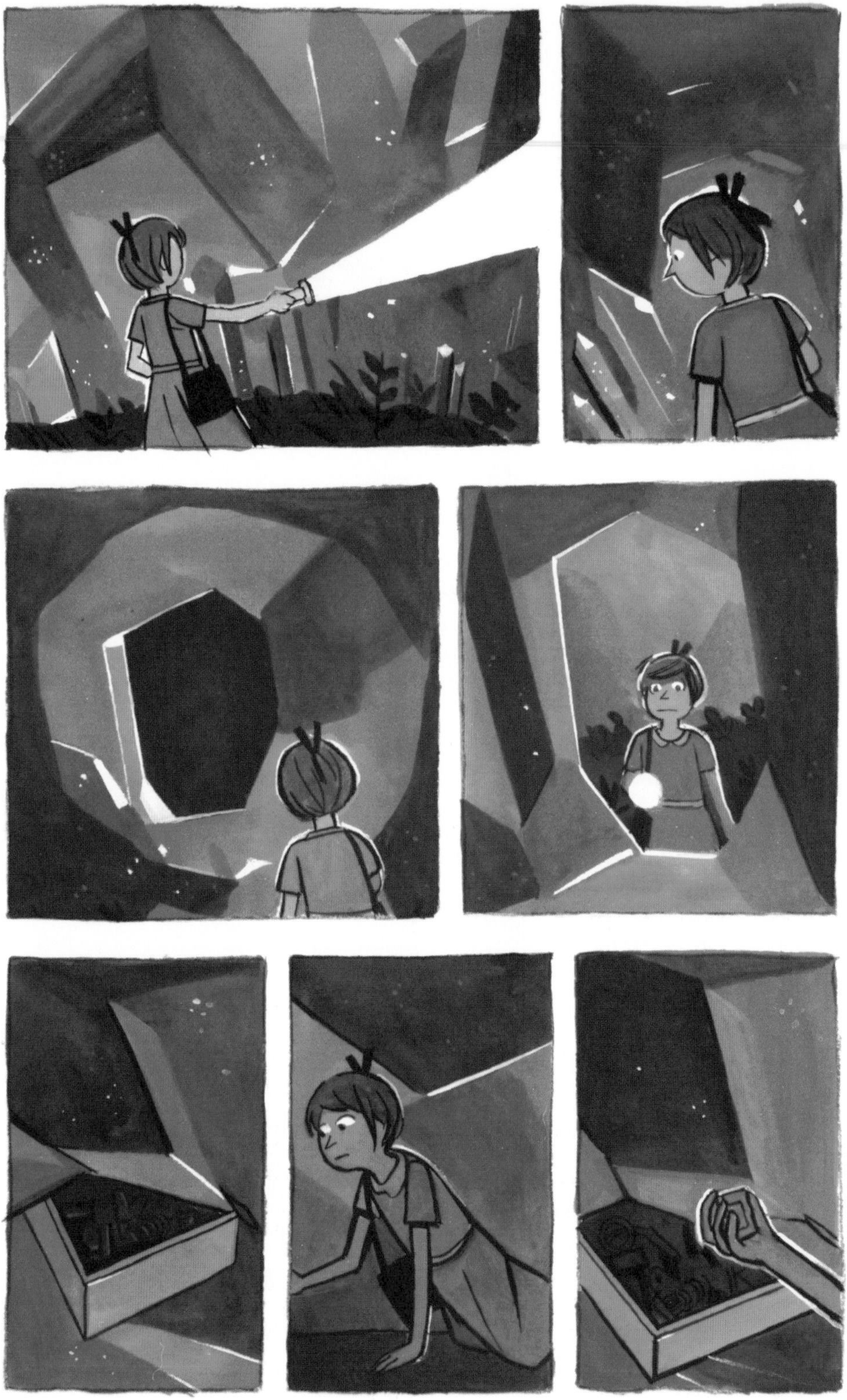

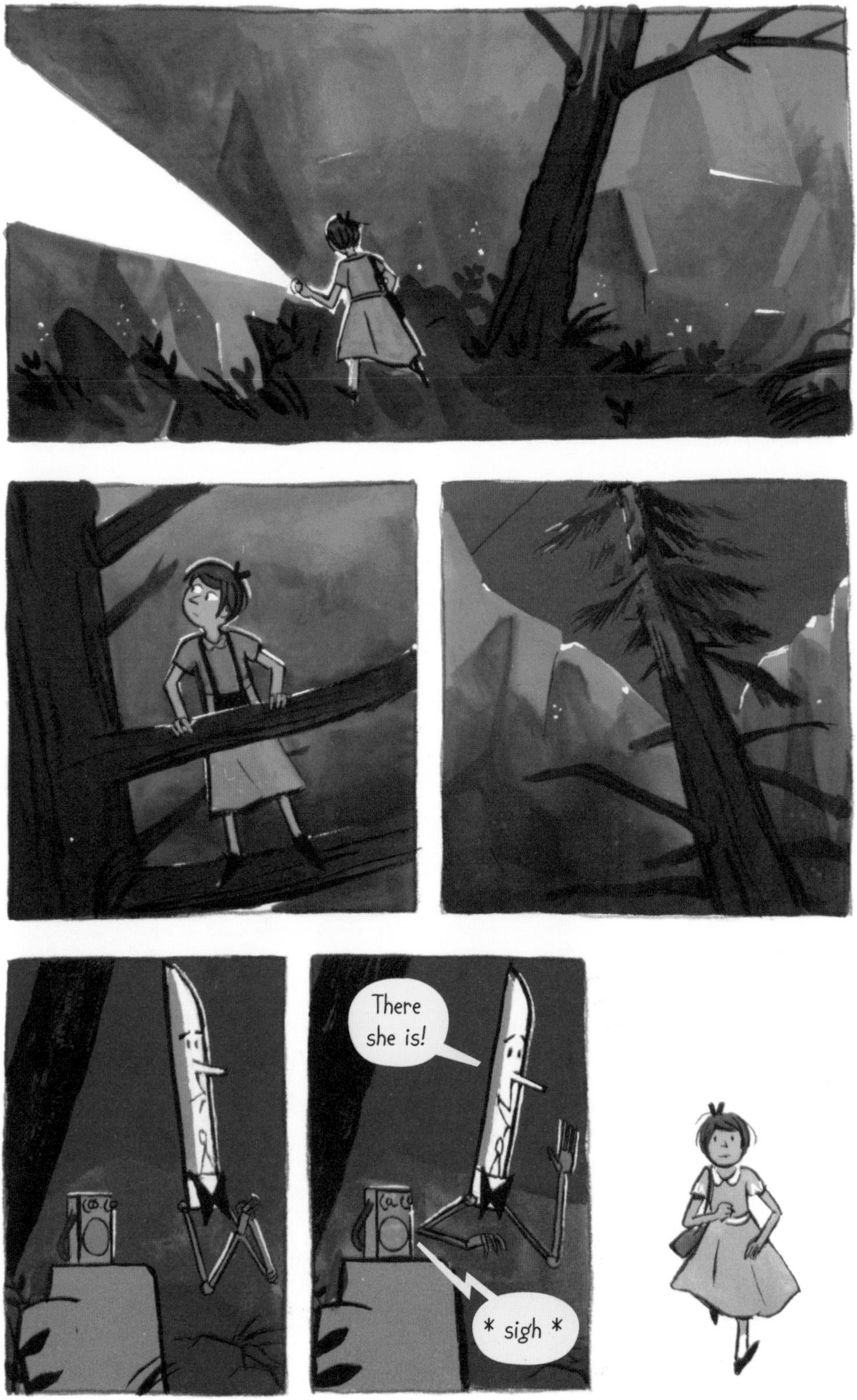
There she is!
* sigh *

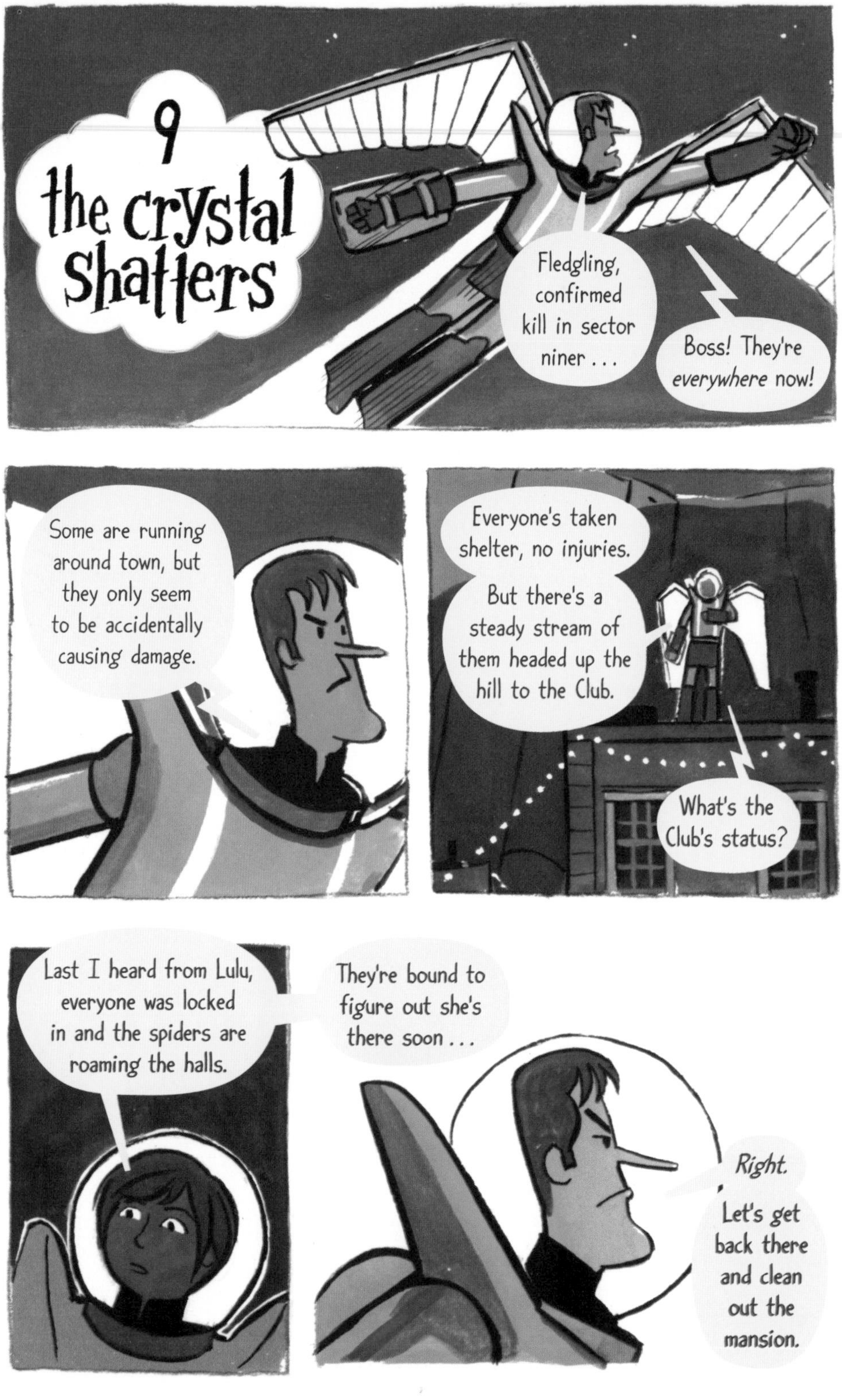
9
the crystal shatters
Fledgling, confirmed kill in sector niner . . .
Boss! They're *everywhere* now!
Some are running around town, but they only seem to be accidentally causing damage.
Everyone's taken shelter, no injuries.
But there's a steady stream of them headed up the hill to the Club.
What's the Club's status?
Last I heard from Lulu, everyone was locked in and the spiders are roaming the halls.
They're bound to figure out she's there soon . . .
Right.
Let's get back there and clean out the mansion.

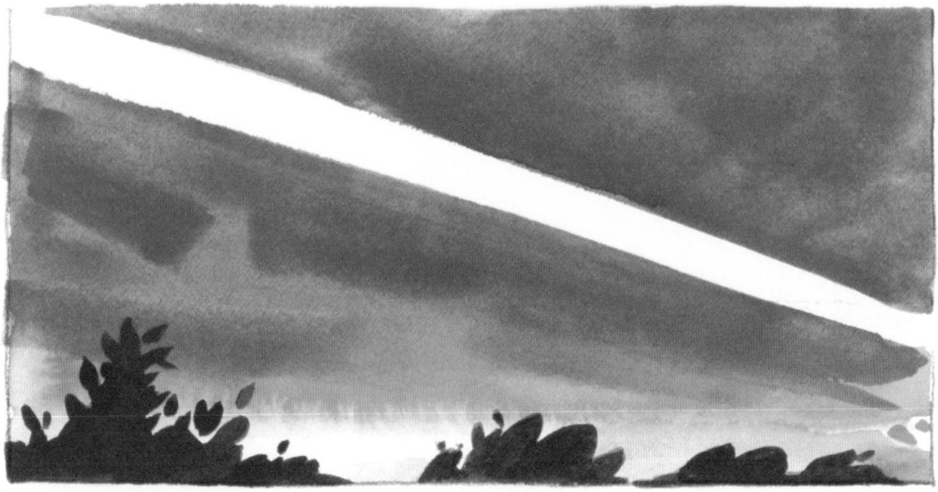

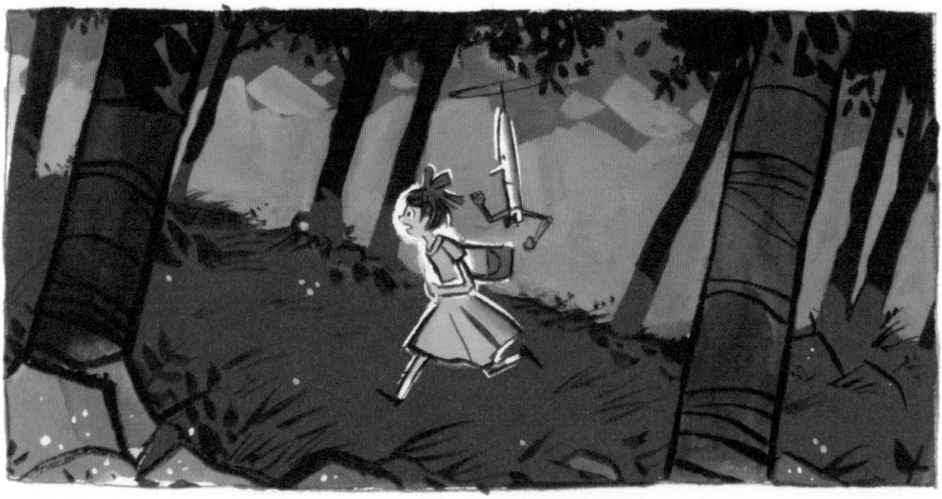

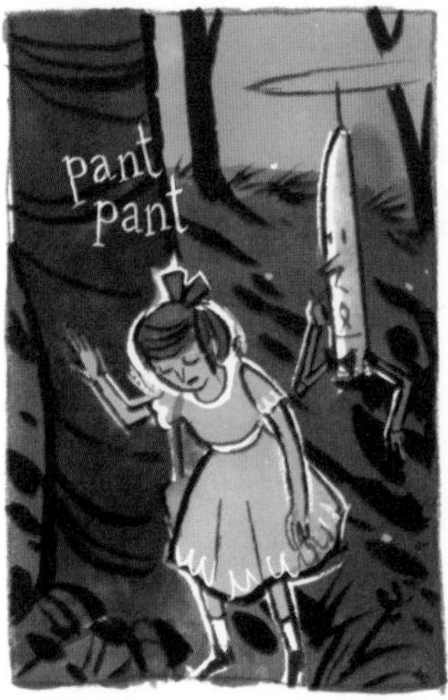
pant
pant

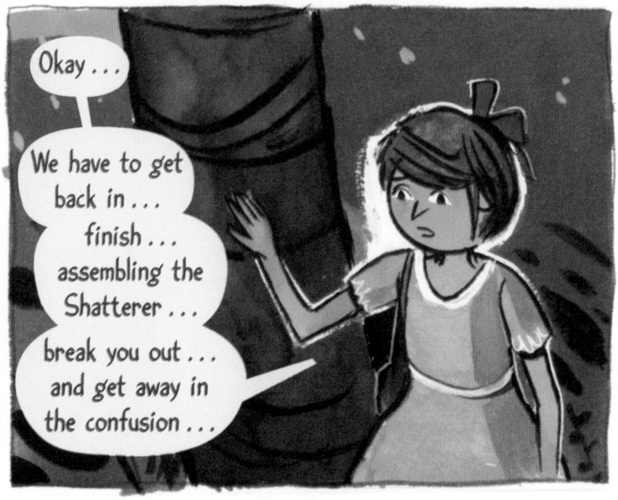
Okay . . .
We have to get back in . . .
finish . . .
assembling the Shatterer . . .
break you out . . .
. . . and get away in the confusion . . .

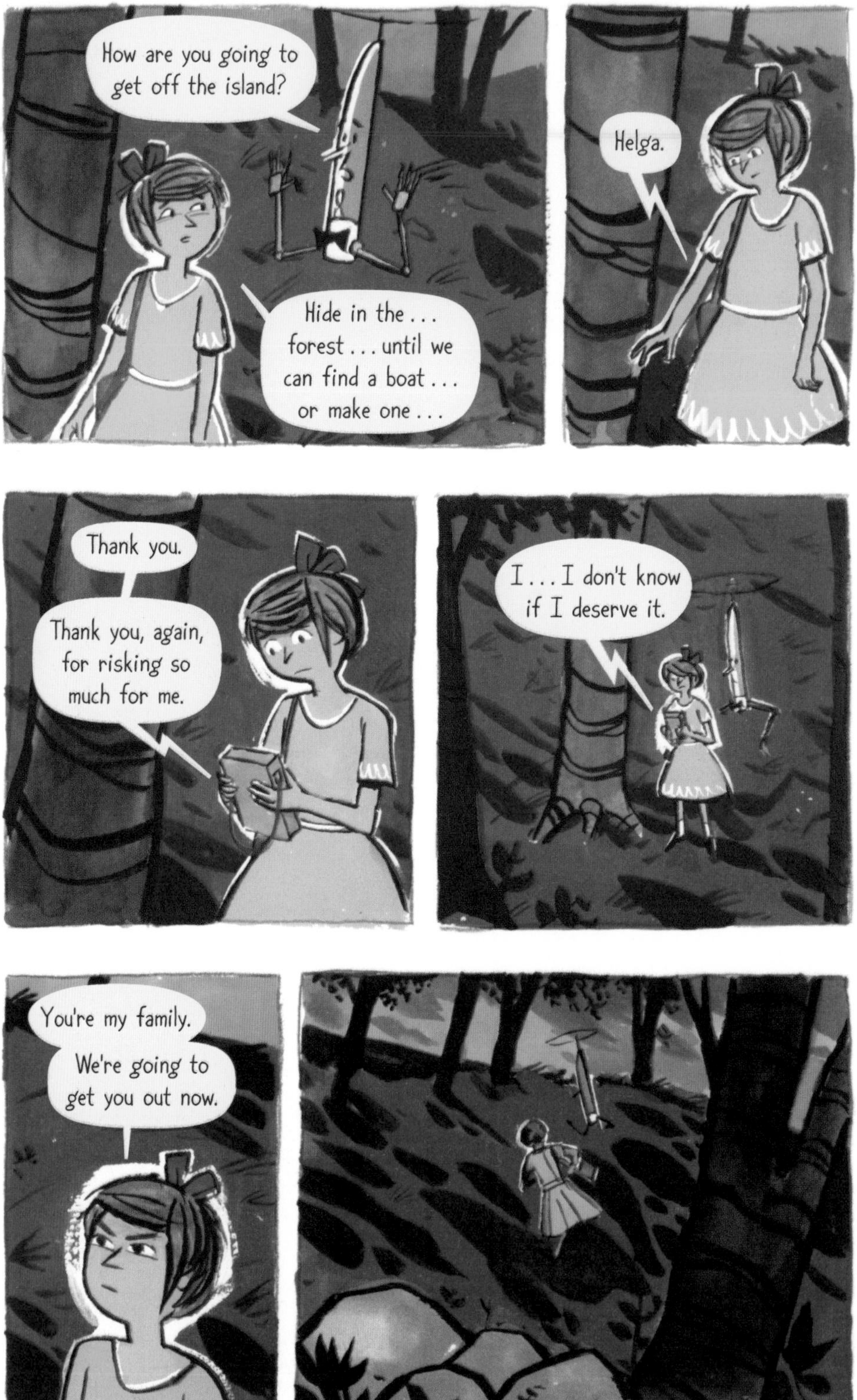
How are you going to get off the island?
Hide in the . . . forest . . . until we can find a boat . . . or make one . . .
Helga.
Thank you.
Thank you, again, for risking so much for me.
I . . . I don't know if I deserve it.
You're my family.
We're going to get you out now.

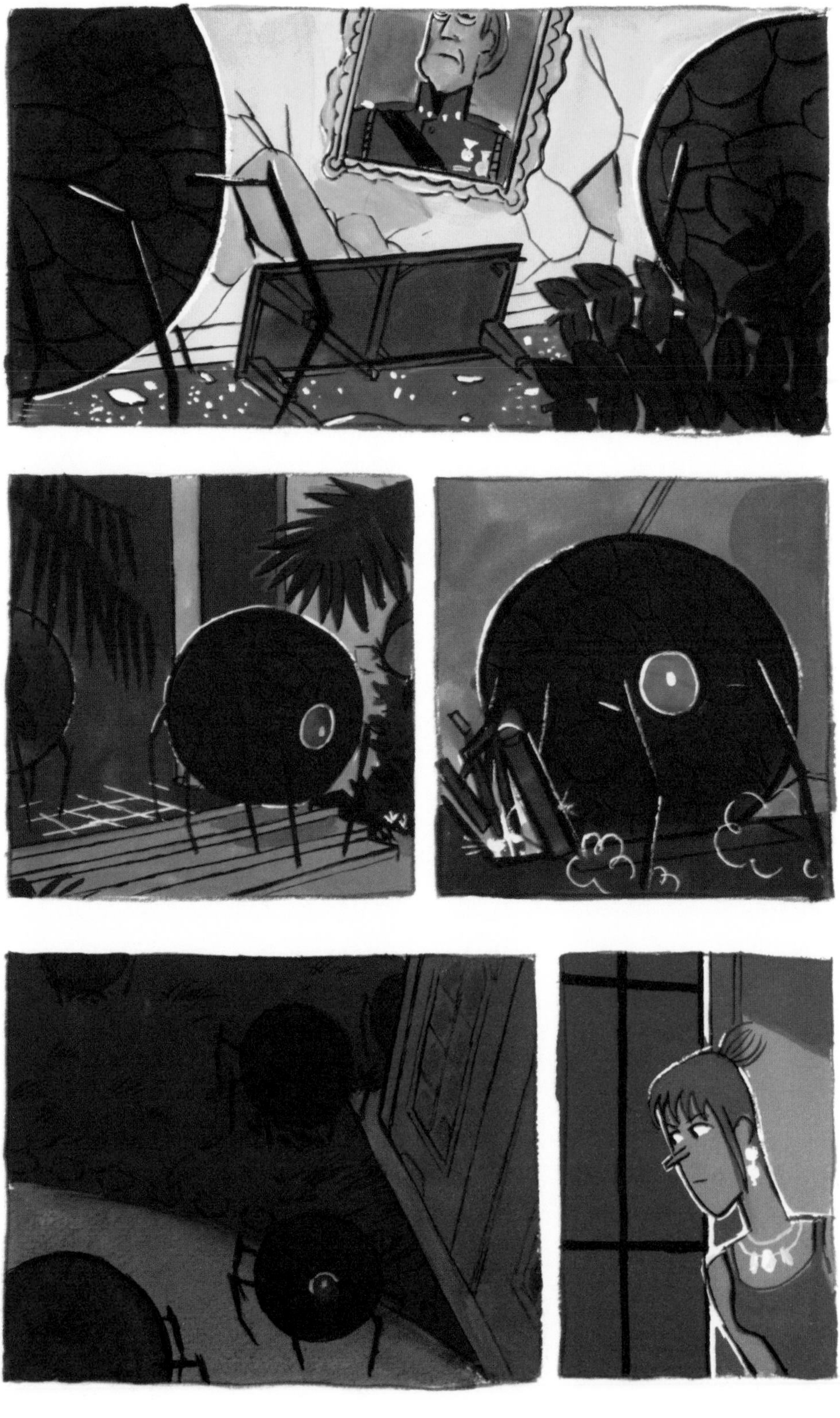

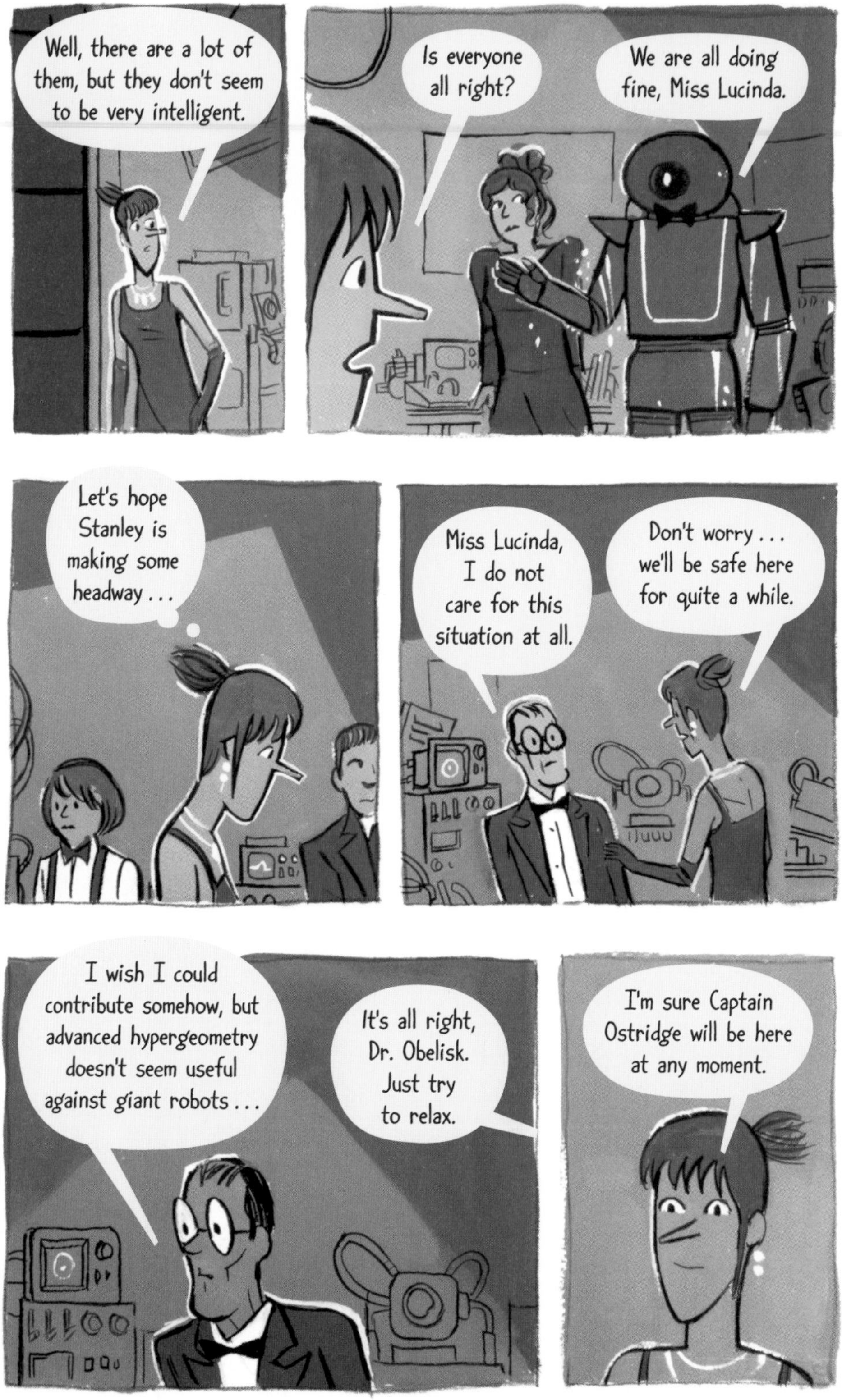
Well, there are a lot of them, but they don't seem to be very intelligent.
Is everyone all right?
We are all doing fine, Miss Lucinda.
Let's hope Stanley is making some headway . . .
Miss Lucinda, I do not care for this situation at all.
Don't worry . . . we'll be safe here for quite a while.
I wish I could contribute somehow, but advanced hypergeometry doesn't seem useful against giant robots . . .
It's all right, Dr. Obelisk. Just try to relax.
I'm sure Captain Ostridge will be here at any moment.

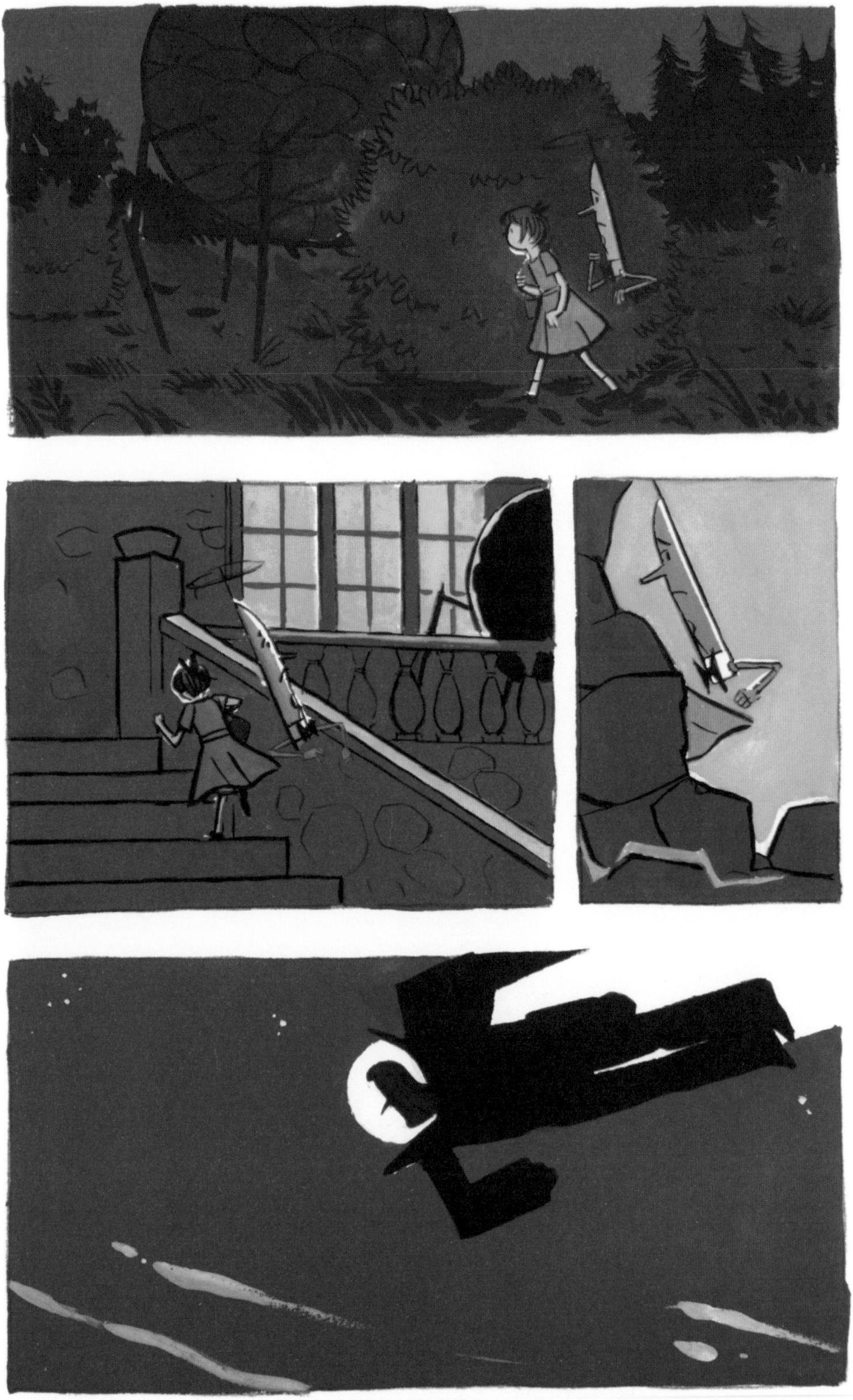

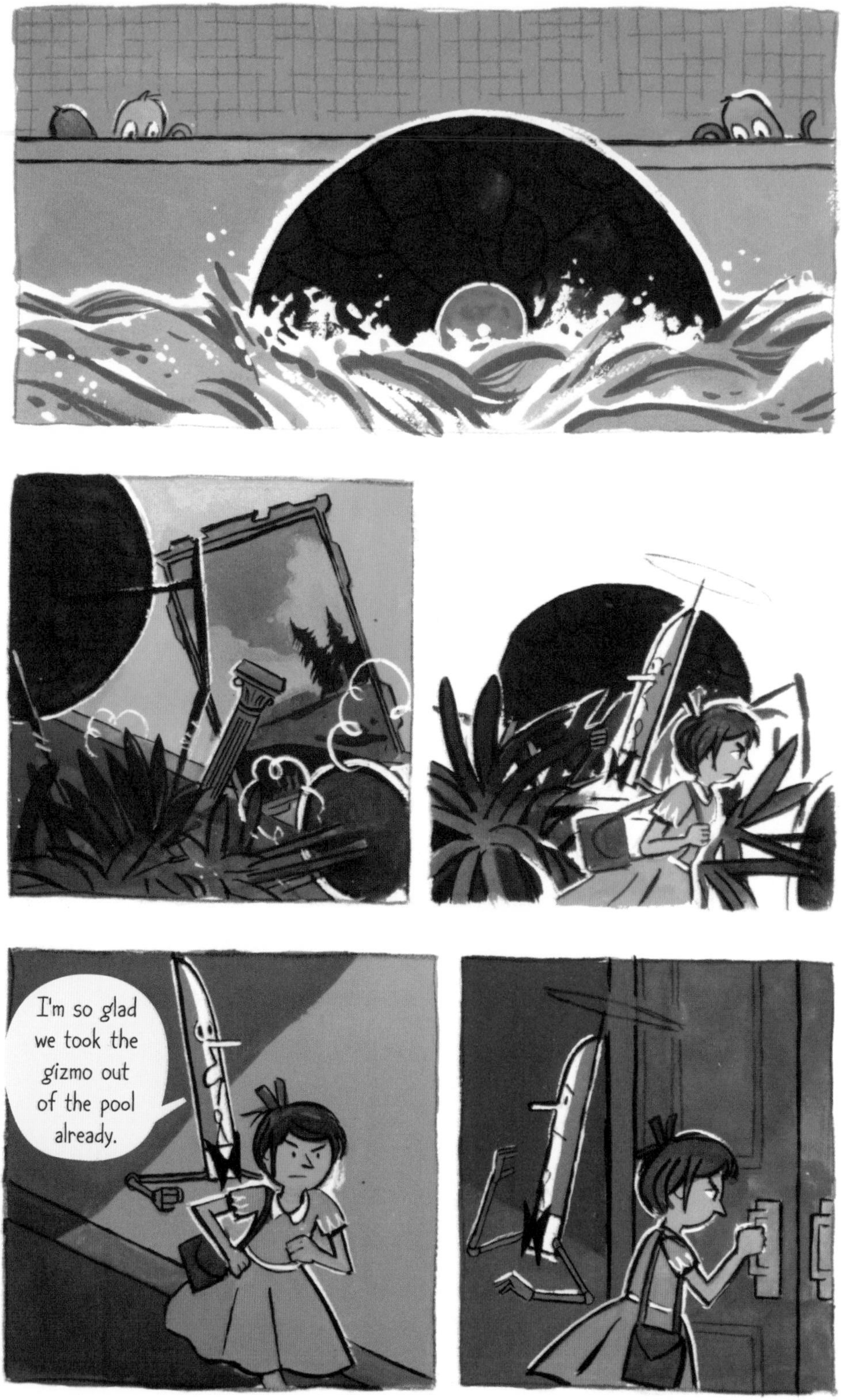
I'm so glad we took the gizmo out of the pool already.

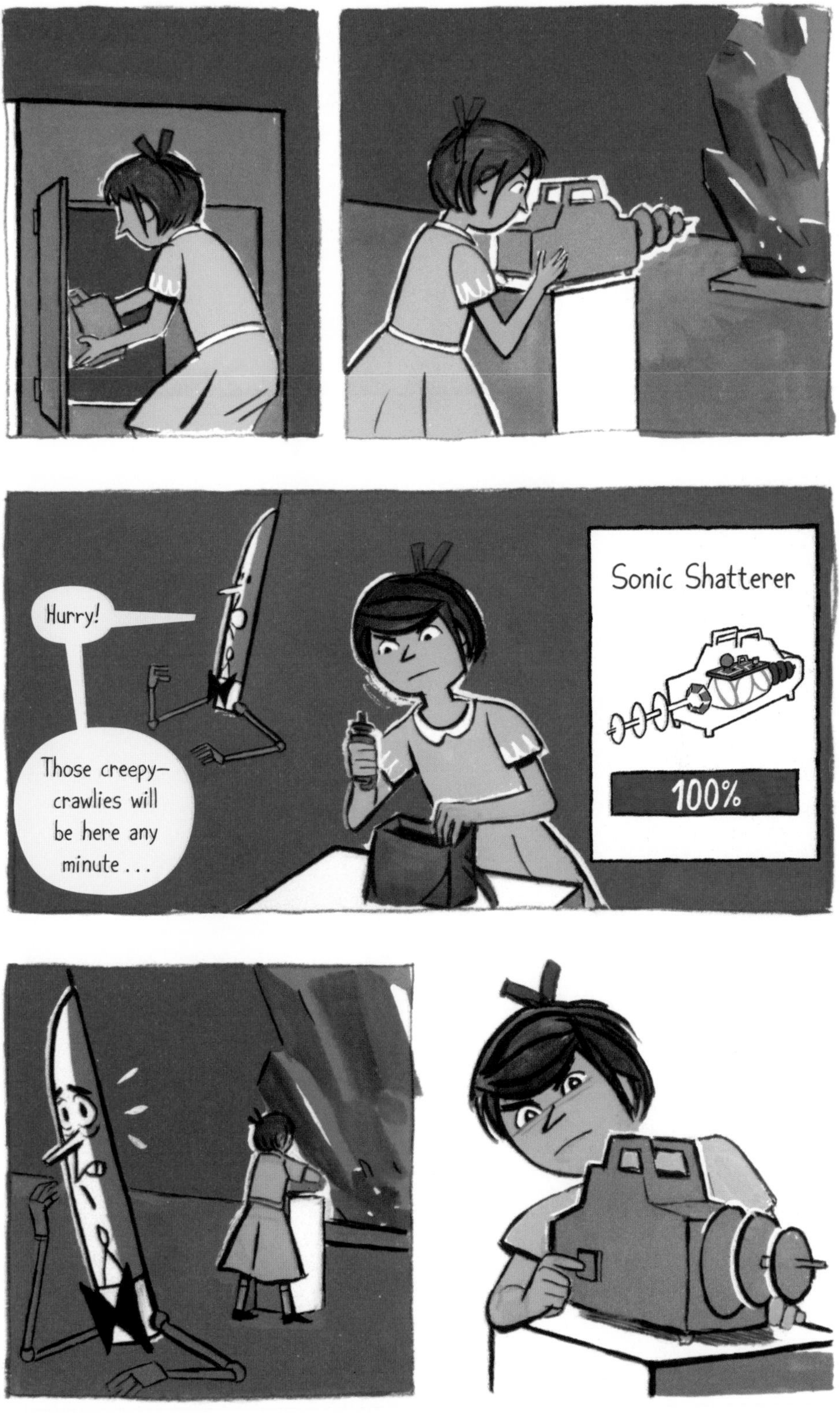
Hurry!
Those creepy-crawlies will be here any minute . . .
Sonic Shatterer
100%

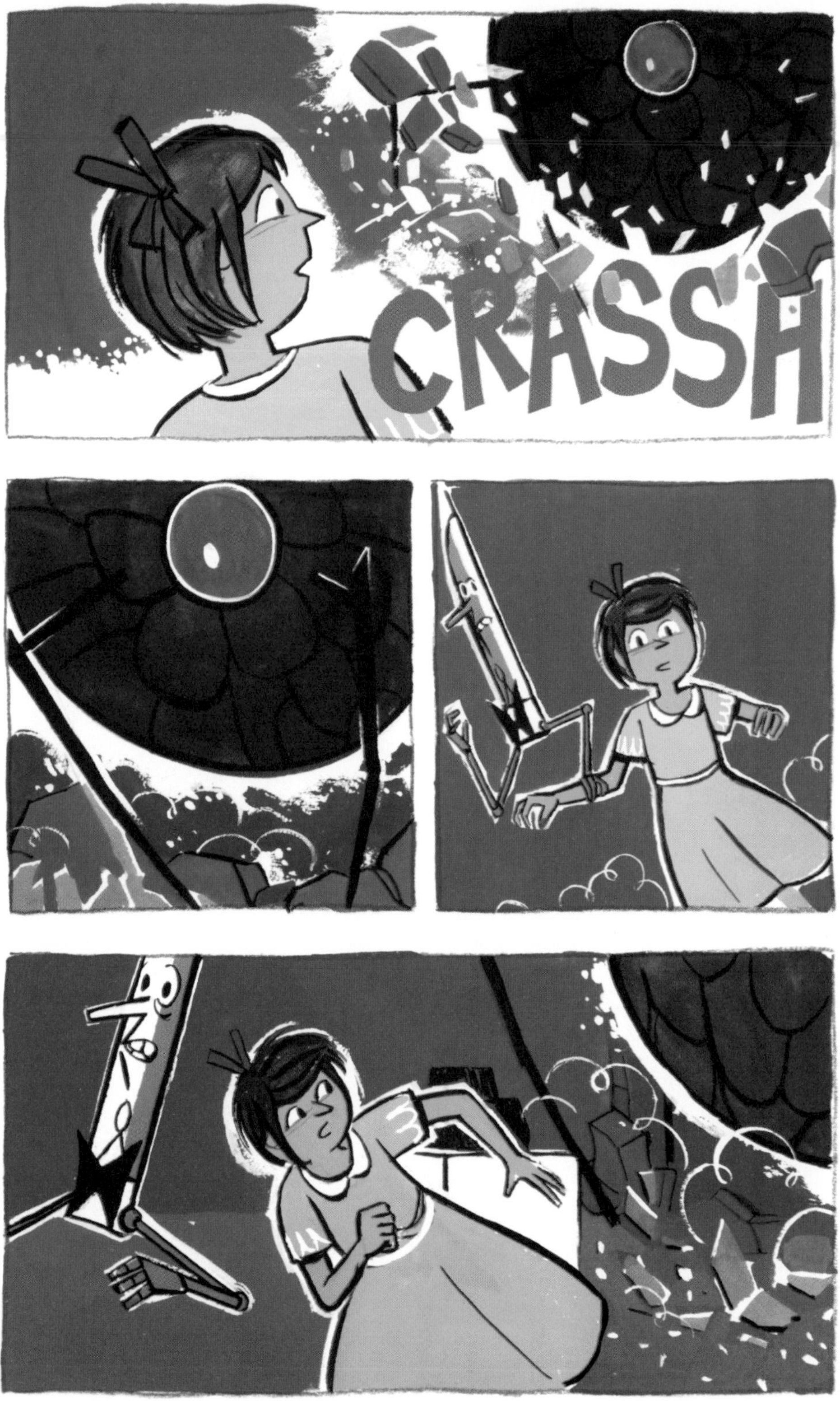
CRASSH

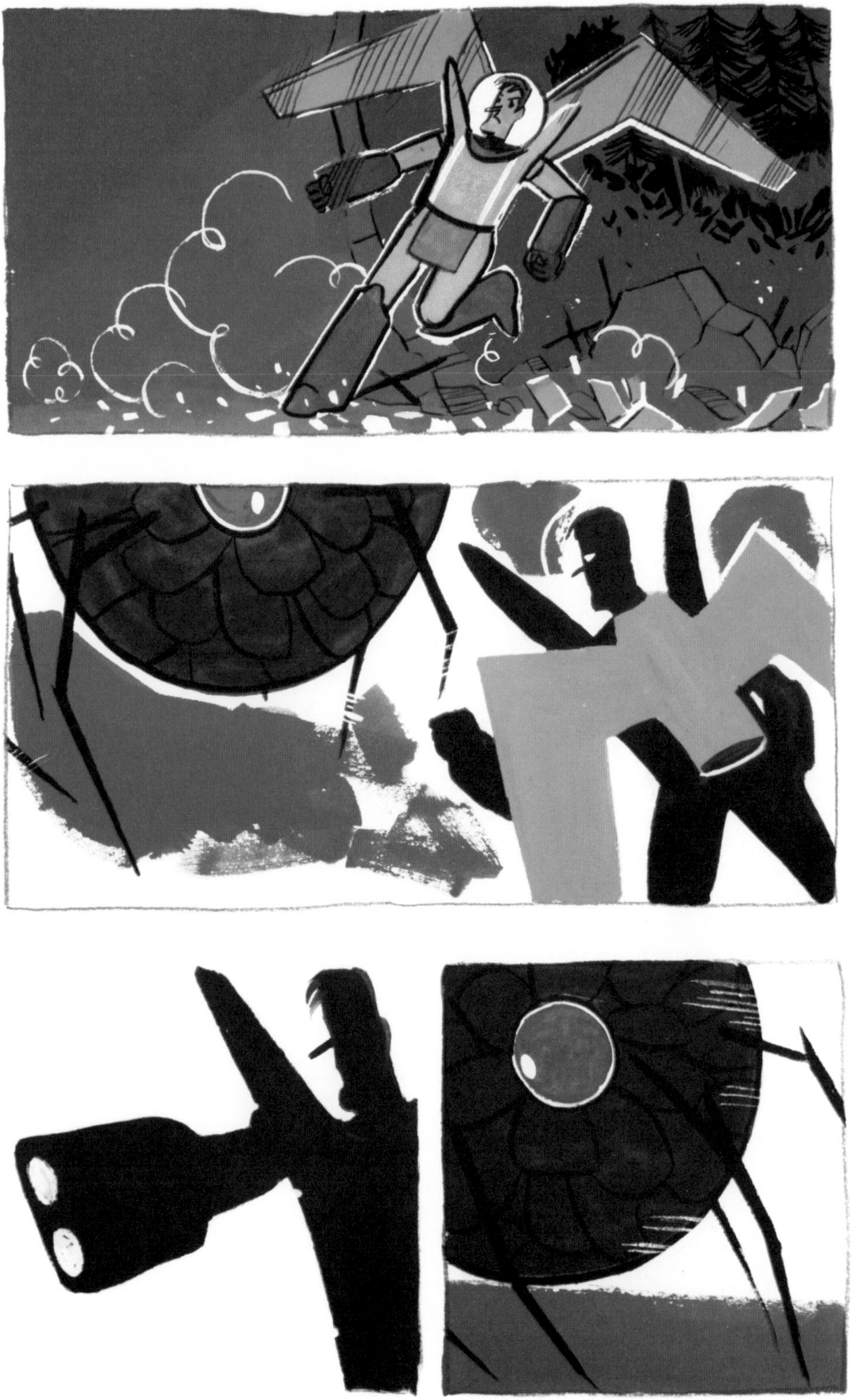

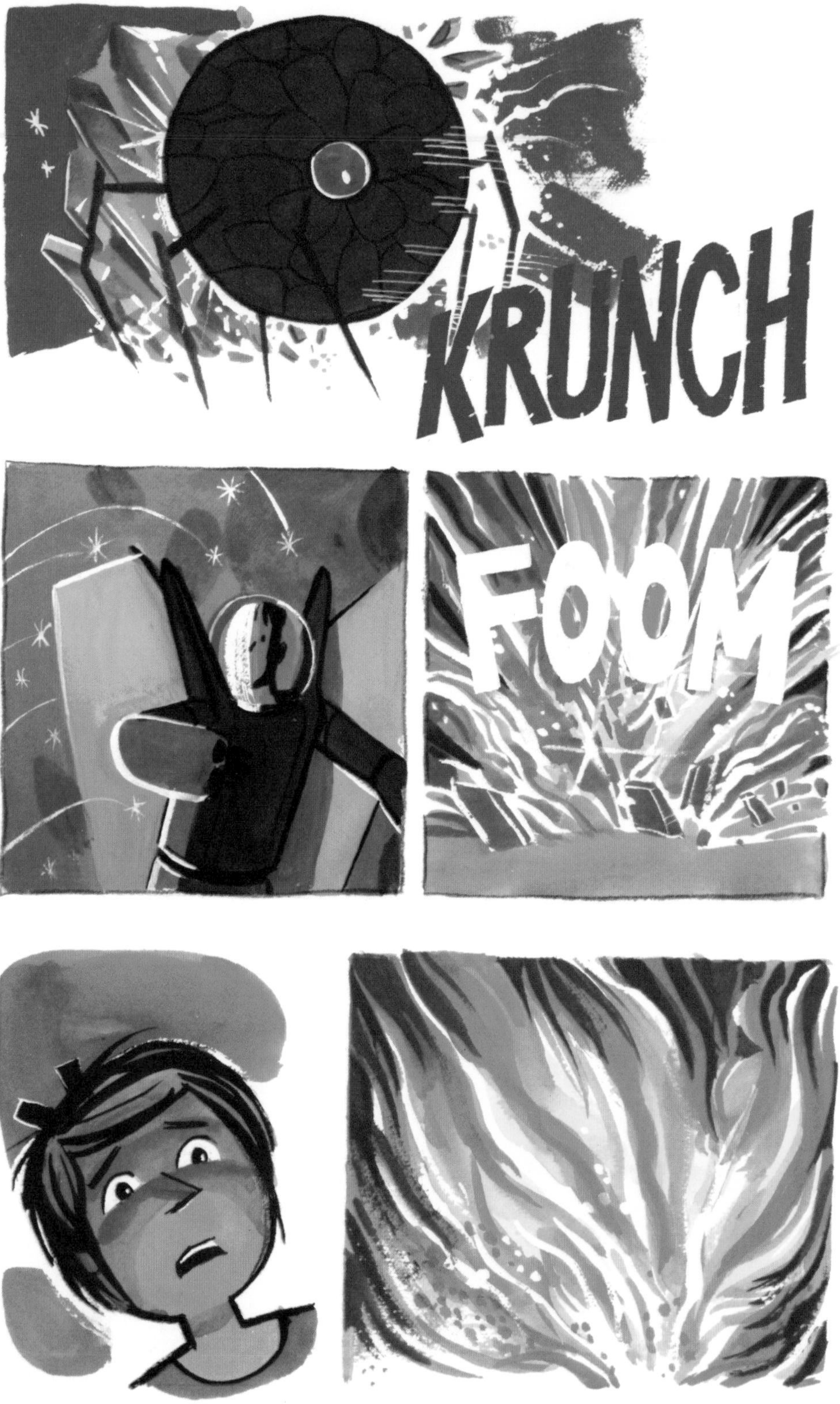
KRUNCH
FOOM

SQUEEE AALLLLLLLL

EEA LLLLLL

Grandfather?

Grandfather!

Grandfather!

EEAALLLL LLLLL

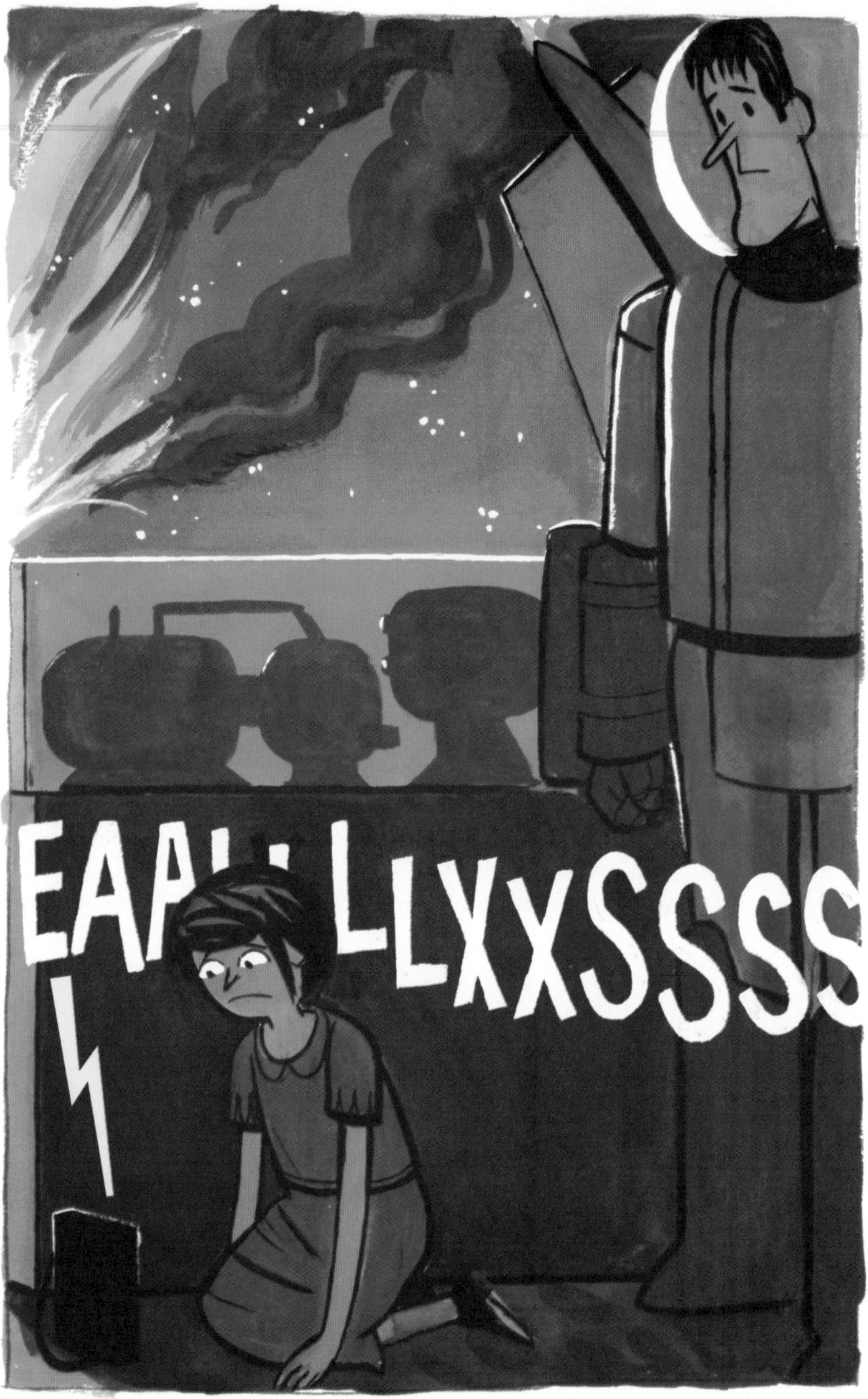
EA
LLXXSSSS

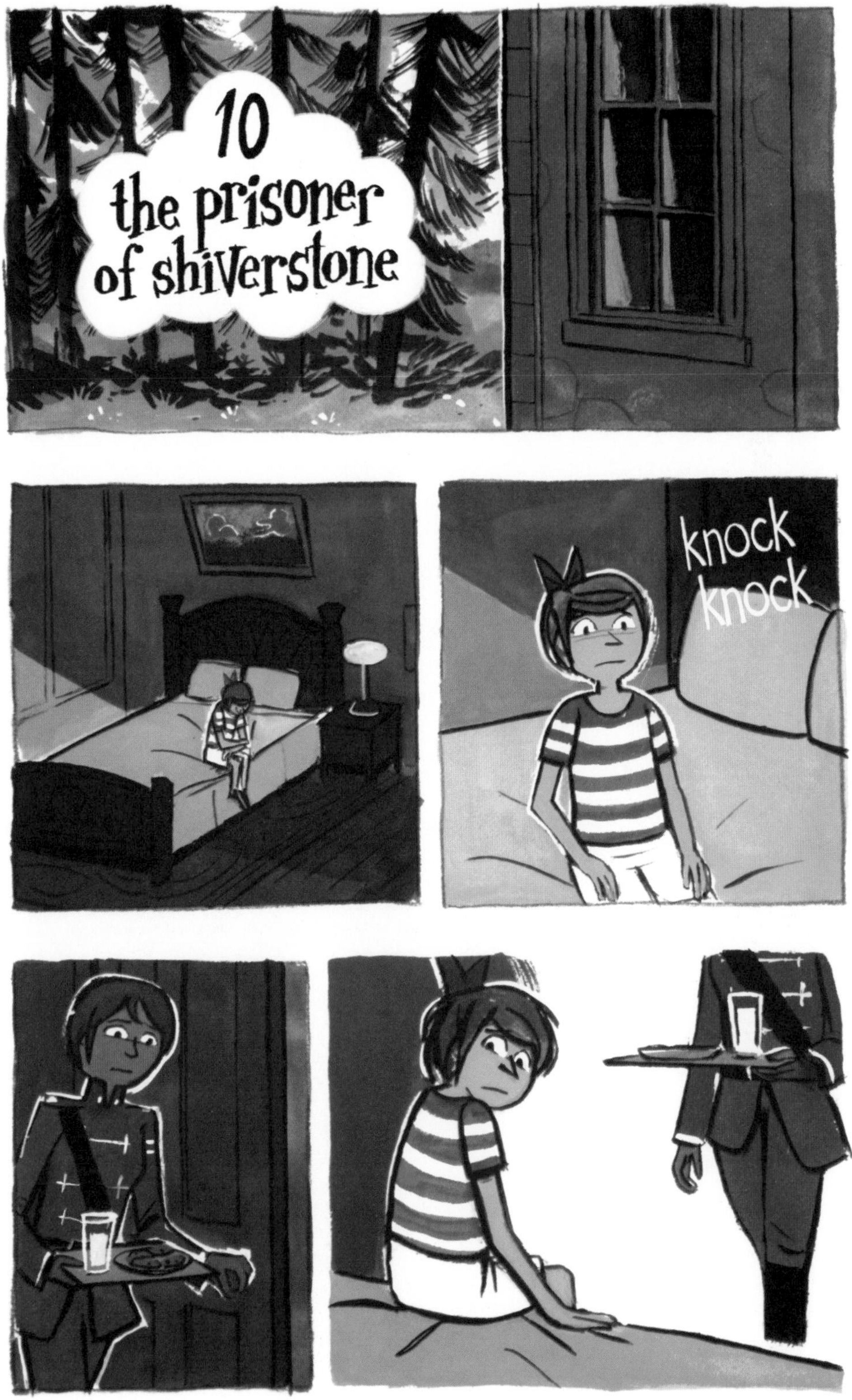
10
the prisoner of shiverstone
knock
knock

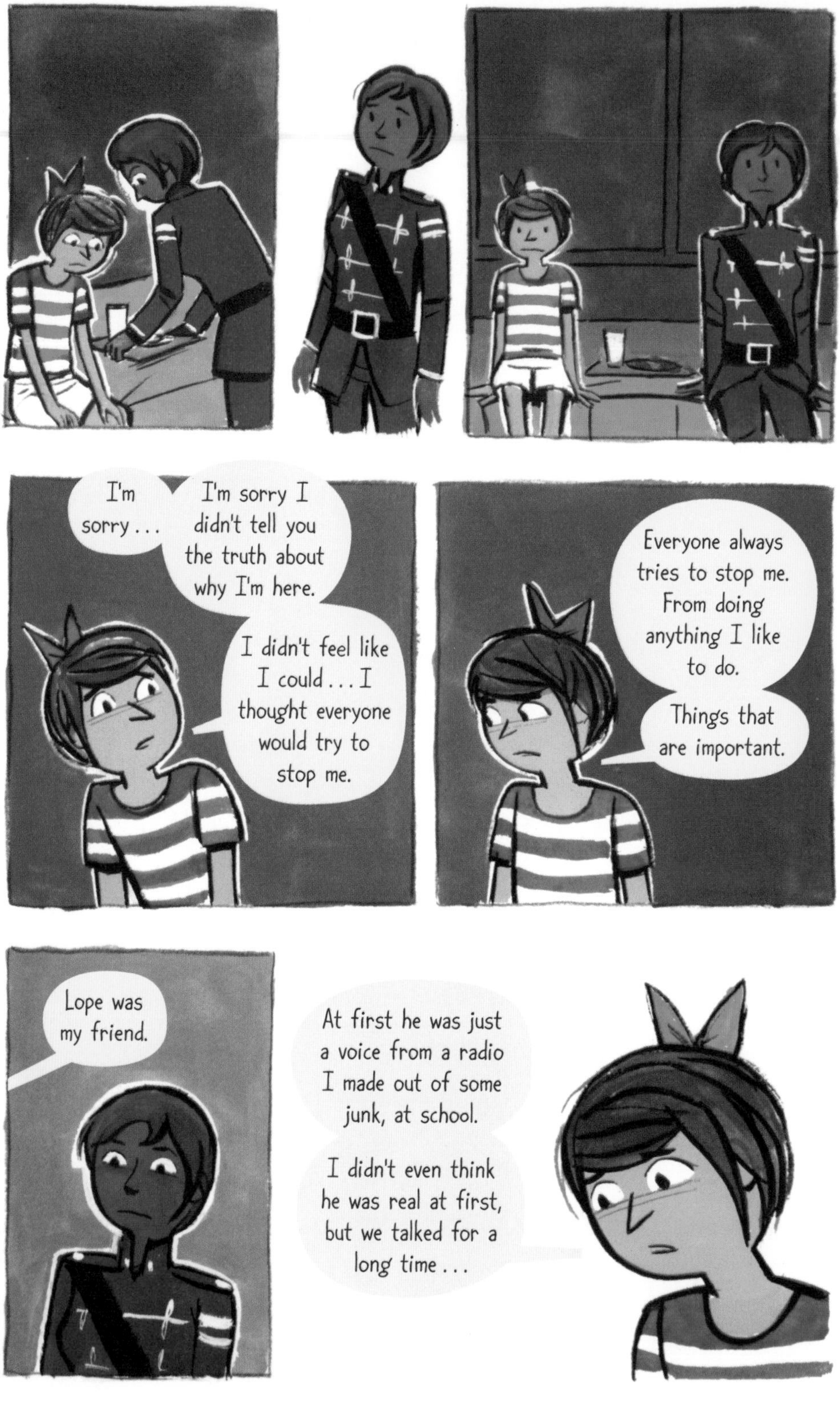
I'm sorry...
I'm sorry I didn't tell you the truth about why I'm here.
I didn't feel like I could... I thought everyone would try to stop me.
Everyone always tries to stop me. From doing anything I like to do.
Things that are important.
Lope was my friend.
At first he was just a voice from a radio I made out of some junk, at school.
I didn't even think he was real at first, but we talked for a long time...

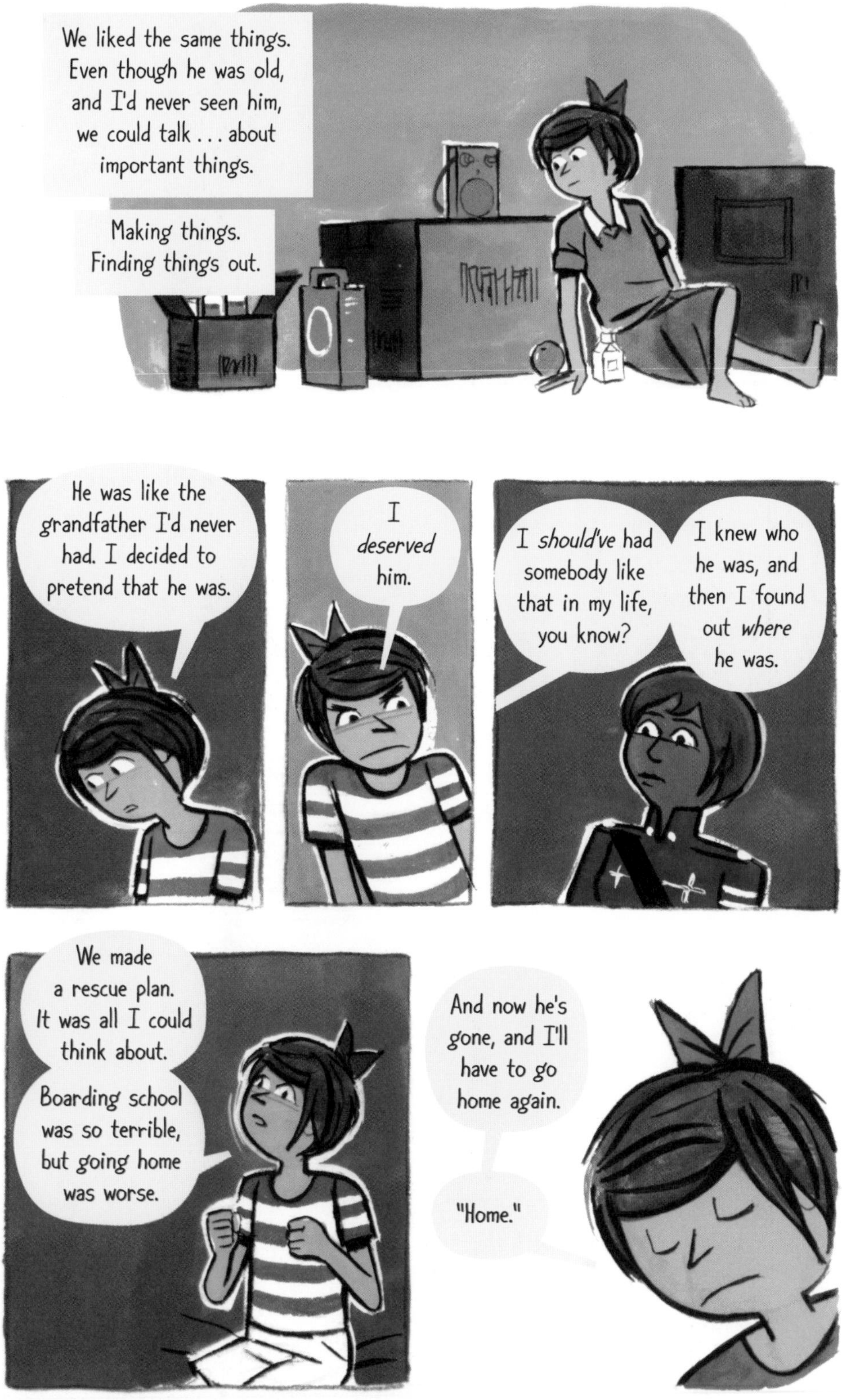
We liked the same things. Even though he was old, and I'd never seen him, we could talk . . . about important things.
Making things. Finding things out.
He was like the grandfather I'd never had. I decided to pretend that he was.
I *deserved* him.
I *should've* had somebody like that in my life, you know?
I knew who he was, and then I found out *where* he was.
We made a rescue plan. It was all I could think about.
Boarding school was so terrible, but going home was worse.
And now he's gone, and I'll have to go home again.
"Home."

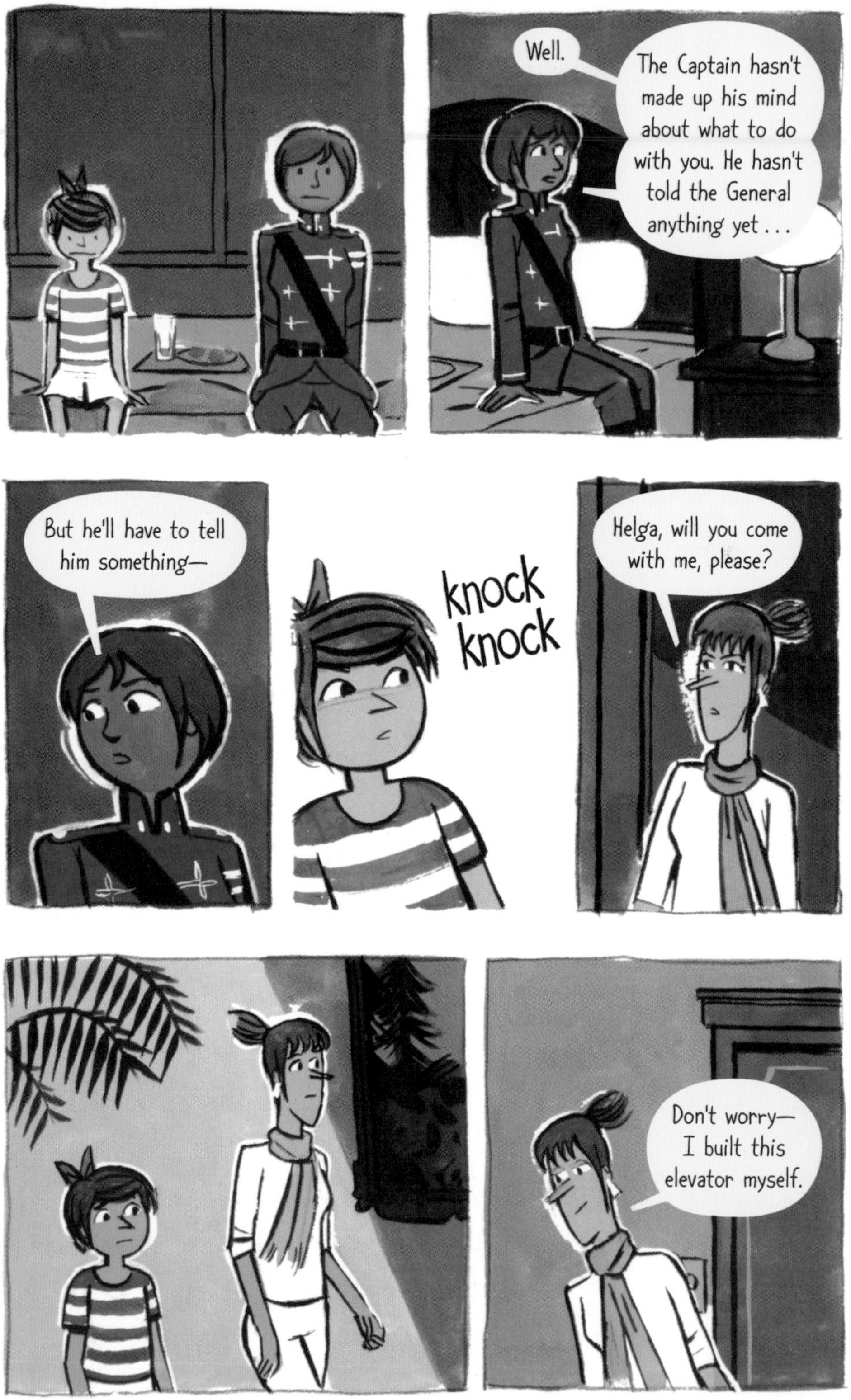
Well.
The Captain hasn't made up his mind about what to do with you. He hasn't told the General anything yet . . .
But he'll have to tell him something—
knock knock
Helga, will you come with me, please?
Don't worry— I built this elevator myself.

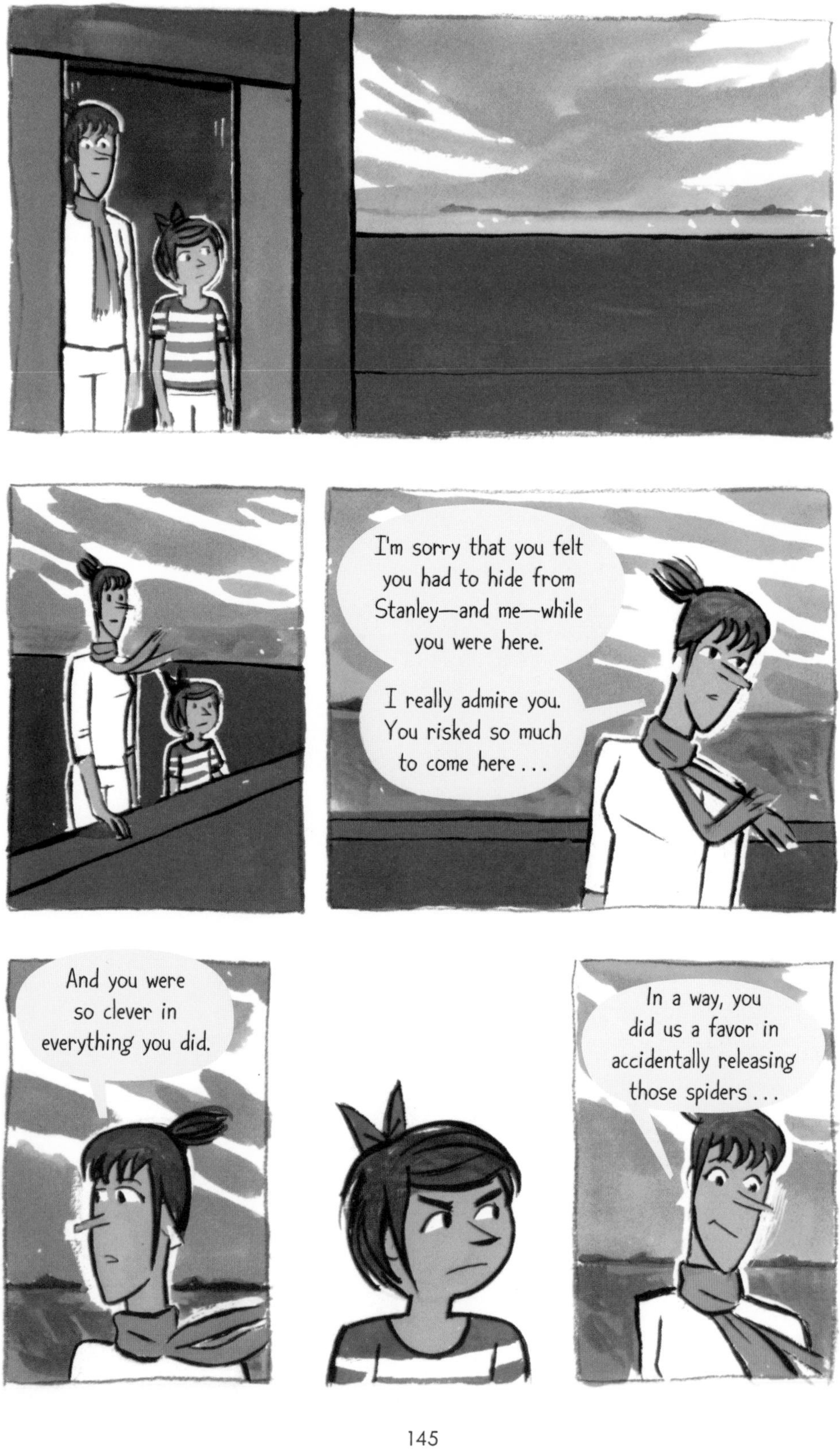
I'm sorry that you felt you had to hide from Stanley—and me—while you were here.
I really admire you. You risked so much to come here . . .
And you were so clever in everything you did.
In a way, you did us a favor in accidentally releasing those spiders . . .

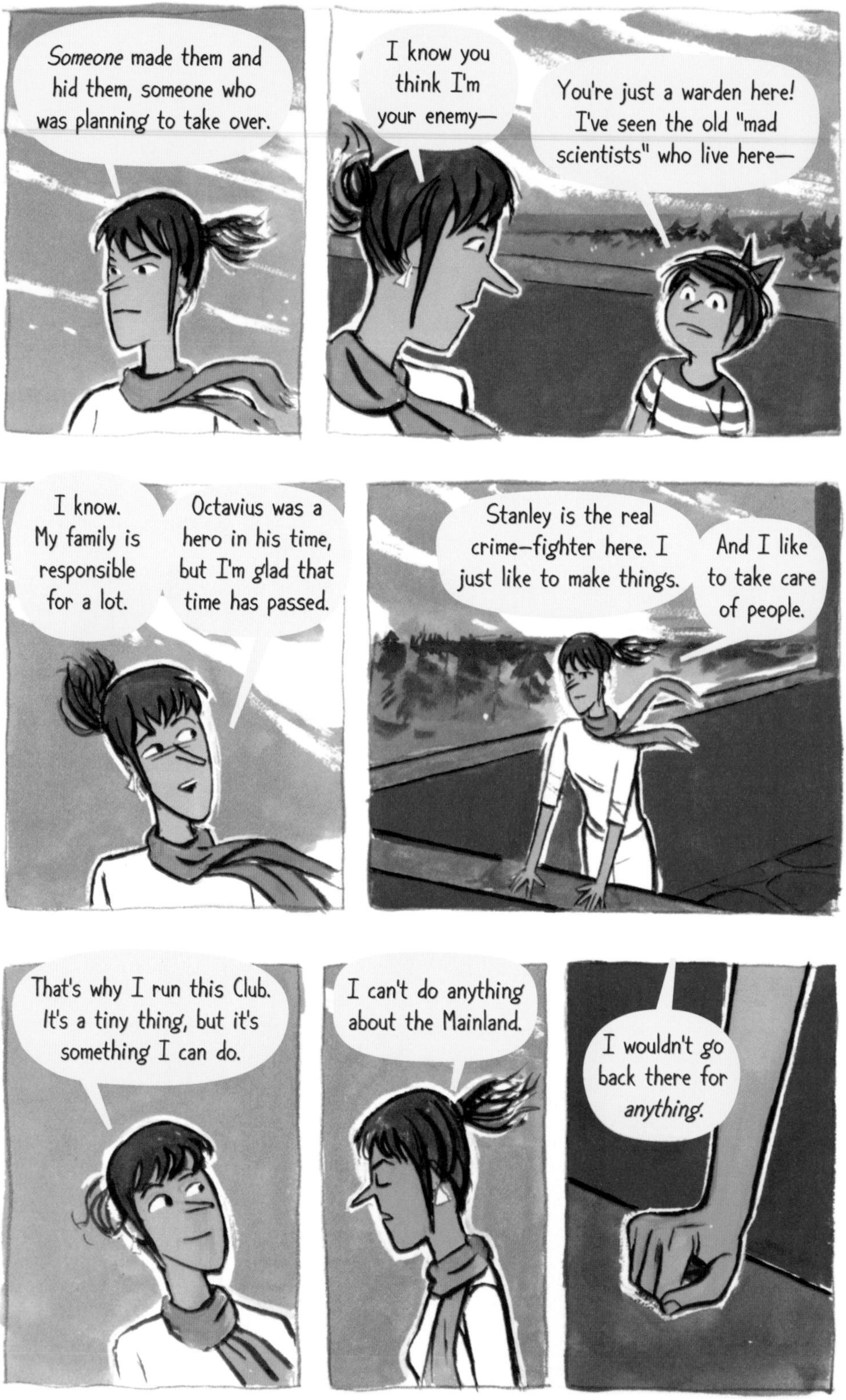
Someone made them and hid them, someone who was planning to take over.
I know you think I'm your enemy—
You're just a warden here! I've seen the old "mad scientists" who live here—
I know. My family is responsible for a lot.
Octavius was a hero in his time, but I'm glad that time has passed.
Stanley is the real crime-fighter here. I just like to make things.
And I like to take care of people.
That's why I run this Club. It's a tiny thing, but it's something I can do.
I can't do anything about the Mainland.
I wouldn't go back there for *anything*.

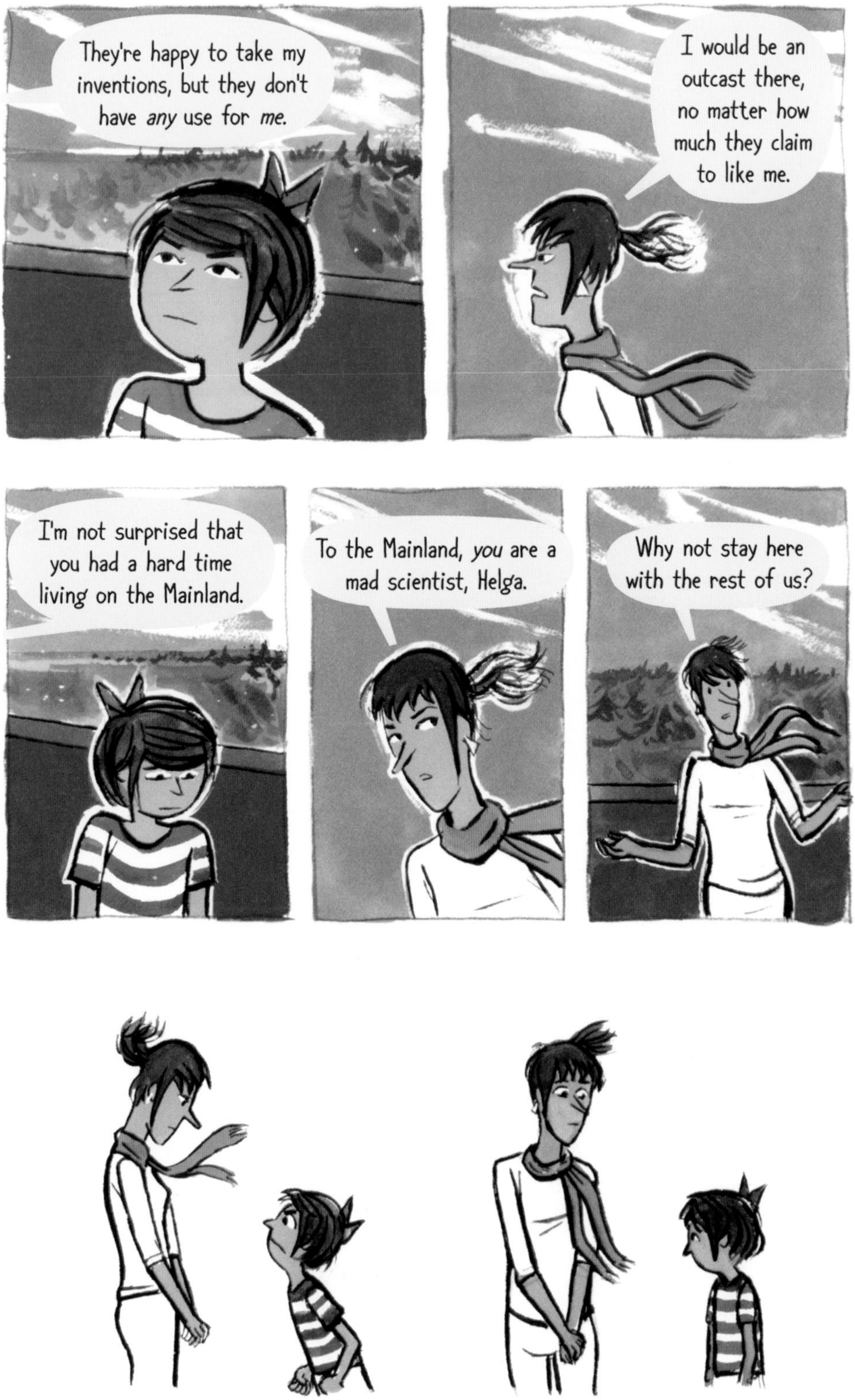
They're happy to take my inventions, but they don't have *any* use for *me.*
I would be an outcast there, no matter how much they claim to like me.
I'm not surprised that you had a hard time living on the Mainland.
To the Mainland, *you* are a mad scientist, Helga.
Why not stay here with the rest of us?

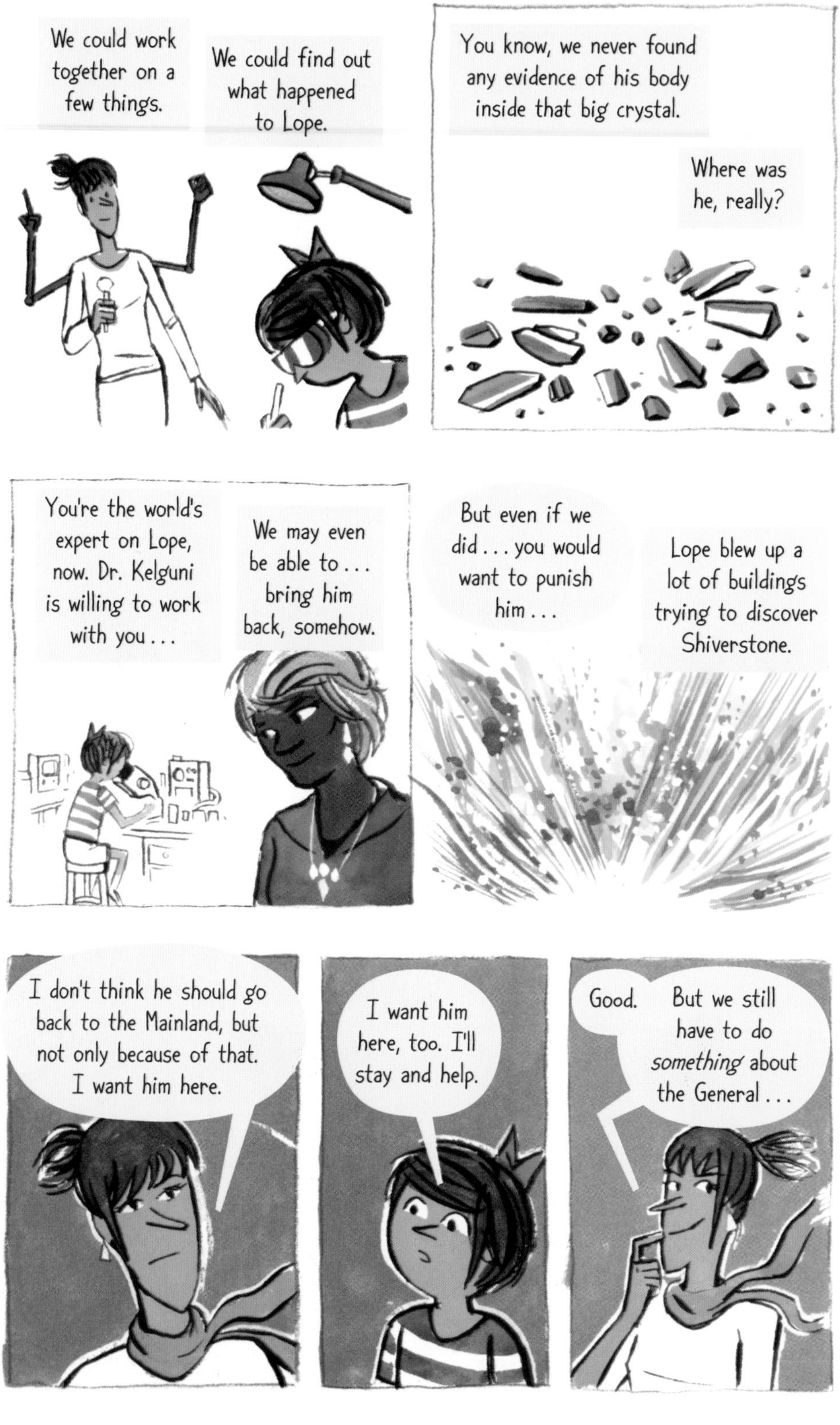

We could work together on a few things.
We could find out what happened to Lope.
You know, we never found any evidence of his body inside that big crystal.
Where was he, really?
You're the world's expert on Lope, now. Dr. Kelguni is willing to work with you . . .
We may even be able to . . . bring him back, somehow.
But even if we did . . . you would want to punish him . . .
Lope blew up a lot of buildings trying to discover Shiverstone.
I don't think he should *go* back to the Mainland, but not only because of that. I want him here.
I want him here, too. I'll stay and help.
Good.
But we still have to do *something* about the General . . .

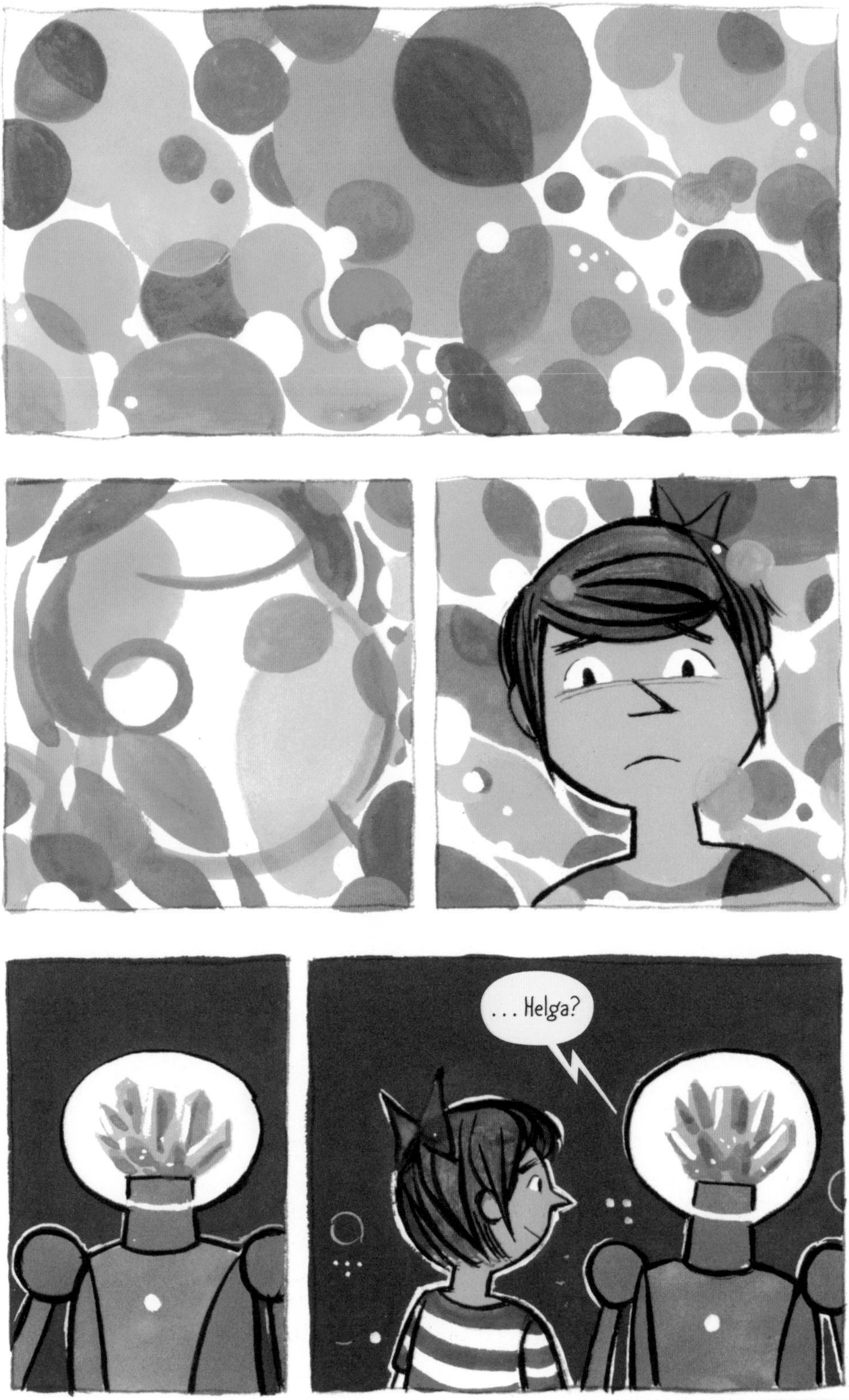
... Helga?

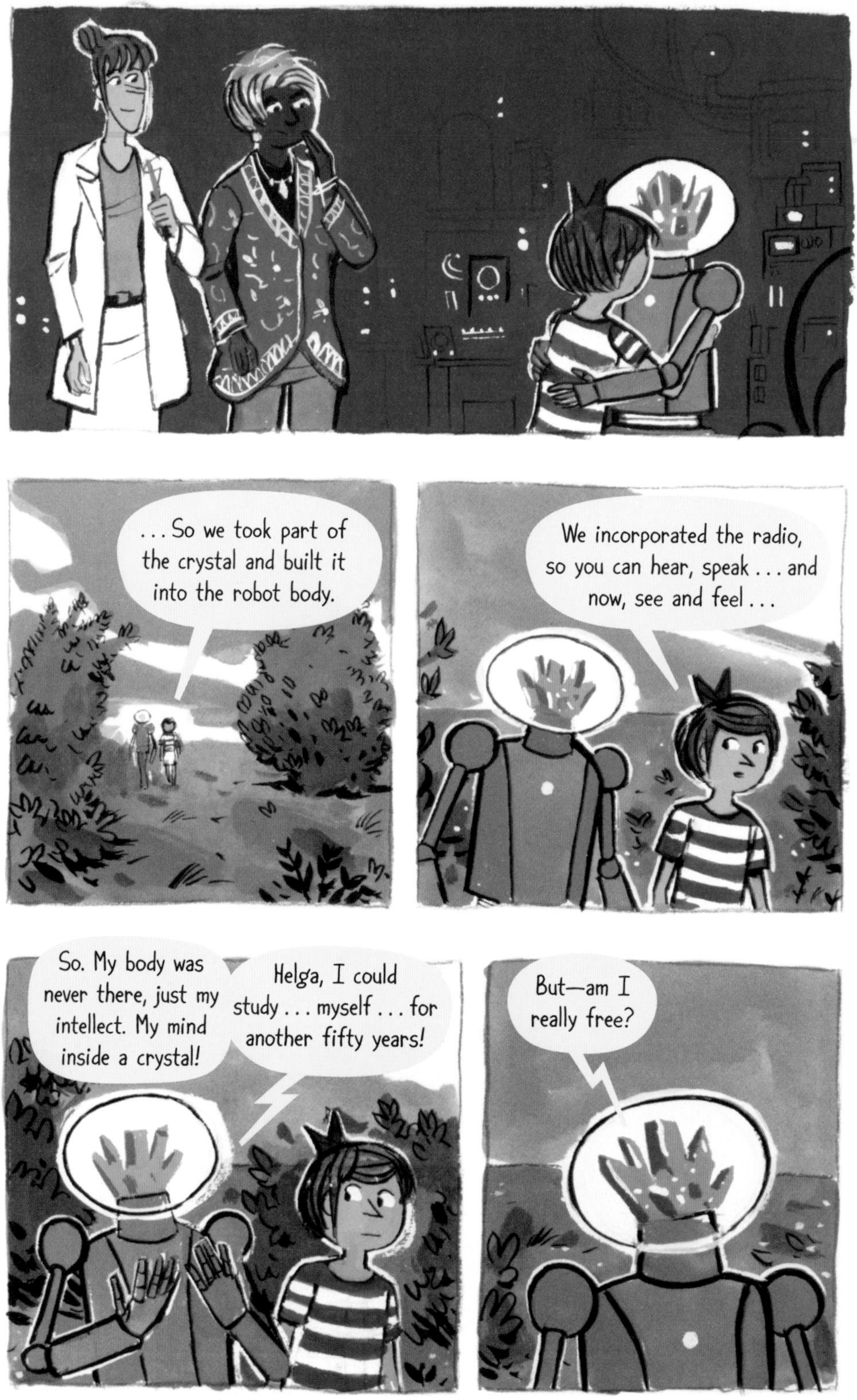
. . . So we took part of the crystal and built it into the robot body.
We incorporated the radio, so you can hear, speak . . . and now, see and feel . . .
So. My body was never there, just my intellect. My mind inside a crystal!
Helga, I could study . . . myself . . . for another fifty years!
But—am I really free?

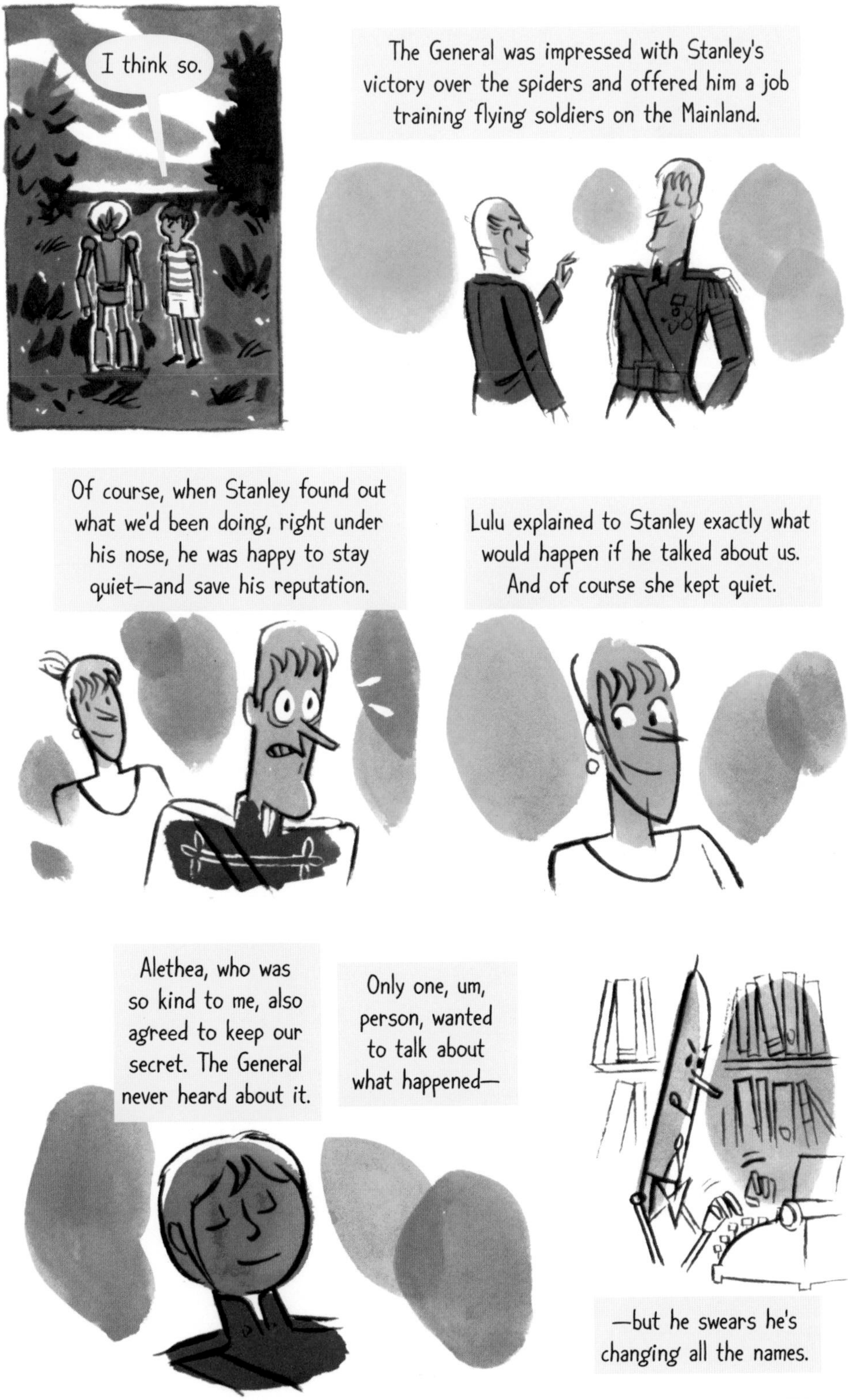
I think so.
The General was impressed with Stanley's victory over the spiders and offered him a job training flying soldiers on the Mainland.
Of course, when Stanley found out what we'd been doing, right under his nose, he was happy to stay quiet—and save his reputation.
Lulu explained to Stanley exactly what would happen if he talked about us. And of course she kept quiet.
Alethea, who was so kind to me, also agreed to keep our secret. The General never heard about it.
Only one, um, person, wanted to talk about what happened—
—but he swears he's changing all the names.

But, what about you?

Well—

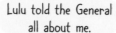

Lulu told the General all about me.

I have observed Helga closely, as well as looking into her school records.

In my opinion, she is dangerously inquisitive—pursuing projects without thought for consequences.

Capable of building restricted technology . . . and easy to underestimate, since she's so young.

Mmm. And your recommendation, Miss Ostridge?

Helga should remain on Utley, where I can mentor her . . . safely away from the Mainland.

It's clear to me that she truly belongs here, anyway.

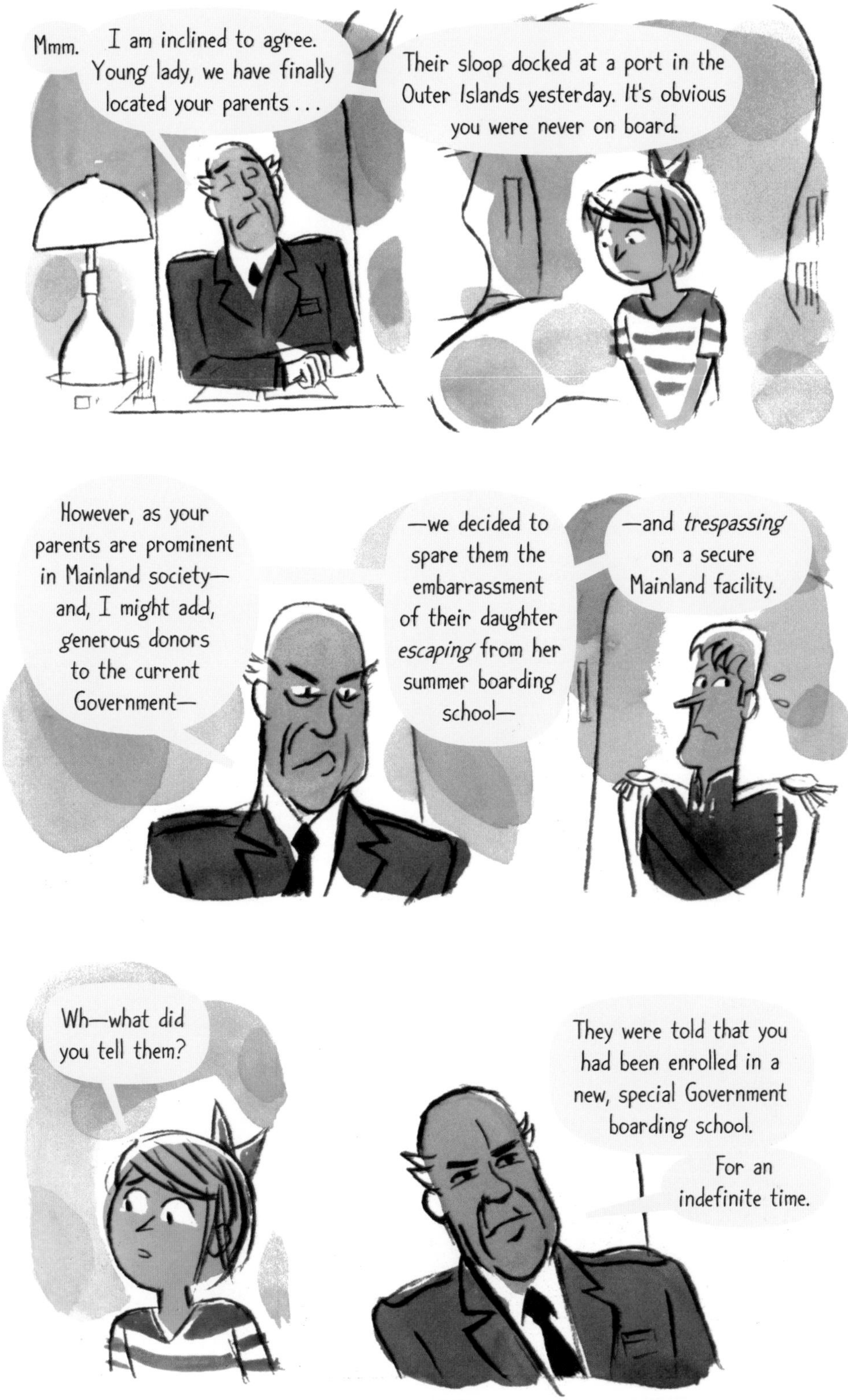
Mmm.
I am inclined to agree. Young lady, we have finally located your parents . . .
Their sloop docked at a port in the Outer Islands yesterday. It's obvious you were never on board.
However, as your parents are prominent in Mainland society— and, I might add, generous donors to the current Government—
—we decided to spare them the embarrassment of their daughter *escaping* from her summer boarding school—
—and *trespassing* on a secure Mainland facility.
Wh—what did you tell them?
They were told that you had been enrolled in a new, special Government boarding school.
For an indefinite time.

So, neither of us is going back to the Mainland soon.

I found out why you're "infamous."

You didn't tell me about ... blowing up buildings.

I thought the Mainland had been unfair to you.

I was ... careless, Helga.

I put all of myself into my work. I didn't care about anyone, or anything else ...

This is where it got me.

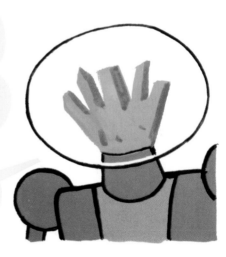

I don't know what I am now.

But I'm not the person I was before.

How long does a crystal live?

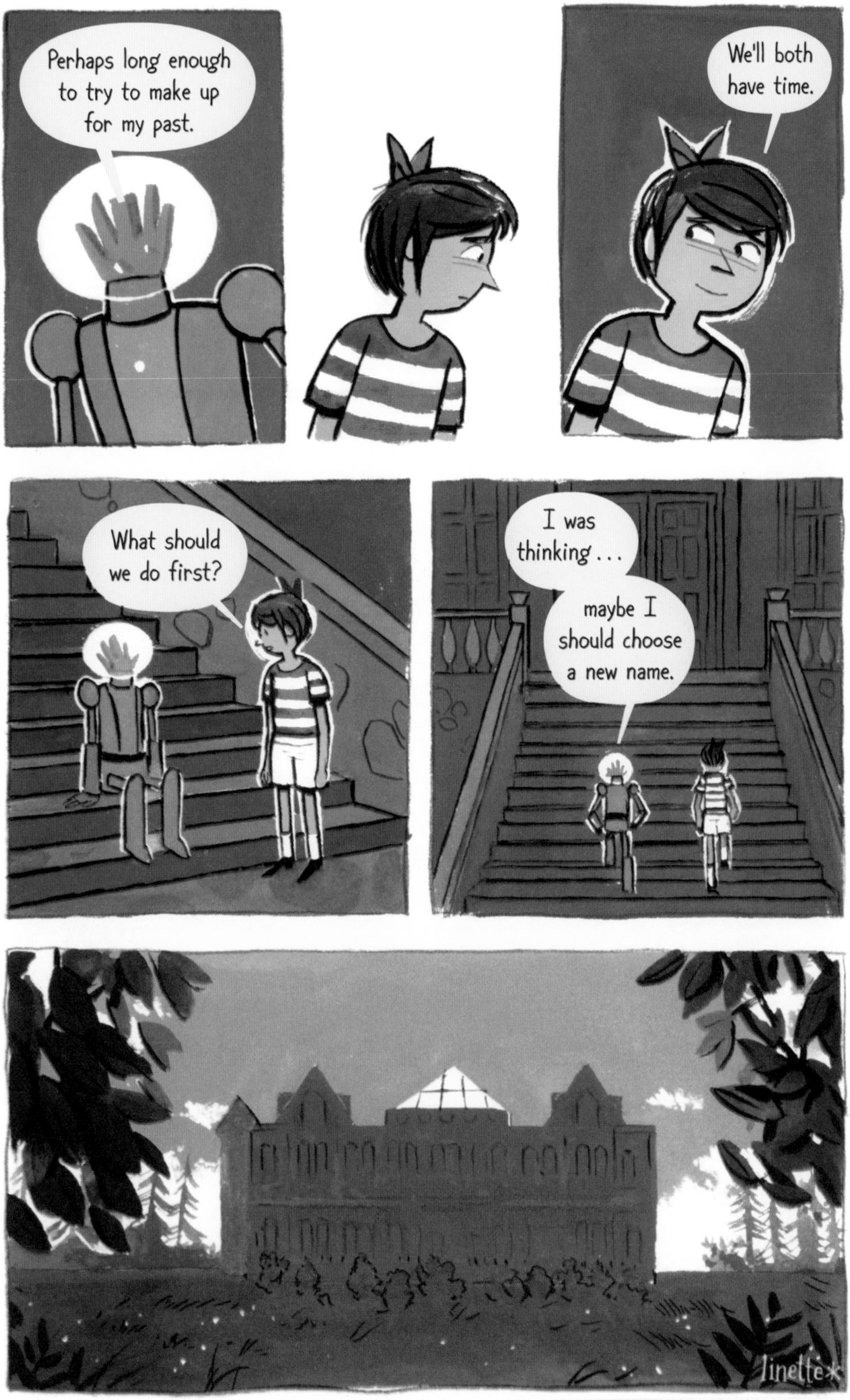
Perhaps long enough to try to make up for my past.
We'll both have time.
What should we do first?
I was thinking . . .
maybe I should choose a new name.
linette

ACKNOWLEDGMENTS

With gratitude to Viv Schwarz, Kate McKean,
Charlotte Greenbaum, Andrea Miller,
Louise Fitzhugh, and Ronald Searle

For the girl who
broke free

Library of Congress Cataloging Number for the hardcover edition 2021944664

Hardcover ISBN 978-1-4197-4391-7
Paperback ISBN 978-1-4197-4392-4

Text and illustrations © 2022 Linette Moore
Book design by Kay Petronio & Andrea Miller
Cover © 2022 Amulet Books

Printed and bound in China
10 9 8 7 6 5 4 3 2 1

Amulet Books are available at special discounts when purchased in quantity for premiums and promotions as well as fundraising or educational use. Special editions can also be created to specification. For details, contact specialsales@abramsbooks.com or the address below.

Amulet Books® is a registered
trademark of Harry N. Abrams, Inc.

ABRAMS The Art of Books
195 Broadway, New York, NY 10007
abramsbooks.com